When
Warhol
was still
Alive

When Warhol was still Alive

A Novel by
Margaret McMullan

The Crossing Press
Freedom, CA 95019

McMULLA

Publisher's Note:
This is a work of fiction. The characters, incidents, and dialogues are products of the author's imagination and are not to be construed as real. Any resemblance to actual events or persons, living or dead, is entirely coincidental.

Library of Congress Cataloging-in-Publication Data

McMullan, Margaret.
    When Warhol was still alive : a novel / by Margaret McMullan.
        p.   cm.
    ISBN 0-89594-651-3 (cloth). — ISBN 0-89594-650-5 (paper)
    1. Women's periodicals—Publishing—New York (N.Y.)—Fiction
    2. AIDS (Disease)—Patients—New York (N.Y.)—Fiction. 3. Young
    women—New York (N.Y.)—Fiction. 4. Friendship—New York (N.Y.)-
    Fiction. 5. Gay men—New York (N.Y.)—Fiction. I. Title.
    813'.54—dc20   93-38634
                                                    CIP

For my friends...
Bruce Davis (January 24, 1959 - May 4, 1989), Ken Johnston (July 9, 1959 -
July 16, 1989), and Andy Kaufman (January 17, 1949 - May 16, 1984)
and for my very best friend, my sister, Carlette.

*I would like to thank all my good friends and mentors who read the first
drafts: Bill Harrison, Phillip Lopate, and my husband Pat O'Connor.*

Chapter 1

Closing the Valentine's Day Issue

Catherine looked at Daniel and wondered what else was on TV. She wished he had MTV but Daniel didn't even have color. He was still of the belief that black and white television sets were superior because all that grey improved your powers of imagination. Then again, Daniel was still calling stereos Hi-Fi's.

"Look at their space ship," Daniel said. "It looks like one of those coffee percolators from Zabar's."

It was Saturday night and Daniel and Catherine were in bed watching the late show. Catherine had wanted to go to a party at Area, but Daniel hated Saturday nights in Manhattan. "It's so obvious," he had said. He wanted to eat pizza and watch the sci-fi movie *The Post* said had inspired "Star Wars." Usually, Daniel disapproved of TV, sit-coms especially. "Real problems don't get solved in thirty-minute episodes," he insisted. Catherine thought that that was the beauty of them. Science fiction was different. "None of it's real," he said. "So you can relax."

Seven men wearing silver suits had just landed on a dusty planet where they could finally breathe. Daniel mumbled something about the lousy reception and scooted up to the edge of the bed to fiddle with the foil around his antenna.

"In less than two weeks, we'll be sipping cheap Italian table wine," Daniel said, scooting back in bed beside Catherine. He put his leg over hers. He was a little pigeon-toed and as he did this, Catherine felt like a hooked fish. "I'm going to teach you all about Caravaggio and we'll eat calamari again. Remember how much you loved it the first time?"

Inside their spaceship, the men were getting restless.

Daniel had been invited to do some conservation work for a small museum outside of Rome. Catherine hadn't taken time off in three years and they had made plans to meet there. Daniel would leave on a Friday, rent a car in Rome, and get the hotel room. Catherine would leave the following Monday. Every morning on the way to work Catherine practiced how she would ask her editor, Fran, for time off. But Fran was still in L.A. and every time she called in, Catherine lost her nerve.

The men were discussing their chances. The captain told them stories of what had happened to the crew in a previous space ship—stories about people going crazy. One man started to get scared. He wouldn't leave the cabin even though the captain told him to. He'll be the first to die, Catherine thought.

Daniel put his hand on Catherine's breast. She moved it up to her neck. "Feel," she said.

"Your glands feel fine. They're not swollen." His fingers were rough and warm.

"Well, something's wrong," she said, turning her back to him. "I don't care what you can't feel."

The man who had been scared was venturing outside the cabin with a companion. Almost immediately, the scared one was attacked by a monster he couldn't see. The other, not knowing how best to help, went back inside. Daniel put his mouth on the back of Catherine's neck and made chomping noises like the monster. It gave her goosebumps. "Let me go," she said, moving further away.

"Jesus, Cat, how long is this gonna last?"

Helen Gurley Brown said never say no. Catherine turned over again and put her head on Daniel's chest. She tried to think of what other advice her editor Fran had given her regarding men. You should always be a warm beacon of light—a home for your man to come into. That was about the way Fran had put it.

Daniel stared up at the ceiling. The monster chewed vigorously and the man quit screaming.

"I can't help it," she said. "Something's not right. I can barely swallow. It could be contagious."

All the men were screaming now. Being invisible, the monster had made its way into the cabin.

"They never should've landed," Daniel said.

Catherine lifted her head to watch. The men were shooting their space guns, not knowing where to aim.

"They never should've left the cabin," Catherine said.

The next morning Catherine could smell the Frango Mints Daniel was eating in bed. Every year at Christmas time Catherine's mother sent Catherine Frango Mints from Marshall Fields in Chicago, and every year Catherine gave the box to Daniel, and every morning he ate exactly two chocolates with his coffee as he read two chapters of *War and Peace*. He said the combination was the right jolt to his system. When the Frango Mints ran out in between Christmases, he made do with Godiva. Daniel licked his fingers, and turned a page. Lying there beside him, Catherine thought about how she had met Daniel four years earlier on a heath in Hampstead outside of London. He had stopped her to ask where he could get a drink. His neck had been wrapped up in an aqua-colored scarf, a color everybody in the West End was wearing that year.

"There's a pub where Dickens used to get drunk," she had said. "They're supposed to have great smoked salmon."

They drank ale outside in the garden and Daniel told her about making things last. He was a conservator, working on some mummies at the British Museum. She was taking her senior year in college abroad.

They visited Keats' house that afternoon, and, for lack of anything better to say, she told him about the Romantic Poetry professor on whom she had a crush and she recited to him what she could from the "Ode on a Grecian Urn."

The next day she blew off a Wordsworth paper and flew down to Portugal with Daniel for a week.

He had gotten a room in a monastery-turned-hotel on top of a mountain so steep the cab driver wouldn't take them there. So they walked, he dragging and cursing the blue Samsonite luggage a grandparent had given her as a going-away present.

The room overlooked the white-stoned, half-fallen city of Lisbon and grapevines fell like curtains on either side of their window. There was only the one bed and he joked when she acted appalled.

They drank a lot of red wine and she tried calamari that night, and after they made love for the first time, he held her in his arms and told her about the time when he and a group of conservators were opening a box from Egypt marked EMPTY. When they opened it, they found a full-sized mummy.

"I love that," he had said, touching her belly and then her thigh, kissing her all over again. "You never know what you're going to find."

Daniel rubbed his toes together. He had evidently gotten to a good section in the *Peace* part. Catherine rolled over and pretended to be asleep. She thought about all the other things Daniel had opened up since he had opened the unmarked mummy. Once, when he had come back from a dig in the West Indies, he had been miserable for weeks. He had found a jawbone, but when he had brushed away the sand, it had crumbled in his hands. It must have been devastating, she thought, having had something important there in your hands, and then having it disappear into nothing right before your eyes.

It was mid-September and it had rained only twice in three months. The city was having a water shortage. Everybody in Manhattan was drinking bottled water because *The Daily News* said Mayor Koch was getting water from the Hudson. It was so dry outside that when the wind blew, the leaves sounded like rain.

At work, Catherine was five weeks behind Food, and three weeks behind on the February issue. She wrote the entertainment page for *Women*, a third-rate women's magazine everyone compared to *Cosmopolitan*. She still had a fourth of a page to fill. She had tried writing a celebrity trivia list about Valentine's Day, but all she could come up with was that Ava Gardner had once announced her divorce from Frank Sinatra on Valentine's Day and that, nine times out of ten, most people thought Venus and Cupid were simply distant cousins.

And Fran had only called in one idea—a two-page spread on How to Kiss. She had already interviewed friends and old boyfriends. "A kiss should be direct and to the point," a trial lawyer had said. "I hate it when they nibble." Howard, the art director at *Women,* had rejected it.

"Who's on the cover for February?" Catherine asked her best friend, Joey. They were eating goat cheese and sliced tomatoes on a shaky linoleum and steel table at Mixed Salads on 48th and 5th.

"Gloria."

"The one with the ears?"

"No," Joey said, bringing his pigtail over his right shoulder. The ends were a light pink that was becoming to his skin. "You're thinking of Elaine. Gloria's the one with the oversized upper lip."

"Which is the one with the ears?"

"Marcie. Howard is giving her March. He says perfection's out."

Joey worked in the art department, laying out pages. He had just spent the morning drawing a picture for the Women Now page and Howard said it was all wrong—Joey had made it look like women were getting paid 50 percent less when it was really 20 percent less.

"He's so anal," Joey said of Howard. He took a tomato from Catherine's plate and ate it.

The restaurant was swarming with fashion assistants in black, eating a lot of lettuce. Catherine had wanted to go someplace else, but Joey said he was slimming for the dance contest he was in that night.

"February's such bullshit," Joey said. "Howard gave Food four colored pages for what? Chocolate. And that's just because they gave him all that goddamned Godiva for Christmas. I mean, who believes in Valentine's Day, anyway?"

"My mother always sends me a card," Catherine said. "But that's just because my birthday's the day after." She didn't feel hungry and pushed her goat cheese towards Joey, but he slid it back to the middle of the table, patting his stomach. "I have to be able to get into that dress tonight," he said. Catherine checked to see if her neck glands had swelled, but they hadn't, even though the back of her throat still hurt.

"Look around. This is not the age of romance," Joey said. Catherine saw a young black woman sit down next to one of the fashion assistants. The fashion assistant put her purse in her lap, and held it there while she ate. Joey took out a compact from his back pocket, opened it, looked in the mirror, and picked some green out from between his two front teeth. "Monogamy sucks," he said, shutting the case and putting it back inside his pocket. Anyone would have mistaken it for a tin of chewing tobacco.

Catherine paid for lunch, saving the receipt so she could get reimbursed. The only way she was able to support herself on her salary was to petty cash everything she ate.

"I wish I had a pretty little compact like yours," Catherine said. She brushed her lips with some Chapstick.

"Get palsy with Beauty," he said. "You'll never have to buy anything for your body again."

Outside, the air was so unbearable, the two of them laughed out loud.

"Why do we put up with this shit?" Catherine said, poking around at her neck glands.

"Because we're young and free and we have such glamourous jobs in New York," he said sarcastically. "Because tonight I'm going to win that damned dance contest and have fifteen minutes with Andy Warhol. Because. Just Because."

At the office, the How-To editor was nearly in tears.

"You've got to help me," she said, stopping Catherine in the hall. Catherine noticed her loose, greasy hair. It looked like she had been up all night. "I don't have anything for February. All I've got is a recipe for Heart Stew and Howard won't use it because he says our readers don't eat organs."

"So use something from January."

"I did that for December."

Everyone but editors wrote the How-To section in *Women*. Without pay. It was supposed to be an honor—a chance to show off your talent by writing up copy on topics such as What to do when your best friend's dog keeps sniffing your crotch; How to rev up a kitchen counter; 27 ways to look like you've exercised when you haven't.

"OK, OK," Catherine said. "I'll think on it."

In her office, she tiptoed over photos of rock stars dressed up in Santa suits. For January, she had done a Can-you-guess-who-this-is Christmas page, except the timing had been off (she had missed the deadline) and nobody recognized the people even after they had read who they were in the list Howard had printed upside down on the bottom of the page. Howard had blamed her, but Catherine wrote him a memo stating in no uncertain terms that she couldn't exactly get Rod Stewart in a Santa suit for a rag like *Women*, unless of course they offered him the cover.

Catherine sat down at Fran's desk. She rolled a sheet of paper into the typewriter and stuck her feet in the wastepaper basket. When she first started working for Fran, Catherine had only used the wastepaper basket for her feet out of necessity—theirs was a tiny office with no windows and no place to put the waste paper basket but under the desks. Now Catherine found that she thought better with her feet in the garbage.

She tried thinking about Valentine's day, but her mind kept returning to Daniel. Sometimes she wondered if she wanted to get rid of Daniel just to see if she could. A year ago she accepted a dinner invitation with a thin, nervous man from a P.R. firm with whom she never did business. They ate at a place in the Village in a crowded room with nice china and afterwards he invited her up to see his condo and his cats. He offered her a glass of wine and when he kissed her on the sofa, he climbed on top.

"Guess how much I weigh?" he had said, balancing himself on her stomach.

Catherine realized that she would have to guess to get him off. "I don't know. 175?"

"155," he said, rolling off. "Now come on." He patted his stomach. "Your turn."

She said she had allergies and when she got to Daniel, late that same night, they made love and it was as good as it had been on the beach in the Algarves, but without the sand.

In a September piece called "How to Make Decisions," the guide editor suggested making a list of pros and cons.

Daniel, Catherine typed.

> *Pros:*
> *1. He says he loves me. I have been in love with him. History has been known to repeat itself.*
> *2. He remembers my birthday. His presents come on time at Christmas.*
> *3. He would be faithful. He would not have a mid-life crisis and run off to Miami with his high school sweetie a la Fran's X. Daniel has been through mid-life and he has no high school sweetie.*
> *4. He's 20 years older than I am.*
>
> *Cons:*
> *1. I'm not sure I'm in love with him.*
> *2. He's never heard of Chrissie Hynde and The Pretenders. He thinks Dick Cavett still has his own show.*
> *3. He would be faithful. Would I?*
> *4. He's 20 years older than I am.*

The How-To editor knocked on Catherine's wall (*Women* didn't believe in doors), and glanced at the page in Catherine's typewriter.

"I hope that's for me," she said.

Catherine smiled and waited for her to leave. She put her hands on her neck glands. It had been a long time since she and Daniel had last made love, and she wondered why and when she had lost her desire. She thought maybe it was the heat and the city. Seven Wild Ways to Say "I love you" Catherine typed. 1. Wrap yourself up in nothing but red ribbon. Let him undo the bow. 2. Design coupons shaped like Cupid, each with a different promise: Good for one bubble bath with me. Redeemable for 13 kisses. 3. Compose a sonnet and write it in lipstick on his mirror. Photograph to document for keeps.

As soon as Catherine and Joey got to the Underground that night, someone slapped Catherine's bottom with a square sheet of paper that read number 19. Joey was Twenty.

Joey was dressed up to look like Jerry Hall. He wore red high heels with his red sequined mini-dress and after he ordered a scotch at the bar, he ran off to the lady's room to straighten his new long blond wig.

"If I don't get Andy, "he had said on the way in, "maybe I'll get Mick."

For years Joey had dreamed of meeting Andy Warhol. If he could just meet him, he once told Catherine, his whole life would change. He wouldn't have to do everything Howard's way. He wouldn't have to draw queer little graphs of defective contraceptive devices for Dr. Clotchcoff's page (Joey called him Crotchcough). If he could meet Warhol, he would help him with his silk screens, get his picture taken with Cornelia Guest, maybe even get mentioned in Liz Smith's column. With Warhol, Joey would have a "creative schedule." Nothing would be mundane or 9 to 5ish. He would finally have the kind of life he had moved from Arkansas to have. But Joey couldn't switch from *Women* to *Interview* yet because everybody knew you had to have money to work for Warhol.

Everyone in the place was wearing black and silver or bronzed leather. Fifteen, Ten, and Two were already on the floor dancing. Periodically they would stop and stretch like joggers. They moved in clever, predictable ways, pouting beneath their neat, geometric haircuts.

A group of bridge and tunnel people stood at the bar next to Catherine. The girls, who were about her age, bitched about their bosses as they kept their heads bent to keep their hair swept over to one side. Daniel had once called girls like them the leaning-tower-of-Pisa girls because of the way they always leaned.

"I'm ready for my close-up, Mr. de Mille." Joey was back from the lady's room and he leaned against the bar, exposing his leg. He had dieted for a month to get into his dress.

"God, Joey. Next to you I feel like a moose," Catherine said.

Joey licked his fingers and fixed one of her spikes.

"You've got big shoulders," he said. "People with big shoulders never really look fat."

Catherine didn't want to be there. This is your thing, she had said, but Joey insisted. "This could be my big fifteen minutes of fame." He had done her hair and it had come out looking like a cross between Tina Turner and a porcupine. Her whole head was beginning to feel weighed down by all the gel and hair spray. Joey claimed she looked pisser.

"Nice hair," a boy next to Catherine said. "Will it hurt if I touch it?"

Catherine couldn't remember his name, but she recognized him from a Disney movie. He had played the good guy's bad friend.

Catherine lavished praise and then they gossiped. It was obvious he had never been interviewed before. Either that or he was going to say anything for a little publicity. He told Catherine that Matthew Broderick was a meek geek and Rob Lowe was just another middle class yes-man with some European style. Catherine asked him if he had any pictures of himself.

"She's got a fourth of a page to fill and one horny homo down her back to get it in by the end of the week," Joey said, cutting in. He had his deep

Lauren Bacall voice on tonight. When he was a woman, Joey always called homosexuals homos. When he was playing a man, they were just gay. "The homo's my boss and he loves cheesecake."

"Yeah?" the boy said. He smiled at Joey. "I got some pictures I think he'll like."

Warhol hadn't shown up yet, and they had to start the contest without him. Joey had bribed the DJ to play "Private Dancer" and when his turn came, he danced solo while everyone else stayed in pairs. His sequins glittered white under the pink glow of moving light as he swayed to the music. He started out slow, lowering one of his spaghetti straps. Then his back curled as he tossed his head and all that blond hair feathered over his face and his Adam's apple as he closed his eyes and danced not with, but against the beat.

"Your friend. Joey, isn't it? Is she like anybody I know?" the actor asked Catherine at the bar.

"Get me the pictures and I'll fix you up with her," Catherine said. The actor nodded and bought the next round.

"Deal," he said.

The judges couldn't make up their minds so they put on that year's INXS and had Sixteen, Twenty and Forty keep dancing. At the end of the dance, they announced that they had to change first prize from the fifteen minute meeting with Andy Warhol (he still hadn't shown) to two free steak dinners at some rib place in the Bronx.

Joey won.

"I don't even do red meat," he screamed when a judge from *Interview* announced his number. He stood in the middle of the dance floor and tore up his coupons. Then he turned around, found Catherine, and dragged her away.

On the way out, they passed Sixteen who was making a fuss at the bar. She had won second place—a $25 bar tab.

"What the fuck am I supposed to do with a $25 bar tab in Manhattan, order a ginger ale?" She bit a nail and spat it out towards the dance floor. Then she grabbed hold of Catherine's arm. "I had the wrong partner is all," she said, looking at Catherine. She had circles under her eyes and her hair was matted down with sweat. She was wearing a mini-skirt and a tee-shirt that said *Ask me about my tan lines*. "Doncha hate that?" she said, tightening her grip. "Doncha hate it when you have the wrong fucking partner?"

It was late but Catherine caught a cab to Brooklyn anyway. She felt like she had to see Daniel. She felt like she was ready to tell him that she wasn't ready to go to Italy. Not now, she would say. Not this time.

They went to an all-night gourmet ice cream place for coconut ice cream cones and outside it was just beginning to rain.

"Finally," Daniel said, opening his mouth to let the rain fall in.

"Don't," Catherine said. "New York rain's poison. You'll get sick and I hate hospitals."

"Slow down," he shouted ahead to her.

He was always telling her to slow down, she thought. Why couldn't he speed up? Catch up already. Every month it was the same story: she was five months ahead and he was about a century behind.

Diana Ross was playing on the juke box and they were the only ones in the place besides the two boys behind the counter. One had blond hair and the other had a peach colored mohawk.

A man with a little girl came in.

"I'd like a beige cone," the little girl said. She was about nine. The blond boy opened the freezer.

"There's no coffee-mocha," the blond said to the Mohawk. "I told you already to bring out the coffee-mocha."

Mohawk went to the back, singing. "Upside down," he sang off-key. "You turn me inside out. Round and round."

"How about something pink?" the blond boy asked the girl.

"Did you hear that?" Daniel whispered to Catherine. "That kid asked for a beige ice cream cone. What the fuck's the world coming to? Is it New York? I mean, what are we producing?"

Catherine wasn't in the mood for one of Daniel's tirades. Once, in Central Park, a bum yelled at Daniel for giving her a dollar. "What the hell is that gonna get me?" she had said, and Daniel had kept Catherine standing there for thirty minutes just so he could yell back at the bum.

"This is such a stupid song," she said.

Daniel looked away from the little girl who was reaching up for her strawberry ice cream cone.

"She did have that one, though," he said and he hummed a few bars of "Stoned Love." "That one was good."

"It's so sixties."

"You just don't have any taste."

The man opened the door for the little girl.

"Don't bring me here again, Daddy. OK?" she said.

Daniel shook his head.

Catherine watched the little girl take her father's hand.

Daniel had never introduced Catherine to his family. He wouldn't. Once, when his father came to visit him from Virginia, Daniel told Catherine to stay away. "I'll call you in a week," he had said. She took a subway out to Brooklyn that Saturday morning anyway, crouched behind a mailbox, and waited there until they came out. She knew Daniel would take him into Chinatown for steamed dumplings. But his father came out alone and when she saw him, she knew—he was just an older, greyer version of Daniel with a Willie Loman slouch. And she wondered then, moving to the other side of the mailbox as he walked away, if Daniel had been ashamed of his father or of her.

"I've got taste," Catherine said.

"OK. Go ahead. Name a great love song," he said.

Catherine thought a minute. "I liked that Stones one. "Waiting on a Friend.""

"Too whiney."

Catherine ate the last part of her cone.

"Well, love is whiney," she said. "First you whine that you love her, than you whine that you're leaving. Then you whine that you miss her."

Daniel looked at his empty cone. He threw it in the trash. "Is that the scenario?"

Mohawk reappeared from the back with a bucket of coffee-mocha. He slammed it down on the counter in front of the blond. Then he went outside, lifted his knee high up into the air, and started to strum an imaginary electric guitar. The rain made his peach spikes sag.

"I don't think he's very happy with his career choice," Catherine said, touching the ends of her hair to feel if her own spikes were still stiff.

At his stoop, Daniel turned to Catherine and held her hand. When he smiled, his laugh lines grew out from under his glasses and his eyebrows rose above the rims.

Catherine could remember when Daniel used to sleep over at her place on 78th. Once, at 2:30 in the morning, he left. "Don't go," she had said. "I'm still afterglowing." But he said he couldn't sleep. He said he had an 18th century fresco to clean. After that he rarely spent the night. Later, Catherine took an Are-you-and-he-on-the-same-sexual-wavelength quiz in *Women*. She scored a 55 and one question stuck in her mind. Would you have his baby? Catherine had checked no and she wondered how she could stay with Daniel, knowing that. For weeks she worried that they were no longer in sync.

"Are we losing our resonance?" she had asked one night after dinner. "You can't even sleep in my bed anymore."

"It's not our resonance, sweetie," Daniel had said, reassuringly. "It's your flannel sheets. They make me sweat."

Looking into Daniel's dark brown eyes now, Catherine wished that the solution to everything could be as simple as changing her sheets.

"Look up," Daniel said. "There's the Big Dipper." He pointed up towards a dim constellation. Daniel once said the only thing he really liked about Catherine's apartment was that it was on the sixth floor and the only view was a wall and the sky. "That's the problem with living here. Manhattan gives off too much light. You can't see the stars," he said.

"I've always liked that word, star," Catherine said. "And I don't mind all the lights."

"Cat. Sweetie." Daniel whispered. "Maybe you shouldn't go to Italy with me."

"What do you mean?"

"I mean, you just don't seem too thrilled about the idea."

"I'm thrilled."

They looked at each other.

"Don't you love me anymore?" she said.

"Do you?" He sounded so calm. "Do you love me, Catherine?"

She looked into those brown eyes again and she wasn't sure at all if she was ready to see them for the last time.

"Don't cry, sweetie," he said, putting his hand on her cheek.

"My mother told me never to cry in front of a man," she said, wiping her face. "I'm ugly when I cry."

"Your mother's wrong."

"I just need some time alone right now." She sniffed. "That's all."

Upstairs in bed, he kissed her belly and whispered that she wasn't getting fat. That the extra weight she'd put on only improved the quality of her skin.

She vowed never to eat again.

Together they moved like liquid and everything she did felt like it was in slow motion. Up close, Catherine could see all the deep pores in Daniel's face. His skin wasn't smooth but it was soft and when she kissed him, his breath tasted of coconut and bitter coffee.

"Sweetie," he said. "Oh my sweet Cat."

She could barely catch her breath and as she hovered over him, she felt as though she were making one more last stop on some remote planet where she would be temporarily safe.

The day after Daniel left for Italy, Catherine stayed in bed for 17 hours and when she woke up, she couldn't open her mouth. She lay still, moving her tongue slowly across her gums and teeth, trying to search for the source of the problem. Then she stuck her finger in her mouth and way in the back, she felt a tooth she had never felt before.

Two hours later, she was in an elevator with a pregnant Chinese woman who was eating an apple. They both looked up at the numbers as they rose above the city. Catherine tried to smile, but her mouth wouldn't move.

Dr. Panter's office was green and cool and Catherine could hear the dribble from the water in the porcelain spit bowls. The bookcases were crowded with plastic mouth molds and on the walls, framed in chrome and glass, were posters of the various stages of gum disease. The hygienist was a grandmotherly woman who wore a real nurse's uniform—the kind women wore in old war movies.

Dr. Panter was a fleshy, soft-spoken man who kept his rubber gloves on when he shook Catherine's hand.

"You're lucky I'm not too busy today," he told Catherine as he pressed a button that tilted back her chair.

He stuck cotton and stiff squares of Kodak film into her mouth while he quietly bragged about the overbites he was designing for an off-off-

Broadway production of Huckleberry Finn. Catherine tried to nod with interest, as she stared up at the Calder mobiles that hung from the ceiling. Taped to the wall was a poster with a cat stuck up in a tree. Crisis? What Crisis? it read.

Catherine first started coming to Dr. Panter when her boss, Fran, had had her incisors bonded. They both received newsletters in the mail once a month which had information on controversial tooth topics such as whether or not to floss twice daily, eating cheese after meals, and the big debate on porcelain fillings. On the last page of every newsletter, Dr. Panter liked to list the names of celebrity mouths he had helped correct.

"Wisdom teeth it is," he said, after he had developed the film. "They're impacted.

"Well. At least now I know," Catherine mumbled. She felt at once relieved and terrified.

Because it was an emergency—Catherine couldn't open her mouth—Dr. Panter performed the surgery that afternoon at 2:00. In the four hours that she waited, Catherine looked through a book on cosmetic dentistry. In all the before pictures, the people looked miserable. They had dark, stained, crooked teeth. The women wore no make up and their hair hung stringy and flat. In one, a nervous, bird-like woman had ground her teeth down to little yellow nubs. She looked scared and trapped inside the photo. The caption said that it had become a habit—this grinding—and Catherine couldn't help but wonder what this woman's life had been like—if she had had a bad childhood or an unhappy partnership or something. In the after shot, the woman had curled her hair, done her nails in crimson and she smiled with her big new teeth.

Everybody looked happier in the after shots. Their faces were relaxed. They were no longer suffering. They were no longer prisoners of their own crooked smiles.

As Dr. Panter stuck an oversized needle into Catherine's mouth, she could smell his sweet cologne over the mouthwash and she tried to imagine that she was just having a cavity filled, that she wasn't there to have anything actually taken away, and that she would leave Dr. Panter's office as happy as the after-picture people.

She dreamed she was being cut open straight down the middle of her belly. In the dream, she woke up and asked the doctor, who was really Joey, "If you take out my wisdom teeth will I be dumb?"

"Don't be silly," he said. And he lifted Daniel, who was curled up around a heart-shaped box of Valentine chocolates, out from under her rib cage. "You just don't have to worry about having children."

When Catherine woke up in Dr. Panter's chair, she felt completely drained. The nurse asked if there was anybody she could call, and Catherine said no, there was nobody.

In a cab on the way to the East Side, the driver asked her what every cab driver in New York asks a woman alone. Are you married? How come a pretty girl like you's not married? A lonesomeness came over her and she wasn't sure if it wasn't just the painkillers. She felt so light and empty and numb, it was as though she were floating on a wave of cool air that was slowly rising above all the heat.

She stopped in at The Star deli before she went upstairs to her apartment. She bought some rice pudding because it looked soft and when the man behind the counter saw her, he gave her a free cup of tea with lemon.

Catherine remembered when her mother once told her how important it was to keep a place clean. "Just in case you get sick," she had said. Scattered across her floor were her stockings and bank statements, newspapers and dirty laundry, and little pieces of cotton she had put in her ears once upon a time to drown out her noisy neighbors. Catherine understood now what her mother had meant.

She kicked everything into her closet and pulled out the sofa bed. Outside, an old woman was leading a slow collie across the roof of her building. Catherine closed all her windows and turned the AC on high.

She took the container of rice pudding out of its bag and used it as an icepack for her jaw. She could smell Dr. Panter's rubber gloves on her hand.

Catherine thought about all of the smells Daniel could be creating in the kitchen if he were there. He would make chicken soup or a nice noodly casserole. Daniel knew about food. He knew about turkey sandwiches with lots of pepper. He knew about icy white wine spritzers with big chunks of lemon. For a moment, Catherine thought about getting up and adding to the list of pros under Daniel's name. Outside, the old woman stood still on the roof while the dog lifted its leg near a gas pipe.

Her mother's voice on the answering machine was irritating. She said "we" when she should have said "I," as in, "We can't come to the phone right now." And her "can't" came out sounding like Margaret Thatcher's can't's.

It was a little before ten when Catherine got hold of Joey.

"I just got my wisdom teeth yanked," she said. "I look like a chipmunk."

"Oh God. Listen. I'm on my way out. You don't need anything, do you?"

"No, no," she said, wishing she had never called. "Just thought I'd give you an update."

"I'll stay tuned," Joey said.

Catherine tried to smile, and then, for the first time, she could feel the big bloody craters in the back of her mouth.

There were complications. For a week she woke up every morning and spat out globs of blood into her sink. Joey told her that wasn't normal.

"Unless you're in a Stephen King thing," he said.

She had dry socket and Dr. Panter had to reopen her wounds the following Friday. He turned on a machine that sounded like a vacuum cleaner and for 30 minutes it felt as though her brain was being sucked out of her mouth.

"Happens all the time," he said, giving her a frightening amount of gauze and cotton. "It'll just take longer to heal."

That night Daniel called from somewhere in Italy.

"Cat," he shouted above what sounded like the roar of an ocean. "Venus is in the sky and I can't keep my eyes off it." She shouted back to him about her wisdom teeth but their connection was bad and his voice was filled with static and she thought she could hear him say he loved her right before the phone went dead.

Joey stopped by later that week. He gave her a lamp with a shade that looked like the hat Audrey Hepburn wore in "Breakfast at Tiffany's." Then he gave her her mail.

Joey was still a little upset about the dance contest.

"For the record," he said, slurping the vanilla shake he had brought for her while Catherine opened a letter with a return address in Rome. "That was only three minutes. According to Andy, everyone gets fifteen minutes of fame, so technically I still have twelve to go."

It was a card from Daniel. It was an Indian drawing of two elephants fighting in the air, locked together tusk to tusk. They were smiling. They looked like they were having the time of their lives. Hope the extraction was a success, he had written inside the card. I miss waking up to you. The Pope says hi.

Joey climbed in bed beside Catherine and told her that Howard loved the piece about the Disney actor from the Underground. "He's giving you half a page. Black and white. Let me see your holes."

When you're sick you don't want anybody in bed with you. That was what her mother had always said, but Catherine was glad Joey was there kicking about and slurping his shake. She felt absolutely secure and safe in the knowledge that they liked each other and that he didn't find her completely repulsive.

"Wider," he said. "It's dark in here."

Opening her mouth for Joey to see, Catherine felt as though she should be happier. It was the first time Howard had given her more space than she asked for.

"That is so disgusting," Joey said, obviously satisfied. He stirred his shake.

"I shoun't be here, Joey," she said. It still hurt to talk and her jaws didn't move very well. "I should be in a cafe with a cappahino. I should be in a cold, damp church looking at saints. I should be married."

Joey moved the straw around in his shake so that it made silly noises and Catherine tried to smile.

"The French have a word for people like us, Cat. Brucher. To mix. We're not into stable. We're into being into everything and everybody. We brucher." He slurped the last of the shake. "Or is it bruchons. You don't want to be in a church. " He climbed over her and turned on the TV. A game show was on. "I mean, Bloomies is right around the corner."

"Oh God, Joey. I'm going to be OK, aren't I?"

"You'll be fine, Cat."

"What am I going to do?"

Joey looked at Catherine. He dabbed at her tears with some of her gauze. Then he put his arm around her shoulder so carefully, it made her cry more.

"What *am* I going to do?" she asked again. Joey kissed her hand and smiled.

"Moisturize," he whispered and he squeezed her wrists until she laughed.

Outside, they heard thunder. While Joey turned off the new lamp to get a better picture on the TV, Catherine looked out her window through her burglar bars and tried to find the Big Dipper, but the sky was clouding up, and she couldn't even locate Venus.

Chapter 2

The HOAX

"God, Catherine, you must have dropped ten pounds!" The girl from Beauty stopped Catherine in front of the elevators going up. Catherine heaved her satchel over her shoulder and held in her stomach.

"Trauma," she said, turning to give Beauty a better look. "I broke up with my boyfriend and had my wisdom teeth pulled."

"Well, at least you didn't lose your apartment."

Catherine had lost weight. It had been hard to eat during the last three weeks because she couldn't chew. And she still couldn't feel the lower left half of her bottom lip. Paresthesia, Dr. Panter had told her. It could last for weeks, months. It could be permanent. It infuriated Catherine—the idea of having half a numb lip. "Cheer up," Joey had said to her. "Daniel's in Roma. It's not like you have anybody to kiss."

Catherine could smell Beauty's jasmine scent as Beauty brushed a thread away from Catherine's blouse. Catherine was thrilled. It was the first time anybody from Beauty had spoken to her in almost three years. In staff meetings, Catherine had suggested doing combination Beauty/Entertainment pieces, but Beauty only did make-overs and Catherine could never get celebrities to admit they needed one.

"We're starting May," Beauty said, smug because their department was always months ahead. "Swimsuit make-overs. Wanna be in? Monday we shoot. It shouldn't take too long."

"I won't eat all weekend," Catherine said.

"No, don't do that," Beauty said, pushing the Close Door button inside the elevator. "You've got to look normal. You can't look great."

The Greek girl with one arm sat opening the morning mail with her teeth. She was Catherine's new temp. Howard had stopped by a week before, and, seeing all the photos on the floor in the office, he had had a fit. "Get somebody in here," he had said. "For the sake of the photos."

It had been an unusually generous gesture coming from Howard. Howard had a reputation: he had fired his last assistant because her shoes clicked when she walked. And he didn't think Entertainment needed a staff of two because he didn't believe in Entertainment. "If you want to go jack off with the stars," Catherine had overheard him scream at Fran one time, "go to *Vanity Fair* or *People*. We're strictly service."

It had also been said that Howard had tried pushing his mother out of her apartment window somewhere in Minnesota, but they had only been three flights up and she had survived and Howard put her in a home and sent money once a month. At editorial meetings, everybody had gotten in the habit of staying away from Howard, who often stood near the big picture window overlooking Madison Avenue.

But that morning, in Catherine's office, Howard had bent down carefully—he was a big man with a gut—and he picked up one of the black-and-whites off the floor and cradled it in one hand, and he said again, this time quietly, "Get a temp." When it came to artwork for *Women,* Catherine realized, Howard had a heart.

It had taken a week to get all the pictures back—the Greek girl was efficient, but slow. When it came time to seal all the envelopes, she put them on the edge of Catherine's desk, licked them, and sealed the flaps shut by holding them steady with her forehead.

At noon she fetched tuna pita sandwiches from Curds and Whey, and while they ate at their desks, she told Catherine how she had lost her arm in an automobile accident the day of her high school graduation. Her father was a shipping tycoon and sent her to New York afterwards to meet a man, because in Greece nobody wanted a wife with one arm.

With the Greek, Catherine was getting a lot done. She had already interviewed and written up the piece on the March cover girl who earned three thousand dollars a day. "The only thing you have to do for a magazine picture is lick your lips and look dumb," she had said. Because she was so grateful to Howard, Catherine got in the picture he had wanted of a sumo wrestler who was appearing in a new movie.

"Now that's sexy," he said, pointing to the photo of the three-hundred-pounder wearing a diaper. "If you don't think so, you're crazy."

Catherine didn't say a word. After all, he had given her the Greek.

"It's a woman named Fran," the Greek said, holding out the telephone.

"Who the hell was that?" Fran said after the Greek had transferred the call.

"That's our new temp," Catherine said, pleased that she had thought to say "our." When Catherine had first started working for Fran, Fran told her to say "we" and "our" whenever she meant "I" and "my." Fran said that was power talk.

"We don't need a temp," Fran said slowly. Carefully. "We've got you. Can't you handle it, Catherine? Do I have to come back? I'm not ready to come back. I hate that city. I don't have a Jacuzzi. I don't have a sauna. I don't have a backyard and I don't have a mountain outside my window. And frankly I've depleted the resources of men there. I don't want to come back."

"You don't have to come back, Fran. Everything's under control." The

Greek girl put the open stack of letters and club invitations on Fran's desk in front of Catherine. There were little wet teeth marks on the edges of all of them.

"We just had a lot of extra work to do," Catherine said. "And someone should be here when I do this swimsuit spread."

"Swimsuit spread?"

"Beauty needs me."

"I don't give a fuck what Beauty needs. I need you there in that office. You work for me, remember?"

It could have been the weather. The following morning, Catherine woke up to the sound of rain rolling off the air conditioners and pipes in her alleyway and she saw the old woman and her dog outside on the roof again. The two of them had on red raincoats and galoshes.

The sky was pink and grey and the subways were impossible. It was hurricane weather and all the weathermen were breathless. Catherine had read an article once called "The Weather and You" that said that when the wind blew hard, the way it had been blowing, the ions in the air changed— there were either fewer or more positive ones, she couldn't remember which—and that messed up your brain.

"Some people get headaches," she told Joey at the office. "Other people get horny." Howard was yelling at another assistant who had laid out the How-To wrong. Her boxes were too narrow, he said. Joey was laying out the Q&A section on Clotchcoff's page. One of the questions concerned vaginal leakage.

"Yeah, well, wind or no wind, Howard's being a bitch and Simpson's in the firing mood," Joey whispered. "So watch your hide."

Howard came around, looked over Joey's shoulder, and told him he needn't bother with an illustration this month.

Joey was right about Ms. Simpson. One of the girls in Accessories was already gone. She had been rearranging bracelets when Ms. Simpson called her into her office. Later, Accessories pouted and said, Well, she had always wanted to be a salmon fisher in Alaska with her fiance anyway.

Catherine squeezed past Howard's belly and went to the little window cut into Ms. Simpson's wall. She pushed in her petty cash slips for the week and she got them back initialed a second later, without a word from Ms. Simpson's assistant on the other side. Then Catherine saw the How-To editor coming out of Ms. Simpson's office, dabbing her eyes with the cuff of her sleeve. As she closed the door, Catherine caught a glimpse of the plastic rock that was lit up green. It was said that Simpson turned on the light whenever she was preparing to fire someone, but Catherine had seen the greenish glow seeping from under her office door late at night sometimes and on the weekends.

"Are you OK?" Catherine asked the How-To editor, walking along-side her down the hall.

"Couldn't be better," she said. "I'm out of here. I'm sick of having nervous breakdowns over lipstick colors. I don't *have* any more ways to tie a fucking scarf. You got any empty boxes? I'm gonna need some empty boxes."

She had not been considered important enough to the magazine to get a going-away party, so that afternoon the How-To editor went from office to office shaking everybody's hand. All but Fashion's. "They never did shit for me," she told Catherine.

At five o'clock, she handed in her last piece: "Why You Should Be Job Hunting Over the Summer Holidays."

"This magazine," she said, putting more file folders into a box. She paused and shook her head while Catherine held the box shut. "They tell you we're a team, that we have to work together." She pulled at the soggy cuff of her sleeve. "They say it's like a marriage. Ha. This place isn't any different from any other shit hole in this city. When it comes right down to it, it's every man for himself. Woman I mean. Every woman for herself. Step lightly, if you know what's good for you, Cat." She ripped out a line of tape. "And don't rule out the possibility of divorce."

"What you need is a good rape," Joey said. They were in Catherine's bathroom. Joey was down on his knees, pulling out the hairs along Catherine's upper inner thigh with a home electrolysis device called Finally Free, which he had stolen from Health. They were only going to do seven hairs at a time, but Joey had rolled a joint and now they were going for fifty. It didn't hurt so much as it stung—a little like static ten times over.

Joey thought it would be a good idea for Catherine to go relatively hairless to the Beauty shoot on Monday. "The photographer will think you're pro and he'll give you better lighting," he had said.

Catherine had been scared to electrolyze herself—she had read somewhere that a woman had gotten electrocuted doing this on her own. As an extra precaution, Catherine wore a pair of green rubber gardening boots with her swimsuit. Joey was wearing a black-and-white striped silk shirt from Saks that a doctor had left him when he had died. Joey called it his Dead Man shirt. Catherine made him put on a pair of old docksiders, just in case.

"Everybody's already done rape," Catherine said. "*People* gave it two covers, remember? And I can't do a disease either, because they switch every week. Ouch. I need something flashier that's just for *Women*. Damn, Joey. That hurt."

"Get a grip. A couple more and we're through."

On the radio, the weathermen talked about Hurricane Gloria. The DJ kept laughing and whooping it up and then he played the Laura Branigan song called "Gloria."

For the first time since she had started working for *Women*, Catherine was scared of losing her job. Fran could fire her and so could Ms. Simpson. She had considered requesting the How-To position, but somehow it wasn't appealing. No one wanted to be How-To because you had to know a little bit about everything all the time every month. Even though she would no longer have to answer to Fran, Catherine didn't feel at all capable of telling women all over the country how to do anything better.

"They're not going to let you wear that suit for the Before, you know," Joey said.

"Ouch."

"It's too cute." He got up, wound the cord up in a neat little circle and put the device away on a shelf.

On the radio Mayor Koch talked about the hurricane. He was upset, he said, because everyone was celebrating. "This is not a joke," he was saying. "A hurricane is a serious thing. It's not cause for a party."

Joey sat on Catherine's sofa and rolled another joint. "Tell me some dirty gossip," he said. "Who's fucking who."

"Whom," Catherine said.

She told him all about this girl she knew, one of Fran's friends, who had gone up to the Hamptons with a director and now she had a part in his new movie. She told him about a so-called casting call for another new movie. The director, having already assigned the female role, had an open casting call, got a hotel room, brought up young would-be actresses, and home-videoed them while they masturbated.

"Nasty," Joey said. "I love it."

He passed Catherine the joint and she toasted him with it before she raised it to her lips.

"You could introduce me to Warhol, you know. You could."

"Yeah, and then you'd end up holding his umbrella for him for the rest of your life."

"What's wrong with that?" Joey said. "It would be *Andy's* umbrella."

Joey got up and browsed through Catherine's closet.

"I've never been much into white fluffy things," he said. He held out a vintage dress Catherine had bought somewhere in the Village. He brought out a pink sheer nightgown and put it on over his Dead Man shirt.

"All I need is one big idea," Catherine said, looking out the window. She tried opening the burglar bars, but they were rusted shut. "Jesus," she said, feeling suddenly paranoid. "If there was a fire, we couldn't get out."

"Calm down," Joey said from the inside of her closet. "It's just a hurricane."

Catherine looked at him. "Are we talking?"

They were still high when Catherine's mother called.

"Mom! I'm gonna model *swimsuits* for *Women!*" She wondered if she was shouting.

"Swimsuits? Couldn't it be just suits? Office suits?"

In her first year at *Women*, Catherine had been a Don't. A svelte assistant from Fashion had come into the office with a photographer, pinned Catherine's hair with a lot of gaudy barrettes and posed her at the typewriter.

Her picture appeared on the Fashion pages five months later. She had a black bar across her eyes, like the Lone Ranger. "*Don't* wear fussy hair ornaments at the office," the caption read. The only woman on the page without a black bar across her eyes was the svelte girl from Fashion. She was a Do.

Still, Catherine's mother had been proud enough to show her bridge group, and during the Feast of the Exaltation of the Cross, she had stood up at eight-o'clock mass and made an announcement. "I'd like to give thanks and praise," she had said. "My daughter's picture is in *Women.* Page seventy-four."

Joey passed the joint back to Catherine and she took a hit while her mother told her about how her tennis was coming along, that she was in charge of another benefit for the year, that Chloe had worms and that her shrink told her she was doing too much.

Catherine's mother called the priest who was her spiritual advisor her shrink.

"He says I should cut one activity out," her mother went on. She was eating a carrot and it was making Catherine hungry. Already Joey was looking inside Catherine's refrigerator. He took out a dirty red plate. "I hate when these priests treat me like a stupid old lady."

Catherine stood there wondering if her mother could tell that she was high. She felt as though the conversation was taking hours. And her leg itched. There were so many pin-point red marks on her thigh, it looked like a gang of mosquitoes had descended upon her.

"I gotta go, Mom."

"When are you coming home?"

"Soon," Catherine lied.

"I haven't seen you since last Christmas. Are you eating?"

"I'm just about to, Mom."

"Do you have a date?"

"No. Well. Sort of. With Joey."

"Joey? Isn't it Daniel?"

"Not anymore."

"You're not having an affair, are you?"

Catherine looked at Joey. He was still wearing her pink nightie over his Dead Man shirt and he had on Catherine's Walkman. He was at the sink, washing the red plate.

"Joey's my friend, Mom. He's gay."

"And you're eating with him? Is that sanitary?"

On a whim, Catherine and Joey took a train out to West Hampton because Joey wanted to see the ocean one last time before it got too cold.

"Maybe we'll get lucky," he had said. "Maybe we'll get to be inside Gloria. She could be my second woman."

At the train station in West Hampton, they got a ride from a potato farmer headed their way. Joey hadn't dressed up like anybody that day and he had taken off Catherine's nightie, but still the farmer stared at him. Everyone noticed Joey's face. Slim and plucked, he was undeniably pretty, and when the light was right, he was painfully hard to look at.

It was off-season and the beach was empty. Still, it was warm enough to soak your feet and they stepped over a row of jellyfish and waded in. Joey found some unchipped shells and pieces of white driftwood that felt like dry sponges. Catherine put them all in her backpack. At sunset, they walked up the beach until they found a place that sold wine and beer and steamed mussels.

"So little time," Joey said after their first round of mussels. There was sand on his lipstick. "So much to eat."

They had brought sleeping bags and they slept on the beach because they couldn't afford any of the hotels near town. Joey found a nice spot between some dunes in front of a house that was all glass and balconies.

"Tell me things," Catherine said, snuggling down into her bag.

He told her about a float trip he had taken down the Buffalo when he was in college. He told her about the time he first made love there, in the river, where the water moved all around him and his third cousin, once removed. Catherine liked when Joey told her about his life in what he called Bum-Fuck, Arkansas. He had a mother who sewed and a father who worked in a chicken plant.

"I'm ready to fall in love again," he said. "Just for like three days."

Catherine thought about that, how nice it would be to keep falling in love—three days at a time. She would always be giddy. Her face would glow and she would never feel tired, even on three hours of sleep. Being in love three days at a time, everything would always seem fresh and new, and Catherine's skin prickled at the thought as she nuzzled into Joey's side for warmth.

In the morning, they raided an apple orchard for breakfast. It was windy and the fruit tasted dusty. They walked the four or five miles into town and caught the first train back to the city.

The swimsuit shoot was in a photographer's loft in the meat district. It was a big drafty room with a high ceiling and a lot of exposed beams. Assistants from all the departments in *Women* stood, wrapped in big terry-cloth beach towels, huddling near the one space heater near the window. Outside, it was raining.

Catherine came in a little past nine. She had stopped by the office first to work on the article idea she had come up with when she and Joey had gotten back from the beach. She hadn't had time to retype the memo to Ms. Simpson and Howard, so she had left it on her desk—Fran's desk—thinking she would get back before the day was through. Beauty had promised this wasn't going to take very long.

Personnel made a point of hiring assistants that looked like good, solid make-over material for *Women*. They were usually good-looking girls with long hair or sloppy figures, girls who made up their faces in spring colors when their complexion was really that of winter. In fact, a person could usually tell how long a woman had worked at *Women* by the length of her hair. The longer she had been there, the shorter her hair was. At Home must have been just out of college. She had a thick auburn bolt down her back. Research had been there a year longer than Catherine. Her hair was bobbed. Catherine's was shoulder length.

While Beauty looked for a suit for Catherine, Research stood, posing on white butcher paper which fell down from a roll hanging from the ceiling. She wore a beige crocheted bikini and her hip bones stuck out. She didn't have any makeup on. She wasn't smiling. The photographer, a handsome, tanned, balding man took some pictures, and then he said that was all. When she walked away, there were brown footprints left on the paper where she had stood. The photographer's assistant, a boy who looked all of sixteen, cut where her feet had been and rolled more paper out for the next girl.

Hair and Makeup stood by, eating ham sandwiches and potato chips. Hair wanted to put on the Beach Boys, but Beauty said they couldn't play any music because they were still shooting the Befores and nobody could look like they were having fun.

The slate blue tank looked even worse than the orange one, so Beauty told Catherine to put it on.

The Before didn't take long at all. Whenever Catherine smiled, the photographer would wait and they'd try it again.

At noon, Hair began trimming Catherine while Makeup blotted out the red electrolysis marks Joey had left on her thighs. When Catherine explained to him how they got there, Makeup shook his head and said, "Stop."

"Isn't that just the way?" he said.

"Snip-snip here. Snip-snip there," Hair sang as he cut. On his collar, he wore a sterling silver pin shaped like a pair of scissors. "She's Dorothy on the way to the Wizard."

"I love that part," Makeup said. The collar on his polo shirt was starched straight up for a painted-on Preppy look. "They polish the Tin Man and put bows in the Lion's hair."

Catherine was enjoying herself. In the past few years, she had had nothing but horrible experiences getting her hair cut in Manhattan. She'd gone to Bumble & Bumble, where all the women from *Women* got a discount and the man there, Ted, had lifted up her wet ends with vague disgust. "See?" he had said, holding up a shriveled end. She had twisted around to see. He pulled on the strands until they broke apart. "You're too dry for a perm." So for twenty minutes she sat, feeling ugly and inadequate, while Ted gave her a forty-nine-dollar trim.

She looked in the mirror. Hair had given her bangs.

"In England they call it fringe," he said. "It's the newest In Look."

For the After, Catherine changed into a red suit. Beauty added a white belt and painted her toenails the color of stop signs. Hair squirted mousse on her head and made it stick up, and Makeup put on more mascara.

"Just remember to pile it on," Makeup told her, combing out her lashes with a miniature eyelash comb. "They can never be long enough." He was so amused by his last comment he felt compelled to repeat it to Hair.

At three-thirty, when it was at last her turn to stand on the butcher paper again, Catherine remembered what the three-thousand-dollar-a-day cover girl model had told her. Catherine licked her lips. She rolled her foot out to the side and pouted.

Then the photographer threw her a beach ball his assistant had blown up and everyone shouted at her to look happier.

"Jump up," Beauty screamed. "People always look better in motion."

Outside, a cold October wind whistled through the windows while the assistants read magazines and crouched closer to the space heater.

The photographer's assistant turned on a fan and Makeup put on that year's Prince.

"Are nipples OK?" the photographer asked Beauty. "Last time Howard said it was too Playboyish."

"Try not to look so cold," Beauty shouted to Catherine. "It's May, remember?"

The photographer got tired of the beach ball and produced a bucket full of sand and a shovel. Then he threw Catherine a towel.

"Play," he shouted. "Move! Spin the towel over your head like this. Keep moving. You're having fun. You *are* having fun, aren't you?"

The sand spilled. Her stop-sign toenails chipped. Beauty cursed. The photographer grumbled, "God, I hate working with amateurs."

By four-thirty, Catherine, wearing a mask and a snorkel, was running in place. She had already tried the fins, but she had tripped and made more marks on the butcher paper and the assistant had had to cut and roll out more. Catherine jumped and skipped in place until five-fifteen—until Hair and Makeup had finished what was left of lunch, until the paper beneath Catherine's red toenails tore for the seventh time, and the photographer said he had run out of film and Beauty said she had had enough.

Early the following morning, walking down the hall, Catherine saw the office light on in Entertainment and she could hear the stereo playing Pat Benatar before she had even reached Articles. She wasn't looking forward to it but she would, she thought, have to have a word with the Greek.

But it was Fran who stood before the full-length mirror, shaving her mustache with a pink Lady's Bic.

"Cat!" she shrieked. "I'm back!"

Fran was a short woman with Joan Collins eyes. She had her hair tied up with lace like Madonna's, wore a tight pink Linda Evans suit, and teetered on stiletto Tina Turner heels. She fiddled with a pair of rhinestone earrings.

Fran was a real *Women's* woman. She had been in the Befores, gotten the makeovers (she lost twenty-five pounds, got a nose job and a haircut) and now, Beauty considered her completely "fixed" using her only for Afters. But Fran didn't feel fixed—she complained about her thighs amd her height and the fact that she was almost thirty-five and unmarried.

During Catherine's first week on the job, Fran had had a brief nervous breakdown. Her fiance, the man she had been living with for five years, flew to Florida and married a redheaded Catholic girl he had known since high school. He had also taken Fran's pasta maker and the microwave. Fran spent most of that month in analysis, and when she did make it to the office, she called her friends and cried on the phone. Because Fran did not make herself available for training, Catherine learned by trial and error. That was the week Bo Derek called to say she still hadn't received her leather bikini in the mail—the one John had had made up especially for her—the one *Women* shot her in for a spread on "Bodies to Die Over," an article which Howard ultimately dubbed a failure because all of their pseudoanorexic readers wrote in saying how disgusting and inappropriate it had been to use the expression "to die over." Bo did finally get her bikini, a month later. And Catherine knew from then on that anything going to a celebrity went Federal Express, never fourth class, uninsured.

Unhappy with the cost of analysis ("Why should I pay a shrink when I can call my friend Pam for free?" she had said), Fran took to telephoning an astrologer in L.A. every morning at ten o'clock New York time. Then she flew out for a week so he could chart out her biorhythm.

Fran and Catherine hugged. Fran, Catherine noticed, was wearing a different, more expensive perfume. She gave Catherine a bottle of rum called Cockspur and a sweatshirt that read *Camp Beverly Hills*. The sweatshirt was in Fran's size.

"That astrologer, Cat. I'd eat a piece of cheese and he acted like I was killing a cow. Then he said he thought Sissy Spacek was ugly and fake. Uch! What got into me? It's nineteen-eighty-whatever and in less than a year I'm going to be thirty-five. I'm sick of living alone. I want a bigger place. Don't you? Don't you want a sauna, and a house out in the Hamptons?"

Catherine smiled and nodded.

Fran held up a book: *How to Find a Husband in 30 Days* published by the same people who had tried to give her *Thinner Thighs in 30 Days*. Fran sat down at her desk, opened the book, and began to read.

They spent the morning being civil to one another. Catherine stayed on the phone and tried to get used to being an assistant again. Every now and then Fran held up something she had found of Catherine's in her desk drawer—some Fig Newtons, a bottle of shampoo from a Beauty giveaway, some notes—and Catherine would retrieve it and Fran would joke, "Get comfy while I was away?"

Catherine didn't bother asking Fran what had happened to her Greek.

"I had a memo on your desk," Catherine said.

"I took care of it," Fran said, and Catherine wondered what that meant.

At five o'clock, Ms. Simpson's assistant called for Fran, and Catherine, remembering the mood the hurricane weather had produced in Ms. Simpson, pitied Fran for the first time. She imagined Ms. Simpson right now, plugging in the green rock. I will be kind, Catherine thought. I will gather empty boxes from the messenger room and when they are full I will hold the flaps down while Fran tapes them shut. Maybe Fran will be considered important enough to get a party. Maybe even Howard will come.

But Fran looked radiant when she returned from her fifteen-minute meeting. She sat with her feet on top of the wastepaper basket, filing her nails.

"Cat," she said. "She loves our idea."

Catherine looked up from the February page proofs on her desk.

"Our idea?"

"Casting-Couch Actresses. You must've spent all weekend on that. I've got to hand it to you, Cat. And I'm glad you let me take a look at it first. I think you'll like the changes I made."

Catherine didn't say anything. She got up, straightened her desk, packed some magazines in her bag, got her umbrella.

"I'm really glad you came to me with it first, Cat," Fran said. "It made it worth coming back for, you know? Like we're a team." She put down her nail file. "Who needs a fucking husband, right? This is cover story material, C. You can start on it tomorrow. God, Catherine. We are so hot!"

The swimsuit photos had been developed, the May Beauty pages laid out, and on the day Hurricane Gloria was supposed to hit Manhattan, Joey called Catherine into the Art Department to have a look.

Everyone at *Women* had come in that morning, picked up their paychecks, and left. They wore their versions of what was chic to wear in a hurricane, but mostly everybody ended up looking like Carol Burnett's bag lady or the girl on the Morton salt box. Ms. Simpson's assistant had made an announcement at nine on the intercom that the subways and buses were closing at ten-thirty and that everyone should be out of the building by then. Even Ms. Simpson seemed to forget about firing for the day; she unplugged her rock and went on home.

Fran had come in bitching about the taxis in New York. Then she left. Catherine went down to the cafeteria on three where they were having a hurricane special—everything was free—then went back to her office to put in a few calls to L.A.

It was noon, the sky was pink, and Gloria still hadn't come. Joey and Catherine were the only two on the floor. Joey offered Catherine a bite of his chicken-salad sandwich and he sat in Fran's chair. The TV was on in Entertainment and there was a lot of grey, blurry news footage of palm trees swaying on beaches, broken power lines, and people wandering around on the streets.

"Have you seen the swimsuit spread?" Joey asked Catherine. All of her phone calls were filled with static and she couldn't get any work done anyway so she decided to take a look. "I only did what Howard and Beauty told me to do," he said, leading the way down the hall to Art. "So you can't have a hissy."

Her picture started the spread because she was the *H*. "Catherine is an *H*," the copy read. "She has no waist." In the Before picture, without her waist, Catherine wasn't smiling. In the After picture, she was jumping up and down, swinging a towel over her head. Sand was spilled all around her feet. She was happy. She was wearing red and Beauty had belted her. "Women without waists should wear belts," the copy concluded. "I wonder," Joey said, looking over Catherine's shoulder. "Have you ever actually seen anyone swimming with a belt on?"

At Home came next. She was an *O*. In the After shot, she wore a suit with shoulder pads.

They had grouped everyone in the *H-O-A-X* body type formula. *O* was all waist. *A* was all hip. *X* was the perfect hourglass figure. Beauty, wearing a becoming V-necked black suit, was the *X*.

There was also a special pull-out section on How to Sit Down in a Swimsuit. "*Do* sit up straight, knees together," the copy read. "*Don't* slump, spread-eagled."

"I feel like such an idiot," Catherine said. "Two million people are going to see this."

"Oh, come on," Joey said. "It's not so bad. At least you got a great haircut." He puffed up her bangs.

"Men are never divided up into the letters of the fucking alphabet."

Joey laughed but Catherine didn't. He punched her arm lightly.

"Don't you think you're overreacting?"

Catherine bit the lower half of her bottom lip, which she still couldn't feel. Her father had once told her if you don't know what's going to happen, you're not in control. And for the first time since her father had died, Catherine felt completely out of control. Daniel was in Rome and she didn't know if she was ever going to see him again. She didn't know where the Greek girl had gone off to. She had lost her article idea to Fran, and in a few months, millions of women would see her standing half-naked, representing the letter *H*. It was thundering and lightning outside and for a brief moment, Catherine saw herself running home, plugging in Finally Free, and electrolyzing herself without the rubber boots.

Joey put the page back under a square sheet of Plexiglas.

"Come on," he said. "Let's go back to your office."

The TV was still on.

"I don't know why they're out there, Mike," a reporter said. "It seems that they just want to *be* in a hurricane."

Mayor Koch was interviewed. He had heard that people were throwing

Hurricane Gloria parties and he was mad. "This is *not* TV," he insisted. "This is real. This is happening. This isn't some fantasy of a dragon coming out in the street. People can get hurt. People can die."

Joey laughed and switched to "All My Children."

In the eye of the hurricane, everything was still, and Catherine was sick of being in the eye. She wished Gloria would hit now. Manhattan would fall off into the Atlantic and everyone would be surprised that California hadn't gone first. She wouldn't have to ask actresses who they had slept with to get where they were, she wouldn't have to worry about getting in her March copy because there would be no March issue, and nobody would ever have to see her in a swimsuit in May.

A weather report interrupted Erica's love scene. A trailer owner on the coast was being interviewed.

"Sure, we're coming back," the man said. "We've lived here fifteen years. We'll just go on down to the schoolhouse and sit it out like always. But we can't leave."

"Idiot," Joey said. "Sounds like one of my relatives."

Catherine and Joey went across the hall to Readers' Service, and looked out a window duct-taped with a big *X*. All the windows on Madison Avenue were taped for Gloria. Catherine felt as though she were in the middle of a blown-up picture of one of those maps in a mall with the *You Are Here* blocked out with a black *X*. Outside she and Joey spotted a woman in a slim black skirt climbing into a cab. Catherine caught sight of a Diane Sawyer leg right before it disappeared into the cab. The woman looked as if she had been in a hurry to get to some place important. Catherine was willing to bet that woman wasn't an assistant, that she had a string of wealthy, banker-type admirers who sent her tulips on Groundhog Day and baskets of Jelly Bellies in spring.

Once, during an interview, Catherine had asked a famous clothes designer how she had gotten the courage to leave her husband and start her own company.

"I saw a woman crossing the street," the designer had told Catherine. "She had one of those great hurried walks. I wanted to look like that. On bad days, I think of that woman."

Catherine thought about all the rain from that morning and she worried about her ceiling in her apartment. When it rained, yellow water dripped down the walls and plaster chips inevitably fell into her sofa bed. She thought about how much trouble she was going to have getting a cab—the subways being closed—and she thought about all the water that would weigh down her sneakers on the walk home.

"Visualize a shot before you make it." That's what her mother had said the tennis pro taught her.

At that moment, standing there behind the window marked *X*, Catherine felt as though she knew exactly what that clothes designer had meant, and more than ever, Catherine wished she was that woman who had sped off in a yellow cab in the middle of a hurricane. She didn't want to be somebody's assistant anymore. She wanted to be sitting in the back of a cab in a short black skirt heading straight uptown.

It was then that Catherine made a silent, shaky vow. I will not be like Fran, she thought. I will not have thunderous Jewish thighs, but sleek Catholic ones. I will never shave my facial hair at the office. The photographer was right, she thought. Movement is the key. Like riding a bicycle—stop and you'll fall over. I will not be sidetracked by L.A. astrologers or museum conservators. Going to bed with a man will become no big deal. I will become hairless and noncommittal. I will not associate with people on the fringe. I will *brucher* so much I will never have to be a letter in anybody's formula again.

"Alas," Joey said, putting his arm around Catherine. "The woman with no waist."

"Maybe now I'll be eligible for a handicap sticker."

"That's the spirit," Joey said. "Except, you don't have a car."

Joey went back to Art to put his things away while Catherine ran back to her office and turned off the TV and the light, then they both took the elevator down and left the building, so they could say they'd been in the middle of Times Square that year, the year the hurricane hit.

Chapter 3

Joining the League

Gloria never came to Manhattan and for weeks afterwards duct tape dangled from the windows of all the buildings downtown. Mayor Koch made an announcement: "I think that New York City scared the hell out of that hurricane," and the reporters wrote it down and didn't laugh because everybody was sick of laughing at everything Koch said.

In mid-November Fran went to a wedding on Long Island and met a man who had made a lot of money in bonds.

"I think this one's *it*," she told her friend Pam on the phone the next day. "He's not perfect. He's bicoastal and he has a problem with commitment, but I figure the way to win him over is to throw lots of cocktail parties, even if it means green nachos."

She got her hair done that Friday and called up the bond salesman.

"You gotta let me come over *now*," she said over the phone. "You've gotta see me before it falls."

At noon the following Monday, she called his secretary to find out where he was having lunch. Then she called the restaurant, got a table next to his, and told Pam to meet her there.

"Can you believe this?" Catherine imagined Fran saying. "I mean, what are the chances?"

For Fran, every day in Manhattan was the start of another hunt. She read articles on the man shortage, tore them out of magazines, and kept them all together in a file folder in her top desk drawer. Once, when Fran's bond salesman was in San Francisco and Fran had had a particularly lonely weekend, she announced she was moving to Sioux City, Iowa, where there were five rugged men for every woman in town. In the folder, there were clips from *Cosmo*'s bachelor of the month, and articles on Steven Spielberg, who hadn't married Amy Irving yet. He had just made her pregnant. "He's still available in my book," Fran would claim.

Fran had a plan: she would get a colossal Entertainment story on the cover of *Women*, take a position on "Entertainment Tonight," interview Spielberg, seduce him, and then become his mistress, wife, or whatever was suitable to him.

Meanwhile, Catherine was entering a period which Joey would later dub her Dating Hell.

She went clubbing with a bisexual who claimed he had played bass for Men at Work. He had long, dragon-lady nails on his right hand because, he said, he used them as guitar picks. He ate escargots for dinner, and, reeking of garlic, he took her home and didn't kiss her but stood at her stoop, reached up under her shirt, and scratched at her breast.

She bicycled in Central Park with a producer from ABC who told her about his idea for a TV series—an interview show about people who have made it in the United States. He wanted to call it "Made in the USA."

"And when the credits roll," he said, ringing his bike bell at two women who were roller-skating right towards him, "I want to see my name, like right over Joan Collins' face." He said "face" with a vengeance. "Come on," he said. "Let's race." Catherine pedaled hard to keep up. He had a ten-speed. She had had to rent a bike—a Schwinn three-speed—and when they got past the ice-skating rink, she turned and pedaled back to her place alone.

She listened to jazz with a bodybuilder who owned the printing place in New Jersey that printed *Women*. All night he stared at other women who wore tight-fitting skirts, ignoring Catherine, who had made the mistake of wearing the Laura Ashley frock her mother had sent her when she'd had her wisdom teeth pulled.

When he took her home, he hugged her and then backed away. He pulled her arms up and then let them fall.

"There's not much to you, is there?" he said.

She ate out with an aging trust fund kid with chapped lips. All evening he said things like "rather" and "in-so-far as to say." She asked him up because she figured her mother would approve of him and they sat nervously on her folded-up sofa bed, staring at the wall streaked with yellow from last month's rains.

Then suddenly he jumped up and shouted, "Male flight! Male flight!" And he was gone.

"Male flight?" Joey said in her office the next morning when Catherine told him all about it. "What the hell is that supposed to mean?"

"I don't know. We're talking about a thirty-seven-year-old man who still lives with his mother," Catherine said. "I miss Daniel."

Joey shook a bottle of nail polish he'd gotten from Beauty. He took Catherine's hand and painted the nail on her pinky purple.

"I wish you'd hurry up and get laid," he said, blowing on her fingernail. "You're beginning to lose your perspective."

Later that day, Fran told Catherine she couldn't be expected to write any of the pieces for April.

"I'm an editor," she said. "Editors don't write. They sit home in their apartments, order in, and edit."

Catherine wasn't getting anywhere with "their" casting-couch piece.

She had made the mistake of being honest and telling publicists what she was really going to ask their clients.

Fran had no advice.

"You're just not trying hard enough," she would say. "Don't take no for an answer." This was Fran's advice every month—that and "Get mad."

April was due but Catherine was still working on a March piece called "The Personals." It was to be a roundup of personal ads written by famous men. Fran had come up with the idea, having once placed a personal in *New York* magazine herself. But Catherine couldn't get anybody famous enough to agree—"What, you think my client has to *advertise* to get a date?" the publicists all shrieked. So Catherine decided to lie. She told the publicists she was working on a piece called "The Newest Hottest Young Stars." She did fifteen-minute over-the-phone interviews with the celebrities so that when the issue did come out, at least she wouldn't feel badly about taking up too much of their time. She asked them what kind of women they liked and if— just say, let's suppose—they were to put an ad in the paper, how they would describe themselves.

"Silly guy wants silly gal," the comedian Lewis Lipman said. He had been the only one whom Catherine had not tricked. In fact, he had liked the idea. "Must be willing to wear tutu, put on toe shoes—maybe flippers and mask—and wade in a pool of wintermint Jell-O."

"With or without the tutu?"

"With," he said. "I'll eat it off. So tell me. What do you look like?"

"I've got bangs," Catherine said. "And I've been known to flop around in a flipper or two."

During one of her Tuesday night calls, Catherine's mother announced that she was concerned that Catherine wasn't meeting the right people, and that she had gotten Catherine into the Junior League.

"It'll be fun," her mother assured her when Catherine moaned. "It'll broaden your power base. Now hold on while I kill a wasp." Catherine heard the phone fall, and Chloe barked in the background while her mother swatted one, two, three times.

Catherine's mother wasn't in the league herself, though she had always wanted to be. When they had lived in Memphis they hadn't let her in because her husband had been Jewish. In Memphis it was "Jurish." Then, when they moved to Barrington, Illinois, she was considered to be too old. Her mother compensated, however, by doing a lot of volunteer work and seeing a priest once a month.

The first meeting for the Manhattan provisionals was held at the Hunter School of Social Work on Sixty-ninth between Park and Lexington. Catherine walked there after work. She had been careful not to tell Fran where she was going because she knew Fran would not approve. The league had nothing to do with entertainment and would therefore be a waste of "our" time.

Inside the building, an elderly woman wearing an Hermes scarf around her shoulders handed out lime green name tags. The auditorium was already filled with done-up girls in bow ties and briefcases, and the only seats left were the ones up front. Onstage, two women introduced themselves: a pregnant president and a blond vice president with her sweater tucked into her skirt.

"The New York Junior League wath founded in 1900," the vice president said. She had a lisp. "We thit here tonight, beginning the leagueth eighty-fourth year."

"During the early yearth," she lisped on, "when the league wath well ethtablithed, theveral quethionth were raithed. Who thould become a member? At what age mutht you thtop being an active member? Thould we wear uniformth?"

Everyone was divided up into predesignated groups in order to discuss what good they could do for the city of New York. Catherine was in Group II. They followed the vice president out the door and paraded up Lexington, past a tired-looking woman with green eye shadow hesitating over a salad bar inside a Korean deli, past three young punks smoking dope at the corner, past a black woman holding her child who was defecating next to a mailbox.

Inside the League's headquarters, it was all flowered chintz and polished oak. Upstairs, in the Astor Room, there were framed botanical prints—faded just right.

"Thay a little thomething about yourthelveth," the vice president commanded when they were all seated. While the others rattled on about their occupations at Chase, Kidder, or Merrill Lynch, Catherine rehearsed to herself. "I'm Catherine Clemons. I've lived in Manhattan for three years and I'm still a goddamned assistant at a piss-ant women's magazine, working for a bitch who claims she owns me and I don't think I can really afford to be in this town or in the Junior League because I can barely pay my rent."

Everyone was looking at Catherine. It was her turn. She scooted herself up to the edge of her chair as the others had. "I'm Catherine Clemons," she started. She was trying for loud and confident, but it came out a breathless whisper. No one was looking at her. The two girls from Kidder, Peabody were on the sofa, discussing that day's big block trades. The girl who claimed to be from Paris was cleaning her glasses. "I'm the Entertainment editor at *Women*." At this everyone looked up. Catherine could feel them itemizing her outfit—shoes to shoulder pads. It was the first time in a long time Catherine had felt significant enough to be envied.

The rest of the meeting, the vice president explained the volunteer work and how much was required from newcomers. In their first year, provisionals were not allowed to actually go forth and do good—not yet, anyway. To better acquaint themselves with league procedures, provisionals were expected to buy a few trinkets at the Christmas boutique, have drinks and dinner at the league headquarters, and swim at the Colony Club, where they would receive a discount.

A large woman in a green dress came in with a camera and took a Group II picture. Afterwards everyone pulled out a Mont Blanc from her purse to sign up for a committee she might be interested in, in a year, or two, or three.

Nobody signed up for the visits to the cancer wards. Most of the women wanted to put on plays or read to children, or help with decorations for the league's annual ball. The ball, Catherine gathered, was a big deal. It was held at the Waldorf, and a few of the women were gossiping about someone who had sued last year because Liz Smith printed that she had worn a white leather miniskirt there. The girl from Paris said she wouldn't be able to sign up for anything—she was pregnant. Catherine took out a blue Bic and signed up with the league's hot line. She would read a booklet and one night a month she would answer questions over the phone concerning sexually transmitted diseases. One of the girls from Kidder told Catherine that was admirable, but to bring a can of Lysol spray.

"For the phone receiver," she said. "Never know."

Catherine didn't bother changing out of her new black suede pumps because the walk home was less then ten blocks. The fat little Korean boy at the fruit stand didn't understand what kind of rice cakes she wanted, so she bought an orange instead, and made it to the Chinese laundry before it closed.

"Baby yet?" Catherine asked, handing her ticket to the plump owner.

"No yet," he said, and he gave her her clothes and held up three fingers.

"Three weeks?"

He shook his head.

"Three months," she said, and he nodded and then his daughter, pregnant and smiling, came out from behind a row of hanging shirts, and at that moment Catherine envied the girl—envied that she would be giving life to something real in February while Catherine would still be trying to figure out July Entertainment, having just closed June.

Two black garbagemen whistled when Catherine walked by, and she passed a bag man who mumbled into his fingernails. "Calm down," he said. "Just calm down."

There was a notice taped to her building's foyer door. "Please don't use water for 24 hours," it read. "Pipes being adjusted. Sorry for the convenience."

In her mailbox, there were invitations, her phone bill, a letter from Daniel, and a bill for two hundred dollars from the New York City Junior League, welcoming her to the club.

Later that week, Catherine went to a restaurant opening in SoHo with Lewis Lipman, who almost got in a fight with a paparazzo who called him a has-been. But even though he was a has-been—a potbellied, balding has-been—Catherine was glad she was going to an opening—any opening—with a somebody.

In the letter she had gotten, Daniel had said his offer still stood—that he would send her her ticket to Rome anytime, and that he would pick her up himself at the airport if he had to. "I'll be the one with the forlorn look," he wrote.

But the idea of running away from Manhattan depressed Catherine. She sent Daniel a postcard—one of those cartoon close-ups of a woman done in dots. *Gasp!* the woman was saying. *A nuclear holocaust? There goes my career!* "At work on a big new story," Catherine wrote. "Can't say what— *Time* may scoop me."

The restaurant in SoHo was featuring a French artist named Margot who stood in front of her paintings—portraits of women wearing red hightops and black-lace Betsey Johnson dresses, their hair held up with colorful plastic butterfly clips. In the paintings, the women's hands were disproportionately large and muscular, painted in harsh blues and reds.

"She got that from Picasso. And that? She got that from Matisse," Lewis said, chomping on a piece of raw cauliflower. "Everything comes from something else."

A guy Catherine knew from *American Health* was there.

"I knew his girlfriend," Catherine whispered to Lewis, as he approached them. "He has herpes." Catherine shook his hand.

"Wash that," Lewis whispered, looking at her hand. Catherine could tell he was mad that American Health hadn't recognized him.

The man from *American Health* went on about the bicycle article he was working on and then a woman came and stood beside him, picking at a pimple on her jaw.

"Lynn used to be at Rogers & Cowan. She's in the middle of a career switch," American Health said. Lynn nodded, making her pimple bleed.

"Investment banking," Lynn said. "That's where all the money is. I'll work for a few more years and then I'll buy a horse farm and ride all day."

Catherine excused herself and went outside to change her shoes. She was wearing a red corduroy dress she thought might look more grown-up with higher pumps, which she kept stashed in her big black fake-alligator bag.

She leaned against the building in the alley and she couldn't help but notice a group of astonishingly handsome people laughing across the street. The men were in dark cashmere coats and the women wore snug little skirts and noisy jewelry. They appeared completely unselfconscious. They were the kind of people you think you recognize, but don't and wish you did. They're out of a commercial for New York, Catherine thought, momentarily wondering how or if she could ever fit in with people who looked like that.

Then she saw one of them—a man—come walking towards her.

"Here, let me," he said, taking her arm. He stood so close she could smell his cologne. *Women* had run a piece once on men's colognes—which were out—Musk—and which were in—Paco Rabanne. But Catherine was only familiar with the scratch-and-sniff samples of their advertisers. His was an altogether different smell. Musty and a little bit too sweet.

"I guess this looks kind of silly," she said, looking across the street at the others. She realized now they had been laughing at her. She watched them watch her and then they lazily closed in among themselves, rearranging one another's scarves and ties.

"You with anybody?"

Catherine went to the restaurant window and pointed out Lewis, who was now at the broccoli bowl with American Health.

"Lewis Lipman. He was on 'Saturday Night Live,' what, five years ago?" the man said. Catherine nodded, impressed that he seemed impressed.

"I'm with them," the man said.

Catherine looked at his crowd again.

"Great haircuts."

The man laughed and his teeth were so straight and white they looked like a row of spotlights around a movie marquee.

"Yeah. Quite the fashion statements," he said, moving a long strand of hair that had flipped forward into Catherine's bangs. "Can't exactly run your fingers through a fashion statement."

"Do I know you?"

He looked at her and smiled.

"Maybe," he said. "From somewhere." And then he smiled again.

"You smile a lot."

"It's the drugs," he said. "Dump him." He tilted his head towards the restaurant window. "Come with us. You like mussels? We're in search of mussels."

"I can't, but you'll find them. It's the season for shellfish. November has an *r* in it."

He laughed again, and took out a fountain pen and his wallet—a slim Italian affair from Fendi's.

"Give me your number."

"I don't even know you."

"Sure you do. I'm Michael."

Usually when a strange man asked for Catherine's number, she gave him the emergency room at Lenox Hill, but she looked across the street, and then at him.

"That's 212," she added, watching him cap his fountain pen with his lips.

Later that evening, Lewis got drunk and hit American Health when the two of them started talking about cancer. But the paparazzi didn't even take his picture and nothing was mentioned in Liz Smith or Page Six the next day, and Catherine quit returning his calls.

To celebrate the completion of the piece on celebrity personal ads for the March Entertainment page, Fran took Catherine out to lunch. They went to the Trattoria in the Pan Am Building. Fran had even made the reservations herself.

Fran was especially dressed up, in a moss green linen suit with pink rhinestone earrings and bracelets. She wore high-heeled green shoes so that she came up to Catherine's chin, and her skirt made her hips look pleasantly plump—the way some Italian women have a way of looking when they walk.

On the walk there, a guy selling crack whistled at Fran, which made her feel good, and she told Catherine what she had learned that morning about lingerie.

"A cabdriver told me," she said. "That's what they like. Lingerie. The sluttier the better." The "they" meant men. Fran's "theys" always meant men. "And they hate all that menswear shit. Pants, suits, forget it. Whore is in. I spent three hundred and fifty dollars at Bloomies on Saturday. I even got a girdle."

Fran had been having trouble with the bond salesman. The week before, she had invited him over to her place and she had cooked linguine with clam sauce because, she had read, clams and garlic were an aphrodisiac.

"And oregano," she had said. "Oregano makes you want to do it."

She had lit up the place with candles and put on mood music—whales singing underwater. But he had turned on the lights, claiming he couldn't see what he was eating, and he had left early to catch the red-eye to San Francisco.

"He didn't even tell me he was going away," Fran had shrieked in the phone to all her friends that day. "He's got to be gay. Do you think he's gay? He doesn't act gay."

The Trat was packed and the whole place smelled of Parmesan and pizza. Fran discussed something with the headwaiter and he led them to a table near the bar where all the food came out assembly-line style.

"I don't believe it!" Fran said. And Catherine couldn't either.

Sitting there, at the table next to theirs, was the man with the pen and the Fendi wallet who had helped Catherine change her shoes in the alley in SoHo.

"Michael! Can you believe this? It's like what, two times in one month that this has happened."

Michael looked at the man seated across the table from him, and then he stood up, smiling at Catherine.

"This is my little assistant, Catherine," Fran said.

Catherine bit the paralyzed part of her bottom lip and stuck out her hand.

"Pleased to meet you," Michael said, and then he introduced his client, a paunchy man with tinted glasses.

Michael pushed the two tables together while Fran squeezed Catherine's arm.

"Isn't he to die," she whispered up into Catherine's ear. "I *knew* he'd be here."

During lunch, Michael sat next to Fran, allowing her elbow to lightly rest against his, while he looked across the table at Catherine who, for lack of anything better to do, attempted to seduce Michael's client.

Look at the eyes, lips, and eyes again. Back and forth for as long as you can go without laughing out loud. This was Jessica Lange's secret and Catherine noticed Jessica tended to concentrate on the lips a bit longer and, consequently, went a little cross-eyed.

It took some doing—Catherine could never actually see the man's eyes under his glasses, so she estimated, using his brows as a starting point.

By coffee, the client had given Catherine his card and asked Catherine for hers.

Having a business card had been an issue between Fran and Catherine. The rule at *Women* was that nobody but an editor could have them. Catherine asked Fran how she could be expected to do business, but Fran had refused, and Catherine had gone down to a place on Seventh Avenue one lunch hour and had a printer do them up, paying for them herself.

Because the lining was ripping and the leather wasn't made from anything special, Catherine opened her wallet under the table, then gave the man her card. Fran didn't say anything. "Don't I get one, too?" Michael said.

"I don't know you well enough," Catherine said. "And I'm a good Catholic girl." She tried to make it sound like a joke, but the three of them just looked at her.

"I'm not good and I'm not Catholic," Fran said.

When Michael called the office, he asked for Fran, and Catherine pretended not to recognize his voice when she transferred his call.

"You handled it all wrong," Joey told her when she told him. "What's this 'good Catholic girl' shit? Since when?"

"I thought I was being clever."

"Sometimes clever's not what they're after."

At a screening that night at Magda, Catherine saw Michael and Fran sitting together in the big swivel chairs up front. Fran sat at the edge of her seat, facing Michael, looking into his eyes, breathing in his every word.

Catherine was with a a short, stocky fellow who did the key gripping for detergent commercials.

"I swear," the key grip was saying, swiveling in his chair, "that Pine-Sol ate right through that bucket."

The movie was about a composer who was famous during his time, but who later became a virtual unknown.

Afterwards Fran spotted Catherine and came over.

"It's amazing," Fran said while Michael helped her with her mink. She put the temple of her eyeglasses in her mouth and assumed the critic's stance. "People were competitive even back then."

The day Fran messengered over a poster of *It's a Wonderful Life* to Michael with her face and Michael's superimposed over Donna Reed's and

Jimmy Stewart's, Lewis asked Catherine out for tea.

He picked her up at *Women*, showing up in the elevator in a hair net, Hawaiian shirt, Bermudas, black socks and shoes. The receptionist laughed and asked him for his autograph and he put his arm around Catherine as though he had known her for years.

"Idn't she somethin," he said in his version of Bill Murray's lounge-lizard voice. He pinched her cheek. "I love this woman."

They went to a place called EAT except the E on the neon sign outside was out and it read AT. They sat at a table covered with white paper, and in the center there was a water glass filled with crayons. Lewis had a cold and was fasting, drinking only herbal teas, because he had read that liquids would carry all the bad away.

She colored while he told her about an off-Broadway wrestling play he had just been asked to be in.

Catherine didn't say anything because she thought the play sounded terrible.

"I have to practice my moves," he said, looking over the rim of his cup. Catherine could smell his Lemon Zinger.

"I don't know anything about wrestling," Catherine said.

"Maybe your readers would be interested."

"So that's what this is all about," she said. She colored in a purple bird. She gave her house some windows and a chimney. She added a dog to the lawn. "You're using me."

"Take me to your readers," he said leaning towards her.

Upstairs at her place, six flights up, they wrestled on the Oriental and she pinned him first.

"You're a weakling," she said.

"Don't tell anyone." He said it so seriously she wasn't sure if he was serious, and when she rolled him over his eyes were sad.

"Kees me," he said. "Put her right there."

Kissing, she had read, is the most intimate act, which is why so many people get it wrong. She decided to keep her mouth closed until he instructed otherwise but when she felt his thin lips get bigger, she really couldn't help herself.

"Catherine," he whispered. "My Catherine."

"Who says I'm yours?"

"I'm falling in love with you. Right here. Right now."

"No, you're not. You just think you are."

It killed her when guys did this. I love you, he says. How would he know? Lewis didn't even know her. He didn't know that she could get up to a size twelve in February, or that the only thing she knew how to cook was spaghetti. He didn't know that she had a mother going through some sort of midlife crisis who was probably out in Wheeling at this very moment, trying out new beds because she thought her daughter was coming back home. He didn't know what she sounded like on the phone when, say, a photographer hadn't sent the April stills in on time. He didn't know her and here he was waiting—like they all did—waiting for her to look back down at him all googly-eyed and whisper, real choked-up-like, I love you too.

Lewis rolled himself on top. He loosened his grip and his hands slipped from her wrists into her open palms.

"I want to be with you," he whispered, and the change in his voice was startling at first.

She tried to laugh.

"You're heavy," she said.

"Don't take this for granted."

"Too heavy."

He let go of her left hand and touched the ends of her hair. His breath was warm and he let out a small sound as he exhaled while he kissed her, a sigh, the kind of sound she might have made. And it was the sound of that sigh, the very warmth of it on her face, that moved her to bring her hand to his face, and as their lips still touched, she said, without thinking, "Take me home."

He wasn't like anything she had predicted. He wasn't fat or pale or awkward and he wasn't acting. He was kind, asking her, actually *asking* her, if he was hurting her.

"I don't ever want to hurt you," he said, and when he said "Oh God" out loud twice, she couldn't help but hold him to her.

"If I was born again, I'd want to be a pond," he said later, holding her to his side. She had the back of her head on his chest. "They have a life of their own and it's peaceful. Ponds aren't like oceans or lakes. They don't get angry."

"Yeah," she said. "You do get angry."

"I know. I was a bastard with that *American Health* guy. I can't help it. For the first time in my life I can't stand what I'm doing. I'm sick of acting like a lunatic to get a laugh."

"So quit."

"It's not that easy. My agent's down my throat, I've got this show coming up." He pressed his hand to her side. "It's different with you, though. I don't have to do flip-flops. I went with a girl once who said the best thing about sleeping with me was that she didn't have to sleep around anymore because every night I was literally a different person."

"Can you do Spiderman for me?" Catherine said, laughing.

"Really, though. When you're a comedian you're switching gears all the time. If somebody's not laughing at my Richard Nixon, I'm Barbara Mandrell like that." Lewis snapped his fingers.

"That must be exhausting."

"Yeah," he said. "It is."

Catherine turned around, burying her face in the dark hair of his armpit, and he rolled over and his lips were that way again, and this time it was she who said, "Oh God."

40 •

Later, while he slept, Catherine stared up at her ceiling, tired, hungry, happy. For a split second she had a vision of herself as an After-picture person—like one of those women she had seen in Dr. Panter's office the day she had had her wisdom teeth pulled. She thought of Daniel. She had betrayed him—or had she? He was in Italy and she had broken up. Sort of. How to Anesthetize a Loss, she thought. Cut your hair, paint your toenails, get a new boyfriend, and boom, you're smiling again.

She looked at Lewis. Asleep he looked like a boy. He'll start cooking for me, she thought. He'll buy a farm in Vermont and want me to raise his chickens. It's starting all over again. Catherine wondered how a woman got through life *without* repeating herself relationship after relationship.

She remembered the vow she had made to herself during Hurricane Gloria.

She got up and pulled on a pair of pants.

"Where are you going, baby?" Lewis said.

"I have to go."

"We're at your place, my little kumquat. My little sweet pagoda."

She stopped buttoning her blouse and turned to face him. "Then you have to go."

"But what about my afterglow?"

"Save it."

He got up and put on his pants. "Well," he said. "Aren't we modern."

"Wait," she said. She reached over to her bookcase and took out a folder with Lewis' glossy in it. "I know this is embarrassing," she said, holding out the picture and a felt-tip.

"Embarrassing for whom?"

She took a deep breath. She wished she could explain everything to him, but she knew he would never understand. "Make it out to Fran," she said.

At the beginning of December, Catherine took Joey to Sting's concert movie, which included footage of his girlfriend giving birth. Sting managed to weep photogenically.

"Let's get a drink," Joey said. "Childbirth always gives me a taste for tequila."

They went to a place that sold margaritas in glasses the size of fishbowls, but Joey wanted his in a mug. Joey always drank from mugs at a bar, no matter what kind of drink he ordered. He did this so that he could drink from the opposite side of the glass—the way a left-handed person would drink, thereby lessening his chance of catching herpes. He insisted that they never really washed the glasses at bars—"They just slosh them around in some lukewarm water," he said—and he figured that there were fewer left-handed people in Manhattan.

"So tell me," Joey said, wiping the salt from the rim of his mug. "What's star-fucking like?"

"Joey. I can't believe you."

"Calm down. Calm down. My God, girl. It's just sex."

"Lewis is a wonderful man," Catherine said.

"Uh-oh, do I hear 'serious'? Should I start talking you out of this, or wait?"

Catherine took a deep breath and drank from her mug.

"I don't know, Joey, it scares me. Do you ever wonder if it gets too easy? I mean, Fran's been on the hunt for years, and I'm with Lew for one night, and, boom, I'm having visions of raising chickens with him in Vermont."

Joey rubbed her back. "Don't worry, Cat. It'll go away soon enough." He took another sip from his margarita and frowned. "Falling in love is just like a deadline. It's exciting up to the very last minute and then it's over, and all you've got left is one big mess to clean up. Avoid the mess, Cat. Don't fall in love."

In the mail, Catherine got a notice from the league that she could join the Colony Club on Park for a reduced price. The Colony Club had a pool, so Catherine began walking there three days a week after work to swim.

There weren't many women her age there, just old women leaguers who fell into the water and swam back and forth on their sides. It seemed to Catherine as though everything at that time of day was in slow motion—the women moved so slowly and gracefully in the water—and she took pleasure in that, in slowing down.

And it was on one of these evenings, after Catherine had swum for an hour and she was leaving the club, that she caught sight of Michael again. He was with a group of older men and a few young women, one of whom she recognized from the league. She had been one of the pert young provisionals who had sat at the edge of her chair that night at orientation, saying she worked at Kidder, saying it just like that—Kidder—assuming everyone knew that it was Kidder, Peabody.

Catherine knew that Michael had broken a date with Fran that afternoon, telling her he had a business dinner.

"But I could come with," Catherine had heard Fran say into the phone and Catherine could tell by the long pause that Michael was saying something, and seeing whom he was with now, Catherine knew that he had been saying something that covered up the fact that he didn't want Fran to dine with him and these Kidder people because she wouldn't have fit in.

Catherine had sneakers on and her hair was still wet and before she could get behind a freestanding column in the entryway, Michael saw her.

"Catherine!" he said. "It is Catherine, isn't it?"

"Hi," she said. She was relieved the others were doing things with their coats.

"Have you eaten? Come join us."

"There's a salad bar on First with my name on it."

"These people are awful. Please. Amuse me. Fran would want you to."

"But Fran would want to be here," Catherine said, regretting immediately that she had even mentioned Fran.

"So it'll be our little secret," he said.

"My hair's wet."

"I'll dry it," he said. "I'll blow on it while you eat."

"Hold on," she said, grabbing hold of his arm. "Let me change shoes."

"This is getting to be a thing with us. This shoe thing."

Lewis' wrestling play never got off the ground and he called Catherine to say he was leaving for L.A.

"Come with me," he said.

"Fran wouldn't like that."

"Life's too short to think about the Frans."

Catherine wondered briefly why all the men she became involved with had this desire to take her away from her own life. Then she thought about her dinner with Michael and how he had leaned over the table to listen to her, ignoring the pert provisional from Kidder with the Chanel bag. She thought about how when the girl had announced to the table that Catherine was an editor, Michael hadn't even blinked.

"And she's got this cute little assistant," he added. "I forget her name. Isn't it Fran?"

"Maybe I wouldn't like it in L.A.," Catherine said to Lewis.

"Maybe you would."

Months later, Lewis would call her again, and then again, to ask if she would go to La Paz, Mexico, with him.

"The people aren't real in Manhattan, Cat, honey," he would say each time. "Nobody knows what they want. I do. I want to be with you. I want to clean my ears with your Q-Tips till I cough."

And each time, Catherine would laugh and shake her head, thinking if only he could just press the pause button on all his feelings, then maybe she could catch up.

Later, long after the April issue had closed, after she had flown off to San Francisco and back, after Joey had met Warhol, after the casting-couch story was well under way, Catherine would get a call about Lewis. She would go to his wake and join his agent, his publicist, and his father, a skinny, balding man who held his hat over his heart the whole time. It would be a closed-casket affair because, it was said, Lewis had a mohawk to disguise how much hair he had lost to chemotherapy. His father would shake his head, and whisper to Catherine, "I keep expecting him to pop out of that rig and yell 'Surprise.' With him it was all a joke."

And that day, the day of Lewis Lipman's wake, Catherine would go back to her office, stick her feet in her wastepaper basket, and write up a funny, poignant piece called "My Last Date with Lewis Lipman," which Howard would love and rush to the printer in Jersey—to that same bodybuilder who had once held out Catherine's arms and announced that there wasn't much to her. And still later, Catherine and her story would get a mention on Page Six and, for a while after that, that same year, Lewis Lipman would be posthumously hot.

Chapter 4

A Cold New Year's Eve

In December Catherine's rent went up from $320.33 to $448.46 and Catherine didn't have the money. She would go this month without paying, she thought. She knew of a few neighbors who had done that. Joey told her to go out to lunch and spend more, but Catherine had already used up $250 worth of petty-cash vouchers to pay last month's Junior League bill, and she figured Howard or Ms. Simpson might get suspicious if she cashed in any more. Luckily, Catherine's three-year anniversary at *Women* was coming up and she was due for a raise.

On the third Saturday of the month, Joey and Catherine bundled up and went for a run around the reservoir in Central Park because neither one of them could afford to do anything else.

"God, do I feel weak," Joey said after they had gone around twice. "I think I just lost a calorie."

He put a leg up on a tree and bent over to touch his toes. A man jogging past turned around and stared. Joey had the longest legs of anybody Catherine knew—man or woman.

"Do this," he said, putting his hands on his hips and turning side to side. "It's supposed to do something for something."

They went to a deli and ordered sardine sandwiches because Joey said he didn't want to get osteoporosis. Catherine had run out of cash, so Joey paid for lunch. They walked west and they sat and ate on an incline across from the Museum of Natural History. Joey was going on and on about a date he had had the night before with a man who spent a hundred dollars on him at dinner.

"He said he liked my company," Joey said.

Catherine took off her gloves and bit into her sandwich.

"Then he turns to me. He looks into my eyes real deep the way they do and I'm thinking, Oh great. This guy's going to ask me to take off my clothes, sit in a chair, and roll an egg under my foot or something. But no. He says, 'Joey, you need a tie.' And he took off his tie—this really ugly polyester thing—right there in the middle of Green Street—and he wraps it around my neck."

"That's sweet," Catherine said.

"Ugh, you should have seen this thing. In the garbage as soon as I was home."

"People are always doing nice things for you," Catherine said. She looked across the street at some people going into the museum. A year ago Daniel had taken her there to an exhibit on mouse skulls. They had moved from head to tiny head as he lectured. He had said that the bones were so small and fragile that to clean them they put beetles on them because the beetles ate what humans couldn't get to. Bored, she had said she was hungry and Daniel had grumbled, saying didn't she know the importance of mouse skeletons? And they left and got a hot dog at a stand outside.

"Yeah, but it's never the right people," Joey said. Catherine nodded. "You know what this guy does? He studies dwarfs. I couldn't believe it. I asked him to tell me about Tiny Tim, and he says to me real seriously, he says, 'Tiny Tim wasn't a dwarf. Tiny Tim was a midget. They're often confused.' As if I cared! I don't want to be with people like him. I want to be *brucher*-ing with the people in the middle of things. We should be eating chocolate sundaes at Serendipity," he said, looking at his sandwich. A sardine fell out and oil ran down his arm. "That's where Warhol always goes."

"So how come the Dwarfman has all this money to spend?"

"Wall Street. Everybody and his mother gets their fucking money from Wall Street. He invests."

Catherine stared down at the sardine sandwich Joey had bought for her. She remembered how her father had told her to always stash a little away at the end of every month. "No matter how little," he had said. But her father had never tried living on an assistant's salary in New York City.

"What would you do if you had more money?" Catherine asked.

"Buy expensive face creams and use English soap. Every day. You?"

"I'd get a real bed."

"Yeah. I'm a little sick of the futonian sleep myself," Joey said. "Are you going to the office Christmas party?"

Catherine shook her head. Her first year, there had been a hypnotist at the party, and when the fat girl from At Home went under, he made her twelve and asked her what she wanted for Christmas..

"A boyfriend," the girl had said. It had been such an honest response everyone looked down into their drinks, even Howard.

After that, Catherine made it a habit to miss all the office Christmas parties. What if she were hypnotized? What if she revealed that she wanted Fran's job for Christmas, or worse, Fran's boyfriend, Michael? What if the hypnotist convinced her she was from another planet and she began speaking in another language in front of everyone, looking glassy-eyed and lost? A girl E.T. looking for a phone.

A children's birthday party was going on in an apartment across the street and they all wore bright blue pointed hats as they ran and ate cake. Joey told Catherine he wanted children, too.

"Soon," he said. "I just want to feel what it's like. I want to watch a part of me grow up all over again."

"My mother wants me to go away with her for Christmas," Catherine said.

"You'll be miserable," Joey said. "I went to Florida once over Christmas. I could see dolphins from the front porch. A pelican ate my lunch. Have you ever seen a pelican up close? Its mouth looks like the hood of a car. Really. Take my word for it. Stay here and keep me company."

"I can't afford to go anywhere right now anyway," Catherine said. "And I refuse to ask my mother for money. God, I wish I had something of my own to invest."

A woman in a grey taffeta evening gown sat down next to Catherine. She put a *New York* magazine and a Bible on her lap and began reading them alternately. Meanwhile, she tied and untied her dirty long black hair up into a knot at the back of her head.

"You got it made, Cat. You're up for a raise this week. What are you complaining about?"

"I may not get it."

"Of course you will. Fran'll go to bat for you. Howard never would for me, but Fran would for you. She's crazy about you. So shut up and tell me what you're doing New Year's Eve."

"Nothing," Catherine said. "I hate New Year's Eve."

"I know. Last year was the pits. I was so depressed I went out and bought myself some fish and lingerie. The year before that I stayed in and baked myself a potato. Loneliness, Cat, is the smell of one potato baking. I've never had a good New Year's Eve. I'm never with anybody I want to be with. Heaven's going to be one long house party with no dishes to wash. Hell will be one endless New Year's Eve."

"Everybody's got their bad time of year," Catherine said. "Mine's Christmas."

The woman next to Catherine paused in her readings to zip and unzip the back of her dress. She then proceeded to pick at the pimples on her shoulders.

Catherine rewrapped her half-eaten sandwich. She wasn't hungry anymore.

"In the summer I come and sit here wearing stripes," Joey said. "The ants climb up my shirttails and use the stripes as expressways."

"Well, think of it," Catherine said. "You've got this vast expanse you've been roaming around in all your life and then suddenly, right in front of you, there are these lines. Straight red lines, leading somewhere." She looked at the birthday party. A mother was counting children.

"Let's spend New Year's together, Cat," Joey said. "Please?"

"Sure."

"Swear?"

"Swear."

"Seriously, I've never had a good New Year's Eve in all my life."

Catherine tried to picture Joey on a New Year's Eve, but she couldn't. She didn't know who his other friends were, though sometimes he would mention a name or two. Ken. Bruce. She would hear those names once perhaps, and then never again. She knew not to ask too many questions about Joey's "other life." She let him tell her what he wanted. Once, when she had been with Daniel and they were walking past a bar on Christopher Street in the middle of the day, Catherine had glanced inside and seen Joey leaning on a bar stool between two men. Catherine saw only the bald head of the man on Joey's far side but the other man, the one nearest her, was terrifyingly big, with one of those muscle-man T-shirts on and black leather pants. She stopped, wanting to go in and drag Joey out of there, but Daniel had pushed her along that day, saying it was really none of her business.

Catherine put her arm around Joey.

"Why don't I feel sorry for you?" she said.

"Because I'm thinner than you are?"

"You bitch."

"What time is it?" the woman in grey said suddenly.

"I don't know," Catherine said to the woman. She had one of those olive-skinned faces from a sixteenth-century painting. She was about Catherine's age. She didn't have a shopping cart filled with all her belongings and it looked as though all she had in the world were her dress, her Bible, and her *New York* magazine. "I'm sorry," Catherine mumbled. "I don't have a watch."

"I'm sorry too," the woman said.

Joey finished his sandwich. "We need to find ourselves a couple of sugar daddies. I always end up with guys who remind me of dirty bedroom slippers. What I need is a patent-leather pump." He crumpled up his bag, nudged Catherine, and they got up to leave. "Fabulous dress she has on," Joey whispered as they turned out of the park.

"Your gloves."

Catherine turned around. The woman in grey held out Catherine's gloves to her. "Don't you want them?" the woman said.

Catherine took her gloves.

"Thank you."

"It gets cold," the woman said.

"Yes," Catherine said. She put the rest of her sandwich on the bench next to the woman.

The woman unzipped her dress and exposed a bony, pimply shoulder. She put her index finger to her lips. "Shh," she whispered. "It gets so cold."

The following Monday Personnel didn't send word of a raise. They sent Catherine a purple African violet instead, with a card attached to one of the browning fuzzy leaves that read: "Congratulations on your three years with us!"

Howard had calypso music playing in all the offices and the elevators smelled of coconut oil. He had gotten mad when Fran sent a memo to Ms. Simpson suggesting that *Women* send out a Christmas card with the staff on the cover to advertisers. Howard suspected that all of Fran's ideas were too self-serving, and besides, he didn't want anyone to be thinking about Christmas cards. The April issue was already two weeks late and he was convinced it was because everyone had Santa on the brain. He didn't want anyone humming "Rudolph" or "White Christmas."

"Think Jamaica," he said. Jamaica was the theme for the May fashion pages. "Dreadlocks and tropical prints. Sandals, for cryin' out loud."

That morning Joey passed out the Very Chocolate chocolate-chip cookies he'd made Sunday night.

"He'd probably be happier if I was passing around reefer," Joey said.

At noon, Fran came in reeking of a new perfume she had bought at Saks.

"I had a dream you quit," she said, sticking one of Joey's cookies in her mouth so she could hang up her mink. Fran had paid for her mink with approximately one year's worth of petty cash. Her mother had chipped in. "See this sleeve?" Fran would say. "My mother paid for this sleeve."

"You went to Milly," Fran went on as she seated herself behind her desk and picked up the phone. She called *Mademoiselle* Milly. "God, was I ever pissed."

Once upon a time, Catherine had felt she owed everything to Fran. She often joked, "Fran, I'm going to give you my firstborn." And Fran would smile and say, "I'd rather have a poodle."

Fran had given Catherine her first break. When Catherine interviewed for the job, she knew she was the least qualified for the position. It had come down to Catherine and some woman who wrote for the *Voice,* and Fran admitted that she couldn't decide. "Look," Catherine had finally said to Fran at the end of her fourth interview. "I'm no Pollyanna. I lost my scruples in college when my favorite journalism professor got picked up for shoplifting a bottle of shampoo, a Cornish game hen, and some birdseed. I'm prepared to give you twenty-four hours a day. I don't have a husband or a boyfriend. I don't even have an apartment yet. This job will be my life."

At the time, Catherine feared that she had overdone it—she had made up the part about her journalism professor. He was actually a kind old man who had glaucoma and was in the process of memorizing all of Shakespeare. And the part about the boyfriend was a lie—she was living with Daniel at the time. But when Catherine saw the left corner of Fran's mouth slowly rise to a half-smirk, she knew this was exactly what Fran had been waiting to hear, much like a false confession beaten out of a prisoner of war.

Fran got on the phone with Food. She told them she was giving her first New Year's Eve party, what should she serve? She wrote down what they told her, then she called her best friend, Pam.

"Pam?" she said. "Everything in my life is, like, perfect. I have this great boyfriend, a new apartment, and my hair is getting, like, really really long. When's my CD player coming? I need some new sheets."

Pam was Fran's best friend and decorator. She also designed sheets for a living. A psych major from the University of Illinois, Pam explained to Fran three years ago that the only way a woman could forget an ex was to get rid of everything in her apartment and redecorate. Pam suggested that Fran pawn her engagement ring and do everything up in pink. Pam also claimed it was necessary for Fran to switch perfumes.

"Wednesday's too late," Fran said. She took out a file and began filing her nails as she listened. "Really?" she said after a while. "I have tickets to Rod Stewart tonight. What should I wear?"

Fran had plans to take Michael and after the concert they would meet up with Rod backstage for an interview. Meanwhile, Catherine was to attend a Disney Home Video P.R. deal in some office building in Times Square. There would be fried chicken wings and miniature egg rolls and she would bitch about deadlines with other peons from *GQ, Glamour,* and *People* who would be scarfing down all the appetizers as dinner. She would come back with network information and a Polaroid of herself with Friar Tuck and some bear wearing a green hat—his furry paw resting on her right shoulder. *I was at "Opening Night" for The Classics from Walt Disney Home Video,* the caption would read in cheesy gold lettering.

Fran put her hand over the receiver. "Cat, you think you could get us some more of those cookies? They're to die. And a cup of coffee?"

Catherine passed Hair and Makeup on the way back down the hall. They had just come back from the shoot in Jamaica and they were tanned and giggling in their Bermudas and wing tips.

"Your ends are dry," Hair said. "You need another cut."

A trim with him would cost fifty dollars, Catherine thought. She smiled.

"I'm trying to grow it out," she said. "Length is in."

"When was it ever out?" Makeup said, and he and Hair giggled over that for a while.

When she got back to her desk, the other line was ringing and Fran was opening a Christmas card from a born-again actress on "Dynasty."

"Hey, beautiful." Catherine recognized the voice. It was Michael's. Fran was on the other line with the "Dynasty" actress's press agent. "God damn," Catherine could hear Fran say. "Tell her I'm Jewish, OK?"

"Can she call you back?" Catherine said. "She's on the other line."

"Who says I called to talk to her?"

She wondered if he still had her number in his wallet. She wished she had never given it to him.

"What's your number?" she said, all business.

Catherine had the high honor that month of doing a roundup for the April Entertainment page: "What the Stars Do in Their Alone Time." She'd put in calls to publicists, working her way down from the A-list to the B-list, and now she was stuck with two soap opera stars, a sex researcher, and an actress with bleached blond hair whose only claim to fame was that she once told *People* that she had a drug problem. With Catherine, she had hardly been cooperative.

"Look," the actress had said over the phone. "There's only about three things a person does in her alone time. Eating and sleeping are two."

And today, the day of her anniversary, the day she had expected to be given a raise and/or elevated to some position of prestige, Catherine fetched coffee and cookies for Fran and began work on a piece about a Beatrix Potter special on PBS. The series started out with Peter Rabbit and wrapped up with Squirrel Nutkin. On her desk before her were copies of the little Beatrix Potter books—in paperback—which Catherine couldn't even keep or pawn because she had to return them to the publicist by five.

In the pictures, the lopsided houses looked charming. Poverty was picturesque. Peter Rabbit only had to worry about his one blue jacket and there was no mention of rent for his sand-bank underneath the root of the fir-tree. Catherine thought about her own apartment and its view of a wall. All I want is a kitchen I can turn around in and a bathroom door that closes, she thought. Even Peter Rabbit has that.

Sometimes, for Catherine, living in Manhattan was just another series of challenges. I'm Mary Tyler Moore, she said to herself, looking over her desk at Fran who was busy nibbling cookies and gossiping with Pam. Why can't she be Lou Grant?

Catherine stuck her feet in her wastepaper basket. Come Wednesday, she assured herself, Personnel would send down a bonus, or, at least, a gift certificate to Bergdorf's or Tiffany's or someplace.

"What would *you* wear?" Fran asked Pam. "Maybe I should get my hair permed. Are you free right now? Come with me to Betsey Johnson's. Then we can go get a facial."

Catherine stared down at the little picture of a porcupine doing laundry.

Remember Mrs. Tiggy-Winkle? she typed.

"That's it?" Joey said. He and Catherine were standing at Joey's desk because Catherine was afraid she didn't have enough light in her office for the African violet to survive. "This is what I have to look forward to? A plant? A lousy plant?"

"Wednesday's the real day," Catherine said, picking off a dead leaf at the stem of the plant. "That's when it will be three years exactly."

"Yeah, right. Wednesday," Joey said. He clicked his tongue. "That's when they'll pull out all the stops and give you one whole rose."

He erased the rubber cement hardening on Crotchcough's copy.

"I can't believe Crotchcough already has his June copy in. I'm still on April," Catherine said. She ate another one of Joey's cookies while she read the copy. A woman had written in saying that she itched every time she had intercourse. Crotchcough suggested she try a vinegar-and-water douche.

"Howard never gives him hell," Joey said. "I mean what *kind* of vinegar? That's what I would want to know. What if I used like red-wine vinegar or balsamic and burned my pussy? I'd sue."

"Let's go to lunch," Catherine said. "Are you ready?"

"Ready?" Joey said, putting a sheet of Plexiglas over the sex-advice page. "Honey, lunch is my *life*."

It was so cold outside they only walked a few blocks away to Curds & Whey off Madison. On the way there, they passed a man asleep in a cardboard box over a subway grate next to an antique store. Catherine couldn't eat. She kept thinking about the woman in the grey taffeta dress and the man in the box and she wondered what she herself would carry around Manhattan if she were homeless—a copy of *Cosmo* and a pair of spare pumps, just in case she got asked out?

She wished Daniel were in America. At least he would have kept her fed. And Lewis. Lewis. She should have gone to L.A. with Lewis.

"I don't think I'm going to be able to make this month's rent, Joey," Catherine said.

"How much do you need?"

She thought about that month's rent and then next month's.

"Four hundred dollars."

"No problem."

Catherine didn't believe him. Joey never had any money. No assistant had that kind of money.

"God, I'm sick of being poor in this town," Catherine said.

"Quit worrying."

"I'm sick of being poor. I'm sick of getting stuck with the shitty little stories and I'm sick of being a month behind all the time."

The waiter came by their table and looked at their plates.

"Do you have everything you need?" he asked.

Catherine looked at Joey.

"I hate when they ask that," she said.

"I don't like this Fran woman. When are you going to get out of there?" It was Tuesday night and Catherine had made the mistake of telling her mother all about work.

"I don't want to leave, Mom," Catherine said, looking up at her ceiling. The blistering plaster was taking shape and to Catherine it looked like Tabby Kitten was giving Twinkleberry a blow job. "For one thing I have this great apartment."

Catherine lived on the sixth floor of a walk-up on Seventy-eighth and York, one block away from the East River in what used to be the German section of Manhattan. Her apartment building stood in a block of identical beige brick buildings which had been built sometime in the 1920s for tubercular patients.

There was a park across the street and even a public pool which Joey told Catherine not to swim in because it was rumored someone had caught herpes from the pool water. The better buildings, the ones with the views of the little park, had floor-to-ceiling windows with New Orleans style balconies, for the really weak TB patients who had once upon a time needed to be rolled out for air. Now, only fifty or so years later, there was a five year waiting list of healthy Manhattanites who wanted to get into these buildings.

Catherine's one-room apartment did remind her of a designated holding pen for the sick and the dying. She had tried fixing it up with whatever she could from the At Home giveaways. On the floor was half an Oriental which, pushed up to the wall, looked as though it continued on into the apartment next door. Daniel had helped drag up and build an industrial iron bookcase which she had painted white to match her burglar bars.

She kept her mail in a glass punch bowl—screenings, invites, and the Christmas card her mother was sending out this year, a color photo of Chloe seated in front of the fireplace in the living room.

The punch bowl sat on top of an antique table Daniel had given Catherine on loan. He had found this table on the street. He said it was very valuable. He said she could borrow it until he needed it. Sitting on the edge of her sofa bed, talking to her mother, Catherine wondered when she would have to give Daniel's table back.

"When are you coming home for Christmas?"

"Mom, we've been through this," Catherine said. "I can't take that kind of time off."

"You were going to spend three weeks in Rome with a man I've never met," her mother said.

Catherine didn't say anything. Outside, someone's rug hung over a fire escape, covered with ice. Somewhere out on the East River, a boat sounded its horn.

Catherine didn't want to go to Barrington for Christmas. Last year and the year before that, it had been just the two of them, and all her mother wanted to talk about was her father. Each time her mother had gotten out the camera and all the pictures were of just Catherine or her mother, but none of the two of them together. Going home seemed pointless now—two women did not a family make. And besides, if she told her mother that she could barely afford her rent, let alone the plane fare home, her mother would say, "I knew you wouldn't be able to make a living there. Come home." Catherine could imagine moving back to Barrington, Illinois, where she would learn to greet the dogs first and then their masters. She would live with her mother and work on some little paper, something like the *Countryside Reminder News,* and on weekends she would play tennis, apologizing every now and then for poaching perhaps too eagerly. Her mother would fix her up with men who had names like Ogden and Ham and they would drag her to cocktail parties where she would be the only one under sixty and where all the food served was beige.

"You never engage me in conversation anymore," her mother said.

"What's your point, Mom?" Catherine said.

"My point is I never see you. Every mother has a right to see her only child. I don't even know what your apartment looks like. I don't even know what color hand towels you need."

"I don't need any hand towels, Mom."

"Every woman needs hand towels."

On the Wednesday before Christmas, the day that marked Catherine's third anniversary at *Women,* nothing happened. Personnel sent nothing down. No gift certificates. No roses. No raise.

Joey had made macaroons. Through the window that divided the Art Department and Howard's office, Joey watched Howard bite into one of his cookies.

"Shit," Joey mumbled. "You know you're in trouble when they use their back teeth."

Catherine took a cookie and went back to her desk. She didn't feel right about asking Joey again for the loan.

After Fran called in to say she wasn't coming in ("So many things to buy before my party!"), Catherine reached in her drawer and pulled out a messenger pad and her wallet. Then she got up and went to the stairwell landing on the ninth floor—the only place in the building where Catherine could be left alone to think.

Leaning against the army green wall, Catherine wished she had the flu—then she could stay in bed with the covers pulled up to her chin and watch TV while Joey made her gingerbread.

She sat down on the stairs and stared down at the balance in her checkbook for the third time that week. $3.22. Payday was two weeks away. She would have to live on petty-cash vouchers.

Two fashion assistants charged down the stairs, their jewelry jangling. Sometimes, *Women* assistants skipped the elevators for the exercise. The two from Fashion had hangers of shirts and skirts flung over their shoulders. They were probably headed for the mailroom on three.

Catherine put the messenger pad on her knee and pretended to be filling out a request form. The assistants passed without saying hello. They were gossiping about the new How-To editor.

"Any Before potential?" one girl said. Catherine recognized them. They were both from Accessories.

"She's a waif," the other said.

"Simpson always does this," Accessories Number One said. "She hires the most fucked-up, fucked-over people for that job."

Catherine had not been too impressed with the new How-To editor either. At the beginning of December, she had passed around a memo asking for help with a How-To piece: "XX Reasons Why You Shouldn't Be Scrooge This Holiday Season." Everyone had heard Howard screaming at her down the hall. "We're in April, you ninny. Get with the fucking program."

Sometimes Catherine thought the fashion assistants had it worse off than she did—they could only get discounts on clothes, not food or cab fare, and they usually wound up all living in one big studio, three or four people at once. She waited for them to pass. She looked down at the numbers in her checkbook. They were still the same, and she still didn't have enough for rent. She flirted with the idea of asking the fucked-up, fucked-over waif for advice. How to Get Two Months Rent in Less Than a Week. How to Live on a Penny a Day . . . in Manhattan.

Catherine got up, brushed off her skirt, and went back to her desk. There was a note from Research—there were two *r*'s in Squirrel and could she please fact-check exactly which shoe (right or left) Peter Rabbit lost in Mr. McGregor's cabbage patch? Catherine spent the rest of that day rereading *The Tale of Peter Rabbit* while she waited for more alone-time calls.

On Christmas Day the plaster on Catherine's ceiling fell down. It had rained the night before, and Catherine lay in bed Christmas morning, watching Twinkleberry's cock spreading out until finally Tabby Kitten's head exploded and they both came crumbling down in bits of yellowed plaster all over the bed. She left word on her landlord's answering machine, and went to the office with a bag full of carryout.

Howard's calypso music wasn't playing, so she put on Kid Creole and the Coconuts.

It was oddly satisfying to work there, all alone with a container full of mu shu pork, typing up the Beatrix Potter piece and the roundup on what famous people did in their alone time.

"I drink Evian in a bubble bath by candlelight," Cynthia Shoemaker, the author/sex researcher, had said.

"I wrap packages," Rhonda Weaver, the leggy leading lady, said. "I love to do things with ribbons."

Catherine forgot all about December and Christmas and kept her mind on April.

"How to Throw an Academy Awards Bash," she wrote for the How-To Guide. "Pop a lot of popcorn. Rent a big-screened TV. Dress up like a star, and pretend you're someone you're not."

At dusk, Catherine had finished the April copy and she had even come up with a few ideas for May. But she was having some trouble finding anyone who would talk regarding her casting-couch story.

She had interviewed an older woman that week—a famous choreographer whom dancers called the Dragon Lady. Catherine figured the woman was so old she had nothing to lose. Dragon Lady smelled of gin during the interview and she chewed on scallions as she spoke.

"Women must learn to breathe through their vaginas," she said at the end of the interview. She put the last of her scallions in her purse and stood up to leave. "That is all I have to say."

Catherine put away her notes for the casting-couch piece. She put her feet in her wastepaper basket, tilted back her chair, and tried to think: Of all the people I want to know something from, whom do I want to call up and talk to this very minute?

Whenever Catherine played this game she came up with a long-shot celebrity name. Once, she had thought of Raquel Welch and, after a month of calling, one day Raquel Welch called back. "Hi, is this Catherine Clemons?" she had said on the phone. "This is Raquel Welch." Just like that.

Sometimes her job could be that easy.

Today, Christmas Day, Catherine thought of Mick Jagger. She had first heard Jagger singing "Walking the Dog" in the sixties when her mother and father had come back from a trip to England with the Rolling Stones' first album. Their rhythm was scary, and at first it had made Catherine nauseous. But soon she was playing her tennis racket along with Keith Richards every day after school.

Yes. Mick Jagger. She wanted to know how he had lasted. She wanted to find out if it was hard, doing what he did, day after day. She wanted to know why the hell he had left Bianca, anyway. They had made such a great pair, looking exactly alike, and, given a rock star's track record, they had lasted a relatively long time. Wasn't it hard just giving up like that on someone and something? Didn't he ever regret leaving her? Didn't he ever get lonely for her?

Catherine had a hunch that someone else in the city might be working on Christmas Day, so she called a publicist who was in his office and she announced to him in a calm, confident tone that she wanted an interview with Mick Jagger for the May issue of *Women*. Liz Smith had written in her column that he was in town; when was he available for an interview? The publicist laughed, and asked who exactly Catherine was again.

"Catherine, with a *C*," she said. "I'm the Entertainment editor at *Women*."

He laughed again. She wondered if he was drunk. She prayed he didn't know Fran. He said he'd see what he could do.

Catherine picked up the phone again.

"Mom?"

"Little Cat. Are you all right? Your voice sounds so strange."

"I'm at work."

"Did you get my present? It wasn't a cheapy."

"I'm going home to open it now."

"Ruth, my Jewish cochairman for the hospital benefit, is shocked I don't have a Christmas tree up. I told her I was waiting for my daughter to come home."

"How was church?"

"Terrible. I think Father is losing it. 'We're all at the breaking point,' he says. 'Christmas is such a trying time,' he says. Just once I'd like him to be joyous."

"Tell him."

"I am currently corresponding with seven Jesuits. I just can't take on the whole order."

"So, you don't have any decorations up?"

"The lesbians across the street put colored lights on all their azalea bushes. They're not even the little Italian kind." Her mother laughed and Catherine smiled. She heard Chloe barking in the background.

"Come home," her mother said after a while. "Chloe misses you."

"Tell Chloe I miss her, too," Catherine said.

When Catherine got home that night she made herself a plate of eggs and some raisin toast and she opened the present her mother had sent—a bright pink sweater with *CC* monogrammed in a diamond in the front and a little purse to match—both of which Catherine would never wear. Inside the sweater was a suede pouch from Bergdorf's. Inside the pouch was a frame. And inside the frame was a picture of her father.

The week her father died—the week between Christmas and New Year's—the temperature in Barrington got down to twenty below, not counting the windchill. No matter how many layers Catherine put on, or how much chicken broth she and her mother sipped, she couldn't get warm. Their house was drafty and whenever they came back from the hospital, Catherine kept feeling the cold air sneaking in from the outside.

That had been three years ago.

He seemed to know he was going to die. Two days before his heart attack, he called up his father in Memphis and they talked for an hour, even though he despised both his father and phones. When he hung up, Catherine's father opened a bottle of wine he'd been saving for fourteen years and the three of them drank it even though it still had seven more years left to age.

"On Christmas Eve the animals talk and you're supposed to keep quiet and listen," he had said, bending down to put his ear next to Chloe's mouth. Chloe licked him.

"That's ridiculous," her mother had said. "Chloe talks a lot more than just once a year."

On Christmas morning they opened presents, and ate turkey and sweet potato pie. They took a long walk and then a nap. Catherine could recall that time so vividly—her parents asleep in their room with the radio playing something by Merle Haggard and she lying stretched out on the couch reading a back issue of *Vogue* while Chloe lay curled up on the rug gnawing at a beef-flavored candy cane. It had gone from light to dark outside so quickly then.

Her father had held on long enough to make two trades from his bedside phone, and when he died, there had been plenty of money left for Catherine and her mother. But the money seemed somehow disappointing to Catherine then and it wasn't until she refused it and moved to New York that she realized why—it was really all her father had left her with. She had no idea who he had really been. She had his shirts, his cowboy hats, the leather box in which he'd kept his cuff links and Swiss army knife, the dictionary he'd used at Memphis State (the cover had come off and Chloe had eaten all the *A*'s). He'd shown her how to empty a garden hose and how to claw into a bar of soap to get your fingernails clean. He told her tomato juice neutralizes the smell of skunk on a dog. And he'd given her some advice: Wear socks when you're driving cross-country because your feet sweat; always stretch five minutes before a tennis match; keep your roses cut and mulched with manure and cocoa shells; and remember—olive oil and wine makes everything taste better.

His picture was colorized. His cheeks were painted pink, his eyes an eerie blue, and he had a yellow crew cut. Catherine put the picture back inside the suede Bergdorf bag, reached up to the top shelf of her bookcase, and put the picture of her father on some yellowed collected works of nobody important. Then she turned on the TV. *It's a Wonderful Life* was on. Again. She shut it off. She looked around the room.

It wasn't snowing, but Catherine wished it was. She wanted the whole city to be buried in snow—she loved how the snow muted all the traffic and shouting. She wanted the city to quiet down. She wanted only to sleep.

She was already half-dreaming, convinced that she was breathing in TB from inside her apartment walls, when the phone rang.

"Merry Christmas, Cat."

"Joey, where are you?"

"I'm with the Dwarfman at Patty's Pub. He wants to go see Miss Divine. I remembered, this wasn't your night. Can I come over? I need an excuse to get rid of this guy."

Joey showed up half an hour later without the Dwarfman. He had a bottle of Cordon Negro—"Nigger Champagne," he said—and a scarf from Lord & Taylor's with Hermés-like chains looping down to the edge.

"I stole it just for you," he said.

Catherine put it around her neck and looked at her reflection on the TV screen. She looked like the black-and-white version of the colorized picture of her father.

Catherine rummaged around her bag and brought out a stack of invitations. She gave those to Joey.

"I couldn't afford to get you anything," she said. "I'm sorry."

"Don't worry. I took plenty for the two of us."

They toasted themselves. They toasted Arkansas. They toasted their mothers, dried papaya, the world's biggest boar, and the April issue.

"What do you do in your alone time, Joey?"

"Bake," he said, reading over the invitations. "Take naps."

They laughed and Joey poured them the last of the champagne.

"I'm sick of alone time," Catherine said. "There's only so much carryout a person can take."

"Look at this. Fran's been invited to Shere Hite's New Year's Eve. She wrote all those sex surveys. I bet you five million Warhol will be there."

"Five months ahead of the rest of the world and two months behind in rent," Catherine sighed, looking around her room, trying not to listen to Joey. She could clean up the place, but then she thought, Why bother?

"Seems like that's always the way it's going to be."

Joey poured more champagne. "Let's go to Shere Hite's party, Cat. We'll have a hellacious New Year's Eve. We'll dance to a whole B-52's album. You can introduce me to Warhol."

Catherine understood why Joey wanted to meet Warhol. It wasn't necessarily that he wanted to be discovered, although Joey certainly wouldn't have minded. He was really after the high, that high you get when someone famous shakes your hand, touches your arm, or says your name, and it's as though a real star had actually come down from the sky and you get to see it for a while up close. It changes you for a day or so.

Catherine could remember the way she had felt when Ally Sheedy had kissed her on the cheek at a press party at Tavern on the Green. Catherine had included Ally in a list of rising young stars in *Women,* and Ally wanted to thank her. "Thanks, Catherine," she had said, and then she kissed Catherine's cheek, just like that. It was better than holy water.

"Sure," Catherine said to Joey. She finished off her glass of champagne. "Let's go to Shere's party and go meet Warhol."

When she passed out, Catherine dreamed she was at a pool in a snowy part of the universe. Her mother was walking on water, but when Catherine tried, she couldn't. Then her father, a Rastafarian, suddenly appeared and began beating her with a fish. Everyone was smoking cigarettes that smelled of chocolate. She felt she had to get out. She tried one exit, but it led right back around to the pool. Then her brother, who was Joey, showed her the right exit to the parking lot, where there was a Volvo station wagon. She didn't have the keys, but when she got in and locked all the doors, the car slowly started moving. In the backseat was the moon. She felt cold and when she looked down, she was wearing a grey taffeta evening gown and there were pimples on her shoulders.

It wasn't really a nightmare, but it was bad enough for Catherine to wonder, in her half-sleep, why the hell Daniel wasn't there in bed beside her, waking her up to say, "Shh. Shhh, baby. It's all going to be OK."

On the thirty-first, Fran called Catherine around noon and invited her to her New Year's Eve party.

"I can't believe I forgot," Fran said over the phone.

Catherine started to say she had made other plans—plans with Joey—but Fran was quick to add that this was work. This was part of her job.

Catherine couldn't get ahold of Joey all day. She would leave Fran's early, she said to herself. She would go to both Fran's party and Shere Hite's.

Fran lived in a big, unimaginative high rise on the Upper East Side, only blocks away from where Catherine lived. She had a doorman. There was a chandelier in the lobby and the elevators were lined with mirrors. Riding up, Catherine felt as though she were inside an ice cube.

Pam had done everything up in pink and grey—*the* Bloomingdale's combination for that month. The walls had been painted a light slate grey and the sofa and chairs covered in a pastel pink. The cabinet which Fran had gone on and on about was made up of mirrors. So were the wastepaper baskets.

Fran's place was like most places Catherine had seen whose renters were women in their mid-thirties—artsy fruit bowl on the coffee table, M&M's by the bed, packaged food from Charles & Company in the cupboards.

"You're here!" Fran said, taking Catherine's coat. "Everybody, I want you to meet my little assistant. She's always hanging around gay guys." Some of her friends laughed. Then Fran turned to Catherine. "I can't believe you're wearing pants." Catherine was wearing a tuxedo she had borrowed from Joey almost a year ago because she hadn't been able to fit into any of his dresses. They were too small. "If I had your thighs, I'd wear a miniskirt a day," Fran said.

Fran led Catherine into her kitchen, a narrow little room which, like most kitchens in Manhattan, looked as though it had never been cooked in.

"This is for you," Fran said. She gave Catherine a long box.

Rent money, Catherine thought as she opened the box. She would pawn whatever was inside. "Fran. This was so nice of you." If it was a gift certificate, she'd cash it in.

It was a pair of black lace gloves without fingers.

"They go up to your elbows," Fran said. She clapped her hands. "Aren't they hot? Guys go crazy over them."

Catherine tried them on. She felt like Oliver Twist. Not as cute, but just about as poor.

"Thank you so much," she said.

Catherine had never disliked Fran—she was usually amused by her, just waiting for the time when Fran would finally land a man, marry him, and quit. But as Catherine stared down at Fran pulling the sleeves of her new red Norma Kamali down to bare her round little shoulders—her hair tied up, teased, and spritzed in studied messiness—Catherine tried to think of all the ways she could ruin this woman's life.

Then she remembered her rent and a raise.

"I just wanted to say one thing, Fran," Catherine said. Fran looked up at Catherine, waiting. Somebody from Paramount behind her stopped talking. "You are everything I want to be," Catherine said. Fran hugged Catherine. Then she turned around and picked up a tray. Catherine took one of the little quiches off of it.

"Can you do me a favor?" Fran said.

If she had known she would be serving at Fran's New Year's Eve bash, Catherine would have charged. It turned out to be a miserable chore. Some man burned a cigarette hole in her cummerbund. Another pulled her down into his lap and said, "Feel that? Feel how hard? That's my empty glass. Get me a drink, will ya? That's a doll."

Pam was there. She stood in front of the mirrored console and lifted up her blouse.

"It used to be there," she said, pointing to a spot just to the right of her belly button. She explained to her rapt audience that when she had gotten a tummy tuck, her belly button had shifted and she was in the process of suing the doctor.

"Fran's going to testify," Pam said. "She knew me when my belly button was centered."

It was a good party as far as networking parties went. There were a lot of celebrity divorce lawyers and a few models who didn't eat and went around describing their countries as they would their hair: "Beautiful but damaged."

At one point, Catherine spotted Michael with Fran, who was introducing him to a record-company vice president, but Catherine wasn't able to get a better look because Pam stepped in front of her, talking loudly to a guy with a Nautilized body who claimed he was a poet.

"I was out in front of my apartment building," Pam said, "and this bag man says to this little boy who was crying, 'Don't cry, little boy. We'll all be crying tomorrow.' I mean like, isn't that deep?"

Pam waited for a response.

"Cool," the poet said. "Is there curry in this dip?"

At eleven-thirty Fran passed out masks. Catherine took the one done in white satin. It had silver sequins sewn around the eyes and three white feathers coming up from the middle, like brows. She put it on and snuck away, into the bathroom. There, Catherine sat on the edge of Fran's bathtub, waiting for midnight to pass.

She tried not to think about Joey waiting for her at the Odeon. She had called, but the woman who had answered couldn't find him, and when Catherine tried him at home, his answering machine wasn't on. Later, Joey would tell her how he had waited there at the bar at the Odeon and when he had gotten home, he had baked until three a.m., using up the rest of his chocolate and unsalted butter. And later, when she went upstairs to her apartment, she would find there by her door a tin of some of those cookies Joey had made, and in the tin, an envelope, and in the envelope would be the four hundred dollars which Joey had stolen from Dwarfman.

But right then, as Catherine sat on the edge of Fran's bathtub, she was worrying about how she was going to pay her rent while she overheard a man and woman in the living room arguing over who was really more talented— Cyndi Lauper or Madonna.

Catherine got up and straightened her cummerbund. Joey's tux smelled vaguely of rose water and mothballs, and Catherine remembered what the woman in the grey taffeta evening gown had said. It gets cold.

She looked in the mirror. When will I have enough money? she thought. When will I stop being a "little assistant"?

Catherine opened one of Fran's bathroom drawers and began methodically smelling all of the English soaps.

When everyone started blowing little horns and rattling bells, Catherine could hear Fran. "It's 1984," she shrieked. "Does anybody know where my boyfriend is?"

At twelve-twenty, Catherine came out of Fran's bathroom. She straightened her mask and grabbed her coat off the bed, glancing at Fran's new sheets—whales spouting out bunches of flowers. Then she heard a man's voice.

"Run, Toto, run!"

Catherine turned around. Michael was standing there in the dark, wearing a tux identical to Catherine's. There was no light in Fran's bedroom because Fran had taken out all the light bulbs. Women her age, she said, weren't into light. But Catherine could tell it was Michael even with the mask—his teeth glowed and she could smell his cologne. Sweet, but musty, too.

"If you didn't want to be a waiter, you shouldn't have dressed like one," he said.

"I'm leaving," she said.

"Let me put you in a cab."

"I can do that myself. Thanks."

Everyone in the living room had Fran's bright pink lip marks on their cheeks, just below their masks. Catherine thanked Fran and wondered how she was going to refuse Fran's payment.

"Grab some food," Fran said, turning to plant a kiss below someone else's mask. "There's a ton of pasta left."

Catherine spent a while on First Avenue trying to get a cab. But then someone behind her whistled and a cab stopped, and as she raised her hand for another one, she heard Michael say, "Get in."

He looked like a mouse in his mask and Catherine couldn't help but notice the lipstick on the corner of his mouth.

"You look like a mouse," she said.

"Just call me Mighty," he said. "Where to?"

They drove to her place, and, as they stepped out of the cab, she thought about asking him up. Then she remembered the mess her ceiling plaster had made.

"We missed midnight," he said. "And you didn't even tell me your resolutions."

"Floss once a day. Maybe I'll start returning my mother's phone calls. Maybe not."

"Noble."

"Yours?"

"To find a faithful companion." He moved closer to Catherine. She couldn't tell what color his eyes were beneath his mask, but he knew how to look at her. And he knew the Jessica Lange eyes, mouth, eyes, mouth trick.

Catherine got her keys out.

"Fran's your faithful companion," she said.

"I already have a dog."

"That's not very nice."

"Nice doesn't pay the bills."

A group of revellers passed, blowing horns and waving their balloons at Michael and Catherine. The women were wearing thigh-high skirts in white leather.

"I wonder where they get those," Catherine said.

"Whores-R-Us," Michael said.

He held her arms as she bent over and laughed. He had on Gucci shoes.

"Ask me up," he said.

"Can't."

"Then kiss me."

Catherine looked at the lipstick on Michael's mouth.

"Go home," she said. "Feed your dog."

"On the mouth. Kiss me."

"Your lips are taken."

"Kiss my taken lips."

She kept her mask on so she could watch, and somehow it didn't startle her to see his own eyes half-open, watching, too. She hadn't realized how cold she was, until she felt how warm his hands were on her face. He kissed her once, then twice. He didn't use his tongue until she did, which bothered her at first because it was more of an air pocket than a kiss. But he knew about keeping his mouth close in between his kisses, so that she could breathe in and taste his warm, sweet breath.

"Mouse," she whispered, trying to move away.

"Cat," he said, holding her closer.

Chapter 5

Crossing the Border

Michael knew where all the hot spots were downtown—little coffee shops that played twangy music, jazz bars you had to step over bums to get to. And there, in one of those jazz bars, on their third or fourth date, Catherine told Michael about her money problems and he pulled out his Fendi wallet, made out a check for five hundred dollars and gave it to her with the word "loan" written in the blank next to MEMO.

"Once I get through this month, I can pay you back what you gave me New Year's Eve," Catherine told Joey at work the next day. They were sitting on stools in the Art Department, eating bagels and sipping coffee from Joey's Wonder Woman mugs. It was Friday and everybody was at Chemical Bank, putting away what was left of their paychecks.

"Sure," Joey said, blowing on Crotchcough's July page to get the rubber cement to dry faster.

"He couldn't believe I'd never been west of the Mississippi," Catherine said. "He was so funny. He said, 'Jeez, even the Brady Bunch saw the Grand Canyon.' "

"He says jeez?" Joey said. He looked up from his page. He had just washed his hair, and it was still wet. Today he didn't look pretty. He looked handsome. Joey didn't say that he disliked Michael. He didn't have to. "You're sleeping with a man who says jeez?"

"He was being tonal," Catherine said. "And I'm not sleeping with him."

Joey stopped blowing and the two of them looked at the page. Ms. Simpson was devoting the July issue to breast cancer and Crotchcough had responded to one woman's letter concerning how to make love after having your breasts removed. The words "tenderly" and "carefully" were repeated twice each in the response.

"*Yet*," Joey said. "You're not sleeping with Mr. Jeez *yet*."

That weekend Catherine went to dinner with Michael Friday *and* Saturday night. Each night he walked her home and each night they kissed and each night she went to bed alone. She lay awake and stared up at the ceiling, thinking, Why should I feel guilty? Daniel's in Rome, Lewis is in L.A., and I can't stand Fran. So why do I feel so damned guilty? We haven't done anything yet. And then she couldn't help but wonder why they hadn't done anything yet.

On Sunday afternoon, Catherine went to Michael's apartment. He buzzed her up. They were going to a matinee of a low-budget movie about a jazzman. Just as Michael answered the door, he hurried Catherine into his apartment.

"Fran's here and she's on her way up," he said. "She wants me to go on a bike ride with her. I told her I couldn't, but she still wanted to come up."

"She can't see me here."

"Hell, I don't care," Michael said.

"*I* do."

Catherine stepped into his bedroom and closed the door. A few minutes later she could hear the clicking of a ten-speed bike being rolled in and Fran's shrieky greeting.

Catherine listened as Fran went on and on about all of her work problems. There was the June deadline and Food was still getting more page space than Entertainment. And then there was her office, which was so cramped. Catherine hated to think so, but Fran was the kind of woman a man would cheat on. She bitched too much.

Catherine was careful not to complain about her job or admit how sick she was of Fran and of the way people talked—everyone, it seemed to Catherine, was talking in quotes, clever little witticisms, as if they were always being interviewed. And she never told Michael how much she hated the interviews. When Catherine interviewed people she always seemed to know what they were going to say: It's been a real joy working with blank. But really, I never could have gotten where I am today without the help of my blank. Me and blank? No, no. We work really well together but, honest, we're just friends. Half the time Catherine was just setting up celebrities for their predictable punch lines.

Sitting now on Michael's bed, Catherine wondered, Had he been here with Fran? Why hadn't he ever asked Catherine up to his apartment before? In the next room, Catherine heard Michael telling Fran he had a business appointment across town.

"On Sunday?" Fran said.

"No pain, no gain."

He lies so easily, Catherine thought.

And then it grew quiet and Catherine moved closer to the door to hear. And she heard movement and then she thought she heard Fran say that she wanted to go away somewhere with Michael.

"I'm so tired of these spoiled, moody little assistants at work," Fran said, louder now. "They don't know anything. It took me a long time to get where I am and Catherine expects to get there overnight."

Catherine bit her lip and waited for Michael to say something. He coughed and then he asked Fran if she needed a glass of water or anything because he had to get going.

When Fran finally left, neither Michael nor Catherine said anything as they walked outside and up Fifth towards the movie theatre.

"You know, she did have one good idea," he said, buying popcorn. Inside the dark theater, Catherine liked that he let her lead them so close to the screen. "The part about going away. You said yourself you've never been to California."

The following Monday, when Fran came in at noon, and it seemed certain that Catherine was not going to get a raise—not this year, anyway—Catherine said that she would like to take two personal days. *Women* employees got five personal days and up to two weeks vacation. They received 65% health coverage, 85% cosmetic, 100% dental and 100% psychiatric. The product of such a system, one was to assume, was a pretty, relatively sane employee with a good, solid smile. Whatever tumor or cancer lurking beneath that employee's skin was not of too much concern to the company.

"Thursday and Friday OK?" Catherine asked as Fran picked up the phone.

Fran nodded. "Fine, fine. Just get your copy in," she said as she dialed Pam. "Pam?" she started, and then Fran went on about her surprise visit to Michael's, saying how effective it had been.

"It was the first time that he's, you know, reacted," she said.

Catherine spent that afternoon trying to complete "Where They Are Now," a May Entertainment piece about what celebrities from the sixties and early seventies were doing in the eighties. Peter Max was a recluse living downtown with a model; everybody from "The Partridge Family," it seemed, was either bulimic or on drugs. Catherine was still waiting to hear from a publicist regarding Tabitha, the child star from "Bewitched."

By four o'clock it was snowing, and Fran asked Catherine how she looked.

"Great," Catherine said. She was on the phone, but she had been put on hold by someone who claimed to know where Tabitha was.

Fran was standing in front of the full-length mirror. "Yeah, I do look pretty great, don't I?" She dumped her makeup bag on top of Catherine's typewriter and started dabbing at her face with various sponges. "I'm going to pay Michael another little visit."

Catherine hung up the phone. She got up, left the office, walked up and down the hall twice, then came back. Fran was putting on lipstick. She stood back, pressed her lips together, then pouted.

Catherine tore the adjective list from her bulletin board. She and Fran kept a list of adjectives. Elegant, coy, tiresome, playful, fey, titillating, snooty, genuine, tony, zany, pricey, doe-eyed, goody-goody, taut, high-minded, boffo, eerie, sumptuous, nerve-wracking, and the one adverb toe-curlingly—as in, "Richard Gere is toe-curlingly handsome." Catherine leaned down, and, without sitting down to put her feet in the wastepaper basket, she added the word "comeuppance" to the list.

"That's not an adjective," Fran said, reading over Catherine's shoulder, as she was putting on her mink.

"I'll make it one," Catherine said.

No one could locate Tabitha. Wednesday morning, Catherine handed in the piece, filling it out with a dozen or so more photos, and that night she was sitting next to Michael, first class, headed for San Francisco.

They landed in a rainstorm, and when they got to his place she washed her hair because he had said he wanted to take her out. She had forgotten her hair dryer, so he turned the heater up to ninety-two degrees just so she could dry her hair. By the time they got to the restaurant, it was closed, so they got carryout from an Indian place, and Michael set up a parachute tent on the roof, and there, while the rain turned into hail, they made love for the first time.

Their bodies were damp from the rain and they slid against each other like two snakes, his arms and legs coiled around hers. They kissed, but then, when it came time, he lifted his head up towards the sky, stuck his tongue out, closed his eyes, then bowed his head, and closed his mouth, all without a sound.

In the middle of the night Catherine lay dreaming about her father in Michael's bed. In the dream, Catherine's father lay on top of her and died. She could feel the dead weight of him and just as she felt she couldn't breathe anymore, Michael shook her and kissed her awake. It was cold. Her throat was dry and it felt sore, as though she had been screaming. The black blinds were tapping against the open windows and she could hear the sea lions barking for more food down near the wharf.

Michael reached down at the end of the bed, and, without a word, he pulled a black fake-fur blanket up around her bare shoulders. A foghorn sounded from the bay and he held her. In San Francisco, Michael smelled like a new tennis ball.

At 4:15 the alarm went off and Michael reached over Catherine to turn it off, tugging her with him. At 4:25 the alarm went off again and he kissed her and said "Hi." Then at 4:30 Catherine felt the room shake.

"Where are you?" she said. She was scared to open her eyes.

"I'm right here."

She reached across the bed and when she found Michael's hand, he pulled her next to him.

In the kitchen, glass rattled, and when she heard a book from a bookcase in another room drop to the floor, Catherine finally opened her eyes. At her feet a framed poster of Bogart holding a picture of Brando eating a hamburger hung crooked and banged against the wall. Joan Crawford drinking a Pepsi was already down.

Catherine's father had had his heart attack on a day the earth tremored in southern California. While nurses came in and out of intensive care, checking her father for vital signs, Catherine and her mother kept hearing news about the aftershocks.

"You feel it too, don't you? I'm not just dreaming?" Catherine said, lying beside Michael.

"Don't worry, we're safe," Michael said. He was wide awake and he said everything very quickly. He squeezed her so close to his side, her shoulder ached. "This building's compact. You're in the best possible place." For one brief moment, Catherine imagined how officials would break the news to her mother. "Your daughter died in an earthquake," they would say and her mother would give them one of her hoity-toity stares and say, "What the hell was Catherine doing in San Francisco?"

Joey would wear black and cry at the funeral beneath a Jackie O. veil. Fran would attempt to sue for something.

This could be worse, Catherine thought, trying hard to think of something worse. Catherine looked at Michael, who looked at her and brought her hand to his mouth, pressing her knuckles to his lips. I haven't told him I loved him, she thought. With Lewis, she hadn't allowed it. With Daniel it had been assumed. With her father, there hadn't been enough time. I'll die never having said "I love you," she thought.

It was all over in a matter of seconds and Catherine admitted she was a little disappointed.

"It didn't last long," she said. "I wonder how it measured on the Richter scale."

Michael kissed her on the top of her head, and loosened his grip.

"That's why some people move out here," he said. He rolled over to face her. "Once you've felt one you want more." His words came out slower now and his voice sounded tired and low. He put his hand on her arm and slowly moved it down towards the small of her back. Within the past twenty-four hours, she had realized this was a kind of signal to which she would respond by arching and moving closer. Daniel had had his own signal, too. His kisses would slow down and his tongue would stretch to the back of her mouth—nearly choking her—and then it would travel up over the roof, passing over her teeth as though it were diving in search of something.

"Do you have to go to work?" she said to Michael, arching her back.

"I can be late," he said. His hand was moving from her shoulders to the middle of her back up to her shoulders again. "After all, there *has* been an earthquake."

She had read somewhere that after an earthquake, survivors are so overcome with joy that they are still alive, they experience something called Earthquake Love. She wanted to ask Michael about it, but she was scared she would choke on the word "love."

Michael nuzzled her neck and Catherine played with the cut hairs around his ear. "Let's make the earth move again," he joked.

Their bodies were lined up foot to foot, knee to knee, hip to hip.

The phone rang. Michael sighed into Catherine's hair as he reached over to answer it. He listened for a minute.

"I can't talk now, Fran, I've got a call on the other line."

When he hung up, he laughed and shook his head.

"She calls me every day, you know. Your boss is crazy."

"She likes you," Catherine told Michael, wondering when he was going to get rid of Fran for good.

"And I like you." He moved closer. His breath gave her goose bumps. He licked her breast and when his mouth went away, she could feel the cold air on the wet spot he had left behind.

"So," Catherine said. "I'm the 'other line'?"

"I love when you make your voice go like that," he said.

When she woke up again, he was gone. The bond market opened early in San Francisco and even though she and he were on a three-day holiday, Michael said he had some things to take care of. He had pinned a note on the pillow on his side of the bed. "Be back around 1:00," it said.

Catherine put the note down and picked up the phone.

"Joey? You're never going to believe where I am."

Catherine went on to tell Joey what Michael's house was like on Russian Hill, that it was all white inside and out and there weren't even any stains on anything. "*And* he doesn't watch TV in bed," she said. The beginning of the end of a relationship, she and Joey had decided, was when the TV appeared at the foot of the bed.

She told Joey about the clothes Michael had bought her because, he said, she'd never get ahead dressed so-so. She told him how his refrigerator was empty and that all his dishes and his wok were still in their wrappers and boxes, not because he'd just moved in, but because he never ate at home. Then she told Joey about the previous night.

"It was so great," Catherine went on. "There was a hail-storm and we could hear it on the tent. We kept warm and he held my hand and said, 'You know what I like about this? There's an automatic return.'"

"You're not a business deal," Joey said.

"You don't understand," Catherine said. "Business deals are his life."

Joey was at work and she imagined him hunched over on his stool in front of Crotchcough's column, rubber cement oozing out from the straight edges of the copy.

"How come you're not saying anything?" Catherine asked.

"I'm listening."

"I felt an earthquake this morning."

"Oh, *pulease.*"

Catherine looked at the flip side of the note Michael had left her. He had written it on the back of a Xeroxed article about markets and investments from the finance section of some magazine. "Breakup Value Is Wall Street's Buzzword," the title of the article said.

"What's Fran up to?" she asked.

"She's wearing a new shade of lipstick. Neon pink. She's got nails to match. She wrote a memo to Howard suggesting we do a 'When He Leaves You for No Good Reason and How to Get Over It' spread. She wants four pages, and she's really pissed at Ann Bartel because Simpson is giving her more space because of all the reader letters she's been getting. Ann's hot." Joey paused to drink something. Catherine thought for a minute about Ann Bartel, the woman who wrote the first-person pieces for the *She* section. Fran always told Catherine how self-indulgent Ann's writing was, but Ann always got these long letters from readers, saying how moved they had been, reading her work.

"Oh yeah, and Fran's all over the place with this benefit she's throwing for the homeless. I think she's redirecting herself. It's kind of neat to see. She's been going around to all the departments selling raffle tickets. Fran's got so much energy."

"Has she said anything about me?"

"I heard her tell Research she can't believe you took two personal days. I guess she figured you never had a personal life."

Catherine wondered if Fran was onto her.

"Back me up, will you?" Catherine said to Joey.

"Yeah. I'll back you up." She could hear Joey sigh.

"Why can't you just be happy for me?" Catherine finally said.

"Look," Joey said. "You may be in love, but guys like Michael aren't capable of loving anybody but themselves. They just have really long one-night stands."

"Since when did you get so fucking linear?" Catherine said, and as soon as she said this, she wished she hadn't. "Look, you haven't even met him. Why can't you just let me enjoy this?"

"OK. OK. Forget I ever said anything. He's a wonderful guy. Finer then finest. The best to you both."

"Fine."

"Fine."

Catherine took a deep breath. She thought she could hear Joey erasing something.

"So," she said. "I'll see you Monday?"

That morning, while Fran wrote up yet another article proposal entitled "How to Hold On to Him," and while Joey drew up breast-self-examination charts for How-To, Catherine planted a garden for Michael.

There was a little enclosed terrace which she discovered when she opened Michael's back door. It was overrun with weeds, but she found a Weed Eater outside behind the door and she mowed the weeds down to look like grass. There was an empty wooden planter, which she filled with Pro-Mix and sterilized manure she bought from a florist up the street.

"The most important thing is your seedbed," her father had told her every year as he shoveled up the dirt for the tomato plants she would plant.

"You'll never get any fruit until your roots are in deep."

She planted geraniums, snapdragons and petunias in pinks, yellows and purples. She found a mildewy hammock behind some boxes under the stairs and she hosed it down and hung it out and lay in it, flipping through catalogues she had found in a basket on Michael's bookcase. She spent a good part of the morning swinging back and forth, imagining that she was planting up whole gardens with plants like Canterbury bells, phlox, and tea roses. She would wear flowery frocks, weed, and wait for Michael to come back home.

After they had made love for the first time last night, they had gone back downstairs, and gotten into his bed, and she had rested her head on his chest and he had answered all her questions. He told her he was from Plainville, Kansas, that his father had grown corn all his life, that his mother had put away money every year so that he could go away to boarding school in the East, and then to Princeton on scholarship. His dream, he said, was to live in London.

"What about Kansas?" she had asked.

"Could care less about it," he said and he had yawned then and fallen asleep while Catherine lay there in bed next to him, wondering whom she had suddenly become involved with. What kind of grades had he made in high school and whom had he taken to the senior prom? She wondered whom he resembled more—his father or his mother. And if he did look most like his father, she wondered what his father looked like and if he had ever come to visit his son, living here in San Francisco, right on the fault line.

Catherine put down the catalogues and unfolded the morning paper. She turned to a quiz, a word game, and the point was to unscramble words that had to do with weddings. She got "honeymoon," "groom," and "bride." Then she came to "ielv." She wrote down "live." For "nirg," she wrote "grin." But the answers were "veil" and "ring," and after she totalled her points, Catherine discovered she had scored a Terminally Independent—a predicament over which she would have, once upon a time, rejoiced.

Catherine was twenty-four years old and for the first time in her life she wasn't trying to figure out how she was going to break up with somebody. What she had with Michael felt decadent—like drinking wine before noon. She was, after all, still in the habit of reading Daniel's horoscope in the paper every day.

Catherine was not sure if she knew enough to be any good at love. When, for instance, was the appropriate moment to say "I love you"? Did one wait until he said it first? She had no one to ask—Joey either loathed Michael or was just jealous, and even though Catherine knew her mother wanted to hear from her, she also knew she didn't want to hear about this. Sex before marriage wasn't necessarily a sin, it was just a stupid move on the woman's part. You lose all bargaining power. Gospel According to Mom.

She wondered what Ann Bartel would think. Ann had written a piece one month called "Why I Stay Single" which, like all of Ann's pieces, had gotten a lot of reader response.

Catherine could see her reflection in the window. She sat up, faced her image, and mouthed the words "I love you." This is how she would look, she thought. If I tell him, this is what he would see. She tried it again, slower, and then again, this time with her eyes bedroomy, her tongue hitting her front teeth on the "l," her lips poking out on the "you."

Michael got home an hour early.

"I couldn't stand it in that office anymore," he said. He didn't have a briefcase. He picked up the phone hanging on the wall and dialed.

"You're done," she heard him say on the phone, and then, after a while, he hung up.

"Was that Fran?"

"No, why?"

She laughed. "I was just hoping you were saying that to Fran."

"Let's get out of here."

She got up and put on her shoes.

"No, I mean, let's go someplace."

"OK," Catherine said. "Take me someplace dimly lit where I can touch your knees and sip wine."

"I know where," he said. "But it's not in San Francisco."

"I want to get frisked," Catherine said, looking at the Mexican guards. There were two cars ahead of theirs. It had only taken two hours to fly to Border Field from San Francisco and fifteen minutes to rent a car and get to the border. All the Mexican women were carrying babies and selling packages of Chiclets. All the Mexican men were selling hats and colored baskets. "I think they should take us aside and check the car for drugs. Maybe they'll ask us to declare something."

"I think that happens when we leave."

When their turn came, Catherine was impressed at Michael's fluent Spanish. Catherine was busy trying to make out the signs across the street. She guessed by the shape of one of the signs that *Alto* meant Stop. Then the guard and Michael stopped talking. They were looking at Catherine. She looked from one to the other. Michael was wearing a white sweatshirt that had *North Beach* printed in red on the front and Catherine read it again and again. She knew where North Beach was. Now North Beach seemed very far away.

"*Je ne comprends pas,*" Catherine said. She looked at Michael for help. "I don't know a word of this language."

He took her to the nearest *playa general,* which, Michael told her, meant public beach. It was off-season and the long stretch of sand was empty, but as they drove further—you could do that, you could drive right on the beach in Mexico—they came to shacks that appeared to be held together with plywood and duct tape. The houses belonged to the Mexican fishermen, stalky, weathered men who were at the shoreline untangling nets and getting in and out of boats.

It was windy and her hair kept blowing into her mouth as they walked up and down the beach and collected shells which they carefully laid in the hem of Catherine's rolled-up T-shirt.

"What are we going to do with all these shells?" Michael asked.

"Joey should be here. He'd glue them onto toothpicks and make cocktail dealies out of them or something. You've gotta meet Joey."

Michael suggested they get something to drink.

There was a row of shabby, homey, outdoor places on stilts. The tables and chairs had been painted in yellow, green, and aqua blue, and the paint had chipped so that everything looked like something out of a van Gogh painting. The woman who served them had a lot of warts on her neck and a substantial tuft of beard grew from the tip of her chin. Michael ordered for them both and the woman came out with a plate of lime and salt and two Tecates because they were out of Corona.

"Doesn't it feel as though something's going to happen?" Catherine said. She didn't like beer—it reminded her of people spitting up in college—but she squirted the lime into the opening of her can anyway. The glasses looked too dirty to drink from.

The blue in his T-shirt brought out the blue-yellow in his eyes. Fran had once said he had money eyes—that he had the kind of look that said, "I have a lot of money. Help me spend it." But Catherine didn't see that. She thought Michael had the kindest blue eyes she had ever seen in and out of the movies, and when he smiled as he was doing now, lines spread out from the corners reaching towards his temples, like two halves of a star a child would draw.

Thankfully, he had a bad nose. It was a wide, thick nose that matched his hands.

"God, I hate Ted Block."

"He's the son of the founding family, right?" Catherine had read about the Blocks in *Town and Country*.

"It's a partnership. Ever since his father died, Ted has the most shares, so if we ever go public, he gets the most cash. He's just a figurehead. He doesn't know shit about the industry. I'm making so much money for that firm he doesn't know whether to hate me or love me."

Three years ago a man named Phillips had hired Michael because he thought it was funny that Michael said he'd do anything. "I'll sharpen your pencils," Michael had said.

Phillips started him out in the mailroom.

Three years later, Michael had sold forty-five million dollars' worth of junk bonds for Block in a single deal. He had a new title—Mr. Hot Shit—an office with a view, two secretaries—and one month later, Michael had fired Phillips.

"There's a lot of pressure on me right now. Sometimes I'm not sure if I'm cut out for this bullshit."

A skinny dog ran across the beach and barked at a rock.

"I had a dog once," Michael said. "A black Lab I called Prissy. It waited everywhere for me. Closest I've ever been to anything in my life. Then it got run over."

"So the closest you've been to anything has been to a dog?"

He looked all around her face and she worried about what he might find. He smiled, drank from his Tecate can, and said, "I guess I'm risk adverse."

"What the hell does that mean?"

"It's a broker term. Adverse to risk."

"Oh."

Catherine looked out over the beach towards the ocean. This was what she hated—suddenly everything he said mattered more and she would weigh it: What does this have to do with me? How can I be different/better than his former girlfriends, or in Michael's case, than his dog?

Was now the time to tell him?

She tried to find the words for the way she felt—important words because what she felt seemed so important. She couldn't get her mouth to shape anything. She concentrated hard and tried to tell him with her eyes. I love you. I love you, she thought.

"Do you have a cramp in your leg?"

She shook her head. Then she put more lime in her beer.

While Michael paid, Catherine got a pen from her purse and told Michael to write his name and the word "yellow" on a paper napkin.

"I'm supposed to be able to tell what you're like in bed by the slant of your *y*," she said, after he laughed and did what she said. She turned the napkin around and examined it. "Everything slants to the left. That means you're inhibited."

"That's it?"

"No. You have an angular loop. That means you're aggressive."

"Inhibited *and* aggressive?"

"And your loop's pretty big."

"Let me guess what that means."

"It means you have unfulfilled fantasies."

"I *did* want to be a DJ once," he said, reaching across the table to hold her hands. "You know what I like about you? You're not after anything from me. All day long, people are after me—for money, for deals—but not you."

For a moment Catherine wished she had something more substantial to offer.

"So what are your fantasies, Catherine Clemons?"

She looked out towards the water. It was too cold and choppy to swim.

"I used to think that the only man I could ever love was Joey, but when I told him he said it'd never work. We'd laugh too hard." Catherine smiled at the thought. "Then I used to think what I wanted was everything that Fran has. Now I'm not so sure."

"So that's why you went after me."

"I most certainly did not go after you."

Michael laughed, "Oh yeah?"

They stood up and Michael held her hand.

"It really does feel weird," Catherine sighed. "I can't believe we're in another country."

"Who knows?" he said. "Maybe something will happen."

"Teach me," she said, turning towards him. She could smell the lime on his breath. "Teach me some Spanish. Show me how to roll my *r*'s."

In town, the markets were still open and Catherine wanted to walk through them. They started out where the street vendors were selling cold fruit drinks in big glass jars with the fruit still in them—mango, papaya, pineapple. A row of marionettes caught her eye, and Catherine went over to touch the one that looked like a cross between Woody Allen and Carol Channing. When she turned to show Michael, he was gone.

Catherine went to the next stall where a man tried to sell her a sterling silver belt buckle, and then she went to the next where two women, a mother and daughter, pressed her to buy a blanket for seven dollars.

"OK. *Seex*," the daughter said. "You can have it for seex."

Catherine shook her head and walked on.

"Michael?" she said. And then she shouted. "Michael?" Two men sitting under an empty brass bird cage smiled at her and said something between themselves.

She searched for street names and house numbers.

When she was young her second-grade teacher would have Catherine's class say where they lived and what their telephone numbers were every morning after the Pledge of Allegiance and a morning prayer. The idea was, in case they got lost, they could tell someone—a policeman, for instance—where to take them. Catherine's father had gone out and bought big black numbers and screwed them onto the front of the house himself. Her mother said the numbers were atrocious-looking, but Catherine remembered having appreciated the gesture so much that she had ironed a maple leaf between two pieces of wax paper and given it to her father that very weekend. At school, Catherine would walk around the playground, saying 144 Northover Drive over and over, so petrified was she at the idea of not knowing where she lived, of forgetting how to get back home.

Walking up another narrow block in Tijuana, Catherine realized now that she didn't recognize any of the names or buildings and they didn't even look like homes to her at all. Nobody had a lawn—only rows of amaryllis that every now and then led to a wrought-iron gate. Nothing looked familiar and the more she walked the more everything began to look the same. She couldn't even remember the name of the street where Michael had parked the car. She wanted to kick herself for having been so gaga and moon-faced. She tried to think of whom she could tell, how she was going to make it back to wherever Michael or the car was. She suddenly wished Michael was

Daniel. With Daniel, at least, she would have remained rational.

For an hour, Catherine wandered through the open markets in Tijuana, trying to find Michael. She made an attempt to forget she was looking for him, hoping maybe then he would appear. She let the mother/daughter team sell her a blanket.

"*Ten* dollars?" Catherine said. "But you said six just a minute ago."

"*No comprendo*," the daughter said, her palm open towards Catherine.

It was dark. Catherine bought the blanket and sat down on a bench under a tree where birds were gathering to roost for the night. She could see the border from where she sat, but she didn't want to go across without Michael. She wished she was back in her office at her desk. There she could turn her overhead lamp on and stick her feet in the wastepaper basket and she would be able to figure out how to get back to wherever it was she should be.

She remembered Tabitha from "Bewitched." No one, not even the TV people, knew what had happened to Tabitha. How could anybody be expected to find Catherine in Tijuana if nobody could even find Tabitha in L.A.?

A Mexican woman with a dirty baby held out a box of Chiclets.

Catherine shook her head and the woman went away.

Catherine opened her purse and started looking through her wallet. She did this at times when she (a) wanted to look like she wasn't lost; (b) wanted to look like she was doing something; (c) wasn't in her office and didn't have her wastepaper basket to put her feet into.

There was her new lime green Junior League membership card, an old appointment card from Dr. Panter, a receipt thanking her for her four-dollar contribution to the Metropolitan Museum of Art, an outdated press pass to the top of the Empire State Building, business cards from photographers, publicists, one from the Disney actor (she remembered him only because of the dorky picture he had of himself on the card), and one card from someone from something called Network Ink. In between a recipe Joey had given her for coconut macaroons and a business card from the P.R. man with the cats, Catherine kept an emergency number for people who suffered from something called Panic Disorder. "Shortness of breath? Trembling? Fear of dying or losing control? Avoiding places or situations from which escape may be difficult or in which help might not be available?" Under these questions on the card, there was a number—toll free—where you could leave a message and a research staff member would contact you or come pick you up. If she called now, Catherine wondered, would they mind terribly coming to Mexico to get her?

Across the street she saw a blue neon light shaped like an open palm. *Palmist*, a little sign below the hand read. Catherine got up and walked towards the sign.

The front room was a small, comfortably cool waiting room with an overhead fan going and a beaded doorway from which a huge Mexican woman emerged.

"How much?" Catherine said. She was tired and her voice was the voice of a little girl's.

"For you? Today? Ten."

"I only have five," she said, holding out a five-dollar bill. It was a lie, but Catherine wanted to leave herself enough money just in case she never saw Michael again.

The woman took the five.

She led Catherine through the beads and into a little hallway which was decorated with blue and red plastic flowers. There were two wooden chairs— one green, the other yellow—and there was a cross on the wall between the two chairs. They sat down. The woman asked for Catherine's left hand. The woman crossed herself and then she touched Catherine's open hand, and her one beautifully shaped, perfectly polished silver fingernail reached into the heart of Catherine's palm.

"Where have you been? I've been looking all over for you." Michael came up from behind Catherine, who was sitting on the bench, flipping between a coupon for a free manicure to La Coupe and an old backstage pass to a Joan Jett concert she had never attended but which, for some reason, she had been saving. He put his arms around her and it was then that she wanted to twirl around and tell him, "I love you. I love you so much you make my knees sweat."

But she didn't say this. She didn't even tell him she had been scared. She didn't say anything about the Panic Disorder hot line. She didn't say she was ready to go home, that she wished they had stayed in San Francisco in bed, under the fake-fur blanket, where the only fear was one which everyone in California shared when the fault shifted.

She did not tell him any of that.

"Where the hell have you been?" she said. "Was this some goddamned joke or something?"

He looked at her and blinked.

"I brought you a present." He walked around in front of her and presented her with a parrot made of papier-mâché. It was green and painted with yellow and red feathers and it was perched on a piece of iron which was shaped into a bell. In the parrot's mouth was a packet of cocaine.

She shook her head and took the parrot. "Oh, this is great. Great," she said. She took the packet of coke from the parrot's mouth and threw it at Michael's face. "Here I am in Mexico with a member of the drug cartel."

"Jesus, Catherine, lighten up." The coke had fallen in Michael's lap. He put it in his pocket, looking all around to see if anyone had seen.

"I don't even really know you," she said. "You're out making drug deals while I'm wandering around getting lost. What the fuck? I mean what the *fuck?*"

"This?" he said pointing towards his pocket. "These aren't *drugs.* I figured we'd have something to do tonight. I've been looking all over for you. We got lost is all."

In the How-To section of *Women,* a girl in Research once wrote a little piece called "How to Spot a Liar." "The pupils of the eyes grow larger," she had written. "The voice gets higher, the smile fades and the hands are held out of sight."

Michael wasn't smiling, but Catherine could see his fingers, thick, stubby, unlikely fingers stretched around the neck of the parrot she was holding in her lap. She wanted to ask him why he hadn't broken it off with Fran yet and if maybe he was seeing anyone else. She wanted to know if he thought she could really trust him. She suddenly felt she had no idea how he felt about her and she wondered if she ever would.

They went to a bar and while Michael went to the men's room with the coke, Catherine took a shot of tequila. It was bitter and it made her feel nauseous. She took another.

"Did you pick up any more Spanish?" Michael said, sitting back down on the bar stool next to hers. The ends of his nostrils were red.

"*Hasta la vista.*"

"Useful."

It was one of those cool, breezy nights and the room smelled strangely of licorice.

"I went to a palmist."

"What did the palmist say?"

"She said I couldn't tell anyone what she'd said for three days."

"Or what?"

"Or none of it will come true."

"I thought you had your fortune told. Sounds like you two made wishes."

Catherine shrugged. The woman had crossed herself three times at the end of their session, clutched both of Catherine's hands, pressing her open palms together, and said, "Dese. Dese was a beautiful reading."

When their dinner came, Catherine drank more than she ate because of what she had heard about Mexican food and because she figured the tequila would kill whatever bad germs there were. Besides, someone had once told her she made a good drunk. And Catherine wanted to be that way now. Simply drunk and amusing. She wanted to think up clever, quotable things.

Michael didn't touch his food. A little boy with a torn shirt held out his muddy hands and said something in Spanish.

"What is he saying?" Catherine asked, staring into the child's big brown eyes. His stomach was swollen.

"He wants the crackers," Michael said.

Before she could give the crackers to the boy, their waiter came to take away their plates and he quickly swished the child away. Catherine took the crackers wrapped in cellophane anyway and put them in her purse.

When they got outside, they couldn't find the boy and Catherine put the crackers down next to a man asleep on the sidewalk, his head at the very edge, near the street.

"God, that's depressing," Catherine said.

"Don't get depressed," Michael said. "There's no percentage."

They decided to stay in the only hotel in town that had showers, a lovely place with a pink courtyard and glossy tiled floors in Mondrian reds, yellows, and blues.

Catherine let him pay for everything.

They took showers separately. She felt silly coming out naked and damp, and she quickly covered herself with the sheet as she got into bed.

"Where are you?" he said, trying to get to her under the sheet. He rolled over to face her so that they lay on the bed diagonally.

"We're crooked," he said. "Let's straighten out."

She was so tired she didn't want to move and she pretended not to hear.

They kissed and touched one another. And then, after they kissed some more, Michael rolled over and sighed. His nose was bleeding again. When they had had sex before, Michael's nose bled. Now Catherine knew why.

"I guess my body's just not used to you yet," he said. "And I want you so much. Maybe too much. I'm sorry."

Once at a bar on First, Catherine and Joey had gotten drunk on daiquiris, and they had come to an agreement: no matter what, neither one of them could end up with a man who (a) didn't like sex, or (b) wasn't into it.

But now Catherine was relieved. She tried to be reassuring. She got him a Kleenex for his nose. She said that it was the alcohol, or the coke, or whatever. And he had been under so much stress at work and, besides, she had read that for men, the daily testosterone high was early morning and the seasonal high was fall.

"So you see?" she said. "It's night and it's January."

His body was completely covered with his own sweat. He held the tissue to his nose. Catherine had read in Michael's *Forbes* about a thing called buyer's dilemma: when you get close you retreat.

"I could sing," she said. She thought of the song from *Annie*.

"'The sun'll come up tomorrow,'" she started. And he laughed and she laughed, and then she rested her head on the good, solid place between his neck and his chest. She could hear his heart beating fast.

"Did you ever see *Love Story?*" He was whispering now.

"Yeah, why?" she whispered.

"Remember that part when Ali McGraw's in the hospital dying and she says, 'Hold me,' and Ryan O'Neal touches her and she says, 'No, really hold me,' and then he climbs into her bed, and he puts his arm around her through all the tubes and stuff and he really holds her?"

He was breathless and she found it touching. She had seen *Love Story* with her mother and father, and, even at sixteen, she had been embarrassed by the sentimentality. Still, afterwards she had gone out and bought a beret just like Ali McGraw's.

"That part got to me," he said. "Seriously. I know that's really queer. But that part really got to me."

There was a scene in *Sweet Charity* when the insurance salesman sees the tattoo that reads "Charlie" on Shirley MacLaine's arm and he realizes he can't marry her. That was the kind of scene that always got to Catherine.

"That's not queer," Catherine said. She was glad she had never told Michael about Daniel. She put her arm over his chest and her leg over his legs.

"I want you to know something," she said. "I want to tell you."

She took his left hand and spread it out, turning it so that his palm was open and facing her.

"She held my hand like this," Catherine said, holding his hand and looking into his palm. " 'There's a new man in your life,' she said. 'Go on,' I said. 'Dese man. I don't know what he looks like. I can't see the color of his hair. But dese man. He does things to you,' " Catherine crossed herself, imitating the Mexican woman.

Michael laughed. " 'Oh, how he does things to you.' "

"That's not a Mexican accent. That's Jewish. You sound like Fran."

The palmist had not really said what Catherine said she said. She had, in fact, given Catherine the old standbys—that someone cared for her very deeply, though she didn't know who because she couldn't see the color of hair, that she would live to be a ripe old woman, and that there would be no more pain in her lifetime. What had impressed Catherine was that the palmist had added that she would have children. Not many—one, maybe two. And that there would be another man who would complicate her love life. Another man, Catherine thought. Not another woman. Not Fran. She wondered how the palmist knew about Daniel.

" 'He surrounds you like mist,' " Catherine said, and she looked to see if he thought that queer, but he didn't say anything. He just stopped laughing, closed his fingers around her hand, and looked at her.

She went on. " 'He makes it so that every time you see him you want him more than the last time and you never thought that possible or even bearable.' "

And then all at once, Catherine's mouth was near his and she was whispering things she wasn't even thinking about. It reminded her of learning to speak French. It seemed strange at first, speaking a foreign language, and it made Catherine feel like she was lying. But then you're thinking in that language and dreaming in it and then the words come out—words you never thought you knew are at your disposal.

"She said that?" Michael whispered.

"But then she said to be careful."

"Why?"

Catherine shrugged. "You know. Because. She said to just be careful."

"But why should you be careful?"

Michael turned to face her. He held both of her hands now in his one hand.

"I guess it's that whole Keats thing," she said. "You know. Nothing lasts."

"Who's Keats?"

Sometimes she wanted to throw up her hands and say, "Who are you, anyway? Who can you be and how could I be with you?"

"A poet." She kissed his fingernail. "Never mind."

Catherine had never done anything slow in her life. Now she wished just this once she had.

He got up and put on a pair of boxer shorts.

"I don't see how you sleep like that," he said, looking at her. "Don't you feel naked?"

She got up and slipped into another pair of his boxer shorts and then she climbed back into bed beside him.

Michael moved closer. He put his hand on her belly, slipping his fingers beneath the elastic, and they lay like that all night in each other's arms, their bodies each touching the length of the other's.

When they crossed the border again, the line was longer and this time they had to get out of the car. Michael had finished off the rest of the coke and he was jumpy.

"Don't we have to declare something or something?" she whispered to Michael while the guards checked under the seats and ran their hands around the inside of the trunk.

"What for?" he said. "All you're bringing back is a bird, a basket, and a blanket."

"That's true," she said, watching the guards handling her purchases.

It cost twenty cents to get into Mexico and a dollar to get out, and as they were driving away, Michael remarked on how much easier it was to get into another country than it was to leave.

On the drive back to Border Field, he turned on the radio and kept time with Bryan Ferry by banging the side of his hand on the steering wheel.

"What's the first thing you're going to do when you're not with me?" he asked.

Order a pizza, she thought. Call Joey. Watch a Rita Hayworth movie to figure out how to be alluring. Take my clothes to the Chinese laundry and see if the daughter's given birth. Try not to call you.

"Open my mail," she said.

"That's exactly what I'm going to do. Turn up my stereo and read mail."

Catherine thought of Lewis Lipman just then. She remembered the time he had told her about having to pretend to be different people all the time, and how a former girlfriend of his had liked that. Catherine knew now what Lewis had meant.

Outside, everything looked dry and withered, and she wondered if

Michael would remember to water the garden she had planted. And at that moment Catherine wondered when and if there would ever be a time when she could give herself to a man and not end up wanting to take it all back.

They passed a sign welcoming them to California. Below the sign was a currency-exchange office. A pouty, British song came on the radio and Michael turned it up.

Don't you want me baby. Don't you want me aah, aah.

"Doesn't it feel like we've left something behind?" Catherine said. She was shouting above the music.

"Like what?"

"I don't know. A toothbrush or something?"

Michael shrugged. "I got everything."

Catherine tried to think up something in Spanish, some amusing little phrase, but her mind went blank and all she could remember now was *mañana.*

Chapter 6

Valentine's Day

The subway was backed up because of track fires in midtown and Catherine decided to walk to work one day in the middle of February.

She bought two coffees at the Star—one for her and one for the bag lady who sat propped up on a stoop on York, her leg stuck out to trip anyone who passed without money or food. She couldn't see the woman's face, but after Catherine put the cup down on the curb, the blankets shifted, a dirty hand appeared, the cup disappeared, the leg recoiled, and Catherine moved on.

Balancing her laundry bag, her satchel, and her Styrofoam coffee cup, Catherine crossed the street with a gaggle of old people who were heading for the Pastry Garden. Catherine didn't know any of their names, but still she smiled because they were old and because they were probably her neighbors and because they didn't smile and because at that moment New York did not seem so bad. It was a good time to be in Manhattan at that hour in the morning, between seven and eight, when the city and everybody in it ignored you.

She dropped off her laundry at the Chinese cleaners and while she rubbed her arm where the rope from her laundry bag had dug into her skin, the owner held up two fingers.

"Hello. Hi," he said, still holding his fingers up. There was a sign behind him: *Please collect all past old laundry.*

"Two days?"

The owner shook his head.

"Weeks?"

The owner nodded.

Catherine stomped the slush from her boots and gave him the thumbs up and said, "No starch."

On Park, in the Seventies, she passed an all-boys elementary school where the children wore blue blazers and ties under their coats and none of them looked at her.

"I don't like Picasso much," one boy said to another. They couldn't have been older than nine. The boy speaking was staring down at the green gardening boots Catherine wore. "I prefer Calder," he said.

Catherine thought about how infuriated Daniel would have been, had he heard. "Can you spell *pretentious*?" he would have shouted, or maybe he would have grabbed the little boy by the knot of his tie and said to his pale little face, "Calder sucks."

She would have had to stand aside, waiting for his anger to pass.

But Michael would have responded differently.

"Calder, Calder. Isn't that the guy down in SoHo doing all that graffiti art?" he would have asked her, and Catherine actually laughed out loud thinking of him. Passing the elementary school, Catherine wondered if she would have to wait for Michael to call her or if they were at that stage where she could call him. She knew what her mother would say: "A woman should never make outgoing calls to a man."

Since they had come back from Mexico four weeks ago, Catherine had seen Michael every Saturday night, but still, the weekdays seemed to be off-limits. She did not think much about calling him because, usually, he would call, but recently, Catherine had had an unfamiliar desire to see more of him, to meet him somewhere after work for drinks, maybe even stay past noon on Sundays at his place.

Midtown was grey with smoke from the subway-track fires and the cabdrivers honked at fire trucks parked all around Grand Central. Catherine passed over grates where the smell of ash and rubber rose from under her and everyone around her looked straight ahead, pretending not to notice the stench.

In the elevator going up, the women who worked at *Women* kept their eyes on the numbers. The building housed seven other magazines besides *Women* and Catherine usually liked to guess which floor each person got off on. It wasn't difficult. The chubby girls in Laura Ashleys got off on three: *Bridal.* The pale willowy creatures in black on four: *Chic Chicks.* And then there were the pretty boys with colored socks and pleated pants who would always look at you, their eyes traveling from the shoes on up, while with one long, thin, middle finger they would press seven for *Men Now.*

Most everyone who rode the elevator with Catherine was among those who would remain assistants for two, three, sometimes even five years. They were the compliant ones, the ones who were willing to overlook sparse paychecks just so they could lean across some downtown bar in Manhattan and say in a nonchalant way to a well-dressed stranger, "Yeah. I'm in editorial."

But it was so cold now that no one undid their coat buttons or scarves and Catherine could not get a good look at anybody as they rode up and the majority got off on three for coffee anyway. Catherine rode on, filled with anticipation and dread at the thought of facing her desk.

The July issue was causing mayhem, and Catherine's desk was deluged. Manhattan during a garbage strike, she thought when she got to it and looked over the mess.

On one end, under the lamp, was a mound of slides and photos from April and May including a black and white of Mrs. Tiggy-Winkle carrying a basket of laundry. There were the head shots of the alone-time celebrities that needed to be returned, and a photo of an Oscar. To the right of the pile were the May put-throughs, a clipboard full of phone messages, and some negligible memos, including an old one from Fabrics—polka dots were the spring theme. Next to the clipboard were invitations to movie screenings, plays, concerts, book signings, and P.R. parties. There were candy canes scattered throughout the papers, a pair of wax lips (a gift from Joey), and there at the far right-hand corner of her desk was Catherine's very dry and very withered three-year anniversary gift from Personnel.

Catherine sat down and looked across the room. Fran's desk was clear, save for a neat stack of paper on her blotter, the jar of neon pink nail polish and an African violet next to the phone. Fran was coming in just once a week now. She was protesting—Howard had refused to give an interview with Madonna more than a page because, he said, Madonna was nothing more than a cult figure who was too much on the slutty side for *Women*. Fran said she would remain at home until Howard agreed to at least two pages. Preferably color. And she was busy planning a benefit for the homeless. She had volunteered to chair a party to be given in April aboard the *Intrepid*, which was an old warship docked in the Hudson. For the moment Fran was trying to pin down a travel agent to sponsor a trip for two to Bermuda. Meanwhile, at the office, Fran's African violet was thriving beneath her desk lamp.

The phone on Catherine's desk rang.

"Are you sleeping with a man?"

It was her mother.

"Well, are you? You're never home. I tried calling you Saturday."

She had been with Michael Saturday. They had ordered from a Szechuan place on First and had watched a comedy special on MTV while they ate.

"Mom, most people go out on Saturdays."

"I worry about you. My God, do you know how many diseases there are now? AIDS, syphilis, herpes, and what is it, spiders?"

Catherine opened a candy cane and yawned. She had slept nine hours, but still she was tired. "It's crabs," she said, taking off her belt. It was pinching her sides. "How was your weekend? Tell me about your tennis."

"I went to a dinner party Saturday night, but we didn't get fed until nine-thirty because the hostess forgot to turn on the oven."

"Was that Rosie?"

"How did you guess?"

"She's from Baltimore. That explains a lot."

"Listen. We had a long talk about you. You need to come home. Rosie wants to fix you up with a candy-bar heir."

And then all at once, Catherine knew she was going to be sick.

"Mom."

She put the candy cane down.

"What is it?"

"I gotta go."

She hung up. She ran down the hall, past Readers' Service, past Research and Food, Travel and Fabrics, and into the bathroom where, moments later, Catherine had the notion that she just might be pregnant.

It could have happened in San Francisco, during the earthquake. She was never really sure if she was getting the diaphragm thing right. Or it could have happened that first time, when she had said, Wait, let me go do something, and he had said, No, stay here.

Back at her office, Joey was standing in the doorway, holding two Wonder Woman mugs full of coffee and two bagels.

"Honey, I've got to do your hair, you're in Page Six," he said. Catherine took *The Post* from under his arm.

They had picked up Catherine's piece about the Disney actor who had posed with nothing on but a heart. They didn't mention Catherine's name, only that it had appeared in *Women*.

"Why aren't you jumping up and down, girl?" Joey took a pair of scissors from Catherine's desk and began cutting out the piece from the paper. He stapled it onto a piece of grey company-memo paper and wrote FYI on the top.

"For Simpson," he said.

Catherine took the memo and sighed.

"Here," he said, putting the coffee and the bagel in front of her on top of her phone messages. "Eat. You look green."

"I'm not sure I'm up for today," Catherine said. She sat down. She felt dizzy. "Look at this mess."

"The desk or you?"

"Thanks, Joe. You make things so much easier."

"You look weird. You should be glowing, but you look weird."

"Yeah, well, I feel weird." Catherine looked at the phone. She wondered when Michael would call, and if he did, what she would say. She had to be sure first.

"I've gotta call Paramount," she said, picking up the phone. Joey sipped his coffee and looked at her questioningly. He was growing out his hair (he wanted to look like a Thompson Twin) and his bangs were held back with two pink plastic Donald Duck barrettes. Catherine didn't wait for him to back out of the office. She was already dialing. "We still don't have slides from Spielberg's movie. They don't want to show his new little creatures. We go through this every damned month. Like clockwork."

At noon, Catherine snuck into the ladies' room with a home pregnancy tester she had stolen from Health.

The directions said to use the test first thing in the morning, but Catherine did not want to wait.

The results were unquestionably, indisputably pink.

After work, Catherine walked up Fifth Avenue towards home. She recognized the woman in front of her. She recognized the red frizzy hair, and the calm way she had of walking—an effortless hurry. It was Ann Bartel, the woman who worked down near Shoes, in the cubicle with no windows.

At first Catherine started to go after Ann—maybe she could tell Catherine what to do. But then Catherine remembered that Ann was one of these single mothers, the defiant kind most likely, the I-wouldn't-have-my-life-any-other-way women who grew herbs in the kitchen window box and found time to grind up all their baby food in colorful Williams-Sonoma bowls. Watching Ann cross the street and dash after a bus (of course it would be a bus and not a cab—saving for the little one) only made Catherine wish she had a bag of Chee-tos and a banana split with caramel sauce.

Catherine went into a discount beauty place on First instead and got another pregnancy tester—the kind that said "Positive" or "Negative" instead of using a color system, and Catherine thought that might make all the difference. She stole a lipstick called Anytime Wine because it was eight dollars, and she lingered in the middle of the hair-and-lotions aisle, squirting free hand-lotion samples into the palms of her hands and reading the labels on tubes of shampoos and conditioners. She finally settled on something called Cello-Fix, a spray which claimed to texturize and condition and put all the stray ends back into place.

That night, Catherine lay in bed alone, with a pillow over her stomach. Michael had not called. The home pregnancy kit she had bought sat unopened on the sill in her bathroom. She stared across the room at her open closet. Could a crib fit in there? she wondered. She would hang her clothes all around, like curtains, but no, a sweater or a skirt might fall and smother the child and even if she did call 911, the medics would never get up the six flights in time.

She thought quite suddenly about Mick Jagger. She wondered if he ever worried that he had gotten all the women he had slept with pregnant. She wanted to ask him. She wanted that interview with him more than ever now. Maybe then she would understand why Michael had not called.

Catherine threw her pillow across the room and pounded her stomach with her fists. Get out, get out, get out, she said to herself over and over. She took deep breaths. She heard some more plaster fall in the shower. Maybe I'll catch TB and it will die, she thought. All my problems will be solved. She stopped hitting her stomach and concentrated on breathing in more TB from the walls. She filled her chest with air and held it there, imagining all the Upper East Side TB germs coming into her, and killing off what she and Michael might have made.

That night Catherine dreamed that she had to take care of all of Jessica Lange's children—the ones from Baryshnikov *and* Sam Shepard—and she ran out of Huggies.

The next morning, Catherine was up at dawn. The test came out positive.

"Look, don't worry," Joey said. He stood at the doorway to Catherine's office. She held her head in her hands, her elbows propped up on her desk, paper scattered all around. She was wearing a blue-and-green plaid dress she called her muumuu dress. "I've got a friend," Joey said. "He's really into the woman thing. He takes these pills that thin your blood and make you bleed. Maybe they'll work for you."

"I don't think so, Joey."

"I took hormones once to change my voice. They gave me boobs instead. You could at least try. Drugs do wonders."

"I can't even call him to tell him."

"Michael? Why not, for God's sake? It's his problem, too."

Catherine shrugged. "It's not my turn to call."

"You two take turns? Great relationship you got there."

Catherine got out the phone book.

When she was nervous she had trouble spelling, so when she looked up Abortionists, she found Tree Service.

"You're looking under Arborists," Joey said. "Give me that."

While Joey made the calls, Catherine put a sheet of paper stained with coffee rings into her typewriter.

Having a baby, she typed.

Pros:

1. *I will never have to be alone again at night.*
2. *I could sue for child support, win, quit* Women, *move to New Guinea, and never have to see Fran again.*
3. *Michael could fall in love with the child, marry me, and we could move to San Francisco and quake happily ever after.*
4. *Uncle Joey would make a terrific godmother.*
5. *I could get many many How-To ideas.*
6. *I would learn to like children.*

Cons:

1. *Manhattan is no place to raise a child. It will order beige ice-cream cones and learn to dislike Picasso by age 7.*
2. *I could sue for child support, lose, and be forced to raise little Junior beneath my office desk next to the wastepaper basket because* Women *doesn't have child care.*
3. *Michael could loathe the child and marry Fran.*
4. *A cockroach or a piece of plaster could fall into the child's mouth while it slept, killing it, and all those Lamaze classes and hospital bills would have been for nothing.*
5. *I could not take a child with me while interviewing celebs for the Casting-Couch-Actresses story.*
6. *I hate children.*

"There's a nice place off Fifth," Joey said, putting down the phone. "I liked the sound of her voice. They can do it for seven hundred, but you know,

Cat, the company insurance can pay for it. You can put it down as a nose job. That's what that girl in Shoes did."

Catherine read over her list.

"I don't know, Joey. I'd be killing something. It just seems so, I don't know. Self-indulgent."

"Don't think of it that way, honey," Joey said. He pulled back her hair and they looked in the mirror, she at him, he at her. His bangs were pinned back with Minnie Mouse barrettes. "We're just doing a little renovation."

That afternoon, while she was opening the office mail and trying to think of what she would say if she did call Michael, she came upon a package from Mexico, addressed to her. She opened it and inside was a piece of redwood carved in the shape of a beaver. Its stomach pulled out like a drawer and inside was a one-way ticket to what she first read as Lamaze, but she saw, on second look, that it was La Paz.

"Kind of nervy of you, isn't it?" she said when Michael answered on the sixth ring.

"Is that you?"

"Yeah. I got the beaver."

"What are you talking about?"

"The ticket."

"What ticket?"

"The ticket to Mexico."

"I didn't send you a ticket to Mexico." And Catherine could tell by his tone that he was in earnest.

"Oh," she said.

"I'm glad you called," he said.

"Yeah?" she said, embarrassed that she had called.

He told her about his week and the deals he had made and that he had sprained his hand the other night at the Odeon because he had banged it on a brick wall.

"That doesn't sound too smart."

"I was proving a point."

"I'd better get off. You're making my ear red."

"Not every woman tells me that."

She knew he could hear her smile and she wanted more than ever to be next to him, to be calmed by the nearness of his body.

On her desk were proofs for the June issue, which included the special pull-out section on breast cancer that Joey had laid out.

"If I got my breasts lopped off, would you still like me?" Catherine said. She tried to sound light and flip.

"What are you talking about?" Michael said, laughing. "You're nuts."

"I've got a screening tonight," she said. "Want to come?"

"I don't think that's such a good idea," he said. "Do you? I mean, Fran might be there."

When Fran had visited Michael he had not cared if Fran saw Catherine there with him. Now he cared.

"You're still seeing her."

"Sure, I see her, but not like that," Michael said. "She's a great contact. Listen, I've got a call on the other line."

At six Catherine went to a screening of a movie about a girl who is visited by aliens. The aliens give a young woman living in downtown Manhattan a special power whereby every time someone has an orgasm in or around her, they disappear, leaving her alone, on her back, usually spread-eagled.

A rapist, a lesbian, a boyfriend, and a man whom she despises all vanish mid-ecstasy. The lesbian scene was particularly odd and amusing. The dyke laid out the heroine on a bed, lifted up the woman's leg, and—both of them still fully clothed—proceeded to rub up against the woman's thigh, her cheek pressed against the heroine's calf. Once her partner was gone, the heroine was left in this position, with one leg sticking up in the air.

Sitting in the wide, overstuffed leather swivel chairs on the thirty-fifth floor of a building on Broadway, Catherine sat in front of a movie reviewer from *The New Yorker* who she knew was asleep. Catherine wondered where this girl in the movie came from and why the space people chose her to visit. Was the heroine also an alien in Manhattan? Who were her father and her mother? Where were *any* of the fathers and mothers in the movie?

I should have been a lesbian, Catherine thought, touching her stomach.

Afterwards the publicist introduced herself to Catherine and said the "film" should not be taken too literally.

"It's all symbolic of a woman's sexuality," she said. "We're all aliens. We're always alone."

"Sorry," Catherine said, putting on her coat. She had on her movie-critic I-work-for-*Women* tone. "It's a little too rough for us."

Catherine could not stand the thought of going back to her apartment, so she went back to her office. There, sitting behind her desk, was Fran, eating a brownie, taking notes. She had the VCR playing a new TV show which Catherine had not gotten around to previewing. On the TV a group of people in their thirties were playing touch football in somebody's backyard. A man wearing an apron was grilling. Fall previews.

"Want one?" Fran said, lifting up half a brownie. Catherine took the brownie.

"How is it?" Catherine said looking at the new show, licking her fingers.

"Everything's family, family, family," Fran said. She started to bite into the brownie, but then she stopped herself. "I shouldn't be eating this," she said, throwing the brownie down with disgust. "Men are such shits, Catherine. You should know that. And here they're like little boys in a candy store. Why should they go out with someone my age when they could have someone your age?"

They both picked up another brownie.

"Did you know that today is Valentine's Day?"

Catherine shook her head. Valentine's Day. That meant her mother would be calling, or sending her a card, because tommorrow it would be her birthday.

"No, I didn't," Catherine said.

"My apartment was driving me crazy. I mean, I like her, but Madonna's not that important. Besides, I figured Howard wouldn't see me come in after five." Fran took another brownie. "I call him and he's never home," she said. "He says to me, 'Quit calling me. Don't call me for two weeks.' It's funny, isn't it? I mean, here I am, breaking up with a *bond* salesman. Even I see the humor in that." Catherine sat down. She put her feet in her wastepaper basket. Breaking up. Fran was finally admitting she was breaking up with Michael, Catherine thought. I should be happy.

Fran was watching the TV. Everybody was eating barbecued chicken.

"Fuck," Fran said, turning off the tape of the show. Her eyes were red and teary. "I want a real home. I want a house with a washer and dryer. I want a patio. I want a husband who cooks."

"You'd get bored after a week," Catherine said. "You're going after more."

"I *know* he's seeing someone else," Fran said, glaring at the phone. "But I am unwilling to declare the body dead until I have observed it."

Crotchcough advised *Women* readers to use two forms of birth control—something plus a condom because, he wrote, you never know where he has been or who he has been with. Catherine looked at the frosting on her brownie and wondered what Michael was doing for Valentine's Day.

"I was cum laude. I've been on 'The Today Show.' I have two folders full of clippings. My own clippings, for Christ's sake. I got a major New York travel agent to sponsor a trip for two to Bermuda for an organization they'd never heard of. I don't need this shit." Fran looked at her brownie. "Why am I eating this?"

"Chemical," Catherine said. "It does the same thing in your brain that love does." Catherine took another brownie and looked at it. "Besides, it's a way to hold off tomorrow."

"He's like introduced me to all this jazz. I have all these fucking jazz tapes. He was like the first guy I've gone out with in New York who wasn't a project." Fran took another bite. "What would I do without you, C?"

The phone rang.

"I'm not in," Fran said. "Unless it's him."

Catherine answered the phone.

"Did you get it?" It wasn't Michael.

"It's me. Lew."

It was Lewis Lipkin.

"Get what?"

"My beaver."

"You sent that?"

"What say we go for a spot of tea? I'm at the Carlyle."

"I can't."

"I'm invited to a costume party. You can dress up like Marie Antoinette. I'll go as Nixon."

"Lew, I don't have time for this."

"You sound terrible."

"How are you?"

"I found a cockroach in my bed and I'm suffering from Cat withdrawal."

"Try boric acid."

"I was thinking we could fly off to Mexico together. My agent thinks I should get out of town. She says I should quit wrestling. She says look at what it did to Cyndi Lauper."

"I can't go to Mexico, Lew."

"It'd be like 'Gilligan's Island.' I could be the Professor and you could be Mary Ann. They were always meant for each other, you know. We could go deep sea fishing, if you get my drift. Get it? Drift?"

"I've gotta get off."

"That's what every woman tells me."

Catherine didn't say anything. Then she sighed and said, "Lewis."

"Cat. Look. No pressure. Honest. But just remember. You'll be in the same boat I'm in right now someday. You'll look around this dirty little town, and you'll say to yourself, 'What the hell do I have here, anyway? Who *do* I have here? Why should I stay?' You gotta go through that, or you're not human."

"You didn't tell me you were seeing anyone new," Fran said when Catherine hung up. Fran had her bachelor file out and she was flipping through old photos of Spielberg.

Catherine shrugged. She wondered, Did she show? Would Fran notice? Some women supposedly glowed when they were pregnant. Catherine glanced in the mirror. Her face was breaking out and her eyes were puffy.

"I'm so glad you got rid of that Daniel guy. He was such a downer. He wore the weirdest ties." She pulled out a head shot of Spielberg from her folder and thumbtacked it on the wall above her typewriter. "Amy Irving is too Ralph Lauren to last."

Catherine wished Fran had not said his name. For the first time in a long time, Catherine missed Daniel. She missed the feeling she used to have that, no matter what, he always wanted to see her. She missed being close to him.

Fran balled up the napkins and the brownie bag, and tossed it in Catherine's wastepaper basket.

"You know what we need?" Fran said. "We need a bigger office. We need one with a window. There's an office near Accessories, you know. We should make a bid for it."

Catherine smushed the garbage down with her feet. She was staring at the adjective list pinned to her bulletin board. She leaned over her desk, scratched out "comeuppance," and under it wrote "guilty, guiltier, guiltiest."

"Let's get out of here," Fran said. "We've done enough for today. Come on. I'll petty cash us a cab home."

In the cab, Fran hunched down into her fur and stared out the cab window at the falling snow. Somewhere way off an ambulance wailed.

"He loved sexy but he never really loved sex. He only wanted it once a week. I want it like every day. That's terrible. Does that happen? Is it like that? You see someone and then it just comes down to once a week?"

Outside, there was a woman sitting on a garbage can.

"Read a book!" she was shouting. "Read a book every day. Every single day!"

Once a week. At least with Fran he was regular.

"I'm what, thirty-five, so when do I have babies?" Fran said. "At one point, I wanted to have babies."

"The world doesn't need any more people," Catherine said. She wanted to tell Fran she was pregnant. She wanted Fran to hold her. "Anyway, you've got too many things to do."

Catherine thought about how much she had to do. She had to pick up her laundry even though she could not stand the thought of facing the owner or his fingers or his pregnant daughter. She had to call her landlord again about her ceiling and write up the June copy. She had to come up with more ideas for July and August. Whole months were before her to fill, and all her fall folders were empty.

"Get a poodle," Catherine said.

"You're right. You're right," Fran said. "I've got so much to do. I'm gonna get a new boyfriend and a bigger office, one with a window. I'm gonna call that producer at 'Entertainment Tonight' first thing Monday." She looked at her watch. "L.A.'s what, three hours behind? Maybe someone's there now. You know the Academy Awards are next month. Maybe I'll get the hell out of this town for a while."

The cab pulled up to the corner on the east side of York and Seventy-eighth. Catherine got out. Fran paid for the cab and got out too.

"I feel like walking," she said.

"I may be a little late coming in Monday," Catherine said.

"No problem," Fran said. It was the nicest Catherine had seen Fran since that first day when Fran took her out to breakfast at the Helmsley. There they ate thirty-five-dollar croissants while Fran told her the trick to writing for *Women* was to pretend you were writing for fifteen-year-olds. Standing there now, listening to the electronic buzzing from the yellow neon Star sign, Catherine could feel her eyes filling up with tears. She considered admitting everything—about her and Michael, about her intentions to get Fran's job—but she thought better of it, so she hugged Fran instead. Their breasts came between them.

"Happy Valentine's Day, Cat."

"Happy Valentine's Day, Fran."

They stood apart awkwardly and smiled, Fran trying to loosen the bracelet that was caught in Catherine's scarf.

"Hold on. Hold on," Fran said, laughing.

Fran had taught her so much—that Fifth was the only avenue in Manhattan that had to be spelled out, that odd numbers in titles got better reader response, that a copy of any memo *had* to go to Ms. Simpson even though Howard made all the decisions, that visuals were essential to every editorial meeting, that when you wrote someone a letter you had to put a Mr., Mrs., or Ms. in front of their name and that nobody went by Miss anymore, and that clothes were an investment, as was good, expensive makeup because "You only have one face."

Freed, Catherine tucked her scarf back inside her coat. The deli man came out of the Star and pulled down the heavy metal front to his store. Fran closed her mink back up and turned to leave. Catherine heard her name and turned around. Fran was standing in the middle of the sidewalk, one hand cupped over her mouth.

"Hey. Cat. Listen. If I go to 'Entertainment Tonight,' I'm taking *you* with me."

When Catherine got to her stoop, she unlocked her mailbox and pulled out a handful of letters, most of them crumpled and torn from being stuffed into the tiny brass pigeonhole. There was a reminder card from Dr. Panter's office. "February news flash," it said in letters the color of healthy gums. "New Year's Resolutions: 1. Lose 10 pounds. 2. Take Scruffy to the groomer. 3. Make appointment with Dr. Panter to have teeth cleaned and examined." His phone number was at the bottom of the card.

There was also a Xerox red notice. *Help,* it said. *Help. Lost dog. Boy Collie named Motek. Sometimes goes by Kotex. Orange, brown, and white. Old. Don't know how old. Blind and can't hear so good. Lost somewhere on the roof. Contact Mrs. O. in 4A.*

Catherine threw out Dr. Panter's card and the Xerox and she flipped through the phone bill and some dance-club invitations. She had told Michael what she thought about Valentine's Day—that it was just the chocolate makers' way to drum up business every year—so she wasn't expecting to find a card with his return address on the envelope. It was a picture of a man dressed up in a tuxedo with a long string of ribbed red plastic coming out of his lapel. Inside there was a message from Michael. "*A you-know-what card from your who-knows-what friend. Pull the plastic.*" Catherine flipped the cover of the card back over and pulled the plastic and she heard something that sounded vaguely like "You put me up."

"I don't think I'm doing this right," she said, upstairs. She was somewhat relieved to have had an excuse to call.

"Pull it again. Use your nail."

She pulled, using her thumbnail.

" 'You put me on'?"

"No. It's 'You turn me on.' "

Catherine pulled again, but still couldn't hear the message correctly.

"That's really neat," she said. "Now I feel bad I didn't send you anything."

"You've given plenty."

"Can I ask you a personal question?"

"Is this an interview?"

"What do we have here?"

"What do you mean?"

"Are we like, friends?"

"Yeah. We're likefriends." She could hear him settling back into his bed. She wished she was there, by his side. She wished she could match up the length of her body with his as though they were Lego blocks, and then she could put her head on his chest just to the left of his heart.

Michael blew his nose and went on, "Likefriends. That's good. That's really good. No wonder Fran hired you."

Catherine could remember a friend of hers named Cynthia who had had a baby. First there had been the long, gruesome birth, when Cynthia had almost bled to death. Then when her daughter was about a year old, Cynthia seemed to turn into another woman altogether. Catherine could remember the night she and Cynthia had last spoken. Cynthia had called late in utter despair. Little Eleni wasn't making all the right animal sounds.

"She can do all but the goat," Cynthia had wept into the phone. "What do you think it means?"

Catherine had tried to calm her friend, but it was no use. What, after all, did she know about children or goats?

Catherine looked up at her ceiling. The superintendent had not returned any of her calls and a poster she had framed had fallen because of the loose plaster on the wall. It was a picture of Picasso's screaming woman, a gift from Daniel. The glass had cracked.

"OK," she said. She took a breath. "Here it is. Your little chum's pregnant."

Michael didn't say anything. She imagined him looking at the phone and then away, out of a window. Then he said "Shit." Then he said he was sorry for saying shit. Then he asked her what she was going to do.

She hated him for asking.

"I don't know. I'll take care of it, whatever."

"Let me handle the financial end."

For the first time since she had lived in Manhattan, Catherine wished she had a car. She would get in and drive. She would go to a place where she could get up to sixty or seventy miles an hour and she would switch lanes without signaling.

"Say something, Cat."

In a piece she had written a few years before on women and art, Catherine had reviewed an exhibit called the "Birth Project." The quilts and needlepoints were hung up on white walls in a room and they all depicted the agonies of giving birth. Catherine remembered one image in particular of a naked woman lying torn apart, her body cut in half by a river of reds, golds, and blues. The woman's face resembled a tree, and she wept in blacks and browns and screamed out more pink and red.

"What do you want me to say?" Catherine said. She was crying, trying to make it sound as though she was laughing.

"A lot of women go through this, you know. I know this woman. She's a trader. She says it's no big deal."

Catherine listened.

"Look," he said after a while.

"I know, I know," she said, interrupting him. "You've got a call on the other line."

"Well, yeah," he said. "I do."

That night Catherine found another place to hang her Picasso poster. Up above her bike, where the plaster had not flaked. She didn't have a hammer, so she got out the beaver Lewis Lipkin had sent and she used its tail and she hammered and hammered, until the Soviet man who lived next door banged back on the other side of the wall and shouted something she could not understand and she stopped and she went to bed, hugging her pillow close, tucking the corner under her chin, kissing the edges.

Early that Saturday morning, Catherine walked up to the corner of York and Seventy-eighth to wait for Joey. She passed the bag lady who had her leg stuck out, her stocking rolled down just below the knee.

"I don't have coffee today, I'm going to the doctor's. Please," Catherine said. "Don't trip me."

Catherine listened to her own words as though she were standing five feet away from herself.

The woman was completely covered with old army blankets and newspapers. All that was visible of her body was her stockinged leg, which, Catherine noticed, was slowly retreating back into the greenish tent.

Joey had not wanted to take a subway to the clinic because he thought the smell of smoke might make Catherine throw up, so he waited at the corner of York in a cab. He was wearing a beige skirt and jacket made out of a nappy fabric. His hair was pulled back in a French twist.

"I call this my sofa suit," he said as Catherine climbed in next to him.

"You look like Nancy Reagan," Catherine said. She was wearing a dark corduroy jumper her mother had sent her one year for Christmas. The letters *EK* were embroidered on the front because the woman who had sewn them was a little crazy and she was also a friend of Catherine's mother, so Catherine's mother had not bothered telling her to fix it.

That morning, as she put on the jumper, Catherine had wondered what her mother would have told her to do. She started to pick up the phone, but then she stopped herself. Her mother would probably have told her to go ahead and have the baby at some nunnery west of the Mississippi.

In the cab, Catherine couldn't get warm. You should always have a tin can and a candle with you in a car whenever you drive anywhere in the winter, she had read in the February Safety on the Highway column. That way if you get stranded, you'll be able to make a little oven and stay warm for at least six hours. Rubbing her bare hands together—she had forgotten her gloves—Catherine wondered if that would be enough time. What if no one came for her?

Joey took both her hands and warmed them in his.

"We're gonna be OK," he said.

She moved closer to him as he squeezed her hands.

Protesters with signs and pictures of mangled fetuses paced in front of the clinic off Fifth Avenue. Joey took Catherine's arm and told her to keep on walking. One of the protesters, a fat, middle-aged woman, grabbed hold of Catherine's arm.

"Murderer! Murderer!" she shouted in Catherine's face.

Catherine was not wearing the right shoes because she had wanted to look nice. She had on pumps and she had to keep placing her feet carefully in the protesters' footsteps in the snow. Thankfully, the Murderer shouter had very large feet.

Catherine could feel Joey's hand closing into a fist around hers. She had had no idea he was that strong.

"Joey," Catherine said.

"I won't. I won't," Joey said, and just before they got to the entrance, the woman shouted again this time into Joey's face.

"Murderer!" she said to him.

"Oh, get a life," Joey shouted back.

In the elevator going up, Catherine turned to Joey.

"I don't know if I can do this. I mean, I cry at Kodak commercials."

"If you want to go, we can go."

They waited in colored chairs which were grouped in greens, yellows, and blues. Catherine filled out forms and she went to a group counseling session that reminded her of a Junior League meeting.

"Hi! I'm Tracy," Catherine imagined one of them saying. "A baby would kill me on account of my tipped cervix, which I inherited from my great-great-great-grandmother who came over on the *Mayflower*."

The women sat in a circle. Some boyfriends were there. Some of the women didn't say a thing. Others went on and on about how they had made their decisions. When Catherine's turn came, she wanted both pity and awe.

"My name is Elizabeth," Catherine said. "I was gang-raped."

A few of the women in the circle glanced up, but most of them kept their heads down, pretending to read pamphlets called *You and Your Ovaries*.

They were all asked if they were sure about their decisions and they nodded sleepily, Yes, they were sure. And everyone was advised to get on the pill.

Each woman was led to a curtained room where the walls had been painted orange. The colors, Catherine assumed, were to make her feel better. She changed into an aqua green hospital gown, then came out and watched a young Spanish girl going into the cubicle next to hers. The girl was holding on to a crucifix around her neck. The nurse closed the door. Catherine sat on a yellow chair, wishing she had something to hold on to, too.

On my honor I will try. That was in the Girl Scout handbook. Catherine thought of everything she had learned in Girl Scouts. She could tie a sailor's knot though she had never gone boating. She could make a vinyl seat to carry around—just in case she ever wanted to park herself next to the bag lady on York. She could make a pork-chop dinner for four. It was funny how the Girl Scouts had never taught her how to cook for one.

In high school, after she had been thrown out of Troop 178 (she had raided the s'more supply at the annual camp-out), Catherine grew bookish, although she never really studied. She read magazines. Women's magazines. She learned how to make housecoats out of towels, rugs out of place mats. She found out how to work a party—the safety zone was always near the food—and she discovered the secrets of stains—seltzer for red wine, baking soda for tomato. But of all the lessons she had endured, of all the How-To pieces she had ever read, and later had written, nothing had prepared Catherine for her abortion.

How to Get Pregnant: 1. Forget, in your state of ecstasy, whether or not you "reapplied." 2. Take the Pope seriously. 3. Secretly hope that you will have your boyfriend's baby.

She wondered what Michael was doing that very minute. On the phone, probably. But with whom? A client? Fran? Catherine thought of the way Fran's breasts had felt through their coats when they hugged the previous night. Catherine had once come to the conclusion that Fran was the kind of woman a man cheats on. Now Catherine wondered if she, herself, was that kind of woman.

At Thanksgiving once, Catherine's father had said that they needed more people around the table, and he had looked at Catherine and then at his turkey. "It's selfish not to want a family," he had said.

If she were going to have a baby she could eat as much as she wanted, as long as it was good for her. She would have to cut down on the carryout. She knew another woman who had been pregnant and every time she was about to eat something questionable, her husband would raise his hand, stopping the fork to her mouth, and say, "Is this the best you can do for your baby?"

Catherine looked down at her stomach and thought, Is this the best you can do for your baby?

"Cat." Joey slipped into the room. He was wearing the same pink smock that the nurses wore. "I can be with you. I told them all about the rape. I told them you had this thing about machines. I told them I was your sister. They're going to let me in, Cat. Isn't that great?"

"No, it's not, Joey. You can't do this. You'll faint or something."

"My father always wanted me to be a doctor. This is good."

"This is so embarrassing."

"I'll close my eyes."

"This is so disgusting," Catherine said. She felt naked in the hospital gown and she wanted to cry, but she knew if she did she wouldn't stop. Joey sat in the plastic yellow chair next to hers. They were small chairs and their knees were almost up to their chests. Joey picked up her hand. He held it the way a boy holds his girlfriend's hand at a movie or on a ride at a carnival.

"It's my birthday," she said.

"Oh God," Joey said, and squeezed her hand. "Happy birthday."

"Relax," the doctor said. Catherine was glad she couldn't see his face. Only his eyes showed. Young. Early forties. There was a nurse standing next to him. Her mouth was also covered.

"Your cervix is a little tilted."

She thought of Tracy, the girl she had imagined in the counseling session, and laughed out loud.

The doctor looked up. His eyes were narrow. Was he mad or was he smiling?

"This could be ectopic," he said. "This could take some doing."

Catherine looked up at Joey and squeezed his hand. She felt a terrible pain. A cramp.

"You'll feel a little cramping now," the doctor said.

"No shit," Catherine said.

On the ceiling there was a poster of a lion charging through some big, green, glossy leaves. Concentrate. *Lions and tigers and bears,* she thought. *Oh my.*

"Is that poster supposed to be soothing?" Catherine said.

"Breathe," Joey said.

"I am breathing."

"Breathe through your mouth."

Catherine felt another cramp, worse than the one before.

"Don't tell me this crap," she said. "I'm not giving birth."

The nurse helping the doctor looked at Catherine, then she looked back down at whatever she held in her hands. Those would be the steel rods, Catherine thought.

Catherine looked up at Joey. He was making an effort not to look anywhere but directly into Catherine's eyes. There was sweat on his forehead and on his upper lip.

"Tell me things," she said to him.

"I bet moaning helps," he said. "Let's try."

Joey moaned. Then he nodded for Catherine to join in. Together they moaned. The nurse looked up.

"OK," the doctor said. "Your cervix is dilated."

The nurse rolled the machine closer to Catherine's legs. The Hoover, Catherine thought.

Catherine looked at Joey, who was looking at the machine which the nurse had just turned on.

Catherine had interviewed a celebrity skin doctor once who told her, matter-of-factly, that the sound of water was close to white noise. Staring up at the lion on the ceiling, Catherine thought if this sound had a color, it would be purple. A deep blue-red purple.

"Tell me a joke," Catherine said. "Make it quick. Make it funny."

Joey took her other hand and bent down closer, near her face. He was wearing a good perfume.

"Why does it take so many women with PMS to screw in a light bulb?" he asked.

The cramps were coming in long waves now. Catherine could hear the machine humming and clogging. The plastic tubes which ran from her to the machine filled with red.

"Keep moaning," Joey said.

They moaned.

The nurse turned off the machine. The doctor stood up straight and covered Catherine's legs with a sheet. He turned around. Catherine could hear him taking off his gloves, washing his hands, then he turned around again, licked his index finger, and said, "So yeah?" He was looking at Joey. "Why does it take so many women with PMS to screw in a light bulb?"

Joey wiped his brow. His hand was shaking. His other one, in Catherine's, was wet with their sweat. Joey sighed.

"Just because," he said, pretending to sound testy.

The nurse laughed.

They went to Cornelia Street to Joey's to make chicken soup because Catherine said she couldn't face all that crumbling plaster at her place.

He rang the buzzer three times before they went up, just in case, he said, someone was in the middle of a burglary.

Joey's place was more like a walk-in closet than an apartment. Belts and feathered boas in all colors hung from hooks all around the room. There was an exercycle in the corner near the window with lingerie hanging from the handlebars. A big basket of hair ribbons sat in the middle of a little coffee table in front of his sofa bed. Joey went to the window as soon as they got in. He watered his geraniums, which had blooms the color of a car's taillights, and when he opened the window, he shook the wind chimes, which were made from mussel and clam shells, sand dollars and starfish.

There was only the one view of the brick building across the alley, but Catherine could tell from the tops of the air conditioners across the way that it had stopped snowing and everything would soon turn to slush.

"God, look at this day," Joey moaned. "Press the sunshine button if you can find it."

He took an empty pie tin from the ledge outside and brought it to the counter of his little kitchen—which was really a board over his bathtub. There he stood and crumbled some bread into the pan, then put the pan back on the ledge where a pigeon was waiting.

Joey watched the pigeon peck at the crumbs.

"So they're filthy birds, so? People give pigeons such a bum rap," he said.

Catherine sat down on the sofa and a cat climbed quietly on her lap.

"Damn It," Joey said.

"No, that's OK."

"I know. That's her name. Damn It."

"Oh."

Catherine petted Damn It while Joey put some water on to boil. She felt as though she were still in the cab—as though she were moving forward fast and someone had just pushed her seat back. It was that sort of sensation.

She watched as Joey brought a cooked chicken from the refrigerator and then dismembered it. And as he threw out the skin and the carcass, she wondered, briefly, what all the doctors in New York did with all that they extracted. What had they done with Michael Jackson's extra lip or the rest of Diana Ross's derriere, for instance? And what of Cher's ribs? She imagined there was a doctor somewhere keeping celebrity parts in separate jars, and when they died, he would auction them all off at Sotheby's. But what of the laity? Were there special bags? What, for instance, had Dr. Panter done with her wisdom teeth? And where would the nurse with the covered mouth empty the machine?

Catherine put her purse down on the floor. In it was the pamphlet the nurse had sent her away with. "If the blood clots get bigger than lemons," she had said, "give us a call." Catherine had stared at that nurse then, trying to imagine something the size of a lemon coming out of her.

Joey had papered the walls of his kitchen, which was really a little hallway, with *Interview* covers and painted them over with shellac to keep them from yellowing. They were all Warhol portraits—of Prince, Richard Gere, Michael Jackson, Jerry Hall, Sheila E.—their lips colored over with bright red, their eyes darkened with black, everybody painted up to look prettier than they already were.

"I wonder why Mick doesn't marry Jerry," Catherine said.

"Why should he?"

"Seems the decent thing to do."

"Maybe that's why he doesn't. Could ruin his image. I can see the headlines in the *Post:* 'Rolling Stone Does Decent Thing.' "

"I bet you got the Scout Cooking Badge," Catherine said, watching Joey bringing out little spice jars from his cabinet.

"I was a Boy Scout for half a day. I couldn't get the knots right. I dressed up like a Brownie that Halloween." Joey brought Catherine a knife, an onion, and a good bone-china plate with a forget-me-not pattern. "Are you hungry?"

"Starved."

He brought out a box of lemon-flavored animal crackers and put them on the table next to his ribbons. Catherine moved Damn It and started chopping.

"We should get a badge for what we just went through," Joey said.

"I don't think it works that way," Catherine said.

The sound of the knife coming down hard on the plate startled Catherine at first, but after a while she didn't want to be sitting in the room without the noise.

As she chopped, Catherine thought about a woman named Michelle whom she had interviewed the year before. Michelle had been the strongest woman in the world and Catherine had spoken to her in person because Howard had insisted that Catherine measure her biceps. They met in a building off Broadway where they sat watching clips of women weight lifters. "I hate being weak," Michelle had told Catherine. "I hate feeling that I let myself down." As a child, she told Catherine, she spent summers walking over glass barefoot to see how much she could stand. Michelle had looked like a man except for her skin. Her skin was a beautiful blue-white—a sheath, like the thin film around an onion, that curved with muscles, and when Catherine wrapped the tape measure around Michelle's arm, that pale bluish sheath was soft and immobile.

Sitting there cutting onions on Joey's sofa, Catherine wished she had a ten-pound weight to lift, or a bar on which to hoist herself up. She wished she didn't feel so weak.

"You should put a piece of white bread between your teeth or cut that near some cold running water," Joey said. He had filled a hot-water bottle and he sat down carefully next to Catherine, holding the hot-water bottle to his stomach. "Then maybe you won't cry." He balanced a plate on his knees, shifted the water bottle to his abdomen, and began cutting a carrot.

"I'm fine," Catherine said. She wiped at her eyes with her wrist and kept on chopping. Then she looked at Joey. "Are you OK?"

"Fine." He slipped the hot-water bottle under his shirt and continued to chop.

"Like they say, it was only seven minutes," Catherine said.

"Longest damn seven minutes of my life," Joey said.

"I need something else to chop," Catherine said. "Got any celery?"

She went to Joey's refrigerator, a short one, like hers. There was the rubber ice cream cone and the *Work Sucks but I Need the Bucks* refrigerator magnet she had gotten him in San Francisco. Inside Joey's refrigerator was yogurt, soy butter, milk, and some wilted lettuce. Catherine found another onion and went back to the sofa.

"When I grow up I want a house near the beach," Joey was saying. "You're lucky, Cat. You come from a family with good chandeliers and chintz. I don't. I come from shit. And you know what else? I want children. At least two to keep each other company. A boy and a girl. I'll give them names like Arnaud and Dionne-Charlotte. French names."

"Yeah," Catherine said, cutting into the second onion, getting to the green heart of it.

"Oh shit, why do I do that?" Joey put his knife down and held Catherine as she tried to cry and chop at the same time. "Why do I always say the wrong thing? Get down, Damn It." He pushed away the cat, who was trying to claw up Catherine's corduroy dress.

"This isn't turning out to be such a great year, Joey," Catherine said. She put her head on his shoulder. It was thinner, more boyish, than either Michael's or Daniel's.

"I know. I know," Joey said. "Things are a bit neonish, aren't they?" He took her hands in his and started to push back her cuticles.

"I feel like such a fuck-up."

"You're not a fuck-up. Sometimes you gotta do what you gotta do. I had an aunt who sold candy in a beautiful little store in the mountains. When she named it, she combined *Arkansas* with *scenic*. She called it Ar-scenic. Now who's going to buy candy from a store called Arsenic?"

"Joey?" Catherine said. "Does this story have a point?"

"She was happy. For a while. The store bombed. She turned it into a funny story that charmed the pants off this rich old guy who married her." Joey began working on the cuticles on Catherine's other hand. "You'll be all right. Tomorrow's Sunday and Sundays are great. You wake up. You make yourself a banana sandwich, grab some cookies and a Coke, and run back to bed."

Catherine nodded and stared at her empty plate.

"I miss my dad," she whispered.

Joey twisted around and put his arm around Catherine. He held her to him. It was odd, feeling his bony chest on hers, and they let go and looked back down at their laps and tried to smile.

"Your nails are cracked," he said. "Let me rub some olive oil in them."

They did each other's nails that afternoon—Catherine's a pale pink, Joey's a bright red—and he taught her how to smash the garlic first before cutting it—to let the flavor out.

"I'm sorry about New Year's Eve, Joe. I'm sorry I wasn't there for you. I don't know what I would have done without you today."

"Don't worry about it," Joey said. He pounded more garlic because, he said, garlic prevented colds. "I had a lot of cocoa to work with."

Joey made cornbread and when everything was ready, he ate the soup and Catherine ate some of the bread and finished the rest of the lemon-flavored animal crackers, because, she said, she felt particularly vegetarian that day.

Damn It weaved himself around their legs under the table and Catherine picked him up and put him in her lap.

"Look at this cat. Look how handsome he is. His hair is so black and shiny. Will you marry me?"

"What do you think heaven's like?" Joey said. He got up and fished around in the pot on the stove for more okra. Catherine bit the head off a lemon-flavored elephant and let Damn It hop down. He settled on Joey's windowsill, moving his tail, inspecting the pigeon on the other side of the glass.

"A place where you can eat anything you want and not throw up," she said. She finished the elephant and put her hand back in the box, even though there wasn't anything left.

"Maybe it'll be like Oz," Joey said. "You know, I never really understood why Dorothy bothered waking up. I mean, Kansas was all in black and white. 'Go back to sleep,' I yell every time I see that movie. At least in Oz everything's in color."

Catherine stopped in at a plant store on the way home, telling herself over and over that she really wasn't so bad off. I'm like most women in New York, she thought. I've had my ears pierced, my hair highlighted, and now I've had an abortion.

At Plant World, one of those humorless health-food types who wear socks with their suede orthopedic open-toed sandals helped her.

"Why not a rubber plant?" he said, pointing to a rubber plant. "It's a dependable plant. Works well in the background."

"Sounds like a bad boyfriend," Catherine said, and she watched his face but it remained unchanged, staring down at the glossy, rubbery leaves.

He warned her about the philodendrons.

"They had lizards in them when they came in," he said.

She bought a small geranium on sale because it looked like it could take care of itself, and she walked home with it, cradling it on First, resting the pot on her hip on York, its leaves under plastic grazing her cheeks and her mouth.

Today she was twenty-five. In another month tulips would be two dollars a bunch.

When she got home, she left a message on Michael's machine, telling him that it was one thousand dollars not seven hundred. The way she figured, he owed at least that much to Joey for taking his place. She lay down on her sofa bed and looked at the geranium in the window. Then she picked up the phone again.

"Lew?" She didn't know what to say. "Say something."

"It's good to hear your voice, Cat."

"Yeah, well. Sometimes a girl figures out things, you know, like what's important. Well, at least she tries to figure them out."

"Yeah."

"Stay on the phone a while, will you?" she said. She rested her head back on pillows and put her hand on her stomach. "I just need a friend right now, OK?"

"Hey. I'm taping this thing onto my head as we speak," he said. "And the connection's so clear, don't you think?"

On Monday, the subways were still filled with the stench of smoke, so Catherine walked to work, skipping the elementary school. Somewhere in the Sixties she passed a podiatrist's office, where there were colored photographs of people's feet in the window. In one, the person's toes were spread to show a scabby wound. In another the foot was angled to better show a callous and a fallen arch. In front of a picture of a foot with giant corns, a woman stood next to Catherine, and used the reflection in the window to put on lipstick. Then she walked on. Catherine stood before a twisted toe, and a sole discolored by a rash, wondering when and if Michael would call.

It was not that she wanted to talk to him—she had preferred talking to Lewis that night on the phone. But she wondered if Michael wondered about her, if he worried.

She got to work early, and even though she was tired and still bleeding, she was glad and even grateful to be in the elevator again. Fran would be in early this time, writing up copy on the new summer TV shows, checking on the catering for the homeless benefit. Then there were the Academy Awards to think about. Smashed up against Copy, squeezed in between Fashion and Research, Catherine thought of all she and Fran had to do and she was relieved to rise above the snow and the slush, the mangled feet and the underground fires, so that she, along with the rest of *Women,* could get back to work on July and get started on August.

Chapter 7

Easter in August

In March, at long last, a new office space opened up at *Women*. Beauty was working on a first-trimester make-over on Accessories, who was on pregnancy leave. The new temporary Accessories editor wanted to be closer to Shoes, so she moved into a closet down the hall, and Fran put in a bid for the abandoned Accessories office.

The office was in the far corner of the floor. It was bigger, had more file space, and it had a window that looked out over Madison Avenue. Fran wrote memos to everyone appropriate and to those not—Ms. Simpson, Howard, even Personnel.

"I deserve that office," Fran said, stepping into a pink sequined dress. "I've given *Women* ten years of my life and I deserve an office with a window." She was standing in front of the mirror in their office. Catherine was on her knees, taking out files from the file cabinet, combining the duplicates, and putting them all into cardboard boxes.

Fran was right—she did deserve the office. Everyone knew she deserved the office. At Home had already given Fran a new desk set (leftovers from a July office make-over) as a "going-away" gift. "Keep in touch," the note on the blotter read. When she got the blotter, Fran told Catherine to go ahead and start packing up.

Fran stepped back from the mirror. She straightened the lower half of her dress.

"You look great," Catherine said.

Fran picked up the phone. "Could someone in Beauty come down?" she said, staring at herself in the mirror. She hung up the phone and sighed. "I wish my hair was longer. I wish I didn't have these hips."

Fran was going to the Academy Awards. She had spent two weeks trying to get a date. First a publicist from PMK had tried to fix her up with a client—somebody who had once appeared on "Mork and Mindy." But Fran said it would be too humiliating to show up at the Oscars with somebody from TV. So she asked the producer she knew from "Entertainment Tonight" and he agreed, and she ran out to buy a new dress, and now she stood in front of the mirror in a bright pink sequined mini, waiting for Beauty to come straighten her out.

Beauty did not say anything about Fran's hips or the fact that the dress pulled a little too tightly over Fran's chest. Without a word, she felt Fran's shoulder pads, said she had the dress on backwards, glanced around the office, picked up a new Pretenders album, looked at Fran—who nodded, unzipping the dress to turn it around—then left, taking the album with her.

"Much better," Fran said, standing back, the front of the dress no longer pulling. Then she looked at Catherine, who was still on her knees on the floor, her hands covered with dust and newspaper print. "In a few years, it'll be your turn to go," Fran said.

At that moment Ann Bartel passed their office. It was odd seeing Ann in the halls—she rarely went beyond her little cubbyhole in the back.

"Oh," Ann said when she saw Fran in the pink sequined dress. "Wow."

"I know," Fran said. "I'm going to the Academy Awards."

Ann nodded, smiling, looking a little uneasy. She looked at Catherine, who was holding a stack of files.

"I feel as though I've just stepped onto the set of Cinderella," Ann said. Catherine and Fran laughed politely, and then Catherine stood up and sat down in her chair.

She followed Ann's eyes—Ann was looking at all of the gold-framed celebrity photos on the wall, and then there was the TV, which was always on with the volume down, and all the stereo equipment. Ann nodded. "Gee," she said, and then she went away.

Fran clicked her tongue. "Thank you, Miss Mother Earth," she said. "It's like, condition your hair already, Ann. Get a new wardrobe."

The Friday Fran left for L.A., Joey painted Catherine's hair with something blue which made it blond, and they made a pact to get working on their upper-body strengths. In the afternoon, Catherine took Joey to the Colony Club.

Swimming up and down the length of the pool, Catherine listened to the peculiar, muted sound of gold bracelets jingling underwater (the old women there never took off their jewelry). If someone had looked, they would have seen a flash of white teeth on the surface of the water every four strokes or so, because even though her goggles were on a little too tight, Catherine was smiling. Fran was in Los Angeles and Catherine was here, underwater, free, safe, and in control. Here was the shallow end, there was the deep end, and Joey was swimming in the lane right next to hers. She knew her boundaries, her perimeters. She knew that if she got tired, she could hang on to the edge of the pool. It was here, in the pool at the Colony Club three times a week, that Catherine thanked God for her mother, the Junior League, and New York.

At the end of the hour, Catherine agreed to meet Joey upstairs at the front. He went to the men's locker room and she went to the women's.

She took a shower and, still wrapped in a towel, dried her hair. An older woman in a white slip stood in front of the mirror next to Catherine, stuffing her grey hair in a pink-flowered bathing cap. The left cup of her bathing suit was caved in. She only had one breast.

For one brief moment, Catherine wondered what had happened to the Greek girl with one arm. Had she gone back to Greece? Had her father found her a man who was willing to marry a girl with part of her self missing? Watching the woman with one breast looking at herself in the mirror, Catherine wondered why women had more parts to lose than men.

The woman stood back, stuck her hand into the side of her suit, punched out her left cup, looked at her reflection from the side, sucked in her stomach, and left.

Getting dressed, Catherine felt lean and strong, and her whole body felt numb, as though it had what Dr. Panter had called paresthesia, the temporary paralysis.

That month Catherine had interviewed the girl who was going to play Wonder Woman in a feature movie about the comic-book heroine's earlier life. To prepare herself for the role, the actress was working out eight hours a day. Swimming, she told Catherine, was the best, because it lengthened your muscles.

"Every woman wants long muscles," she had said, putting on her cape.

Catherine had gotten Wonder Woman to sign her glossy to Joey, not to Fran, and in the Colony Club changing room, she gathered up her things with the photo of Wonder Woman framed in gold.

Upstairs, in the corridor, she gave Joey the photo along with an envelope which contained the five hundred dollars.

"I'm gonna hang it above my bed," he said, holding the photo at arm's length. There were imprints around his eyes from his swimming goggles. He was wearing a pair of black pants that laced at the side. When he opened the envelope with the money he looked at her.

"Think of the hundred as interest," she said.

"Let me take you out to dinner," he said.

As they were leaving, Catherine thought she heard Michael's voice. She turned around just as he did.

"Catherine." It sounded as though he was tired, as though he was really glad to see her. "My God, you look great. I think you've lost what, fifteen pounds since I've seen you. It's in your shoulders," he said, feeling her shoulders. "And I can feel your rib cage. It's great." She was wearing a short black Betsey Johnson number Joey had given her from a Fashion giveaway. She had even put on lots of mascara, the way Makeup had shown her, and it had smudged, giving her a kind of downtown unwholesome look that was so popular that year.

"Your lips are different," she said.

"They get that way when I'm cold."

"Blow," Joey said. "Go like this and blow."

The three of them went to Jezebel's. It was Friday and it felt like the whole world was out. Catherine watched Joey and Michael talk and eat, and she came to the realization that Michael and she never really had a chance. Her mother, for instance, never would have approved of the way Michael handled a knife and fork and she would have said his head was too small.

"Your father never had a little head," Catherine was sure her mother would have said.

Catherine ordered another glass of wine, and, safe in the knowledge that she and Michael did not have a future together, she felt more relaxed than she had ever felt around Michael.

After dinner, Michael took them to a gallery opening in SoHo. His boss, Block, was an investor in the gallery, and Michael said he had to put in an appearance.

All the women were wearing black tights with cloddy men's shoes that buckled on the side. All the men were just in black. In the first room there were wooden loading crates with photos of something pink nailed to them. In the second room there were photos Scotch-taped to animal fur. A picture of garbage was on a bear fur, magnified spit on a rabbit, ketchup on a squirrel, and a woman's shaved pelvic area on a shaved beaver fur.

"I love it," Catherine heard a woman squeal. "First you have the boxes that you catch the poor animals in and then you have their skins." The woman held out her hands to the artist—only man in the room wearing blue jeans.

"The rooms have nothing to do with each other," the artist said solemnly. The woman looked disappointed and a little embarrassed. "I call the boxes my tanning boxes. Those are magnified pictures of my tan line." He unzipped his pants and pulled them down to bare his thigh. He wore no underwear. "See?"

"Oh yes yes yes," Catherine heard the woman say as she, Michael, and Joey passed. The woman had a pen and a piece of paper out. She wanted the artist's number. She wanted to see the rest of his work.

Michael saw Block and the two of them nodded.

"Mikey!" A skinny woman in black tights hugged Michael. She held up her hand and a waiter appeared with a tray of champagne. Another one came behind him with a tray of ice-cream cones stuffed with steak tartare.

"I'm going to Sardinia in the morning," Catherine heard the woman bellow into Michael's ear. "Do you know any Sardine?"

Catherine went upstairs alone, where the floors were as white as the walls. Three women all in black tights stood in front of an empty bookcase made out of plywood.

"It's like, *ugh,*" one of the women said.

"I know," her friend responded. "I'm like, *God.*"

From the balcony, Catherine could see Michael and Joey. They were side by side. Michael had his left hand on Joey's right shoulder. He was whispering into Joey's ear. Catherine watched as Joey turned towards Michael and smiled, and then Joey quickly looked around, as though he were trying to find Catherine. From the balcony, she waved. Joey caught sight of her and motioned for her to come back down. She shook her head and motioned for them to come up. Michael just stared up at her. He looked a little drunk, a little dazed. But he was staring at her, and she wondered what he was thinking. She smiled and then he looked back down again at his empty glass.

Next to the bookcase there was a green board covered with glass. Next to that was the letter *A*. But what everyone was really going nuts over was the broken mirror.

There was a long rectangular mirror in the center of the room with three sections that had been broken. A few of the women were fixing their lipsticks in the far right-hand corner above a square piece of cardboard that said "Untitled."

"What did you use?" Catherine heard a woman ask a man who was even skinnier than the skinny woman downstairs.

"My assistant," the man said. His hair was gelled up into spikes and his white shirt was buttoned all the way up at the collar. He was wearing a black suit and he spoke with a British accent.

"He did this all in one afternoon," the skinny woman from downstairs was saying. She was coming up the stairs with Michael and Joey, who were both laughing.

"Can you believe it?" the skinny woman said. "See that letter *A?* I love that one. He just sat down and cut that out. I could stand in front of that one for hours."

Michael put his arm around Catherine and introduced her to the skinny woman, who kept looking over Catherine's shoulder to see who else there was to talk to. She put up her hand again and Catherine, turning around expecting to see a waiter with a tray of champagne, saw the artist instead.

"Where in England are you from?" Joey asked, after the introductions had been made. The artist looked up at the ceiling with his mouth open in a silent laugh, and said he'd never been to England in his life.

"I'm from Ames, Iowa," he said with his British accent.

"My art. It is not beautiful because there is no more beauty left in the world. The earth is doomed."

"I don't know," Michael said. He was smiling. "Take a look at these two right in front of you." He nodded towards Catherine and Joey.

Joey laughed out loud and punched Michael's arm. Then he looked at Catherine and, shaking his head, said, "This guy. Such a charmer."

Catherine couldn't tell if Joey was serious—she didn't know if he was flattered or insulted. She looked back and forth from Michael to Joey, but they both just looked at one another and smiled.

The artist turned his back and spoke with the skinny woman about Sardinia. "It is not a beautiful country," Catherine heard him begin.

On their way out, Joey turned to Michael, saying, "So those were your friends, huh? No wonder you were with us."

"We'll take you home," Michael said.

"No, thanks. I can walk from here. Really." Joey hugged Catherine and told her to take care.

"I'm not sailing to Bora Bora," she laughed. "I'll see you tomorrow, you know."

Joey looked at Michael. "I know. Still."

Catherine and Michael watched him walk down the bricked street, disappearing, reappearing, and disappearing again in the shadows between the lit second-story windows.

"Nice guy," Michael said, watching Joey turn the corner.

"Yeah," Catherine said. "He's my best friend."

He took her to a late-night double feature in the Village. One was a Woody Allen movie and one wasn't. Afterwards, she turned to him, saying she never thought he would have liked that, and he looked at her and laughed and said didn't she know by now that every man feels like Woody Allen at least once in his life?

They got a cab and he took her to a cafe next to the East River under the Manhattan Bridge.

"How's Fran?" he asked at the bar. The room smelled of baked salmon.

"You don't know?"

"Haven't talked to her in months."

Catherine looked at him. What was it again, the pupil either gets bigger or smaller when you're lying? Catherine forgot which. Michael's looked big.

"She's in L.A. at the Academy Awards. She's getting a new office. She's seeing a guy from "Entertainment Tonight." Catherine wished she hadn't told him that. She might as well have said, Yeah, I'm still a peon and Fran's not.

"Sounds like everything she wants," he said.

"Yeah," Catherine said. "Fran's doing really well." She looked at her shoes, good, sturdy, unaffordable shoes Joey had stolen for her from Fashion. Michael paid, and outside, under the bridge, Catherine thanked him for the dinner and the opening and the movie and the drinks, and when she turned, he turned her back around and he kissed her. Two black children walked past.

"Look," one of them shouted. It was the boy. "She's got to stand on her tippy-toes."

"Hey, you two," the girl said. "Why don't you get yourselves to a hotel?"

"Why don't you guys go play spin the vial or something," Michael said.

"Hey mista, is that a ticket on your car?" the little boy said.

Michael was smiling. He looked at a parked car and said no. "It's a pizza coupon. Take it and get yourselves a pizza."

"This ain't no pizza coupon," the little girl said, waving the slip of paper. "It's for fireworks."

"Good," Michael said, looking at Catherine. "Take it and go blow up something."

The children left, kicking and throwing gravel at each other.

"You looked so funny when you were crying—like Kermit the Frog," he said.

"When did I cry?"

"At the movie. When the girl almost died and then when the guy died."

"Oh yeah."

Michael took Catherine's hand and kissed her knuckles. "Come on," he said. "Let's go home."

And Catherine could feel the goose bumps on her arms and legs rise when she heard his voice say "home."

They spent the whole weekend together, leaving her apartment only once to pick up some carryout. On the way back, Michael stopped at a store and came out with a big imitation-diamond necklace. It was gold with millions of tiny glass diamonds and he clasped it around her neck even though she was wearing jeans.

Upstairs that night, they watched an old John Wayne movie, and afterwards, when she had taken off all her clothes, she stood at the foot of her sofa bed, trying to get the necklace off.

"Don't," he said from under her sheets. "Leave it on."

Later, a bright light woke Catherine up, and when she looked out the window she saw that all that light was coming from the moon—two ribbons of light, one crossing over the other like the old-fashioned searchlights they used to use at the opening night of a movie—and she felt as though this was some kind of a sign, but she wasn't sure what any of it meant.

She touched the necklace at her throat as Michael slept beside her. He had a way of holding her while he slept. With one hand. He had not shaved in two days and his face smelled vaguely of mildew. Careful not to wake him, Catherine unclasped the necklace and reached over to put it on top of the TV. She moved Michael's hand down from her rib cage to her belly and she fell back into the diamonds of moonlight coming in through her burglar bars.

Later, Michael woke her up, and they made love again, but this time she began to cry in the middle of things. She wasn't sure exactly why, but, hearing her, he opened his eyes and kissed her lightly, sweetly, on her mouth and then on her neck.

"There," he whispered. "There, there. It's all over now. It's all over."

On Monday Catherine took everything she could hold to the cleaners. On the way to the cleaners she saw Ann Bartel walking ahead of her. Catherine watched as Ann stopped and bought a banana and an apple at a fruit stand, then walked on. Catherine wondered whom Ann confided in, if, for instance, she had a Joey in her life. Ann didn't even have a direct boss with whom to eat brownies—whom did Ann Bartel talk to, anyway?

At the cleaners, the owner wasn't in but the daughter was. Her baby lay in a crib near a sewing machine. The daughter said hi to Catherine and continued wrapping and boxing a wedding dress in blue tissue paper.

"I've got a lot that needs cleaning," Catherine said.

"So beautiful," the girl said. She was referring to the wedding dress. "It almost makes me desire to do it all over again." She looked at Catherine and smiled. "Almost."

When Catherine got to the office, Articles was celebrating. Everybody was standing around drinking coffee, eating bagels, and talking about Ann Bartel. And in the middle of it all, sitting on top of Health and Fitness' desk chatting it up with Ann herself, was Ms. Simpson. Ms. Simpson who never attended staff parties or anything else for that matter.

"Here's another one," Ms. Simpson said, holding up a letter Readers' Service had just given her. Everyone quieted down. "'Dear *Women.* You have my compliments on Ann Bartel's story on cervical cancer. What else can I say except that if anyone missed the March issue, go find a copy and read it. It's been a long time since I cried while reading an article in a fashion magazine. Keep these articulate writers such as Ann Bartel in business! Sincerely, Cynthia Spellbind, Greyville, Illinois.'"

Catherine left while everyone cheered.

Fran had never paid much attention to reader mail, and so Catherine hadn't either. But for Ms. Simpson, reader mail was everything.

Ms. Simpson wasn't a mirror editor—she did not assign and edit only articles she wanted to read. Helen Gurley Brown was a mirror editor. Simpson was guided by her readers. Once, a reader wrote to *Women,* explaining how she wished the magazine would picture larger-sized models, that she herself was a size sixteen. Readers' Service, an anorexic woman who spent weekends reading fairy tales to prisoners, had printed the woman's letter in *Women* the following month with the advice that the woman go on a diet. The woman canceled her subscription. That day, the day the woman's letter arrived at the offices of *Women* announcing that she wanted to cancel her subscription, Ms. Simpson went down the hall with an empty cardboard box, which she gave to Readers' Service along with ten days' notice.

Back in her office now, Catherine opened the only unpacked file cabinet left, and she pulled out a file marked Mail.

Fran had a silent deal going with Readers' Service—she gave Readers' Service a few movie passes (they were usually duds) and Readers' Service gave Fran a first look at any mail concerning the Entertainment pages. Fran filed the letters she didn't want Ms. Simpson to see.

There were the letters from girls with bubbly cursive handwriting, asking for celebrity addresses. And there were the housewives who wrote longer, two-page letters shaming *Women* for publishing pieces like "Bodies to Die For" or "Hollywood Cheesecake." And then there was John "Candy" Okadaford whom neither Fran nor Catherine ever mentioned because the very presence of his letters embarrassed them both.

John/Candy wrote monthly letters addressed to Entertainment, sometimes signed "John," other times signed "Candy." John/Candy claimed that the world would soon be under a radar attack by aliens disguised as celebrities. John Wayne was from Pluto, Jesse Jackson from Mars, "etc., etc. (decorative mask)"—that's what he always added at the end. More often then not, the letters were hysterical rantings and made no sense.

Catherine threw the file in a box marked MISC. Down the hall, she could hear Ms. Simpson reading another letter. "'I was quite touched by Ann Bartel's poignant piece on cervical cancer.'"

Poignant. Catherine tried to think of anything she had ever written that could be called poignant. The Beatrix Potter piece? She wanted to write something poignant, she just didn't know how.

Catherine stuck her feet in her wastepaper basket, and picked up the phone. When a publicist from United Artists said "Hello" on the other line, Catherine lit in, wanting to know why the hell the August stills were taking so long.

"How long am I gonna have to wait?" Catherine could be heard all the way down the hall, screaming into her phone.

At noon, Catherine had an interview with a director who was well known, not for his movies, but for his casting-couch reputation. They met at a noisy diner on Lexington because, he said, he liked the eggs there.

"Everybody thinks I'm hot shit right now 'cause I made a movie with people talking in English accents," he said.

Catherine worried that her tape recorder was only picking up the dishes clattering in the kitchen. She pushed it across the table, closer to his side order of hash browns.

They talked about his new movie. He gave her quaint, on-the-set stories which she pretended to write down. And then, as if the idea had just come to her, Catherine asked him, casually, somewhat jokingly, why everybody was always talking about his sex life.

"Who's talking?" he asked. He dumped the rest of his eggs on a slice of buttered white bread and shoved it in his mouth. Then he smiled, his jowls filled with food.

"We're all sleeping with somebody for something and nine times out of ten it's not for love," he said in between his chewing. "Some people have a problem with that." He swallowed and pressed the stop/eject button on Catherine's tape recorder.

"Come on," he said. "Lemme show you how they do it in L.A."

Poignant. Where was the poignancy in a guy like this?

Catherine thanked him graciously. She said she really wished she could, really, but she had work to do, his piece, for instance, and she was needed back in her office.

He reached across their table and tousled her bangs as one might do to a Little Leaguer on a baseball field.

"Whatever you say, kid," he said, and he stuck a toothpick in his mouth and he left her there with her tape recorder and the bill.

When she got back to the office, Catherine put in a call to interview the actress who was starring in the director's newest movie. She was new—she had been a first-grade teacher in Boise, Idaho—so she called Catherine back early that afternoon. Catherine got right to the point and asked the actress about her first meeting with the director.

"I went to his house in L.A. and this incredible blond was coming out. I thought, I don't have a chance in hell. He was in 'the game room' playing pool. He didn't say a word to me, until all of a sudden he says, 'Get a stick.' So then we play this game of pool. I'm not so great, but I can play. He beat me. Then he sits down and so do I. 'In movies every actress has to seduce her audience,' he says to me. 'If you can't seduce me, you can't seduce them.' So he sits there and stares at me and I stare back."

Catherine waited. "And then?"

"Well, of course I didn't *do* anything."

"But you got the part."

"Yeah," she said. Catherine could hear the actress smiling. "I got the part."

Even though she had not gotten anybody to spell out anything, when Catherine hung up she felt she had had an exceptional day. She felt so good, so important, so on-the-ball, in fact, she put in another call to Mick Jagger's man. "You again?" he said. "Why don't you go pick on Warren Beatty, or somebody?"

Catherine left the office on time that Friday, because she felt she had earned it. She stepped into the empty elevator and heard a woman screaming, "Hold it!"

It was Ann Bartel, clad in jeans that didn't quite hit her in the right places and wearing Earth Shoes with socks. Her face was flushed from running down the hall and she thanked Catherine for holding the doors for her, and the two of them stood side by side in the otherwise empty elevator, staring up at the numbers as the doors closed.

"I've been doing this piece called 'Star Gazing,' and I've been finding out all this wild stuff," Ann gushed. She smelled like pineapple. "Did you know that you can't ever really look directly at stars, that you have to kind of let them slip in through the corner of your vision?" She was looking at Catherine. Catherine tried to smile. Ann put her hands on her hips. They were large hips. Ample hips. Childbearing hips. "See, at night your vision is working on a different level. Everything has to go through rods and cones."

They were nearing the lobby. Ann apologized and introduced herself.

"I'm sorry, who are you?"

"Entertainment," Catherine said, and at that moment the doors opened and Ann said good-bye, and just then Catherine wanted to run after Ann Bartel and tell her. Tell her that there was more to Catherine Clemons than Entertainment. That she just did this for a living. She wanted to say, No no no, you don't get it, really, that's not all there is to me. I can be poignant, just give me a minute. But Ann had already disappeared into the five-o'clock crowd heading up Madison, and Catherine walked on towards Grand Central where she beat Travel to a cab, and, on the way home, Catherine tried very hard not to think about how she looked at stars.

That Saturday night Catherine and Joey went to dinner with Michael and then they all went back to Michael's place. Joey found a pair of roller skates in the closet and put them on. Michael opened up a bottle of old liqueur—something French that had real bits of gold that had settled on the bottom.

They sat on black sofas in front of lacquered tables painted to look like marble. The floors were stripped and stained to look like unpainted pine.

"Do you swallow the gold?" Joey asked, skating towards Michael, who held out two glasses.

"Oh yeah. It's good for you. Roughage."

They toasted each other. Catherine thought the drink was too sweet and the gold felt like little goldfish scales going down. She lifted her glass for more as Michael brought out the bottle again.

When Joey spoke next he was a Southern belle—his drag version of Scarlett O'Hara.

"It's what, nineteen-eighty-whatever, and I still don't have a fella." He got up and skated in a circle. Catherine marveled at how he was able to keep his balance. They had had at least two bottles of champagne at dinner.

" 'I'm just a girl who cain't say no,' " he sang. " 'I'm in a terrible fix.' Jesus Lord, I got the show tune gene in me." As Joey skated and sang other tunes from *Oklahoma*, the wheels on his roller skates lit up and Michael turned off the lights. Catherine could barely see anything, except for the wheels of Joey's roller skates and the bits of gold that were illuminated by the lights outside Michael's window.

"What about Dwarfman?" Catherine said when Joey sat down. "What happened to him?"

"Oh him. He's crust. I finally told him off. I said, 'Look, Bub. You may have bucks, but you're not such a great date. You don't fuck until four in the morning and you don't turn into a pizza.' "

Michael got up and turned on an ABC CD.

"You're so cruel," Catherine said. "You've probably devastated him."

Joey shrugged.

"We just weren't sexually compatible," Joey said, serious all of a sudden. "He wouldn't fuck me."

"Jeez, Joey," Catherine said. She took another sip of liqueur.

"Listen to you. Now *you're* saying 'jeez,' " Joey said, laughing.

" 'I seen the future,' " Michael sang. " 'I can't afford it.' "

Catherine and Joey picked up the chorus.

" 'Tell me. Tell me. How to be a millionaire. A billionaire. A trillionaire.' " Michael took Catherine's hand and pulled her up out of her chair.

"When she's happy she calls me Mouse," he said, swaying towards Catherine.

Michael still had his drink in his hand, and when he danced he barely moved, which was effective because he was wearing a suit. Catherine could smell the liqueur on his breath mixed with his cologne and then she could smell the perfume Joey had swiped from Beauty as Joey came up behind her and put his hands over Michael's.

"Cat and Mouse," Joey said. "That's so cute."

"Have you ever seen Joey dance?" Catherine said. She bumped her hips between Michael and Joey. "Teach us, Joe. Teach us how."

"Find the bass and go with that," he said. "Then go against that. That's it," he said. "Now go low. Lower. Like this. This."

Catherine and Joey and Michael dance-skated to the whole ABC CD, until the back of Catherine's thighs stung from the beads on the hem of Joey's dress brushing against her.

"OK, here's the trick," Joey said when the Eurythmics came on. "Close your eyes and pretend you're all alone. No partner. No nothing."

Catherine saw that Michael's eyes were closed and he moved closer every time Joey spoke.

" 'Sweet dreams are made of this,' " they all whispered along with the song.

"That's what gets them," Joey whispered into Catherine's ear. "They see you getting off on your own. Then they wanna break into your world." She could feel Michael's hip-bones just above hers and she imagined he would have pressed harder if Joey hadn't had his hand on her belly.

The three of them moved slowly, moving their hips against the song, losing Annie Lennox's rhythm altogether. Catherine didn't want the record to end.

"Yes. Yes. Yes," Joey said when the song was over. He collapsed on a sofa next to the chair where Michael sat. He took a long sip of the liqueur. "If I were straight, Cat and I would be having the wildest affair, wouldn't we, Cat."

Catherine smiled and looked at Michael. She could not see his eyes, only his mouth, which rested at the edge of his glass. She sat down on the sofa next to Joey.

"I mean, I don't think of myself as queer or anything," Joey said. He reached inside the top of his dress and pulled out a pair of rubber nipples which he flipped, Frisbee-style, on the coffee table in front of him. "When I saw *Gone with the Wind* the first time, I was looking at Rhett, *then* I watched Scarlett to see how you could get a guy like that. I just like to look pretty, you know? What's the big deal? It's what I like now. Who knows what I'll like, say, ten years from now. I'll probably have a wife and a Volvo by then."

He took his shoes off and brought his legs up on the sofa and twisted around to look out the big picture window. Michael's place was across from Lincoln Center and from his window you could see couples coming out of the theater, avoiding the beggars who held out cups and pans around the lit-up fountain.

"Sometimes I just can't get over that feeling," Joey said. Catherine could barely see Joey's head shaking, but she could hear his earrings jingle. "They lock you in this embrace and then they ride you real fast and real strong."

Nobody said anything.

"Jesus, Joe," Michael said. He poured himself the last of the liqueur and got up to get more.

"Catherine said you said everybody's got some percentage of gay in them," Michael said from the kitchen. "That's such bullshit."

"Haven't you ever wanted to wear lipstick?" Joey said. He was looking at Michael now across the room and Michael was staring back over the counter, holding a bottle of something.

"Not on my mouth."

"Oh. Baby," Joey said. You're so *tres*." Joey went French, lit a cigarette, and let the smoke trail between his nose and mouth.

Catherine laughed and picked up one of Joey's rubber nipples.

"So what are we gonna do with these?"

"Put 'em in a time capsule," Joey said. His voice was low and soft. Catherine put her arm around him. He rested his head on her shoulder.

"Give 'em to Fran," Michael said, coming back with another bottle of something else.

"Fran, poor thing," Joey said, lifting his head. "She's just freaked because she's thirty-two and still single."

"Thirty-five," Michael said.

"God, are you mean," Catherine said.

"I hope I look like that when I'm thirty-five," Joey said.

"What else?" Catherine said. "What else should we put in this time capsule?"

"Couple of Miles Davis tapes," Michael said. "*Citizen Kane.* Maybe a Boy George album. He's got such a pretty voice. Something by Van Morrison."

"I quit listening to Van Morrison when I found out he wasn't black," Joey said. "We'd have to put in that Marilyn Monroe poster—the one by Warhol—and this dress." Joey fingered the beads of his red sequined dress. "This is my all-time favorite dress. How 'bout you, Cat?"

Catherine thought about it for a minute. She thought about everything on her desk and in her wallet. She thought of what she had at home, with her mother. Her old Girl Scout badges and swimming ribbons.

"I don't know," she finally said. "Maybe just a really good bad movie. Some old black-and-white with a lot of aliens in it. A couple of issues of *Women* and a bag of popcorn and a jar of peanut butter because together they taste like chocolate."

"Oh God, this is great," Michael said. He had his shoes off and he put his feet up on the edge of the coffee table. "I love not talking about work. You two are great."

"I've got balloons," Joey said, getting up to get his purse.

"Joey always carries around balloons in his bag," Catherine told Michael.

"You never know," Joey said. He dumped a bag of colored balloons on the coffee table, took one, and began blowing it up.

"Sometimes, when I can't get to sleep," Joey said, tying a knot at the end, "I'll blow up balloons in bed."

The three of them blew up all the balloons Joey had brought out, and as they let them float down to the floor, they thought of other things to put in their time capsule. Catherine wanted to leave messages on her answering machine, Joey wanted to put in some of his feathered boas and a picture of Damn It, Michael wanted to add money and cocaine.

"Looks like our little girl needs some nose candy," he said, looking at Catherine. She had her head on Joey's shoulder, her eyes half-closed.

"Is anybody awake?" she said.

"She's exhausted, poor thing," she could hear Joey say. She could feel someone taking off her shoes. She heard Joey's skate wheels roll across the floor. A balloon popped. Joey was giggling. Catherine thought she heard him say that he wanted to add more Warhol stuff. A stack of *Interviews*, the tape recorder Warhol referred to as his wife, Sony.

"You'll see," she heard Joey saying. "We'll all remember this as the time Warhol was alive."

She could feel Michael's arms around her and when she opened her eyes next, he was covering her with a fake-fur throw from the end of his bed.

"Come with me," she said.

"In a little while," he whispered, and then he smiled and kissed her eyelids and she said she was sorry, but she didn't think he heard and she fell asleep and dreamed of skating to Mexico with Joey.

The place smelled like rubber when she woke up and it reminded Catherine of the time when Michael had used a condom in San Francisco, because he had not wanted Catherine to leave the bed. Afterwards, her hands had smelled of rubber.

A yellow balloon tumbled into the room. It was a little deflated, so it stopped as though it were suddenly glued to the floor. Catherine wrapped herself up in the fake-fur throw.

Everything in the living room looked pink because of the early morning light. On the coffee table there were their cognac glasses, and Joey's rubber nipples. Michael's shoes were near his chair on the floor. She heard the TV on in the room down the hall, and she saw a strip of blue-green light coming from the half-open door.

On the TV, Arnold Schwarzenegger was the Terminator, standing, legs apart, holding a huge gun. She started to say something like, I can't believe you guys are watching this, but then she turned to her left and saw them there, on the couch, moving together naked in the flickering bluish tint.

She did not know why she didn't turn around and leave. She did not know why she stood there in the doorway and watched. Later, she would wonder why she hadn't intervened. Maybe it was because she had suspected something like this would happen all along.

It looked like it hurt. Michael held the back of Joey's shoulders, his own head turned away towards the back of the couch. Catherine could not see Joey's face. He had his head in his hands, but then he clutched the arm of the sofa, and Catherine saw his profile.

He was clenching his teeth. He looked like an angry little boy. Twelve maybe. His shoulders were pale and his whole body was skinny and hairless. It looked like rape—so much like rape, that Catherine took one step forward to stop it, but a balloon popped and Joey opened his eyes and saw her.

He said, "Oh." Michael didn't see or say anything and he kept on. Joey moved his hands down to his hips. Was he pointing or was he trying to stop Michael? Catherine stood still in the doorway. More than anything, Joey looked as though he were pleading with her. As though he were saying, Please, just this once. Then just as suddenly, Joey squeezed his eyes shut and put his head back down into his hands.

She hurried, grabbing last night's smoky-smelling dress, and dressed in the elevator going down.

She could not remember what part of town she was in or even what day it was. For a minute she thought she was late for work, but then she saw how slowly everyone else was walking, how empty the streets were and she remembered it was Sunday. Easter Sunday.

She passed two bored-looking little girls in Brownie uniforms. They were wearing neon green lipstick.

In a chapter titled "Finding the Way" in the Girl Scout handbook, Catherine could remember reading that a good traveler can find the way on city sidewalks or on mountain trails. She knows where she is going and where she has been. She can tell another person how to find the way. Catherine could remember that chapter being important when she had read it.

She fell into a crowd of people dressed up in pastel polyesters and followed them inside a church.

The mass was in Italian. She sat next to a large woman who wore a black dress and prayed with a mother-of-pearl rosary. A little girl in the pew in front of Catherine's kicked her little brother until he cried.

"Let us pray," she guessed they were saying.

It made her nauseous to think Michael and Joey had done this, knowing she was sleeping just down the hall, in Michael's bedroom. She wondered if Michael and Joey had lied to her, if they had started up together long before. She wondered when and how the idea first came about—that night at the gallery opening? How fitting, she thought, thinking of how everyone had been dressed in black that night, as though they were attending a funeral—the end of whatever she had had with Michael. From the balcony, she had seen the two of them alone together for the first time. She had been happy then, too, thinking, At last Joey will let up on me. Now they can be friends. Still walking, Catherine shook her head. She wondered what they had been whispering about that night.

The altar boy rang the bell a third time. Catherine looked at the candles at the altar as the priest held up the host. She looked at the stained glass windows and the big Italian woman seated next to her, counting her rosary beads.

She wondered why she hadn't figured it out before. What about the soulful way Michael looked at me? And what of Joey? Where did this leave their friendship?

She considered seeing a priest. Bless me, Father, for I have sinned. It has been, oh what? fifteen years since my last confession. Where should I start? And what would a priest say after all was said? Priests never gave advice on anything real. It was always so many Hail Marys and a few Our Fathers. They never told you how you were supposed to live with yourself, or how to get up in the morning, or how to look your best friend in the eye after you've seen him with the man you thought you loved.

When they got to parts she could remember, Catherine mumbled her own English equivalents.

"Look, Lord. I know I'm not worthy to receive you, but only say the word and I shall be healed. Just say the word. Anytime, Lord."

As she headed towards the altar for communion, she could feel a woman's pointed fingers in the small of her back, edging her forward.

At her pew, Catherine sank to her knees, sucking on the wafer that was stuck to the roof of her mouth. She caught sight of herself in a brass plaque on the back of the pew—a plaque that said who had donated the pew in front of her. She thought at first her image was one of a little boy's.

She was thinner than she remembered ever having been, and as she moved her face to see her image, she saw that her neck looked as though it could barely hold up her head. Her hair was cut short, died white-blond— Joey had done it in the style of a picture he had seen in *Vogue*. More than ever she noticed her mother's mouth. Her father's blue-grey eyes.

For the first time, Catherine realized she finally looked the way the girls in the elevator looked when she saw them coming in to work every morning at *Women*. Chic. Hip. She had often wondered, that first year there, how they managed to look the way they did. How they managed to look expensive and unkempt, their clothes hanging on them in an edgy way that somehow also managed to convey an I-don't-give-a-fuck attitude. They were the young girls in Manhattan who looked like they owned the city. They knew that Fifth was the only numbered avenue that you spelled out; they knew that anything, *anything,* could be gotten on sale and nobody bought anything at full price. They knew that first boyfriends in New York were like first apartments—temporary stops before you got that roomy, high-ceilinged, light-filled loft somewhere in SoHo.

A baby cried. Catherine looked away from the brass plaque and put her head in her hands. She wished she were in a car just then, just so that she could slam the door shut.

She tried to focus on the August issue. That was real. How to Make a

Summer Quilt. What to Wear to a Bruce Springsteen Concert. Fifteen Ways to Hold On. Seven Places to Go to Find New Friends.

Staring down at the tiled church floor, Catherine could remember a newly married couple who had lived down the street from her family in Barrington. One day it had rained, and Catherine had passed their house and they were out there, together, laying out bricks, building their own driveway. Together they crawled about in the rain and the mud, laughing and handing one another bricks. A year later, they divorced, and Catherine saw the husband there one Sunday afternoon, standing in the middle of their driveway just staring down all around him at the intricate brickwork he and his wife had created together, once upon a time.

After mass, Catherine thought of going to work, of going up to *Women* and just sitting at her desk. Maybe Ann Bartel would be there—but Catherine didn't feel like she could quite stomach Ann Bartel. She would probably tell Ann everything, and then Ann would probably say the right thing. She would probably say, "Catherine. These people are no good. Do your work. Just do your work."

It was the first warm day in a long time and the bars on Columbus had opened up their doors so that people could drink Bloody Marys with one foot on the sidewalk. Catherine looked into one, the Saloon, and there, at the bar, she saw Lewis Lipman.

"Happy Sunday," she said, sitting down at the bar beside him. She ordered a white wine.

"You don't look very happy," he said, looking at Catherine in the mirror across the bar. Catherine took a long sip of wine. Then she put her hand under Lewis' arm and leaned her head on his shoulder.

She let out a laugh. "I guess I'm lacking warmth and friendship in my life these days," she said. "It's good to see you."

Lewis patted her hand. Then he moved his arm, got up, and put on his coat.

"Look," he said. "I heard from you late one night. You sounded like you needed me, and believe me, I was happy to be there. But then I don't hear from you. I'm not a light switch. I'm not like one of these fucking dolls that kisses when you push the button on her back." He got up and paid his tab. Then he looked at Catherine. "I know what I want, Catherine. What do you want?"

Catherine watched Lewis watch her in the mirror and then she watched him leave.

She caught a cab with a cabdriver from Madagascar who said he liked heavy metal and movies with guns. She asked him to let her out in front of the Star.

"Some rice pudding?" the man behind the counter asked. He did not speak English very well but he had kind eyes that were magnified behind his thick glasses. "I just made."

"Sure," she said. She bought a pint of milk, too, because she could not remember when she had had milk last.

On the corner a black teenager kicked his leg up the minute the light changed to red. Some street musicians were playing. There was a horn and a violin and the boy started break dancing to the Messiah on York.

Catherine looked up at the sky and she couldn't help but think how hot and scared and cramped a spaceman must feel in his bulky silver suit and helmet, crammed inside his space shuttle. And all for what? All to get a good close-up look at Mars, or Venus, or a few lousy stars?

There were weeks' worth of messages on her answering machine from her mother, including one in which her mother told Catherine that she ought to change her outgoing message because, she said, Catherine sounded like a hockey coach.

"Mom?"

"Is that you?"

"Mom, happy birthday."

"My birthday's not until August."

"But it *is* August."

"Cat. It's March. Are you OK?"

"Oh God. I'm sorry. I guess I'm all mixed up."

"I know what you're going to say. I forgot to send you an Easter basket. I guess I figured you figured we were beyond that. But listen, I'm on my way out, what is it?"

"Nothing."

Catherine could hear Chloe's tail thumping hard against the wall. Their dog had a habit of creeping under the stairs whenever Catherine's mother got on the phone or banged around in the kitchen. That was what Catherine wanted to do at that moment. She wanted to find a set of stairs and she wanted to creep under them. Curl up and settle there for a good long time.

"You didn't go to church, did you?" her mother asked. "I hate going to church on Easter Sunday. Everyone's so damned sure of the Resurrection."

"Yeah," Catherine said. "I went to church." It was the first time in a long time that she had actually told her mother the truth. She wished she could tell her the rest.

"Are you eating right? Stay away from all that instant stuff. I tried Ragu the other night. It was vile."

"I'm fine."

"You're lonely. Ha!" her mother said.

Catherine stood there and silently swore that she would never talk to her mother again.

"Look," her mother said. "I'm late. I've got a Russian buffet to get to. It's going to be really exotic. Blini and caviar and a cake with *Christ Has Risen* written in raisins."

Her mother didn't say anything else for a minute. From her window,

Catherine looked down below, and in the little alleyway, she saw a little girl crouched on the sidewalk with a rag. She was going around and around, wiping at nothing.

"I'm looking at your picture right now," her mother said. "The one of you in high school. You look so innocent, not a blemish on your face. You had your father's eyes. It's fading, you know. The picture's fading."

Catherine hugged herself. She pressed her forehead against the cool glass. "My heart is breaking," she mouthed to the glass. She stood there, trying to stop shaking. Outside, the little girl was scrubbing and scrubbing and it was then that Catherine realized that the girl was trying to erase her own shadow.

"I'm sorry, Cat, honey, but I can't just drop everything now that you finally decide to call. You're the one with the exciting life—hanging around all those beautiful people."

Get mad. That was always Fran's advice. Don't take no for an answer and get mad. And when Catherine heard the dial tone, she slammed the receiver down.

When she got back to Michael's apartment, Joey was gone. Michael had just come out of the shower. She stormed past him as he opened the door with a towel around his waist. She kicked a balloon.

"So what we had," she started. She was pacing because she didn't want to look at him. She didn't think she could. Not yet. "We just did the summer-romance thing in the winter, right?"

"I hate it when you do this, when you wrap things up like I'm one of your goddamned Entertainment assignments, like what we had was a fucking trend or a movie-of-the-week or something. Like you have to come up with an angle on me. Sometimes, Catherine, you're not going to be able to figure everything out."

She had expected him to be silent and humble. She had expected him to at least be ashamed.

"Can't you just take what we had and enjoy it?" he said.

"Live for the moment."

"Yeah."

She looked him straight in the eye.

"I tried that," she said. "Then I got pregnant."

"I paid for it, didn't I? You want more money? Here." He took some bills rolled up and held together with a silver money clip on the table by the door. "Take it. It's yours." He held out the money.

"I don't believe you."

"Grow up, Catherine." He came close to her. He took her by the belt, his mouth close to hers. "You're not in Kansas anymore," and then she could feel him shoving the money under her belt.

Catherine backed away. "Fuck you," she said. She took the money and threw it at him, aiming for his foot, but she missed and the money landed at Fran's feet—Fran who was standing at the open door, her sequined Acadamy

Awards dress in a garment bag in one hand, the key to Michael's apartment in the other.

Chapter 8

The Horror

Catherine was in the Magda screening room watching a man blow up in a movie about chemical warfare. A military man who was experimenting with different chemicals put some concoction in another man's toothpaste and now this man who had just brushed his teeth was literally falling apart in his car. First his gums bled, then his teeth fell out. He scratched and his skin fell off in his fingernails. He stopped the car, got out, stood out in the middle of the highway and proceeded to explode, much like all the cows and sheep who had been given the same chemical concoction before him. Catherine knew the next move. Somebody would pass by in a car and think him road-kill.

Fran had assigned Catherine to watch all the horror movies that month. Penance.

Fran had not said much that day she had seen Catherine in Michael's apartment. She had just turned around and left. Later, Catherine would find out that she had gone to Michael's apartment to tell him it was over (it hadn't been before?) and that she was seeing someone new—the producer from "Entertainment Tonight" had flown back to New York just to spend another week with her.

The next day at work, Fran got word that she hadn't gotten her office. Ms. Simpson had given the office to Ann Bartel.

"I lost my office *and* my boyfriend," Fran had screamed into the phone. She had been talking to her friend Pam, glaring over her desk at Catherine. "Everyone takes, takes, takes, takes."

Sitting in the Magda screening room, Catherine knew Fran would not fire her, not yet anyway, not until Catherine had handed in the casting-couch-actresses story.

Only losers went to these screenings. In the front row was some poor schmuck from a teen magazine. He was actually taking notes with a pen that lit up every time he pressed down on it. In the back row was an assistant to somebody important at *People*. He had fallen asleep.

The hero in the movie, a tall young actor who looked good in jeans, knew of course that the bloody mass in the road was not a deer or a cow. He was onto the man in the military. He will proceed to warn the people, Catherine thought, opening a package of red licorice sticks. He will most likely die doing so, and P.R. will say what an important movie this is. "It's not *just* a horror movie," P.R. will say when the lights go on.

Catherine couldn't think of any place else she'd rather be than in a dark screening room. The May issue was on the stands with Catherine standing there on page ninety-three in a slate blue tank suit next to the letter *H*. A girl she hadn't seen or talked to since high school had already called Catherine at the office. Mimi Laser said she had been soaking in the tub and saw Catherine's picture.

"So they made you do that, right? I can't believe you did that," Mimi said over the phone.

Catherine could only think to say that it was nice of her to call and did people in Barrington still call her Creamy?

After the actor died a sad, bloody, well-filmed death, P.R. turned to Catherine. "I don't know about you, but I need a drink."

Outside it was raining and P.R. blew on her rape whistle and managed to get a cab.

Melissa Wicker was P.R. Someone from *Brides* had once told Catherine that Melissa looked like Marisa Berenson. Melissa looked nothing like Marisa Berenson. She was a wide, mouthy woman who worked at a big P.R. firm and represented everything that was third-rate, including bad horror movies, soap stars, and game-show hosts.

"Let me just give you the spiel so I can write this off," she said when they got to a place near Rockefeller Center. She and Catherine climbed onto bar stools while Melissa started in on the movie, and the leading actor's potential. Then she said "There," took a deep sip from her scotch, put it down, and said, "So. Ask me anything you want. I know all the gossip and you can even quote me. I'm out of here."

She was dumping everything, her job, her apartment, her cat, to move to L.A. She wanted to be Stephen King's personal press agent, and after ten years, she finally had an interview with him.

"There's gotta be a better place to live," she said. "A place where the cockroaches are smaller, or at least have the decency to hide when you come home at night. Somewhere where you don't have to smell piss when you walk out the door."

That night, Melissa told Catherine everything. She told her about the blond who was on the cover of *TV Guide* that week—how she had to fuck before she went out because it made her walk sexier. Catherine found out about everyone's lifts, tucks, silicone injections, and liposuctions. Then she got started on movie directors.

"Let me tell you about this other movie," she went on. "They've already started making the trolls for this one."

"I'm working on a story about the casting couch," Catherine said, interrupting Melissa. Melissa leaned back and let out a loud "Ha." She ordered another round.

"You might want to get your notebook out," she started.

Catherine stopped back at the office. She didn't expect to see Fran sitting there at her desk. She was on the phone, telling one more Academy Award story for the umpteenth time. It was the bathroom story this time. Whenever someone in the audience at the Awards left to go to the bathroom, an usher would send in a pretty, young extra, so that when the camera panned the audience, there was never an empty seat.

Sitting at her desk, listening to Fran tell the story again, Catherine tried to get started on transcribing Fran's interviews, but she couldn't help but wonder, What if the extra refused to leave the seat when the person got back from the bathroom?

Then Fran started in on her facial.

"I'm never going back to that woman again," Fran was screaming. "All those oils are stupid. I told her, 'Look, could you just blow out the incense and squeeze my blackheads?'"

Whenever she was in a bad dream and knew it, Catherine would force her eyes open, right there, in the dream. She would say "Wait a sec" to the bloodied dog that was chasing her, or to the four-headed rapist with b.o., and then she would open her eyes as wide as they would go until she was awake.

"I forgot something at the screening," she said to Fran, and left.

It was still raining when Catherine got back to her apartment, and when she turned on her lights, she turned them right back off again. There was a leak in the corner of the room near the window and she got out the bucket which she used for such occasions from under the sink. She called her landlord again, a man she had never spoken to or seen, and left one more angry message on his answering machine. She opened her window because inside the air tasted of mildew and she undressed quickly and got into her sofa bed. Staring up at the yellowed ceiling, Catherine had the odd sensation that she was being filmed—as though there was a director there on the roof, setting her up for some big, bloody blowup like the one the man had been set up for in the cow movie.

She picked up the phone and dialed. She got Lewis' answering machine. "Hi," his voice on the machine said. Lewis had a warm voice. "I'm out. I think you know what it is you have to do."

The beep sounded and Catherine was at a loss for words.

"Hi," she started. "I just wanted to talk. Could I see you, maybe?" She hung up, wishing there was a way to erase what she had just said, wishing there was a way for her mind to stop playing back that last time she had seen Lewis on Easter Sunday at the Saloon. "No," she should have shouted. "Don't go. You're right. I don't know what I want. But please, stay here by me until I can get that figured out."

That night Catherine dreamed she was in a car with Joey. They parked and went across the street for a face-lift. The place looked a lot like the shoe-repair shop on Seventy-eighth. Catherine took off her face and waited, but when she saw what they were doing to her ears she tried to make them stop. "This is the way it's done," they said, so then Joey took off his face and gave it to Catherine and she tried doing what they did, but she messed up and she said, "Let me start over. Let me start over." And she looked over at Joey's empty face, waiting, and then she looked down at his face in her hands and she saw the mistake she had made with the skin and she said, "I'll pay double. Just let me start over."

The following day, "Entertainment Tonight" was setting up their lights in front of Fran's desk. The man she had taken to the Academy Awards had completely fallen for Fran (it had helped that Morgan Fairchild had come up to them at a party after the Academy Awards and asked Fran where she had gotten such a lovely sequined dress), and he had arranged for the interview. Fran was going to speak on celebrity fashions and she was only a little concerned that Fashion would get miffed. It was, after all, their turf. Still, this was what Fran had been after all year.

"Pastries, pastries, pastries," Fran said, on the phone with the chef for the homeless benefit. She was standing in front of the mirror, doing her makeup. "That's all I see anymore is puffed pastries. Crab-filled. Doesn't anybody do anything original anymore?"

She dabbed at the lid of her right eye then stood back and looked at herself. "Pheasant is good," she said, turning her head to the right then to the left.

Fran was wearing a lightweight black suit she had gotten at a "Dynasty" wardrobe press conference. When she hung up the phone she switched from rhinestone earrings to pearls and back to rhinestones again. Catherine had tried to get back in Fran's good graces by gathering up as many quotes as she could for Fran's story on how stars decided what to wear for the Academy Awards. Catherine had gotten everybody but Jessica Lange.

"Lange would have made all the difference," Fran grumbled. She no longer greeted Catherine in the morning.

"Ready when you are," Lights yelled out.

"Is Beauty around?" Fran yelled. She looked at Catherine. "I want Beauty to do me."

Catherine ran down the hall, fetched a Beauty associate (Fran would have been insulted had she come back with an assistant), and brought her back to Fran.

"Ditch the rhinestones and go wash your face," Beauty said, rolling up her sleeves. She had a black leather satchel with her, the kind doctors carry. "I'm going to have to start all over."

Lights moaned audibly.

In the end Fran was stunning and smooth, maybe too smooth, Catherine thought. Catherine and Beauty leaned against the doorway, nodding and smiling while they watched Fran under all that white light.

She told the approximate number of beads it took to cover Cher for the Academy Awards. She talked about the Ralph Lauren belt one young actress needed at the last minute and how the actress had paid Fran's airfare from New York to L.A. and back just to deliver it.

"And she wasn't even nominated this year," Fran said. She smiled. She had wanted to make sure that the producers saw that she had straight teeth.

When it was all over and Lights turned out the lights, Fran said no one gave a fuck about what Jessica Lange wore anyway and she sent Catherine to Zaro's with two hundred dollars—lunch for the crew. When she got back the phone was ringing. Catherine answered and put her hand over the receiver. It was Helen Gurley Brown's assistant. Of course Helen would love to attend Fran's benefit for the homeless aboard the USS *Intrepid,* and she has also been keeping up with the Entertainment section in *Women*—would Fran be interested in doing a column for *Cosmo?*

Fran took the call. The other line rang. It was the chef from that East Side restaurant where David Byrne went on Friday nights. Fran was right. Pastries were cliche. What would Fran say to chocolate-dipped shortbread diamonds and sugared walnuts? The evening was only weeks away. Catherine pictured the chef standing there in his white chef's hat, his cookbook poised, waiting to get the OK from Fran. The whole world, it seemed to Catherine, was waiting to get the OK from Fran.

Catherine was in the office late that night, typing up the final menu for the homeless benefit (smoked pheasant on whole wheat with walnuts and watercress butter, sliced strawberry sandwiches with cinnamon cream cheese and fresh mint) and transcribing tapes of Fran's interview with John Cougar who had just recently added the Mellencamp. It was a difficult tape to transcribe because he mumbled and swore so much. And there was all that giggling from Fran's end in between questions such as "How come rock stars are so sexy?" and "How come you guys always date models?"

Fran never asked why. She always said "How come" instead.

Catherine almost missed the phone. She took off her headset.

"Cat? Cat, are you there? I knew you'd be there."

"Joey?" She wished to God it had been Lewis.

"Cat, you'll never guess where I am."

"I'm not really interested in trying."

"Oh, chill out, girl, this is important. I'm in *his* studio."

"I'm hanging up now, Joey."

"No no no. Cat. Are you still there? Not Mike, Cat. Andy. Andy Warhol. I'm in Andy Warhol's studio. As we speak. We met at this party that, well, you know, *he* took me to."

"It's Michael, Joey. Or, I guess we're calling him Mike now, are we? We're grown-ups. We live in the twentieth century. It's cool. You borrow my dresses, my makeup, my boyfriend."

"Oh, cut the shit, Cat. That's not important. I'm right here, Cat. Don't you understand? I was dancing, right? I've got the red dress on, OK? And there I am, dancing, and I see him and I dance in front of him and I wanted to put my card right down his pants, but I know he's shy, so I stuck it in his shirt pocket. He doesn't smile or blink or anything. He just has one of his assistants come over to me later and this guy goes, 'Wanna come to a little party with me and Andy?' Isn't that just too precious?"

"I'm supposed to be happy for you, right?"

"I gotta go. I'm thinking of you, baby."

Joey's version of an Academy Award speech.

Catherine hung up and put on the headset again. Fran was giggling on tape. She wanted to know "how come" John was still living in Indiana. She wanted to know "how come" he never invited the press out to his place. Catherine shut off the tape.

"It's *why,* Fran," Catherine shouted. "It's why, why, why. Not 'how come.' "

All around her were files marked *October, November,* and *December.* It was Fran's month this month. And it was Joey's month, too. Picking up a file marked *January,* Catherine wondered when or if she would ever have her month.

She sighed, pressed the pedal that turned the tape back on, and started typing again.

The following Monday Fran came to the office with a vase full of daisies which she set down on the desk in front of Catherine.

"Happy Secretary's Week," she said. "You'll be one for a long, long time."

Catherine stopped opening the mail. She moved the flowers to the left side of her desk, then to the right, then she finally dumped them into her wastepaper basket, smashing them down with her feet. "Is there anything you want to say to me?" she asked Fran.

Fran looked up from the stack of Page Six clippings Catherine had put on her desk. Catherine's March piece, "The Personals," had been mentioned in all the papers under Fran's name.

"That was a shitty thing you did to me," she said. "You lied. I'll never be able to trust anything you do or say again."

"I'm sorry. I don't know what else to say. I made a mistake."

"This isn't church. It's gonna take more than an apology. I'd fire you, but I don't want to deal with training another little bitch like you. Not now, anyway."

"I made a mistake," Catherine said again. She could feel tears welling up in her eyes. "People do terrible things sometimes without really meaning to."

"Oh, please," Fran said, rolling her eyes. "Everyone in this fucking town is morally bankrupt and all they can say is 'Ooops.' "

"Sometimes. Sometimes you don't always know what's right or wrong anymore. There should be a guide."

"Catherine," Fran said, reaching across the clippings with a Kleenex. "Your tears are cheap at this stage in the game."

The phone rang. It was Fran's friend Pam. As co-chairman of the homeless benefit, Pam found out that half of the invitations were lost and Mayor Koch hadn't even gotten one. Catherine transferred the call, wishing they had gotten that bigger office after all because now there was nowhere for her to go.

Catherine stuck her feet in the wastepaper basket and looked over the rest of the mail. There was another letter from John "Candy" Okadaford. "Dear Entertainment," it read. "Christopher Reeves is from Saturn. Nancy Reagan is from the moon. And now my real aim is that I need help desperately from this invisible radar attack since I couldn't purchase the electronic countermeasure due to monopoly."

This month Okadaford signed his letter "Annie from Brooklyn (I think)."

Poor John. Poor Candy. Poor Annie.

How to Take Care of Yourself When No One Else Will, Catherine thought. Roast a chicken. Work, even on Sundays.

She picked up the phone and dialed Lewis. She got his answering machine again.

"Where are you?" she said into the machine.

That night she went to a screening of a new movie about nuclear war. Everyone—even the priest—died at the end.

The last week in May Catherine went shopping for white vigil lights. Fran had called Catherine at eleven o'clock the night before with a vision: she wanted hundreds of white vigil lights scattered around the flower arrangements on the USS *Intrepid* the night of the benefit. She told Catherine to go out and get them.

The benefit was in three days.

Catherine found the lights in a shop off Fifth and arranged to have them delivered to Fran's place. She thanked the saleswoman and went into another shop nearby.

Catherine guessed she would have recognized him anywhere, but later she would think, Maybe it wasn't an accident that she had stopped in that same pottery store in the Sixties which she and Daniel used to frequent on weekends.

He was greyer and heavier, and he was alone and his hair was wet from the rain.

She stood next to him just as he picked up something blue with black stripes.

"Do you still call Xeroxes 'dittos?' " she asked.

He looked up. He had that ability to never really look excited, but for a moment she thought his eyes twinkled. It could have been the track lighting.

"What do you think?"

"I think you do."

He brushed a strand of wet hair away from her mouth.

"Have you learned how to cook anything else besides spaghetti?"

"Stop," she said. "You're making me hungry."

They caught a cab and ate at a dive in Chinatown because he said he was sick of how pretentious Manhattan was getting. Over steamed dumplings, he told her about the shoes and the suits and the espresso in Rome. When the waiter came with their long fong kew, Daniel told her about the sandwiches he ate at the bars there and all the Caravaggios he had seen. He talked about everything that went with Italy—art and good leather—things that were supposed to last.

When she had eaten all there was to eat, Catherine took her lipstick from her purse.

"I've started painting again, too," he said. "Mostly in gouache."

She raised her napkin over her mouth and put on her lipstick.

"Straight?" she asked, putting the napkin next to her plate.

"I can't tell. Stop smiling. You missed a spot here and here," he said, pointing to his lips. "Let me. It's easier."

She gave him the lipstick, leaning towards him so he could fill in her crooked lines.

Outside, he held the cab door open for her, and when she slid in beside him, he put his arm around her and it was like he had never left.

Upstairs in her apartment, most of her ceiling was on the floor.

"Maybe we shouldn't," she said. "Everything's such a mess."

"I don't mind mess," he said, turning her towards him. She could smell his mustache.

She knew that when he took off his pants he would fold them on the crease and hang them over her bike parked below the Picasso poster. And she knew that after he had kissed her, he would hold first her left breast, then her right, and then he would kiss those and back her up to the bed.

After the breast business, Daniel backed Catherine up onto the bed and pulled out a condom. She laughed and said that wasn't necessary.

"I'm on the pill now," she said. "We're safe."

"Let's use it anyhow," he said, and she knew by the way he said it, he was protecting himself, not her.

He took more time with everything, and the two of them went on pretending that it all meant a lot more than it really did. Afterwards, after she had wrapped her legs around his back the way he said he liked, and after he had done the slow circular thing he thought she liked—even though she didn't—and after she bit his ear the way he once said he liked—though this time, she thought she saw him wince—they lay in bed side by side and Catherine stared up at her yellow crumbling ceiling and thought to herself that sleeping with Daniel again was one of the stupidest, most depressing things she had ever done.

In college, her first lover, an earnest farm boy who was more experienced than Catherine, told her the one thing she should never do was have a one-nighter. That wasn't the advice he should have given her, Catherine thought now, looking at Daniel's pants hanging neatly over the bar of her bike. He should have told me never to sleep with an ex.

"Wow," Daniel said.

"Yeah," Catherine said. "Pretty wow."

She knew she had to say more. She felt that saying something meaningful would be the right thing to do.

She sighed, feeling as though she were being filmed again. She wished Fran would stop sending her to so many screenings. She wished she could yell out "Cut!" so the director would send in somebody else—somebody cuter, sexier—to play the part of Heartbroken Girlfriend, Screwed-up Neurotic, or whatever other role she happened to be in that week.

"I've been going through such changes," she started. And she went on. She told him she had forgotten what had been the best part of her life—him. It had been all so overwhelming, she said, keeping up with him and her job and she just hadn't had the time or the energy. Maybe, she said, we can bring these two worlds together now.

"I've really missed you," she said. She paused for an effective minute or two.

An ambulance screamed from someplace close by. She heard her Soviet neighbor move something solid over his floor and then she heard his TV. The theme song to "The Andy Griffith Show" played.

If she were a car, she thought, she would be on a gravel road stuck in park without any wheels. That was the way she felt just then, lying there, beside Daniel again.

"We don't have to say anything," he said all of a sudden. "Let's just sleep now. OK?" She nodded. Then she realized he wasn't looking at her, so she said, "Yeah. 'K." She thought of Lewis and she wished he were there beside her, not Daniel. Lewis would have had his arms around her as though together they were going somewhere. She would be smiling. Where was Lewis? Why hadn't he called?

She looked up at her ceiling right then and thought of everything she had to ask Mick Jagger. How did he feel about Bianca, knowing she had slept with almost as many men as he had women? And why *hadn't* he ever bothered marrying Jerry?

Catherine was late picking up the TV actress, Cynthia Sanborn, at the Fairmont. Catherine had the limo wait outside the front while she went in and called her down.

"Good morning, Cynthia," Catherine said once they were back in the limo. Fran had taught her to call them all by their first names, no matter how famous. It would make them immediately more down-to-earth. Cynthia was with a boyfriend. She looked at Catherine, put on a pair of sunglasses, and without a word stared out the window.

"You're late," she said to the window.

Howard had been against shooting Cynthia Sanborn for the cover all along. Because (a) Cynthia was a celebrity and Howard didn't believe in celebrity covers, and (b) she was too old. "Tell her we don't airbrush," he had said. Cynthia was thirty-five.

Howard was right, Catherine thought, looking at her now. There were lines around her chapped lips and her eyes, and the cute, flip-top nose, popular in the seventies, was now just no good. But she had a new TV series that was a winner, and she had gotten her first break modeling for *Women,* and Ms. Simpson was insisting that Fran and Catherine do a big spread on the Comeback Girl. It was the first time Catherine had known Ms. Simpson to insist upon anything concerning a celebrity.

Catherine had about thirty minutes before they got to the studio in SoHo so she got out her notepad and started.

Cynthia had cut a country/western album that had bombed and then there had been the movie that had opened and closed in less then a week. She had married an auto mechanic, a movie producer, a recording magnate and now she was single again. The man in the limo, a big man whose cowboy hat rubbed against the roof of the car, was a stuntman.

"I've done it all," Cynthia said, staring out the window. "And I've never regretted any of it. Put that down." She turned and looked at Catherine's notepad. "I said put it down. I don't see you writing."

Catherine moved her pen around. This was the part she always hated— when they told her what to write and what not to write. Once, LaToya Jackson told her how her brother Michael always ragged on her about how fat her face was. "He's right," she had said. All ninety-eight pounds of her. Mrs. Jackson sat next to her daughter, eating from a tin of butter cookies Catherine had gotten from Paramount two Christmases before. LaToya lifted up a very slim, very manicured pinky. "He's like this." In the middle of the interview, LaToya had panicked and pressed the rewind button on Catherine's recorder. She had, she claimed, said too many personal things that had nothing to do with her new line of makeup.

"Did you get it?" Cynthia said, looking for a moment at Catherine.

Bitch goddess. Ice princess. Cynthia Sanborn had been called them all.

Catherine looked at the stuntman. Don't you get tired of doing every-body else's stunt work? she wanted to ask. He stared back at her and, to her horror, she realized by the look on his face that he was pitying her.

The driver pulled up near the curb and Cynthia didn't waste any time getting out.

"Don't forget to get my underwear," she said to the stuntman.

"White cotton."

"Where?"

"I don't care where. Just get it." And she slammed the door and disappeared behind a black steel door in a building made of brick and iron.

"We can drop you at Bloomingdale's," Catherine said.

"Thanks," the stuntman said, even tipping his hat. "She's not usually like this. It's just that time of the month. You know."

It was a zoo outside Bloomingdale's and the stuntman got out, and stuck his head back inside the limo. He had a lot of scars on his face.

"My card," he said, giving his card to Catherine. "Larry Hackman. Hack man. Not Hagman."

As she watched him walk away, Catherine wondered how many roles he had gotten because of Cynthia Sanborn and if it had been worth it. And then she remembered her casting-couch story and she reached into the front seat and told the driver to stop and stood up in the back and stuck her head out the sun-roof, yelling, "Hey. Hackman. Lemme buy you breakfast."

Catherine had wanted to swim after work that day, but she stopped in at the office to see about any phone messages or mail. Maybe, she thought, Mick Jagger's man had called.

Everybody was leaving while she was coming in, and even though it was May, they were all dressed in black. There were silk autumn leaves in the elevator—Accessories was getting sloppier and sloppier—and a girl from Fashion stood peeling away her nail polish next to a rack of plaid quilts for the Back to School pages.

Joey had come and gone, a girl from the Art Department told her, and Catherine quickly told the girl she wasn't looking for Joey.

"Well, Howard sure the hell was," the girl said.

Catherine knew Joey was missing a lot of work. He would come in between ten and eleven o'clock, wearing sunglasses, and then he would be out by four. And Catherine could tell he was being sloppy. Crotchcough's September page had little balls of rubber cement around the copy which Joey had neglected to erase away, and when he had drawn up a calcium-and-vitamin-C graph to go alongside a Food piece on You and Vitamins, everyone in the office heard Howard shouting at him.

"Everyone knows calcium is white and vitamin C is orange," Howard bellowed. "Yellow. Maybe. But purple? This isn't *Interview*."

Fran was hysterical.

"Don't you ever leave me alone like that all day. I was answering *your* phone calls and I couldn't get a thing done." She got up, and handed Catherine a stack of pink *While You Were Out* slips, on top of all the August copy Catherine had handed in. "It's not snappy enough. Start over," she said, putting on her mink. "I left the number of the florist on my desk. Call them and tell them the flowers they sent are a foot too short. Tell them that's a huge goddamned boat. Tell them they'll have to do better." Finally she left.

A minute later Fran stuck her head back in the office.

"And listen, Catherine. If you're thinking about leaving, just remember one thing. The Rolodexes are mine."

There was a message from a man named Hank. "Lewis's father" was in parentheses.

"It's about Lewis," Hank said on the phone. He cleared his throat. He coughed. "I found your name in his things."

"Oh no."

"Yeah," Hank said. "I was wondering if you wanted me to pick you up for the funeral."

Catherine didn't want to go to Lewis Lipman's funeral. She had watched her father die and she had helped both her great-grandmothers on their deathbeds, but nobody Catherine had slept with had ever died and the idea brought chills.

Using the I've-got-to-see-a-horror-movie as an excuse seemed pretty lame.

"I'll swing by at five," Hank Lipman said.

Lewis had told Catherine once that he had always wanted to be in a funny horror movie, and when Catherine saw the closed coffin she kept expecting him to pop out any minute.

"He was a good boy," Hank Lipman kept breathing into her. He was a slight man in a dark suit and he smelled of onions.

There weren't very many people there. There was a large woman in a cheap black hat who wept into a Kleenex and said she was the Girlfriend.

"She's probably after the money," Hank whispered to Catherine. "But there is none." Lewis had evidently spent it all on traveling and on what he thought would be cancer cures.

"He was a good boy," Hank Lipman said again.

Catherine couldn't keep her eyes off the coffin. Wake up, she thought. She was trying to command it to open. Stare at a person long enough, he'll turn around. Wake up, she thought harder. A friend told one of those warmhearted, when-he-was-alive anecdotes and he came off sounding like somebody doing Bill Murray doing an imitation of the bereaved.

The Girlfriend read a poem by Robert Frost. The Agent recapped charming things Lewis had said during those deal-making times. The Father got up and made a speech, starting and ending with "He was a good boy."

Afterwards, everyone was busy claiming moments spent with Lewis. The Agent looked at Catherine.

"You're the girl at *Women*," she said.

"I only interviewed him once," Catherine said.

"I've got a client on 'Days of our Lives' you might be interested in," and before she could give Catherine the pitch, the Girlfriend stepped in and spoke in hurried, hushed whispers about the possibility of getting cast in an upcoming Scorsese film.

Lewis' father touched Catherine's sleeve.

"I don't know what you were to Lewis, but I remember him telling me about you, about this girl he met, and that there was something to her."

Catherine smiled and bowed her head. Hank was a hard man to look at. His eyes were brown and kind. Lewis had had these eyes. He didn't belong here, among these people.

"He was a wonderful man," Catherine said.

"He was a good boy."

Catherine stayed behind. Again she looked at the coffin. Baby, he had once called her. My light. My Rock of Gibraltar.

She remembered when he had told her that he wanted to be a pond if he were born again. "Ponds aren't like oceans or lakes," he had said. "They don't get angry." Catherine had felt that she had understood him then and she wished he was there with her now to tell her more about ponds and peace.

Catherine put her hand on the lid of the coffin. She wished she could feel loss less right then. She wished her whole body had a case of paresthesia. She wished she was as numb as her lower lip had been after Dr. Panter pulled her wisdom teeth.

She wanted to make up a list, one last list of grievances and sorrows. On it she would write that she was sorry—sorry that she hadn't been kinder. Sorry that she hadn't been with him more. Sorry she had lost the knack to say what she wanted to say, to say what was in her heart.

Before her father died, a nurse had come into his hospital room, bared his white, shaven chest, and painted his whole upper body with iodine that squirted out brown on a sterile pad, but on her father turned yellow. Catherine had wanted to say something, anything, to cheer him up just then.

"You're the color of Chloe now," she had said, but he hadn't laughed or smiled. No one was laughing anymore then.

Her hand still resting on the lid of Lewis' coffin, Catherine could feel tears welling up in her eyes and she couldn't help but weep. She wept for all the fear she had known. She wept for her father and for her mother who was alone now and for the baby she didn't have. She wept for her stupidity and weakness in ever having gone to Mexico with Michael. She wept for her lost friendship with Joey. She wept for the fate of Fran and for all women in New York who didn't have a patio or a mountain outside their window.

Lewis had said that sooner or later the city would spit her out and she supposed it had. He had said that maybe someday they would end up together. She backed away from the coffin. I'm alive, she thought to herself. At least I'm alive. And then Catherine sat down in a pew across from Lewis, mentally measuring the distance between him and her.

Catherine was due for *Don't Let the Bedbugs Bite* at seven. At the screening room off Broadway, Catherine saw the guy from the teen magazine again. He was talking earnestly with P.R. He had on a tweed jacket. He was trying to look like Gene Siskel, but he had too much hair. Melissa rolled her eyes at Catherine and tipped her hand to her mouth. She excused herself from Gene Junior and came over to Catherine.

"I'm leaving for the coast in less than a week, let's go for a drink after this," she said, walking Catherine to her seat.

Later, Catherine would hear about Melissa, that when she had first gotten out to California she had a fabulous place in Malibu where she kept her collection of Halloween masks, but then when she found out that she hadn't gotten the job with Stephen King after all, that even the interview had fallen through, she had flipped, flushed all her masks down the toilet and walked from room to room of her new house, naked. In the end, a plumber would find Melissa Wicker passed out on her water bed.

But that evening, after Lewis Lipman's wake, Catherine thought a drink sounded like a good idea.

The movie began with a tranquil scene in a forest. The setup. Then the camera zeroed in on a Girl Scout camp and then, of course, came night and the ghost stories and finally the delimbing. Catherine settled into her seat and opened up a bag of yogurt-covered raisins. At least, she thought, I am not out searching for white cotton underwear for my mate. And at least I am alive. I am in a screening room. I am not coming apart in a car and I am not blowing up in the middle of a highway. She stared up at the screen. And, alas, my arm is not getting snipped off with a giant pair of pruning shears as Scout Number Thirty-nine's arm is. How to Survive Getting Dumped, Catherine thought, sucking the yogurt off a raisin. Thankfully the Scout's screams were dying down, but wait, here comes Number Forty-one. Go to a good boy's wake. Watch horror movies for a month. Compare and contrast.

After the screening, Catherine went back to the office. There she finished off the yogurt-covered raisins and wrote about her last date with Lewis.

The night of the benefit for the homeless, Catherine dressed up in Joey's old tux, moving the cummerbund so that the cigarette hole didn't show.

The vigil lights worked, and although the flower arrangements didn't quite reach up high enough for Fran's tastes, the shadows cast from the eucalyptus and the birds of paradise spread out over the army grey ceilings and down past the portholes.

It was a warm evening, warm enough to melt the watercress butter on the pheasant sandwiches, warm enough for women to wear backless, strapless gowns. Too warm for a tux.

Catherine took tickets at the door, so she saw everyone come in. They didn't look at her. They dropped their tickets into the plastic cup she held, usually while talking to their dates. There were some of the people from the *Dreamgirls* cast there and some major and minor soap-opera stars. You could always tell who the celebrities were—they were the ones with a worked-on glow. Their lipstick never bled and they always smiled. That was what the poseurs never caught on to—poseurs pouted. In real life, the real stars always smiled.

By ten o'clock Catherine was ready to go home.

"I think everyone's here," she said, offering Fran the cup full of tickets. Fran pushed the cup back to her, and she was off again, hurrying towards someone who looked a lot like Christopher Cross.

When Catherine turned back around, she saw Joey.

He was wearing a tux better-looking than hers and he was smiling. He had the celebrity glow.

His eyes weren't focused and he didn't really see her, but he said hi, and he gave her one of those affected L.A. kisses, his lips never touching her face. Still, Catherine saw who was behind him, whom Joey was with.

"You know Andy, don't you? Andy, this is my friend Catherine."

Andy Warhol didn't say anything. He had people with him who weren't looking at Catherine. They were looking at who was aboard the *Intrepid*.

They didn't have tickets, but Catherine stepped aside and watched them pass. She watched Joey pointing every now and then as though he were a cruise director aboard the *Love Boat*. She watched young, pretty waiters hurry over with pheasant sandwiches for Andy. "I served Andy Warhol a pheasant sandwich," they would tell their friends. But Andy didn't eat or drink anything. He just stood there, touching his wig every now and then, listening to whatever anybody whispered into his ear.

"Wow." Fran stood by Catherine's side. Catherine knew that Fran was going on less than four hours' sleep, but still, Fran looked beautiful and full of life. "Andy Warhol," Fran said. "Joey's really made something out of himself, huh?" The music was loud, so Catherine didn't need to say anything. Fran left, heading towards Joey, to get an introduction.

There they were, Catherine thought, watching Joey move his shoulders next to Andy in time with the music while Andy stood still. A small, white-haired, pimply guy from Pennsylvania and a guy from Arkansas. And here I am from Barrington, Illinois. She looked at all the people, sparkling now under the moonlight of a beautiful spring evening on the Hudson. Here we all are, Catherine thought, watching Joey move the way he had once taught her. Here we all are—the fearless and the homeless.

Catherine wondered where Lewis was right then. And her father. She wondered why she wasn't with her mother, and why she was here in New York aboard a ship named for those who felt no fear. She looked down at her second-hand tux. She didn't belong here with any of these people.

Out near the dance floor, Joey tipped his head and laughed a loud "Ha," his mouth wide open, then swayed and looked for someone to hold on to for balance.

Catherine put the plastic cup full of tickets down on a table in front of a locked cabin. Then she walked down the pier, away from the *Intrepid*. She could hear people's laughter dying away and then she heard water lapping against the side of the ship. For an instant, Catherine had a vision of herself swimming out towards sea. She was strong, she had been swimming three times a week at the Colony Club. Maybe she could make it out to the harbor, and to Liberty Island by morning.

She had her cabdriver let her off at the corner so that she could pick up the Sunday *Times* at a newsstand on Third and Seventy-eighth. There was a group of black girls standing huddled around page ninety-three of May *Women*.

"Look at that white bitch," one of the girls said. "She don't have no problems. Look at this." The girl directed their attention to her ample backside. "What kinda bathing suit would they put around this? And what does this make me, a *G?*"

Catherine laughed to herself, walked past the girls, and caught sight of a copy of the *Enquirer*. Lewis was on the cover. Dying had made him popular again. It was an old picture of Lewis after a wrestling match, his arms up in victory. "Stand-up Comic Is Still Alive, Friends Say." The headline depressed Catherine and she stopped in at the Star for a turkey sandwich and when she got home she saw that her ceiling had caved in.

Chapter 9

Finding Motek

The whole ceiling hadn't fallen through—only a corner of it—but Catherine stood there at her door cursing so loudly that her Soviet neighbor came to her side, looked up at what Catherine was cursing, mumbled something in Russian and called the landlord. Maybe it was because he had an accent, maybe it was because he was a man, but whatever the reason, the landlord finally came huffing up the stairs to Catherine's apartment within an hour. That evening as it began to rain, the two of them went up one flight to the roof to see where all the damage was coming from.

"You should have called me earlier," he said, standing under the umbrella Catherine held over the two of them as they stood on the roof, surveying the damage. "The rain hasn't helped."

There were tiny holes in the tar all around the area above her apartment.

"That'd be Mrs. Olson in 4A," the landlord said, spitting off to the side. He was the first man in New York Catherine had seen chewing tobacco. "She comes up here with her dog. It's easier to come up here, one flight, than it is to go down five. Piss'll eat right through tar."

"So tell her to stop."

"Already have."

"Tell her again."

"Look, lady. I'll fix your roof, but I can't keep a twenty-four hour watch on an old lady and her dog."

Everything in Catherine's apartment was either wet or damp from the rain. The Audrey Hepburn-hat lamp Joey had given her when she had had her wisdom teeth pulled had fallen and was now bent out of shape. The only dry piece in the room was Daniel's table and Catherine was afraid it might warp along with everything else.

When Daniel came to his door, Catherine was standing on his stoop with his table.

"My roof caved in and I didn't want this to get wet," she said, looking at the table and then at him. "You said it was an important piece."

"It is. It's very important," he said, opening the door wider. "And I've just made some tea."

Catherine stayed the night with Daniel, and on Sunday, she took a cab back to her place, took one look around, threw some clothes into her red *Women* workout bag, and headed back to Daniel's place in Brooklyn.

"This is big," Fran said when Catherine arrived straight from Daniel's place Monday morning. Fran had Catherine's monocle stuck in her right eye. She was sitting at Catherine's desk, looking at a slide of Brooke Shields.

"We should come up with ideas like this every month," she said.

Catherine had convinced Beauty to "rev up" their pages—*Women* liked the verb "to rev"—with a celebrity spread on the new pout. Howard had OK'd the piece because Catherine had promised to use famous business-women and Catherine was put in charge, getting close-ups of Nastassia Kinski and anybody else with a decent mouth.

All day long, messengers came with packages of photos and slides addressed to Catherine Clemons, Entertainment Editor. Catherine was care-ful to hide them or tear off the outside labels, though she would have liked to pin them up on her bulletin board next to where she had scratched out her noun/adjective, "comeuppance."

The word was out about the pout story and publicists were calling Catherine now, not Fran, urging Catherine to attend the better screenings and plays.

Fran's benefit for the homeless had made Page Six, and she had already turned down an offer to head another benefit for Vietnam vets. Her tape for "Entertainment Tonight" on Academy Award dressing had pleased the producers so much they wanted her to do another, and she had had Catherine run and get her a sack of Zaro brownies so she could sit at her desk and think up a new topic.

"What about doing something on short women in the industry?" she said, eating a brownie at her desk. She got out a *Women* notepad and began to make a list of short women.

"Sissy Spacek, Sally Field," she began.

"Susan Lucci, Joan Collins," Catherine added.

Just then Ann Bartel knocked on the wall and said that she was sorry to bother them, but could Entertainment spare any boxes?

Fran looked at Catherine in disbelief. Catherine worried a moment for Ann Bartel.

"No, Ann, we don't have any boxes," Fran said slowly. Catherine could hear Ann's little silver bracelets jingling as she moved her hand down from the wall. Ann nodded and said again she was sorry if she had bothered them. Catherine realized that she was, in all honesty, sorry, and that there had been nothing premeditated or malicious about her request. She looked tired and a little pale, and when she turned and knocked on the wall next to Readers' Service, Catherine saw that the hem of her gauze skirt was ripped. She, after all, didn't have an assistant to bring her roses, fetch her brownies, and clip the loose threads from the hems of her clothes.

"It must be nice knowing what you write makes a difference in somebody's life," Fran said. Catherine turned around. Fran was eating another brownie, staring up at the gold-framed celebrity photos that lined her wall. Catherine couldn't tell if Fran was serious or not.

She waited, but Fran didn't say anything. She was still staring up at the photos.

"Dolly Parton," Catherine said. She was staring at Fran's back. Catherine felt as though Fran were deciding something.

Fran nodded, slowly turning her chair, looking all around the office, at the file cabinets that overflowed with photos and news clippings, the stereo—not the company's, but one which Fran had had in college and brought in one weekend—the TV, which was off because the reception had gone bad. Everything in the office was cramped and a little the worse for wear.

"Yeah," Fran said. "I bet being short's a real pain for them. I bet at first nobody respected them, you know?"

The following afternoon Catherine went to a play.

"You wanna mouth?" a publicist who represented a stage actress had told Catherine over the phone. "Have I gotta mouth."

It was a musical about an English girl traipsing all over the United States, going through men as though they were jelly beans. "It's not the end of the world," the thin-lipped actress sang over and over. "Breakup after breakup, all the wiser."

"It's National Tissue and Organ Donation Week," Joey said over the phone. "Let me make you dinner."

It was late and Catherine had just gotten back from the musical and she had just finished telling the publicist that nobody on Broadway had a mouth big enough for the pout spread and now she was on the other line with the man who claimed to represent Mick Jagger and who had put her on hold.

"Where are you?" she asked.

"Right now I'm at the grocery store, torn between chicken and roast," Joey said. "You sound exhausted. Let me feed you."

Catherine sighed and said she was free Sunday evening and they set a time and Joey gave her his new address. He was living with the Dwarfman now. "Finally. I'm a housewife with a house," he had said. Catherine hadn't seen Joey since he had been fired.

Joey had been showing up later and later until finally he came into the Art Department at noon one Monday, bleary-eyed and shaky, and Howard handed over his empty Wonder Woman mug and told him he needn't bother laying out September, October, November, or any other month for that matter. It had been the day of Joey's second anniversary at *Women*.

"What, no plant?" everyone heard Joey yell at Howard's back. "I want my goddamn African violet."

It had not been unexpected. There was talk in Articles of Joey doing a lot of coke, that he had been seen at Area and at the Palladium nosing up with business types until all hours. One assistant had it that he had played the mermaid at Visages and at midnight he had taken off his scales while hanging upside down from the golden ring.

When Joey hung up, Catherine cut into the other line. Jagger's man still had her on hold. Listening to a Muzak version of "Brown Sugar" playing for all those on hold, Catherine thought of everything she still needed to ask Jagger. Didn't it feel old, being a legend? Knowing all the people he knew, seeing everything he had seen, didn't it make him terribly, terribly tired?

She brought wine, and Dwarfman, who was a short, fat, bearded fellow, answered the door and made her a spritzer at a side table using an old-fashioned seltzer bottle which he let Catherine hold.

"He loves to go antiquing," Joey shouted out from the kitchen. "He got that in Albany."

Joey came out with a tray of shrimp wrapped in pea pods.

"I put water chestnuts in there, too," he said.

He was letting his hair grow out and it was all different shades of beiges and blonds. He had a little gut now and he was radiant. He reminded Catherine of a pregnant bride.

He put his hand on the Dwarfman's shoulder while he leaned over to put the tray on a glass table that was really a giant upside-down specimen jar. Joey's cat, Damn It, was curled around the lip of the jar, asleep. Joey stood back, his hand still on the Dwarfman's shoulder. The Dwarfman playfully slapped it away.

"God, this is great," Joey said. "My two favorite people."

Catherine and the Dwarfman looked at each other and smiled politely before they took another sip from their drinks.

Catherine tried one of the shrimps on the tray on the specimen jar.

"Tell me more about what you do, Steve," Catherine said.

"I specialize in the genetic mutation of adult male achondroplastic dwarfs."

"Oh," Catherine said.

"Achondroplastic dwarfs are the ones with normal heads and bodies, it's just their arms and legs are so short," Joey explained. "Steve's trying to figure out why they quit growing."

Catherine nodded.

"It's wild," Joey said. "All these little guys coming in and out of here all day. They're so cute."

"They don't have long to live," the Dwarfman said. He drank. The three of them looked at the shrimp. Damn It woke up, stretched out her two front legs while she yawned, looked at Catherine, and went back to sleep.

"I've always wanted him to do a screenplay," Joey said. Catherine laughed. "No, really. On the real Tom Thumb. He had the wildest life. He was so rich for a while he raised Arabian horses on his farm. Can you imagine? What would Tom Thumb do with Arabian horses?"

"How many times do I have to tell you?" Dwarfman said, getting up to refill his glass. "Tom Thumb was a midget, not a dwarf. Dwarfism is a genetic mutation. There are approximately one hundred types of dwarfism. A midget is simply a very, very small man."

"Anyway, that's not how he pays the rent," Joey said. He leaned forward as though he were going to whisper a secret. "He taught me the trick on investing: Anytime someone says 'Recession,' buy."

They didn't eat until nine, because Joey said he had been so excited about Catherine coming over he had gotten a late start. It was an elaborate chicken dish with a wine mushroom sauce, and by the time they sat down Dwarfman was drunk and grouchy.

"I can't eat chicken off the bone," he said as Joey served him a breast. "Chicken off the bone makes me sneeze."

Joey passed butter he had shaped into seashells. Catherine watched him trying to think of conversation starters as he studied his turnips.

"How's Howard?" he asked. "Has he done a five-page spread on the earlobe yet? I swear, that man's given magazine space to every conceivable body part."

Catherine said that Howard was fine and that the October cover was hideous.

"How's your mother?"

The last time Catherine had spoken with her mother, her mother had said that it was rainy and she was tired of being bothered by Catherine's nonsense.

"Why don't you just quit that ghastly job and come home," she had said, and she had hung up on Catherine and neither one of them bothered calling the other anymore on Tuesday nights.

"Mom's doing great," Catherine said. "We're really close now."

"That's important," Joey said, looking at Catherine.

"Mmmph," Dwarfman mumbled, nodding with a mouthful of food.

Joey went on about living there in the meat district with trucks loading and unloading at three in the morning. Catherine made jokes about her place and Joey wondered out loud why she hadn't moved yet.

"Either that or make it into a home, Cat," Joey said, getting up. "Eat your turnips, Cat. They guard against cancer."

After dinner, in a sudden mood shift, Dwarfman showed Catherine his study, a red room lined with bookcases and stuffed ducks. The ducks were posed and pinned midflight, their wings spread out to show off their colored feathers.

"I didn't shoot them myself," he said, pouring out two glasses of brandy. He gave one to Catherine and closed the door. "One of my patients died and willed them to me. I don't know why. I never even knew he had them."

"Oh God, Steve, don't show her those," Joey said, coming into the room. "I hate those."

"He hates those," Dwarfman whispered to Catherine conspiratorially. Man to man.

Joey flapped his hands at the birds, said he had a cake in the oven, and left.

Catherine was relieved to get away from Joey. He had that smug I've-got-my-man attitude she had seen so many times in the faces of the more well-to-do women of Barrington.

"He never comes in here. Refuses to clean it. This," he said, lifting his glass and toasting the walls, "this is my room."

The two of them sat down, sighing at the quality of the brandy, even though Catherine hated brandy, and for a moment, when he opened a box, she thought Dwarfman would bring out two cigars, but he clipped only the one, smelled it, and lit it.

"This is where I do my work," he went on. Catherine looked around, trying to find some pictures of dwarfs, or maybe specimens of something grisly, but there were only the ducks.

She wondered, too, why and how Joey had gone from Michael to this short, bearded man in front of her. If she believed in vendettas, she would have tried to seduce Dwarfman, but she didn't have a vendetta and Dwarfman wasn't very appealing to Catherine.

They could smell the cake baking.

"It must be nice," Catherine said, looking at the neatness of things—a pair of gold scissors and a letter opener lined up on his desk. The books and ducks all straight, "coming home every day to somebody."

Dwarfman nodded. "Lately, though, I've been thinking about going back to school and getting an MBA."

Damn It came in before Joey came in with dessert. After they ate the cake—a chocolate-cream-cheese affair with almonds on top—Joey said there were some things in the bedroom he wanted Catherine to see.

Their bedroom was simple, almost Puritan in style. There were hard-wood floors and the bed was raised on cement blocks and covered with an old-fashioned-looking quilt. Joey opened the closet, pushed back a bunch of dresses, and pulled out his red sequined dress.

"Remember this?" he said, lifting the plastic. "Some of the sequins fell off, but it's still in good shape." He covered it again, lifted it up in his other hand and gently laid it in Catherine's arms.

"Joey. I can't take this."

"You have to. I can't fit in it anymore. It needs a new home."

"But don't you think you should keep it? For memory's sake?"

"I don't need a dress for that."

Catherine looked at the dress. She wondered if it would fit her, wondered if Joey had had it cleaned between now and the time he had last worn it—had he worn it alone with Michael?

"Everybody misses you at work," Catherine said. It wasn't true. No one had even mentioned his name.

"Michael wasn't the one for you, Catherine," Joey said in such a low voice Catherine wasn't sure she had heard him right. She looked up. She wished she could have been more angry at him at that moment.

"It took me a while, but did you know that his initials were M.E.? Catherine, Michael was nothing more than a selfish little prick who screwed whatever and whomever he could and he happens to have the money now to do so. He's a taker. He's into other people's energy. And he'll only stick around for as long as you've got it. Then he's out the door. To him everything's just one more trade."

Catherine took a deep breath and then she let the air out. Sometimes she wished Joey wouldn't say what she knew to be true.

"So," she said after a while. "What was Warhol like?"

Joey shrugged, and bit off a stray thread from the hem of the dress.

"I wanted to do a piss painting or something, but he was through with those. He's got a lot of pretty boys in tuxedoes sweeping his floors and doing all his painting for him. He's just an old rich guy with terrible skin and bad hair."

"I'm sorry."

"Don't be. It was freeing."

"That when you quit seeing Michael?"

Joey nodded.

"It's hard, you know," Catherine said after a while. "I don't even have you to hang out with anymore."

"You've still got Fran," Joey said.

Catherine let out a laugh. Then she looked at the dress.

"So," she said. "I suppose this means we're friends again."

"Too late," Joey said. He touched the hem of the dress Catherine held between them. "That happened a long time ago."

When Catherine was ready to leave, she stood at the door with Joey's dress in a Bendel's bag. She thanked Joey for the dinner and Dwarfman told her to wait a minute and reappeared with a book with an ugly black-and-white cover of a small town covered with grey smoke.

"You'll like this," he said, giving the book to Catherine. "It's about coal mines in Kentucky and West Virginia."

Catherine looked at Joey, who had tears in his eyes.

"It's his favorite book," Joey said. Dwarfman blushed and when he shook her hand, Catherine was surprised that it was neither cold nor clammy.

That night Catherine couldn't bear the thought of facing her apartment—she had been back only once since the roof had caved in—so she hailed a cab and told the driver to take her to Brooklyn.

In the back seat of the cab, Catherine opened a window. It was one of those late spring evenings when the city smelled of rain and Catherine leaned back and looked up at the sky. It was bright and she couldn't see too many stars and the moon looked like just another office light.

She would get to Brooklyn and she would have a glass of wine with Daniel and they would go to bed and she would dream that Joey had left her using the Seventy-seventh Street subway. She would stand on a platform in this dream, waiting to see him off. All around her there would be people with limbs peeling off. Everyone would smell bad and their bones and muscles would be sticking out. Joey would get on the train, leaving Catherine behind surrounded by these people. "My little baby sister," he would scream, his arms outstretched—the subway doors not yet closed. And in this dream Catherine would run towards the moving train, unable to catch up with it, watching as it disappeared into the dark tunnel.

But just then in the cab, Catherine lifted the red dress from the bag and draped it across her lap. She wondered where Fran was, what she was doing and whom she was with. She thought about where Michael might be. Under the Manhattan Bridge, maybe? With Fran? Jagger was singing "I'm so hot for you" on the radio. She would meet Jagger and she would keep it light, Catherine thought. She would hum something—"Jumpin' Jack Flash," maybe—and they would dance, and she would ask, casually, "So, Mick, tell us. What's your favorite body part?"

And as her cab made its way out of Manhattan and into Brooklyn, Catherine wondered what else she would ask Mick Jagger when she met him and where she would ever be able to wear Joey's dress.

"This just isn't working out," Daniel said. It was Monday and Catherine was getting ready to go back into Manhattan.

Catherine scanned the room. She couldn't find her belt. "What are you talking about?" She retraced her steps from the night before. In the kitchen they'd had the wine. She went in the kitchen and looked through all the drawers. They had stepped out on the balcony. She went out to the balcony.

"This, Cat. This," Daniel was saying from inside.

Had he taken the belt off her outside or in?

"What did you do with my belt?"

"You come. You go. I can never get any work done. You call when you need me but I can't get hold of you when I need you."

Catherine went into the studio and sat on the sofa. She felt between the cushions. Daniel was spilling his coffee as he paced in front of her. On the wide desk in the corner of the room was the nineteenth-century gold bracelet he had been working on the night before when she had come in late. Every time he tried putting on a link, another one fell off. Catherine got down on the floor on her hands and knees and looked under the sofa.

"Are you hearing a word of this?"

Catherine looked up.

"I can't find my belt."

"Fuck the belt, I'm talking about *us*."

"I gotta go."

"I should have married you when I had the chance."

Catherine got up and picked up the bag with Joey's dress and Dwarfman's book on coal mines, and she headed out the door.

"This isn't a relationship," Daniel shouted out to her. "It's a long-term sport fuck."

She was already at the curb, getting into a cab. She turned for a moment, with one foot in the cab. For a moment she thought about that woman she had once seen, the one with the Diane Sawyer leg, getting into a cab on Madison Avenue. That was the woman Catherine had wanted to be—a woman in a short black skirt, speeding off towards somewhere. She looked back up at Daniel. He was standing in the open doorway, holding his coffee mug. There were coffee stains all the way down his right pant leg.

He was right, she thought. And she wasn't sure at all if this was where or who she wanted to be anymore.

"So? Think how thin we're going to be," she yelled back, and she got in the cab and slammed the door shut and reminded the driver to get his meter running.

That morning everybody at the November How-To meeting was sitting around, eating bagels, and gossiping about Ms. Simpson.

"She's been here forever," Fashion said.

"It's been, what? Twenty-five years?" Research said.

"When I was at *Mademoiselle,*" Fashion said, "it was always, 'Sure, let's have lunch, but do we have to bring Simpson? Tomorrow. We'll bring her tomorrow.'"

Accessories split open a croissant and nodded. "She was never what you'd call a fashion plate. She didn't even wear hats."

"I remember I had to drive to a wedding with her," Fashion went on. She passed the cream cheese to Accessories, who passed it along to Research, who passed it to At Home, who always ate everything. "My husband at the time said to me, 'Do we *have* to drive out with Simpson?' He hated her. I didn't know what to wear. I mean, what do you wear to a *Vogue* wedding? It was July, and everyone was doing pale pinks and pastel linens. Beautiful colors that year. And there was Simpson. All in black."

"For a wedding in the middle of summer?" Accessories said. She spit out what she had just bitten into. It was a Fashion trick: eating your cake and not eating it, too.

Fashion nodded. "It wasn't even linen," she said, while everyone shook their heads.

At that moment How-To came in—late for her own meeting. She looked hurried and bony and her hair was unwashed, just like the How-To before her and the one before that.

"I hope you guys have a ton of ideas," she said, nearly in tears. Fashion rolled her eyes and Accessories giggled. "I had to go into November to fill up October. What are we on? Wait. December's in June. It's May, right?" She sat down and counted on her fingers. Fashion looked at her watch and shook her head. "Yeah," How-To said. "It's May so we're in November."

Daniel wasn't returning any of Catherine's calls. She imagined him hunched over that gold bracelet on his work table in the corner of his studio, his desk light shining down over his right shoulder as he tried desperately to put together links that had once upon a time been inseparable.

Catherine didn't think it would be such a good idea to just appear on his doorstep, so for the first time in a long time, Catherine went back to her place.

Her apartment was such a mess she went upstairs to the roof, where she stared down at the damp tar. The landlord had resurfaced it. Now all she had to do was go back downstairs to her place and clean up, make it into a home, like Joey said. A dog came up from behind her and sniffed at the tar, all around at her feet. The dog lifted its leg.

"No, no," Catherine said, but the dog wasn't paying any attention to Catherine. It was sniffing at the corner of a chimney of the neighboring apartment building. Its ribs showed and its tail was shaking. She approached the thing carefully.

"It's OK," she said. She bent down and petted the dog's head. His eyes looked cloudy and he had his tail between his legs as he sniffed at Catherine's knee.

"Motek," Catherine said, reading the name on the tag on his collar.

The dog licked Catherine's hand.

"Everything's going to be all right, Motek," Catherine said. It was an old dog, but it didn't seem to mind terribly when Catherine picked him up and carried him back towards her apartment building. "Take it easy now," she whispered into his fur. "Relax. I'll take you home."

Two flights down in 4A, an old woman came to the door and when she saw Catherine with the dog, tears came to her eyes and she whispered, "Motek."

Her name was Mrs. Olson and she said she kept losing Motek on the roof once a month. She cracked open a can of salmon and heated up some leftover cabbage soup, and she and Catherine ate the soup while Motek ate the salmon at their feet under the kitchen table.

She asked Catherine if she had family in the city. And when Catherine said no, Mrs. Olson said she knew how that was—that her husband had died twenty years ago and she had lived alone ever since.

"I have a recipe," she said, ladling out more soup for Catherine. The smell filled Mrs. Olson's little kitchen, which didn't look at all like Catherine's. It looked like a home from a TV sitcom. It had a yellow-speckled linoleum floor, a table with four chairs, and lots of spices in the cabinets. "I tell it to everybody. Serve the Lord. Don't have bitterness in your heart—it messes up your digestion. And swim. I go to the Y."

Mrs. Olson held out a scrap of pork from the soup in front of Motek's nose and Motek licked it and then ate it.

"He's really a wonderful dog. Goes purely by instinct. Barks at all the people I would bark at. Chases all the trucks I'd chase."

"What does Motek mean?"

"Sweet," Mrs. Olson said. She bent down to pet the dog. "She's the sweetness in my life." She looked up at Catherine. "Do you have a dog?"

Catherine stared down at her bowl of soup. She shook her head.

"Everybody needs something. Everybody needs a little sweetness in their life."

Catherine nodded. She ate a spoonful of cabbage. "I work," she said, her excuse now for everything.

In the course of the evening Catherine forgot about telling Mrs. Olson about Motek and the tar and her roof.

That month, the month Catherine never seemed to get around to cleaning her apartment, she finished the pout story and the October Entertainment page and she even came up with three extra pieces for How-To. She felt as though she lived at *Women* because she never went home, and she couldn't help but wish that she would one day run into Ms. Simpson. She would smile and say, "Look. I'm with you on this. I'd wear black to a summer wedding, too. So why don't you just get Fran out of my life and give me a decent salary? Then maybe I could have a home like Joey's."

Joey called a couple of times that month, and Catherine kept thinking there should have been more for them to say to each other. "Let's go to Bloomingdale's and try on hats," he would say.

"I've got a deadline," she would say back.

The day Catherine's pout copy came back to her with the words "Put Through" written in black at the top, Books called. They wanted a box for November—what famous people read while they soaked in the tub. No problem, Catherine told Books. Fifteen minutes later Food stopped by. Food never stopped by unless it was to give Fran a menu for a party.

"Fran's not in," Catherine said. Fran was out again, eating and buying funny cards in the Village.

"I'm not looking for Fran," Food said.

Food wanted to know—was it possible Catherine could do a roundup for November on what famous people thought of peas?

"Peas?" Catherine said.

"Peas," Food said. She stuck a stick of sugarless gum in her wide mouth and didn't offer any to Catherine. Food never had giveaways.

Never say no. That's what Fran had said Helen Gurley Brown said.

Catherine looked at the pile of work Fran had left her with. She had agreed to the Book box, too. She wondered what Ann Bartel would do in a situation like this—write poignantly on peas? Food stopped chewing. She was looking at Catherine's desk, too.

"I'll give you a byline," Food said.

Catherine looked at Food. This was better than a raise. This was better than getting the interview with Jagger. Maybe November would be Catherine's month. She wanted to call up Mrs. Olson and tell her. "Hey, Mrs. O! I've got it. I've got *motek* in my life now, too."

Catherine smiled. Food chewed vigorously. The deal, as Michael would have put it, was done.

Chapter 10

The Thing about Hospitals

"Do you know about bananas?" Joey said. "To let them ripen, let them rock on their backs like a cradle. And remember, you've got a good peach when it smells like it should taste. OK?"

Catherine nodded. From his bed, Joey flipped through the advertisement section in the paper, found a coupon for Dole pineapple, cut it out, and put it next to the piece of angel food cake on top of his monitor.

He had already shown her the way to draw a nose. One oblong circle with two little circles on the end at either side. Then you erase the lines between the circles. "No one knows about noses," he had said.

"And corn," he said. "When you're at the store, peel it a little and stick your fingernail in it."

"Why?"

"I don't know why. Just do it. And the white's sweeter."

"What about cantaloupe? I've never known about cantaloupes."

From his bed Joey sighed, and stopped cutting the coupon for Purina Cat Chow. He moved the IV to make sure Catherine could see him shake his head.

"Feel both ends," he said. "They should be soft."

On Joey's nightstand there was a page torn out from *American Health*—an article about how AIDS patients should take care of their teeth because soon they would forget how.

"Are you OK?" Joey was looking at Catherine. The elevator rang from somewhere down the hall. He put his scissors in his lap and ate a spoonful of crushed ice. That meant he felt nauseous. "I mean. Are you OK?"

Joey had been in the Lenox Hill Hospital for a week. First it had been for a few tests. He had been in pain, he had told Catherine over the phone. Hemorrhoids. Then the bleeding had started.

He had called Catherine at work. He had not said much—just that he wanted someone in the United States to know that he was at Lenox Hill.

She knew by the wing they had put him in. There were a lot of doors to go through and the nurses were all big and black. Through half-opened doors, Catherine caught glimpses of bony feet with the purple blotches.

"Tell me things," he said, putting his scissors on the tray table. There were coupons for cereal, coffee, and cat food all over his bed.

"I called Madonna. Guess what her answering-machine message is?"

"What?"

"No, it's 'What the fuck do *you* want?' "

"She's great," Joey said.

"Yeah."

They both stared at the guardrail on Joey's bed.

"I've got the AIDS virus lurking," Joey said, after a minute had passed. It was the first time he had said the word.

"Lurking?"

"Their word, not mine. They want names of everyone I ever fucked." He paused to look at Catherine, then he laughed a short "ha." "And all this time I was worried about plaque buildup."

"Do you want to see a priest or something?"

"Jesus, Cat."

"They're not so bad, really. My mother sent me to one once when she found out I was dating a Jew. This priest had the biggest house I've ever seen. He told me not to think so much and to read all his poems."

"Well, I don't need a priest. I'm not terminal yet."

"Can you believe this? I never knew they could do that." Joey and Catherine were watching earthworms having sex with themselves. It was a PBS special on worms and insects. The earthworm on the TV shaped itself into the letter *O*.

"I never knew they could do that," Joey said.

"They have the male and female stuff," Catherine said. "They can even have babies."

Catherine was not going to let Joey alone. The last time she had seen her father alive, he had been so weak he barely said anything. He was being taken into surgery and right before the elevator doors shut, he had raised his hand and given Catherine the thumbs-up sign. She had stood there, when the doors shut, staring up at the red numbers flashing 3, 4, 5 . . .

"Get this," Scott said. Scott was Joey's new roommate. Before the bed had been empty. Scott was always reading something. He had the Sunday *New York Times* spread out all over his sheets. "Reagan said he didn't have cancer. He says he had something inside of him that had cancer in it and it was removed. This is the guy who says *AIDS* is insidious. Ha!"

"The guy in seven told me that when you die, you come one last time," Joey said. He looked at Catherine. She looked at the earthworm.

"Now there's something to look forward to," Scott said. He coughed and punched his paper.

"Your fingernails keep growing, too," Joey said, looking at his nails. He looked back up at the TV. The earthworm was straightening out.

"What advanced creatures," Joey said, watching the earthworm bury itself in the dirt. "*They'll* never have any medical problems."

The clock radio next to Joey's bed went off. Prince was singing "1999." Catherine got up and pulled a pint of orange juice, whole milk yogurt, a box marked *Energy,* and two glasses out of a grocery sack near Joey's nightstand.

"Oh God. No more," Joey said.

"Three times a day," Catherine said. "We made a deal."

They drank three energy drinks a day and the only way Catherine had gotten Joey to agree—he hated the taste—was if she drank one, too.

"Here." Catherine gave him a glass. The drink looked like brown mud.

"Remember the good old days, when losing weight was a problem?" Joey said. "A guy from Liverpool devastated me once when he said, "Joe. You're fat, but I'll still shag you.""

Catherine and Joey clicked their glasses together, and Scott counted to ten while they chug-a-lugged.

Joey was sitting propped up in bed wearing a white diaphanous dressing gown with ostrich feathers at the cuff.

"Don't I look lyrical?" he said, nearly lifting his arms all the way up. A feather floated from his cuff down to the IV tube coming out of his arm. "Angelic Outfit Number Seven."

Catherine could see the purple Kaposi's sarcoma blotches on his skin beneath the gown. They ran all along his shoulders and collarbones. He held out his hand and a bottle of nail polish.

"Do me," he said.

It was Joey's birthday and Catherine had given him a Minnie Mouse night-light. She had also baked him a cake. He had wanted chocolate, but chocolate wasn't on his diet, so she made him a carrot cake with cream-cheese icing. She had given it to Alma Jean, the nurse, so that it would be a surprise. They were timing it. Any minute now, Alma Jean would come in, turn off all the lights, and sing "Happy Birthday."

"Happy birthday," Scott said, reaching across their nightstands to give Joey a dog-eared copy of Camus' *The Plague.*

"It's wild," he said. "They've all got it, right? And everyone's saying, 'I can't believe this could happen to me in the twentieth century.' "

"You're a sick man, Scotty, my boy, but I appreciate the thought," Joey said.

Scott went back to reading his paper. "Yeah," he mumbled. "I'm sick."

Catherine held Joey's cool, thin fingers and started painting his nails Merry Mango orange.

"They've got birthdays all wrong," he said. "The presents shouldn't go to the birthday kid. They should go to the mothers. They're the ones that did all the work."

"So call your mother," Catherine said.

"I wouldn't know what to say. We haven't talked in so long. Don't let that happen, Kitten. You get sloppy with people, then you can't do anything.

And you end up like me." Joey held his hand out and looked at his wet, orange nails. "It's a strange world. No one lives where they were born. No one even lives where they grew up. Everyone's all over the place. You end up making makeshift little families in make-shit little apartments."

At that moment Dwarfman came into the room. He had pink roses with him and a box of chocolate turtles. Catherine moved to get up, but Joey told her no, no.

"Let's not get dramatic," he said. "My nails are wet."

"I brought these," Dwarfman started. He looked at Catherine.

"They're beautiful," she said.

Alma Jean came in and turned out all the lights and brought in the cake. Catherine was glad for the candles—they hid the fact that the cake had come out lopsided and that one-third of it had crumbled.

Alma Jean was smiling as she sang "Happy Birthday" along with the rest of them, her black face glossy in the light. She set the cake down on Joey's tray table and gave him a bottle of Calgon bath beads. "The kind that really bubble," she said.

Joey inhaled to blow out the candles.

"No, don't blow," Dwarfman said. Everyone stopped singing and looked at him. "You can't blow on it. No one will want to eat it then."

Nobody said anything. They all looked at the cake. The wax from the candles dripped green onto the white frosting.

"Blow on the fucker and then spit on his piece," Scott said. He fell back into his pillow. His chest rose and fell in quick succession.

"No," Joey said. He reached up and turned on the lights. "He's right." One by one, he squeezed the tip of each candle with the tips of his Merry Mango-painted fingers. There were twenty-three candles. Alma Jean had forgotten about the one to grow on.

The Tuesday after Joey's birthday, Catherine called her mother.
"Mom?"

She told her mother about Joey. Her mother usually had good advice on what people should do for people in the hospital. It was a good idea, she once told Catherine, to bring people dirty books and magazines—that way they would feel more alive. Novenas were important, as well. A week before her hysterectomy, Catherine's mother told Catherine how to make a novena, and every day before work, Catherine would stop in at a church and place the prayer written on a slip of paper under a cushion, in a Bible, or up front where the candles were.

Catherine told her mother everything—about how Joey was always cold, about how the nurses woke him up every morning at five for X rays because they didn't want him to catch pneumonia, about how he couldn't make himself eat because he would throw up.

Over the phone, Catherine could hear other conversations, distant and fuzzy.

"This *is* an epidemic, you know," her mother finally said. "Don't lick any envelopes, Catherine."

Catherine didn't say anything.

She heard fuzzy laughter from some other conversation far away.

"Well, what did your friend want to do with his life?"

"I don't know. He wanted to meet Warhol."

"What?"

"I guess he wasn't very focused."

"Well, now he is." And then her mother let the phone drop while she went after Chloe, who had just downed a vial of saffron, and Catherine stood there and listened to the receiver on the other end banging on the kitchen floor.

Then she thought she heard a man's voice.

"Is someone there?" Catherine said, when her mother got back on the line.

"Never mind," her mother said. "This stuff happens, Catherine. When your father died."

"Stop it," Catherine said. She was shouting now. She was holding the receiver out and away from her ear. She didn't want to hear what her mother had to say. "Don't start with Dad, Ma. You don't have a damned copyright on death. Just because Dad died doesn't mean I can't grieve over my friend."

There was a long pause. Catherine heard some girl asking a question. It was a long way off but Catherine thought she heard something about the weather.

"OK?" Catherine said, wondering if anybody had heard her.

Catherine started putting slips of paper under the cushions of the hospital chapel down the hall. She would slip in just before she visited Joey, put a card under the nearest cushion, then slip out. She didn't know what prayers went with what illness so she just wrote down "Pray for him," and "Make him better."

"Fear is a rabbit staring at a snake," Scott said. He was in bed staring at the ceiling. Even in the daytime, the smile on the Minnie Mouse night-light glowed red.

"He's writing poetry now," Joey said, rolling his eyes. He tapped his temple with his index finger. Joey's face was covered with shaving cream. He was propped up in bed with a portable plastic sink. The pop-up mirror was still down.

"He quit reading," Joey said, moving the disposable razor along his chin. "So give me the 411 on your weekend. Tell me things."

"I had a dream last night that I was on the Johnny Carson show," Catherine said.

"That's easy," Joey said. He barely moved his lips. He was shaving under his nose. "Johnny Carson represents Jesus Christ. J.C. Get it? So what'd you wear?"

"Love is two a.m.," Scott said.

"They told him he could go home," Joey said. "But he won't. He said he can't get this kind of reception on his TV at home. Can you believe that? The guy would rather be here." Joey put his razor down for a moment. He was out of breath. Joey wanted to go home, but his insurance didn't cover the cost of medical care he would need there. "On the way over, a garbageman mistook me for Caroline Kennedy."

"All right, Cat," Joey said. He brought his hand up for a high five and when Catherine slapped it gently, she could feel how cold he was.

"Hope is popcorn," Scott said.

"Oh, I like that one," Joey said, wiping his face with a towel.

Without the shaving cream, without his stubble, Joey looked paler and more gaunt than ever. "I just love the smell of popcorn." Very slowly, Joey lifted the plastic mirror on his portable sink.

"That's hope," Scott said. Catherine watched as Joey, without a word, folded the mirror back down again. "You love the smell of hope."

The next time Catherine visited, Scott's bed was empty and neither she nor Joey said anything more about him.

"Glen Campbell is having an affair with Michael Jackson," she said.

"Don't," Joey said. "It hurts to laugh."

Catherine turned on the TV and tried PBS, but the nature shows were over and that was the only thing Joey wanted to watch anymore.

"Put me in the tub, Cat. I wanna die clean."

"Joey."

"I mean it."

She stood up. She turned and shut the door to his room.

She used the Calgon bath beads Alma Jean had given him for his birthday.

He took off his nightgown next to the tub. He was wearing a pair of cotton Wonder Woman underwear.

It seemed as though part of his body was caving in, closing into itself, while another part—his rib cage and his hips—were reaching out. His body looked like a piece from a jigsaw puzzle. Catherine wanted to hold him, fit herself to him, to fill in the parts that were caving in.

"I should probably tell you not to look, but frankly, my dear, I don't give a fuck."

He sank down into the tub so that the bubbles came up to his mouth. In the tub he looked even thinner. His hair was limp and it was the first time Catherine had seen it natural. Joey was a brunette.

"Oh, that's good," he said. "Water's good."

"Should I go?"

"No," he said. "Stay."

There was a plastic stool in the bathroom and Catherine pulled it up next to the tub and sat down.

"Penicillin was the end of Hot Springs," he said. "Before, everyone took the baths to get well. I wish I could go to Hot Springs."

All around his shoulders there was a galaxy of freckles and Kaposi's sarcoma red marks.

"I feel like I should say something," he said.

"Like what?"

"I don't know. Something like 'I coulda been a contenda.' "

"You don't have to say anything."

"Yeah. What's to say? You're born, you grow up, you go on a few diets, then you die. The worst of it is I was ready to settle down. I had my recipes and everything."

Already there was a ring of Joey's dead skin around the tub.

"So," Catherine said. She held her breath and then she let it out. "Did you ever cook for Michael?'

"Oh, Catherine. Don't."

"Come on. Just tell me. How was he?"

"Don't do this."

"Compared to the others. Really. I want to know. Was he experienced? Or was it just a fling?"

"Why are you doing this?"

"No one thought about me in all this. Or did you? Did it make it better that he was my boyfriend? Did it turn you on that I was right there? Down the hall? In his fucking bedroom? Did that make you hotter, Joey?"

Joey looked at his toes.

"*You* didn't love him, Joey. *I* did. The worst of it is, you knew that."

"Why are you doing this now, Catherine?"

"Because I'm sick of being mad at you. Because I don't want to still be mad at you when—" She stopped herself.

"When I die."

"No," Catherine said, shaking her head.

"That's what you meant to say. You don't want to be mad at me when I'm dead. And I'm supposed to make everything all right. Bless you, my child. Right? Well, you know what? Fuck you. OK, Cat? Fuck you. Just fuck all of you."

Catherine walked home that night even though it was a bad hour and a not-so-good neighborhood. She didn't bother with any of the how-to-not-get-mugged rules—walk fast down the middle of the street if there isn't any traffic, head up. If she did get mugged she figured she had it in her to fight off anybody. Had he been there, Joey would have joked, "Cat, the mood you're in, you could kill a small village of pygmies."

Damn It came out from behind a pile of clothes in the closet and rubbed up against Catherine's legs when she got back to her apartment. *Citizen Kane* was on and Catherine made herself some popcorn and sprinkled

Parmesan cheese over it and curled up in her pull-out bed and thought, This isn't so bad. Damn It was beside her, licking bits of salted cheese from the tips of her fingers. I don't need to call Daniel or Joey or Michael. I've got a cat and my roof is not leaking. She even thought of ordering a pizza for the hell of it—her own kind, with Canadian bacon and onions—nothing with pepperoni the way Daniel liked, or green peppers the way Michael liked, or mushrooms the way Joey liked. But she stayed in bed beside Damn It instead, and shouted out "Rosebud" at crucial points in the movie, the way Joey used to do sometimes when he worked on Crotchcough's page. Then it was Christmas Eve and Orson Welles was in his office with his friend and they poured themselves a drink.

"Toast to love on my terms," Catherine said along with Orson. "Those are the only terms anybody ever knows. Their own."

A fight was brewing in Accessories. One of the assistants had forgotten to bring an iron to one of the photo sessions and a towel showed up wrinkled in the pictures. Then that same assistant lost a poodle. They had been doing a shoot using a poodle and the poodle got away. Catherine saw the girl around the halls, whispering, "Here, baby. Come here, baby" (they had forgotten to name the dog), and posting up Xeroxed sheets reading "Lost! One White Poodle from Accessories."

The following weekend Catherine did not go to the hospital to visit Joey. She went to Melissa Wicker's going-away party on the Upper East Side instead.

She hadn't known Michael would be there, and when she got home after the party she wasn't at all surprised to see him standing on the steps outside her apartment building, waiting for her.

"I needed to see you," he said. It came out half-whispered. He cleared his throat and said it again.

"So you know," she said. "You know about Joey?"

She walked up the steps towards him and he took her in his arms. He had changed his cologne, and now he smelled like one of the foldout scratch-and-sniff ads on the men's page of *Women*.

She looked up so that her mouth was near his.

"Oh, Cat," he whispered into her mouth.

It was the first time in a long time that she wanted to fall asleep. There in his arms, she realized how tired she really was. She breathed in his breath. Was the virus in the saliva? She moved to kiss him and opened his mouth with her tongue.

"Take me upstairs," she whispered.

He moved away from her and stepped down. He ran his hand through his hair as he paced up and down a square of pavement.

"I don't do sex anymore, Cat,"

"I'm not lunch," she laughed. "We'll be careful."

For the first time she saw how tired he looked. She had read in *The Wall Street Journal* that he had replaced his boss, and after a particularly successful leveraged buyout, he was quoted as saying, "It's a simple formula, 'Fear and greed. Fear and greed.' "

"I suppose I could have it," he said.

"I don't care," she said.

He stopped. "Don't say that."

"I know." Staring down at the cars parked fender to fender on Seventy-eighth, she wished she could sit in one. Just sit in a parked car for a while, maybe with the radio on. Then she would start the car, take it to an automatic car wash, cry during the rinse.

"I talk to you sometimes," she said, holding on to the top of the iron gate. "In the shower. When I'm getting dressed."

She closed her eyes and thought about the time he had given her the necklace made of fake diamonds. They had, after all, looked real enough in moonlight.

He stepped towards her and drew her to him. "And what do I say back?"

She opened her eyes. "You laugh at all my jokes. You say, 'Yeah. I think about you, too.' "

"I still like to hear you."

"You know the stuff that makes fireflies light up? When we made love, that's the way I felt afterwards—like a firefly."

He took one step down. And then another.

"Sweet Cat," he whispered. "You're my princess. You'll always be my princess." He brushed her bottom lip with the tips of his fingers, then he turned and walked away, lifting his right hand in a wave, without looking back.

Word had gotten out about Joey at *Women,* and Howard was spraying down all the phones with Lysol and making everyone in the Art Department throw out all the coffee mugs. At noon one day, Catherine was interviewing a model when she heard George in the conference room next door, talking to his doctor.

Catherine wondered if she had AIDS, and she wondered if Michael had it.

The model-turned-actress was eating carrots sprinkled with Sweet'N Low. Brunch. Her pet snake, Mephisto, slept curled up inside a Louis Vuitton bag at her feet. The model had recently made Page Six in the *Post* because she had worn a plastic grocery bag as an evening purse to an Yves Saint Laurent show at Area. Tom Cruise had been her escort. Her hair was cornrowed. The model had just told Catherine that that had taken six hours, but that it had been fun. Catherine asked her what she had learned since she had moved to New York two years ago. The model seemed perplexed. Then she looked at Catherine very seriously.

"I really really know how to put on makeup now," she said.

Catherine watched to see if the model might laugh but she didn't. She picked up another carrot and eyed it suspiciously.

"What do you think?" Catherine heard Howard say in the next room. He sounded urgent now. A white poodle ran down the hall. Accessories followed, whispering, "Here, Baby, come here, boy."

"Isn't there a way I can get tested?" Howard said.

"I might have to work on my pectorals pretty soon, too," the model suddenly blurted out. It was as though she were making a confession. As though she were finally admitting something everyone wanted to know. Catherine nodded as though she were the priest. The model leaned forward with her carrot and whispered, "They say that's the first to go."

On a three-by-five index card without the lines, Catherine wrote "Love him." She put the card in her purse and took a cab to Lenox Hill.

Walking through the hospital, she passed waiting rooms filled with women—women with their shoes off, women reading pamphlets on tumors and postoperative care, women reading back issues of *Women,* women asleep, women praying, their heads in their hands, women biting the edges of their Styrofoam cups while talking to other women.

There were hardly any men in these waiting rooms where phone calls carried the news of survival or death. There were mostly just women there. Women who waited.

During the days before her father died, a doctor had come by every morning and used a stethoscope to listen to her father's heart. Then, always impatiently, the doctor would fling the instrument over his right shoulder as though it were a scarf, and he would bend down, putting his ear directly over her father's bare chest. He would move his head a bit to the left or to the right until he had found the sound he had been tracking down. Meanwhile, everyone in the room—Catherine, her mother, a nurse—would not make a sound, slowing their own breathing even, as though they were all together listening, waiting to hear the sound that meant her father was still alive.

That was the thing about hospitals. The only thing you could do was listen and wait.

Catherine slipped into the hospital chapel with the prayer card and saw Joey there, in the second pew, his IV in the aisle.

He was wearing a pink dressing gown. There was no one else there.

He smiled at Catherine as she sat down next to him. They were quiet for a while. Joey stared ahead at a wooden cross behind the altar. Catherine was glad there wasn't a bearded Jesus hanging from it.

"Been drinking your energy drinks?" Catherine asked.

"Yeah," Joey said. "I call 'em scotch-and-sodas."

Catherine looked away from the cross. His face was even thinner than before.

There was so much that she did not know about Joey. That time she had seen him inside a bar on Christopher Street drinking with two thugs in leather, it was as though he had been another person altogether, a person she couldn't even begin to understand.

She wondered then, sitting in the church pew beside Joey, if you could ever really understand those you love.

How to Know Someone. Follow them around all day, every day, until you realize you never knew them.

How to Keep Loving Your Best Friend after You've Hated Him. Just do.

"You know what I'd like to do?" Joey said. "I'd like to strike a deal with God. God, I'd say. I swear I'll never have sex again. Just let me live. If I could just have my life back."

He looked down at his hands. He petted the maroon-colored fur on the cuffs of his dressing gown. Then he looked at Catherine. His eyes were glassy and a little red.

"I'm sorry, Cat. I'm really sorry."

Catherine touched his lips with her finger, then put her arm around his back. She could feel his rib cage.

Somewhere down the hall someone was watching reruns of "Mr. Ed." Absentmindedly, Joey sang, " 'A horse is a horse, of course.' What's the rest? Remorse?" His voice echoed in the chapel.

How to, how to, how to, she thought. How to Keep from Being Scared. Turn a light on. Close the closet door. Have your mother read you a bedtime story. How to Keep from Feeling Lost. Buy a map. Stamp it with *You Are Here.* How to Keep from Crying. Put a piece of bread in your mouth. Chop an onion near cold running water. How to Keep the Nightmares from Creeping into the Day. Plug in a night-light.

"Who knows why I do things?" he said. "I was at my aunt's house in Nacogdoches one summer when I was about nine. She left me with some cans of spray paint and when she came back, I'd spray-painted her pecan tree silver. 'What the hell you do that for?' she says to me. 'I don't know,' I said. And I really don't know why, Cat. I just wanted to change the color. I wanted to see what a tree looked like in silver."

"I don't think I really loved him anyway." Catherine took a deep breath. "I loved that he liked what I said, or maybe what I wore. Some days it was my hair. When I finally told him that I loved him, it was more like something I wanted. It wasn't really how I felt about him. I might as well have been saying, 'Let's get the car washed.' Or 'Yeah, let's have some wine with lunch.' "

"You're exaggerating."

"Maybe, but how can you stay in love with a man once you've had his abortion?"

A woman came in and sat in a pew across the aisle from them. She held a pamphlet called *Christ and Cancer.*

"Tell me what you want," Catherine said.

"I wouldn't mind being on the I-10 to New Orleans. Ever been to

Mardi Gras?"

Catherine shook her head.

"Well, shit, Cat. You never showed your tits at Mardi Gras?"

The woman with the pamphlet got up and left.

"Was it my breath?" Joey asked.

Catherine smiled and took his hands. They were cool and bony and his skin was as delicate as a moth's wing.

"Sometimes I think it would do me some good to stand in front of an elephant, but it would just be too real," he said.

Catherine pressed her forehead on his shoulder.

"You're such a good friend," he said. "It's a shame we can't grow to be old friends."

Catherine did not want to lift her head because she didn't want Joey to see her crying. She thought of everything she still had to do for him. She hadn't brought him a box of chocolates yet—the kind he liked from Bloomingdale's. She wished they had more pictures of each other. She would have made him a scrapbook to look through. Nothing seemed enough. She tried to think of people to call, but she wasn't sure whom he wanted to see and whom he didn't.

Joey hummed the beginning of the "Mr. Ed" song and rocked Catherine back and forth.

"See the sea gulls?" he said.

Catherine looked up. Joey had his eyes closed.

"Yeah?" she said. She still had the prayer card in her other hand and she slipped it under the cushion where they sat.

"Let's feed them," he said. "Let's throw them some bread."

They were watching *Breakfast at Tiffany's* late one Friday afternoon when Michael came into Joey's hospital room with a bag of oatmeal cookies from a health-food store and a dozen red roses.

"They say oatmeal's good," he said.

Catherine stood up to go.

"No," Michael said. He looked at Joey and then at the roses. "I mean, stay." She nodded and sat back down while Michael brought another chair around to the other side of Joey's bed.

"Bet they're better than what Cat made," Joey said. He winked at Catherine and opened the bag of cookies. He took one out, looked at it, then set it on his nightstand. "We're trying to learn her how to cook."

Michael smiled.

"You've put on weight," Joey said.

"If you don't eat, everybody thinks you've got it," Michael said. Then he looked at the guardrail. "Sorry."

Joey shrugged. A new nurse came in.

"Where's Alma Jean?" Joey wanted to know.

"Lucky enough to have tonight off."

"This is a famous man before you," Michael said. Joey and Catherine looked at one another and then at Michael. "He works for Warhol. He and Andy, they're like this." Michael crossed two fingers.

"No kidding?" the nurse said. She was taking Joey's blood pressure. "Can I have your autograph?"

Joey laughed and only realized she was serious when she gave him her prescription pad on which to write. He took the pad. The nurse took a cap off the pen in her pocket and gave that to him, too. He was smiling as he pressed the pen to the pad. He made a motion to start, but then he looked up. He wasn't smiling. He was crying.

"I," he said, swallowing hard. He looked at Catherine, then at Michael. "I can't remember how to spell my name."

That day it didn't seem right to just leave, but Michael had left, the movie was over, and visiting hours were up.

"I could sleep here, you know."

Joey looked across at Scott's old bed.

"You don't want to do that."

Catherine nodded absently.

"OK." Catherine put her hands on her lap as if to rise. Then they looked at each other and she couldn't move.

"Say good night, Catherine."

She wanted to hug him but he bruised too easily now.

"I can feel my lower lip again, you know. It's not numb anymore." She stood up to kiss him, but he stopped her.

"Wait," he said.

He took a Kleenex from the box on the nightstand and laid it over his lips. "OK," he said, the Kleenex moving as he spoke.

Catherine shook her head. She took the Kleenex away and then she put her lips to his for what would be their first and last good-night kiss.

Chapter 11

Learning to Breathe

At the airport in Dallas, Catherine contemplated the look on her mother's face as her mother approached her. Catherine felt like an accident victim found lying by the side of the road, looking into a stranger's face, trying to figure out how bad off she was.

"Poor thing," her mother said as they hugged. She could feel her mother's nose on her neck. "Where did you get that horrible suit? You look like a pea. You're emaciated and you don't even have any decent perfume. You need some B vitamins in you. What did you do to your hair?"

Catherine quickly ran her hand through her hair. Hair and Makeup had seen her in the elevator going up one Friday afternoon and they told her her ends were damaged.

"And what are we going to do about your roots?" Hair had said, glaring at the top of her head. He shook his head and clucked his tongue. "Your poor ends."

She went to their salon on Fifth Avenue and Hair cut away the last two bleach jobs Joey had given her while Makeup went on about craft fairs.

"Cows are in. So are dogs, but for the life of me I can't find a mouse."

Meanwhile Catherine sat and read back issues of *Women,* looking for something—a recipe, maybe—on how to keep on going after a friend dies, or a step-by-step approach on how to be when you feel alone.

"Just keep cutting," she had said, as they droned on about vases and kitchen tiles.

"It dries easy," Catherine said to her mother, who held out a very large, brown vitamin pill. Catherine took the pill.

"The only good thing about grief is you lose a lot of weight. When your father died I lost twenty-five pounds. Couldn't eat a thing. I looked like you—like I had the flu."

"Good to see you too, Ma."

"Would you rather I lie and tell you you look great?" Catherine's mother picked up Catherine's carryon, and Catherine followed her to their connecting flight. "Never trust a woman who tells you you look great," her mother yelled over her shoulder. "It just means she wants to be your friend."

On the plane they both drank two scotch whiskeys and talked about the full moon perched on the tip of the wing outside.

"Maybe Chloe's howling at it right now," her mother said.

"You've got dog on the brain, Ma," Catherine said.

Her mother looked at her. "Have another drink."

"One up here is like two down there."

"It'll do you good."

Catherine went to the ladies' room and as she waited, she overheard a mother talking to her daughter inside.

"You know why I bring you in here? Because you're such a pretty little thing someone might come and take you away from me."

Catherine moved closer towards the door. She wanted to knock on that door right above the OCCUPIED sign and say, That's right, lady. Don't let anybody take away what you love.

"I just want to sleep forever," Catherine told her mother when she got back to her seat.

"Here," her mother said. She moved to the empty seat across the aisle. A man beside her had stretched out, so Catherine's mother slapped at his feet.

"Ma," Catherine whispered.

"Well, it's just not fair," her mother said. She was being loud now, but Catherine was too tired to care what anybody thought. Everybody in aisles six through nine was looking. "It's not fair that he should have all that when we have just what we have."

The man struggled up from his seat, looking annoyed.

"My daughter needs rest. Just look at her." The man looked at Catherine's mother and at Catherine, then he straightened up, gathered his pillow and blanket, and moved to the smoking section.

Catherine got a blanket and stretched out.

Her mother had won two tickets to Maui in a raffle at a hospital benefit in Barrington. A friend had a condominium in Maui and had made arrangements for them to stay there, though he had been unable to join them; he was at an Alzheimer's convention in Munich, and as Catherine's mother had explained, it was a very big deal.

At first Catherine thought July was a silly time to go to Hawaii. But then again it was midsummer and even on days when it got into the nineties, Catherine couldn't seem to get warm.

Everyone kept saying he had passed. Joey has passed, Alma Jean had said. Sorry about Joey's passing, Howard had said. *Passed.* It was the wrong word and Catherine wanted to edit it out of everybody's mouth. You pass gallstones. You pass bread. You pass out, but you don't pass into death. You die.

Alma Jean had held her the day Catherine came to collect his things.

Some clothes. His ostrich-feathered negligee.

"There will be times like these," Alma Jean had said. "There will be times when you feel like you're just not breathing right."

Catherine couldn't see the moon outside the window of the plane anymore, but for a moment she thought she saw her father through the curtains in first class. His hair was grey-blond and thinning and he had a wonderfully tailored grey suit on, the thin stripes matching up at the seams on his broad shoulders. She wanted to talk to him. She wanted to sit down next to him and touch him, maybe hold his hand.

But then the man in first class got up and Catherine saw that he was not her father after all. It was a close resemblance, an honest mistake, and even though she knew now that he was not her father, she still wanted to sit next to him, to be near him. It would be something, at least, she thought, just to share a drink up in the sky with a man who looked like your dead father. She would tap him on the back and say, Would you mind? Would you mind buying me a drink and holding my hand for a minute while I catch my breath?

"Turn after the bamboo grocery store, not before," her mother said.

They had rented a car with an *I Survived the Road to Hana* sticker on the bumper and Catherine drove while her mother sat in the passenger's seat reading the directions from a piece of lime green stationery.

The village of Lahaina was all bougainvillea and sunlight, pink stucco T-shirt shops and shell jewelry. They stopped at the grocery store, a little wooden shack with furry fruit in Produce.

"Not that one," Catherine said, taking a cantaloupe from her mother. She pressed the ends of another one and handed it to her. "This one's ripe."

Her mother stood holding the cantaloupe.

"Don't look at me like that," Catherine said. "You learn things."

Their cabana was a one-bedroom and they were both appalled at the wallpaper—oversized hibiscus flowers. Catherine's mother plopped down on the green vinyl sofa.

"Everything made in the sixties should be destroyed," her mother said. "I feel like a frog on a lily pad."

"I'm gonna go for a swim," Catherine said.

"Fine," her mother said. "I'm going to pray."

That night Catherine stood beside her mother at the bathroom sink as they flossed their teeth.

"Look," Catherine said. "See where my wisdom teeth were?"

"Oh, Catherine."

"Come on, just look." Catherine opened her mouth wide and moved the corners of her lips out. She moved towards her mother.

Her mother grabbed a fingerful of Pacquin's and shook her head. "Juliana of Norwich is waiting for me," she said. "I'm going to bed."

Her mother belonged to a women's literary club which met once a month. Everyone had to write a paper and read it out loud once every three years—the price of being in the club. One woman wrote about her dog and its long lineage.

"That dog is more American than I am," Catherine's mother had said when she spoke to Catherine after that particular meeting. The woman had traced Pippin back to the *Mayflower*.

Another woman wrote about the history of women's underwear.

"Can you imagine?" her mother had said after the meeting that month. "I sat there for two hours to hear about corsets."

Catherine's mother was due to read her paper in a month. She wanted to write about Juliana of Norwich, an obscure fourteenth-century mystic who lived alone and claimed to see the seven bleeding wounds of Christ.

"She called them showings," her mother said. She was on the floor doing sit-ups. "Seventeen. Eighteen. This is horrible." Hibiscus flowers dripped down the walls. Catherine opened the sliding door and pulled the screen. She could smell the ocean from where she stood.

"Twenty," her mother said. "And one for the Dipper."

"That's Gipper."

"Whatever," her mother said, getting into bed. "Showings. Not visions. Isn't that disgusting?"

"That's a pretty nightgown," Catherine said.

"Thanks. I got it when I had my hysterectomy."

Catherine shut off the light. So that is what women do when they are in pain, Catherine thought, climbing into bed. They buy themselves pretty nightgowns, another shade of lipstick, maybe a big fur hat. Catherine and her mother lay there in their separate beds listening to the waves break. There was another bedroom, but Catherine had wanted to hear the ocean. She was almost asleep when she heard her mother get up.

"Close the bathroom door, from now on, Catherine. It feels like I'm sleeping with the toilet. You're just like your father."

They ate papaya for breakfast and talked about movies Catherine's mother had never heard of. Then they took a walk along the beach—a stretch of sand that only went for about a quarter of a mile east and west.

"There's some good shells," Catherine said.

"There *are* good shells," her mother corrected her. "They look better wet."

Catherine bent to pick a black stone up and dipped it into a wave until all the sand was off.

"My stomach feels like an upside-down soup plate," her mother said. "Why can't I be tall and slim like you?"

"Ma. You look great."

"Must you do this "Ma" thing with me? It sounds so Jewish."

"Well, that's logical."

"Part. Only part. And if the Nazis come back, it's the part that doesn't count. You'll be safe."

"Thanks. I feel a whole lot better."

"I've started dating again," her mother said.

Catherine straightened up. "What do you mean? Dating whom?"

"Well. To start with, John."

"John Hadley?"

Everybody in Barrington knew about John Hadley. He had lost four cars in one month. He would park one and then forget where it was. Once, his nephew found one of them—a Mercedes—in front of the Baha'i Temple with a thousand dollars' worth of parking tickets on it.

John Hadley had Alzheimer's.

"It's not so bad, really," her mother said. "Sometimes it's funny. Once he called me Robin. I said, 'No. I'm Jenny.' And you know what he said? He said, 'Robin's a pretty name.' Just like that. He said, 'Robin's a pretty name.' "

Her mother's eyes closed as she laughed.

"You should see him with Chloe. He touches her nose and says, 'Oh, Chloe. You clever thing. Your nose matches your fur.' As if Chloe thought that up all herself."

"I don't believe this," Catherine said.

"Look," her mother said after a while. "I'd like to enjoy myself for once in my life, OK?" They had come to the end of their part of the beach, where the sand became rocks. Parents were setting up chaises and opening up best-sellers. One older, balding man stood up and waved at Catherine and her mother. Catherine's mother waved back. Two children shouted from the ocean.

"Open your eyes," a little boy shouted to his sister. "It doesn't hurt. It's only salt."

Catherine and her mother turned to walk back. They stood, looking out towards the ocean—towards Honolulu.

"I just got so damned tired of priests feeling sorry for themselves and feeling alone and alienated. It's so negative. I needed to get out." Catherine's mother looked out at the water. "And I'm not going to spend the rest of my life waiting around for you to come home."

For lunch they ate raw tuna sushi-style, not because either one of them particularly liked it, but because neither one of them wanted to cook.

That night they went to a luau on Pineapple Hill. A Polynesian couple stood outside, giving everyone who paid a shell necklace.

"It's a little much," her mother said as the man put the necklace around her neck. Catherine's mother took it off and gave it back to him. "I'm just not the shell type."

They sat down and got a free mai-tai—a watery, sweet, red thing with a lot of crushed ice. The master of ceremonies made everyone stand up and toast the beautiful Hawaiian sunset. Catherine's mother got into a brief argument with the father of a fat family who accidently grabbed her drink.

The sky was lit up with golds and oranges and they watched as the orange spread across the sky. It deepened, then turned to red. A man with a knife in his mouth climbed a tree in his bare feet. Her mother sighed and said she guessed it really was beautiful.

Later, during the Polynesian love dance, a man with a camera came to their table and asked Catherine's mother if she would like a picture of herself with her son.

"That's my daughter," her mother said.

"Oh," the man said, looking at Catherine.

The man put a lei around her mother's neck.

"Eeew," her mother said, stretching her neck so that her face wouldn't touch the fake hibiscus flowers on the lei. "It's been around all those people. I might get AIDS."

The man laughed.

Catherine impatiently pulled the lei off her mother, and tossed it on the table.

"Say *Maui*," the photographer said.

"Maui."

The light flashed, the photographer took the lei, and he moved on to the next couple.

"What about our picture?"

"I guess he comes back," Catherine said. They sat back down.

"You shouldn't have worn those earrings. They're pulling at your lobes."

Catherine picked at the ambrosia on her plate.

"Why did you do that to your hair? It was prettier long."

"Lay off, Ma," Catherine said. She sang it, so no one would look up from their plates.

"We should get that picture of us together," her mother said. "We don't have any of us together since your father died."

"Please don't start with Dad."

"I'm only thinking of my Christmas cards."

"It's July."

"Well, at least you've got your months straight."

Catherine watched a man on stage eating fire.

"When are you going to stop picking on me, Ma?"

"When you stop "Ma'ing" me. Why is it that everyone blames the mother anyway? They say, 'Oh, look at her, her mother must have been crazy.' I'm sick of everything being my fault. Pretty soon I'll be responsible for global warming."

The man who had climbed the tree was now onstage swallowing swords.

"You never ask about me," Catherine said. She was stirring the melted ice in her mai-tai. "You never say, 'So how's it going, Catherine? Are you OK?' "

"That's because you're always fine. You're just like your father."

"Yeah. And look where he is."

"Catherine."

Chocolate-skinned women in grass skirts wiggled around the man who had four, now five swords down his throat. Catherine wanted to cry.

The photographer reappeared between them and shined a flashlight on the picture of them, which he had put inside a white cardboard frame with *Maui Luau* engraved at the bottom in gold.

The red lei almost buried Catherine's face. She had her all-teeth smile on but her eyes were wide open, which meant she wasn't really smiling. The sun from their first day there lit up her mother's face.

"God, I'm ugly," her mother said.

The photographer wanted thirty-five dollars.

"Forget it," Catherine said.

"But we don't have any pictures of us together," her mother said.

"I don't care. Nobody should spend thirty-five dollars for a Polaroid."

"Were you ever by any chance a professional dancer?"

Catherine and her mother looked up. It was the balding man from the beach. The one who had waved. Catherine's mother coughed.

"Don't be silly," she said.

The photographer took the Polaroid away from Catherine and moved on to the next table. Catherine saw that tourists were dancing next to the Polynesians in grass skirts.

"Would you like to dance?" Baldy said, holding out his hand.

"I suppose any fool can dance to this," her mother said.

"It'll feel weird at first," Kimberly said. Kimberly was Catherine's scuba instructor. "But just stay calm."

Catherine was sitting by the edge of the pool with an oxygen tank on her back. Her feet were fitted inside fins that kept floating to the surface of the water. She was wondering now if it had been such a good idea to sign up for scuba diving lessons at the visitors' center in town that morning. But her mother had kept on about Juliana of Norwich, Chloe, and the dance with the balding man from the beach.

Catherine recognized some of the people around the pool. The man from the luau was there with his fat family—his children floated face down on the surface of the water, aiming their snorkel pipes at those near the side of the pool. Their father yelled, but they pretended not to hear.

"When we go under, I'm going to ask you questions," Kimberly said. She used Catherine as her partner. She pointed to Catherine and made an OK sign.

"Are you OK?" she said. "That's what that means, OK, everybody? I'll check your tank for you." Kimberly checked Catherine's tank. "You look OK to me," she said. Everyone laughed a little. She turned to Catherine and made the OK sign again. She looked at Catherine while she was doing it.

"Are you OK? Now make the OK sign. Make it. Go on. You have to check your tank and make the OK sign before I can go on."

Catherine looked at her monitor. She looked at Kimberly. She didn't know what any of the numbers meant.

"Go on," Kimberly whispered.

When Catherine got back to the cabana, her mother was on the green sofa, reading.

Catherine squeezed oranges for orange juice. Her mother's vitamins were lined up alphabetically near the refrigerator. When her mother looked at her, Catherine pointed to her and made the OK sign.

"That means 'Are you OK?' "

"You got that for ten dollars?"

"I know how to work oxygen."

"It took a lesson?"

"Do you mind if I go out this afternoon? They're having a scuba dive and I want to try."

"If you're careful."

"What will you do?"

"Walk. Read. Pray. It'll do us both good."

Catherine met up with Kimberly and her crew on Kapalua Bay. They waded out into the ocean and climbed aboard the *Seasmoke*. There were eight of them and they motored out to a coral reef near Lanai.

The equipment seemed heavier than it had been poolside, and on the boat, Catherine felt awkward and dumpy with her fins and the tanks and all those buckles and weights around her waist. She dropped herself into the water fins first and struggled there on the surface. It was an effort to keep her head above water. As she clung to the orange rope that went all the way down, she wondered why she wasn't sinking.

She couldn't get her respirator in her mouth and the water kept flooding her mask. Kimberly was busy helping somebody with a loose buckle. One woman changed her mind at the last minute and climbed back up onto the *Seasmoke*. That's what I'll do, Catherine thought, as she began dragging herself back along the rope. I'll climb back aboard, get a drink, and watch the waves. But then she came face-to-face with Kimberly, who checked her oxygen tank for the third time and said *OK?* Catherine nodded, turned, and headed back towards the other end of the rope that would lead them all down.

As they descended, Catherine held her nose and blew to depressurize her ears the way Kimberly had taught them. They dropped quickly, farther and farther down.

It didn't get darker. The blue light turned their skin to a translucent white the color of Madonna's on good days. Catherine was able to see more than she ever expected. Everything was a pastel—yellows, pinks, reds, blues.

This was what At Home was always trying for when they redecorated all those apartments.

They swam through a school of yellow sunfish and when Catherine reached out to touch one, it scooted away. It was the first time in a long time Catherine had felt warm, and she wanted to smile, but when she did her respirator almost fell out.

Kimberly's hair flowed out soft around her face. In the light her body looked longer and she moved gracefully, checking the air on everyone's tanks.

Catherine couldn't believe all the fish. She wished she had brought down one of the charts aboard the *Seasmoke*. She wanted to say something. She wanted to shout, but she could only bite down on her respirator and point. Everyone was swimming ahead of her—they were better with their fins than she was. An eel passed and, overcome, Catherine clapped. A heavy, mute, underwater clap.

In Manhattan on the days she had walked to Lenox Hill to visit Joey, Catherine had passed the Clinic for Speech and Hearing. Old men came out wearing new hearing aids clamped around their ears and young boys and girls stood on the stoop talking in sign, their fingers dancing out in front of them. Catherine wondered if the deaf didn't get terribly tired moving their arms about to get even the smallest point across. It always seemed to take so many gestures just to say "I want something to eat" or "I think you're swell." It was like aerobics. The deaf must have a lot of energy, Catherine decided.

Before Joey had stopped talking, he called her late one night. She was at work, waiting on a call from L.A. A woman in P.R. was getting back to her to tell her the name of Lily Tomlin's dog. Catherine needed it for a caption. So far she only had "Tomlin makes like a space hero searching for signs of intelligent life in the universe with her pup, blank."

"I knew you would be there," Joey had said. His words came out slowly and carefully. He told her there was something he had wanted to tell her, but now he had forgotten. He laughed and so did she and they waited for a long time, hoping it would come back to him.

When Joey couldn't talk anymore, Catherine considered learning and teaching him sign. Anything was possible. She had gone out with an Ear-and-Throat doctor once and after dinner, he had showed her pictures of some of his patients—men without jaws who had learned to eat and speak (electronically) through holes in their throats.

But then she realized talking in sign took too much. The best Joey could do was point, his nails painted in Passion Plum, flashing towards the bathroom or the clock. When he wanted to laugh, he would raise an eyebrow and smile.

Some nights she would lie awake at night, wondering what Joey had wanted to say that night he had called. She wondered if it had been important. When she had last told her father that she loved him, he had been druggy and he might not have heard because all he said then was that he had a taste in his mouth for peanut butter. That had been the day of his bypass surgery, the day that he had died. A nurse had rolled him away, he had given Catherine the thumbs-up sign, the elevator doors had shut, and Catherine had been left alone watching the numbers light up as her father ascended.

With Joey, she had been careful to tell him everything she could think of. Every day she sat next to his bed, pulled the bed rail between them down, and told him things. That Cher had worn braces in her thirties. That Mariel Hemingway said "Shit" a lot and didn't eat meat. That Michael Jackson watched TV in the dark in the middle of the day.

She was afraid at times to look away. She thought if she did, he would be gone when she turned back.

After his third seizure, Joey reached across the bed one Sunday afternoon and touched Catherine's arm. She thought he had remembered just then what it was he wanted to say, but she couldn't be sure and she didn't want to go filling up the air between them with sounds and questions like What? What is it? He couldn't talk. He was losing his eyesight and she could tell he was trying to focus on her face. So she just looked at him, and tried to hear with her eyes.

He patted her arm then. We'll be OK, she thought his eyes said. We'll be OK.

Catherine stood in front of an underwater cave that was about the size of her apartment in New York. But this place had a view. There was a whole cliff of color.

She had read somewhere that when you die, not all of you dies at once. Some cells live on. She remembered pictures in books of people's souls coming out of their mouths as they slept. Breathing in from her respirator, Catherine tried to imagine that she was breathing in the souls of her father and of Joey.

There wasn't much left of him the morning he died. But at 6:02, four hours before he left her, Joey had said her name. He took a deep breath and when her name came out of his mouth it was loud and uneven. He sounded retarded. She couldn't help but wonder why he had gone through all that effort just to say her name. She held his hand. She said, "Yes, Joey, I'm here." His eyes were the only thing alive on him and in them, Catherine saw nothing but terror.

Catherine readjusted her respirator. She felt, then and there, in front of that coral reef, that Joey was still alive—still breathing—there underwater near her. Close by.

And it was good. For the first time in a long time, Catherine stopped thinking about Joey in his hospital bed. She thought about Joey in his red sequined dress. She thought about him dancing. She thought about his hair pinned up with Donald Duck barrettes. She thought about the high points— when it was October and they were working on March, when Michael held her that night after she had gotten lost in Tijuana and she held him the way he said he had always wanted to be held—the way Ryan O'Neal held Ali

McGraw in the hospital bed in *Love Story*. That was the high point—when he kissed her that night under the Manhattan Bridge, when Joey taught her how to dance in heels and the three of them—Michael, Joey, Catherine—sat in Michael's living room listening to ABC, making up an imaginary time capsule, and Joey put his arms round them and made the toast to them and to Andy Warhol and the whole world seemed no older than twenty-nine and death was farther from Manhattan than Barrington, Illinois, was. That was the high point. When Joey was still alive.

The day he died, her apartment seemed so small. She came back from the hospital and she looked out the window. Everybody's windows were closed.

She went up to the roof looking for Motek, but he wasn't there. She had watched her father die. She had watched her friend die. She had put her hand on Lewis Lipman's coffin. What does a person do with all this death? She stood near the ledge and stared past the park and the hospital. She couldn't remember any street names. She didn't recognize any of the buildings. She stood there staring out at the city, not seeing a thing.

Kimberly was holding Catherine's monitor and making the hand signals. *Are you OK?* She kept pointing to Catherine and making the OK sign. Catherine could see every tendon in Kimberly's fingers as she tried to make her hands shout.

Catherine nodded. Kimberly shook her head and did the hand signal again. Catherine had to play her part. She was supposed to make the OK sign back.

If it was possible to cry inside a mask, Catherine would have then. But it seemed silly to cry underwater. Redundant.

Kimberly showed Catherine her oxygen gauge. It read 350. When it hit 500 you were supposed to go up. Kimberly had said that people used oxygen differently. That sometimes, when you're scared, for instance, you tended to breathe faster.

Kimberly pointed up. Catherine shook her head. She didn't want to go back up. She never wanted to go back up. She wanted to stay down here where the light was soft and didn't hurt her eyes. Where the water made her oxygen tanks and the heavy weights around her waist weightless, where there weren't any smells of rubbing alcohol or vomit or human feces, and where sound was only so many bubbles that you could see and hear and be sure of.

Kimberly reached behind her own tank where there was an extra respirator. She held onto Catherine's respirator. Catherine bit down. Kimberly nodded and then she made the switch.

At first Catherine was terrified. Tasting all that salt water, she realized that she was breathing down here, underwater where she shouldn't be. Where nobody should be. But Kimberly stood there in front of her, so calm, looking into Catherine's eyes, nodding, breathing with her, so Catherine could get back in sync. Slow it down. Breathe along with her. Slow, calm.

Kimberly nodded and when she smiled, her respirator didn't even fall out.

Kimberly did the *Are you OK?* question again with her hands. Catherine looked back at her through her foggy mask. Kimberly signed again. And then Catherine lifted her own hands.

She met up with her mother that evening under the banyan tree. It was the oldest tree in Lahaina and wooden stilts had been built to hold up the heavier branches. They sat at a table there and drank Diet Cokes while they decided what to do about dinner. All around them tendrils hung down from the tree branches, rooting into the ground, becoming independent of the mother tree.

The late afternoon light shone through the tree's leaves while two Hawaiian bums stood in a triangle of sunlight, picking through people's leftover Burger King boxes.

"Mom?" Catherine could hear herself whispering. She heard her voice as though for the first time in a long time and it sounded old to her. "Do you regret anything?"

Her mother looked past Catherine, out towards the ocean.

"I regret that I didn't get your father to buy that acre and a half in back of us when we could have and that we didn't get the tuna for dinner tonight."

There had been so many times when Catherine had wished she had another mother. Somebody like Ann Bartel, for instance. Somebody who would hold her and rock her and hum sweet songs. Wasn't that the way a mother from the Midwest was supposed to be?

"So you're happy otherwise."

Her mother sighed. "Sometimes I wish I could do more. I'll be at the grocery store or at one of these damned meetings and I wonder where the poetry is. I had that when your father was alive."

Her mother pointed at the concrete sidewalks that circled the banyan tree and she said she didn't think the tree appreciated that at all.

"I hope those roots crack this cement right open," her mother said.

"Do you still think about Dad?"

"He comes to me every now and then. I'll forget where I am."

Her mother had never spoken this way before. Catherine wondered if, as in an interview, she just hadn't asked the right questions.

They could smell the honeysuckle and the plumeria trees that grew all along the road.

"Your eyes look like old garden benches today," her mother said. "Under trees."

"Gee, thanks."

"You still have your father's eyes," her mother said. "I've seen them before on policemen and firemen—men who've seen infinite tragedy. They're calm, steady eyes. They'll see it through. Your father had the kindest eyes I'd ever seen—so deep-set and blue. I can't marry a man for his damned eyes, I thought. But I did."

Her mother put her arm around Catherine.

You can blame everything on New York. That was the nicest part about living there. That's what Joey had once told Catherine.

"Ma. I don't know what to do with myself anymore. I don't know how to act. I don't know what I have to go back to." Catherine could feel the tears welling up in her eyes. She realized where that expression came from just then. Welling up. As though there would be a flood and a dam would break. "I mean I have this whole black book full of names and numbers of everybody. I could call Raquel Welch right now if I wanted."

"And what would you tell them?"

"That's it. Nothing. I want to go home, Mom. I want to be back home with you. I'm sick of reading while I eat. I'm sick of living alone."

"Being single is wonderful."

"You're saying that because you think it's glamorous or something. Like I'm always wearing a bunch of scarves and shit."

"Catherine," her mother said. She sighed. "Chloe would love to have you home. She misses you so much."

Catherine looked at her.

"And you know I do, too." Her mother brushed away Catherine's bangs from her eyes. "But it's wrong. You'd be using us as an escape. You know it. I know it. You're tired right now. You're still in shock. You have a wonderful job. Make something out of it. Make something out of yourself."

"But, Mom." Catherine swallowed. "Dad's dead. My best friend died. Everyone's gone. Everyone keeps leaving."

Her mother held her, and whispered, "I'm still here."

Catherine laid her head down on her mother's shoulder. She put both her arms around her, and she could feel her mother's lips on the top of her head. "Sometimes I say what I say because I miss you so damned much," her mother said. "Know that."

Catherine nodded her head and sniffed.

"What you need is a good stiff drink and a spiritual advisor."

"Don't get started with the priests."

Her mother looked in her purse for a handkerchief and came up with a Kleenex which she had used to blot her lipstick. It had different shades of lip prints all over it. "I can already hear what one would say," Catherine said, blowing into the Kleenex. " 'Consider Christ,' he'd say. Well, you know what I have to say to that? *His* passion only lasted three hours."

Her mother considered what she had said.

"Juliana of Norwich . . ."

Catherine interrupted her.

"Don't start with her, Mom. She saw all those bleeding wounds because she lived alone for too long."

Catherine looked over towards the visitors' center. The woman was putting out the *Closed* sign.

"It's just that I'm not sure I like who I'm becoming."

"So stop becoming that person and become someone you like." Her mother shook her head. "Look. Every emotion has an end," she said. "This will run its own course, Catherine. You'll live." She took out some vitamins from her purse and pulled Catherine to her side. "Here, have some magnesium. Now turn around and look at the trees with me. They look like children who've just had their hair brushed. Very pleased with themselves. Look how pleased."

The next day Catherine and her mother swam while the whole island seemed to sleep. The water was cool, and long white pieces of ash from the sugar cane factory fell all around them. Smoke circled the caps of what Catherine and her mother called the furry mountains on shore.

"The fish can't like this," her mother said, spitting out salt water. They were standing in a shallow part of the ocean.

"It's only ash," Catherine said.

Her mother looked around at the water. "That's true."

They swam until her mother said she was too old.

They went into town and ate soyburgers at a place called MacNature's and sat near a prison wall made of coral. They bought whole coconuts, addressed them, and mailed them off to people as is just because they could. They bought blue-and-red papier-âaché parrots and straw Panama hats and they got their picture taken by a street photographer who only asked for six dollars.

Catherine stood at the counter wiping off dirt from mushrooms. Joey had taught her that. Mushrooms were like sponges and it was wrong to wash them because they soaked up all the water. Joey had known about mushrooms.

Catherine's mother was standing in a straw hat and a slip, ironing a dress near the green sofa. Outside, mice climbed up and down the sliding screen door trying to get in.

"All I'm saying is you should have called me. I mean told me," Catherine said.

"I did tell you. You just forgot."

"You did not tell me."

"You know I did."

They looked at each other and then they went back to what they were doing.

Catherine's mother had a date with the balding man from the beach. Catherine could vaguely remember her mother mentioning something about seeing him that night, but she thought that had been a dream.

"You should call that astronaut. You said yourself Fran was expecting that story when you came back."

"Just go already, would you?"

"Oh, come on, Catherine. Grow up. Tell me how I look."

She had the dress on now and she was trying to get the back hook.

Catherine let out a deep sigh and went over and hooked her mother.

"I don't like the buttons at the slit," her mother said.

"Why not?"

"They'll make a man wonder what I'm trying to do to him."

"Oh, Mom."

"I'm so ugly. I'm so fat and unattractive."

"No, you're not. You look like me."

Catherine's mother turned around to face her and they both laughed.

"Wait a minute," her mother said. She went into the bedroom and came back with a handful of expensive-looking navy blue makeup cases. "I bought these and I don't know how to use them."

Catherine thought of her mother getting talked into buying all these compacts from a pushy Estee Lauder saleswoman at Neiman Marcus. Her mother held out all the compacts towards Catherine, her hands shaking— from nerves? Old age?

Catherine started with the base.

"This won't clog your pores. It's water-based."

"I don't have any pimples to cover."

"It'll just blend in."

Her mother was shorter—Catherine's mouth was about level with her mother's nose—and Catherine crouched while she dabbed the base under her mother's eyes. Then she went on towards her cheeks and chin, her mother's skin moving every time she dabbed. She had deep wrinkles that were not unattractive, and for a moment, standing there, in front of her mother, Catherine thought of Joey, and of how he used to like doing up her hair and lending her his dresses.

She wondered how long grief took, and if there was some kind of point system. So many years for breaking up with your boyfriend. So many years for a dead husband or father. So many for a dead friend. She had read an article once that said if your husband died, you shouldn't make any major decisions for one year because you were in shock. Catherine wondered if it mattered how old you were and if young people were supposed to bounce back faster. Putting the last touches of base on her mother's face, Catherine wondered if and when losing someone got any easier.

"It does make me look livelier," her mother said.

Catherine stood off to the side while her mother looked in the bureau mirror. She turned her face from side to side.

"What about my eyes? All these women my age use all this eye stuff."

Catherine opened another compact, and with short, gentle strokes, she colored the lids of her mother's eyes.

"Hey, I got news for you," her mother said with her eyes closed. "We love each other."

"Think so?"

"You *are* my favorite child."

"I'm your only child."

"So? You can still be my favorite."

Catherine stood back. Her mother opened her eyes and blinked, getting used to what was on them. She looked in the mirror.

"Maybe you *are* learning something in that horrible city."

Catherine sat in front of the phone, waiting for the astronaut to call her back. She had put in the call an hour ago and she sat in the chair, eating the mushrooms she had made. When the phone rang, Catherine answered it "*Women* Entertainment, Catherine speaking" out of habit.

She thanked the woman for calling on such short notice. She lied, telling her *Women* was doing a piece all about the Omnimax space movie the astronaut was narrating and that *Women* readers had a lot of questions.

"Like what?" the astronaut said. She sounded tired. She sounded as though she were onto Catherine.

"Well, like, and I'm sorry to have to ask you this, but it is a very real concern." Catherine took a deep breath. These were the questions Catherine had made a living on for three years. These were the questions Fran had taught her to ask, the kinds of questions that had made the Entertainment pages more popular than the Fashion pages, the kinds of questions her mother would have told her never to ask.

"Did you ever have to compromise yourself during your career?"

"Compromise?"

Catherine cleared her throat. "To get to the moon, did you have to sleep with someone?"

"I don't need this. I'm hanging up."

"No, don't hang up. Please don't hang up." Catherine choked. She had not expected to choke. She swallowed back whatever was filling up her head.

"I'm sorry," Catherine said.

Though it was a long way off, Catherine could hear the astronaut shifting. Catherine knew she was still considering hanging up.

"Could you tell me what it's like then?" Catherine said.

"What what's like?"

"What you see. When you're there. When you're so far away from home. From Earth."

The astronaut sighed and paused. Then she started. She told Catherine about the colors of all the different countries. She told her about the darkness and all the light from the moon when it's up close.

"When you can feel that close to something you're used to seeing from this great distance, well, it changes a person."

That night Catherine dreamed that Joey came to her during a lunar eclipse. The sky cleared just after a rain and the only light was getting slowly covered up by the earth's shadow minute by minute. Joey was thin—very thin—and his eyes were bug-eyed because of his thinness. But he was well dressed in his Dead Man's clothes—charcoal slacks and a plaid shirt—and he sat down at a wrought-iron table next to Catherine and held her hand with both of his. His hands were warm, rough, and dry. But it was so nice. They talked, but in her sleep, Catherine couldn't hear what they said. She could only see them, sitting there holding hands, watching the moon get cut away, bit by bit, until at last it was just the ghost of itself.

The following morning Catherine and her mother ate the last of the papaya outside on the patio and they overheard a woman next door on her porch talking about abortion.

"I'm all pro-choice," the woman was saying. "But if it happens to my kids, I don't want to hear about it. And I sure as hell never want to have to go through with it."

"That's ridiculous," Catherine's mother said. "I would have had one, but nobody did them safely in those days. I wanted a mink coat, but I had to have you instead."

"Mom," Catherine said. "You're traumatizing me again."

Her mother leaned over to get a better look at the woman.

"She's crazy," she said, shaking her head. "If you had an abortion, I would most certainly hold your hand the whole way through."

Catherine looked at her mother and she could tell by the way her mother said it that she meant it.

"Tell me about your date," she said, giving her mother the last slice of papaya.

"It wasn't glamorous enough to be glamorous. Oh, there were white tablecloths to the floor, but you could feel the cheap plywood underneath. It was deadly. I got so bored I just stopped talking and prayed for another glass of wine."

"What about him?"

Her mother shook her head. "He was handsome in a cheap way. He looked like he went to Loyola and got all C's."

Catherine laughed and said she thought she knew what she meant.

"Well, there's one thing for sure," her mother said, putting her spoon down and stacking the papaya peels. "We've had a lot of memorable fruit here."

"Come on," Catherine said. She held out her hand to her mother. "Let's get our good cholesterol up and go for a walk. I'll tell you what the astronaut said."

Chapter 12

Salvaging

At the end of August, while everybody was on Fire Island or in the Hamptons for the weekend or for the summer, Catherine got her teeth cleaned. After the X rays, after the picking and scraping, and after the banana-flavored fluoride treatment, Dr. Panter told Catherine she had a cavity.

He wore mint-flavored gloves because, he said, nobody likes the taste or the smell of latex. She told him he was right. He spoke in a soothing Mr. Rogers voice, and each time he drilled with a new drill, he held out the device and said, "Now this is the way this will sound." And he would turn the drill on so she could hear it and get used to it and she would nod her head to let him know she was ready.

He stopped anytime she squeezed her eyes shut and it almost felt good, a nurse and a doctor hovering over her like that, looking deep inside her mouth, paying all that attention to that one decayed tooth.

"Would you like to see?" Dr. Panter asked when he put away the second, slower drill that rattled.

He brought out a mirror and held it to her face.

Her lips were speckled with bits of silver from the old filling, and when she opened her mouth, Dr. Panter told her she would have to face the light to get a better look.

What appalled her was not all that pink gum that showed where there should have been tooth, but the edges. What was left—two last remaining sides of a tooth, half a skeleton—looked dismal. She understood now why they were called cavities, and she couldn't help but worry for the rest of her.

"It looks worse than it really is," he said.

"It's hollow," she said. "There's nothing left."

"Enough to work with," Dr. Panter said, mixing the filling. "You should see some of the others I've done."

He took away the mirror and took his time packing in the filling, holding her jawbone with his other hand, making it secure and, she imagined, leakproof.

There was a place, he said, still pressing and pressing and pressing. A one-bedroom right above his office for rent.

"It's nice. My mother lived there, but she's gone now. It's rent-controlled. Three hundred and fifty a month," he said. "Interested?"

She kept her mouth open until he had taken his hands away.

"Can I have pets?" she asked when she was allowed to close. "I've got this cat. Damn It."

"Sure," Dr. Panter said. "But, Catherine. There's no need to swear."

It was August and Manhattan was in the middle of a record heat wave. Everything smelled of vomit or men's piss, but the elevator at *Women* still smelled of Christmas. Fashion was hauling around pine and holly and At Home was giving away the last of the cinnamon potpourris. Everybody was clearing the decks for the January issue.

January was always the slimmest issue. Advertisers figured everybody had spent all their money in December and most of the writers at *Women* were worn out or away on vacation. Fran had calculated that the January issue was the perfect issue for Catherine's casting-couch piece; Simpson and Howard would be desperate to print anything.

It was the month that Beauty put everybody in Readers' Service on a thigh make-over and Health and Fitness started disappearing every day at three to take naps on a cot in Personnel. It was the month that Catherine finally finished her casting-couch story, which she assumed would be her last.

She started the piece out with a quotation from a feminist author who had written *Hello, Good-bye*, a book all about people who can't commit.

"Nobody tries to work anything out anymore," she told Catherine over the phone. Fran had told Catherine not to bother doing the interview in person. Feminists weren't important enough in the eighties. "The minute something goes wrong, it's like, 'Taxi!' Sometimes I wonder if we don't have too many choices. We're a different generation because of that, but I'm not at all sure that we're better."

Then Catherine had all those quotations from men and women in the movie business, dancers, and models. "Why shouldn't I use everything I've got?" one *Vogue* model-turned-actress told Catherine. "Producers always have the prettiest girl in town, and I *am* the prettiest girl in town."

"I fucked so many men I started feeling like a piece of myself," one famous leading lady said. She had a pretty twenty-year-old face with a thirty-five-year-old neck and a flat, thirteen-year-old's body. "I gave myself away so much, there wasn't much left. You hear what I'm saying?"

"You've got to keep in mind one thing," a Martha Graham dancer said. She had bug eyes and a skinny neck made longer by her man's haircut. "Men and women never have real relationships. He's getting; you're giving. It's as simple as that."

Fran was at her desk on the phone. She had her hair up like Pat Benatar's and she was wearing Madonna gloves with holes in them.

Holding the phone between her ear and her shoulder, Fran scrawled her signature on the remaining August thank-you-for-the-interview-here's-your-copy-of-*Women* letters with a pen that had gold ink. She had found the pen at a stationery store on the West Side and she had bought twenty-five of them. She wanted to sign the very last batch of letters with something special.

Fran had finally landed a job at "Entertainment Tonight," behind the cameras. The producer she had taken to the Academy Awards had been fired. He had spent too much time away from his assignments, too much time with Fran, and after he had called her and complained about his new, unemployed status, she hung up on him, picked up the phone, called his boss, and asked for an interview.

"Who knows," Catherine overheard her say on the phone. Catherine guessed Pam was on the other end. "Maybe I'll pop up from behind the camera one day and there I'll be, right on your TV screen, my whole ethnic self."

Catherine's line was ringing, and when Catherine picked up the phone and answered, there was a long pause.

"Ms. Simpson would like to see you." It was Ms. Simpson's assistant. "Can you please come down now?"

When Catherine hung up, she thought to herself, This should be my finest hour. Fran was leaving and now Ms. Simpson was calling her down to her office to ask her, Catherine Clemons, to become the new Entertainment editor of *Women*. So why didn't Catherine feel triumphant?

Catherine looked at the nearly empty wall behind Fran's desk where she had been taking down her gold-framed celebrity photos. I should be considering my own wall of fame, Catherine thought, but the idea of one more celebrity interview made her weary. What did any actor or actress or singer really have to say that would make a difference in anybody's life?

Catherine looked at Fran, who had her gloved hand over the receiving end of the phone.

"Was that for me?"

Catherine shook her head. "Simpson wants to see me."

"Oh Catherine!" Catherine knew the look, she had just never seen it on Fran before. She was glowing with pride. Fran was happy for Catherine, actually happy for her.

"Go get 'em," she said to Catherine.

Catherine thought she had prepared herself, but as she walked down the long, grey-carpeted halls of *Women,* she felt as though it was for the last time. She passed Articles, where the woman who had written "Confessions of a Shoplifter" was sitting. An assistant ran to get coffee for her, then on second thought, went back to her desk and got her purse. Catherine passed the showroom, where Beauty was lining up the thigh make-overs. Beauty was down on her knees, taking measurements. The youngest thigh make-over, the one with the longest hair, raised her hand and stepped forward.

"Do I have to wear a bikini? My boyfriend says I'm not bikini material."

She passed Howard, who was in the process of training someone new in the art department—a young man with long black hair and thick eyebrows to match. They both looked up at Catherine who was standing in the doorway, watching. She smiled. They nodded and smiled back. Howard pointed back to the layout on his desk.

"Now, you see this? This girl's got too much stomach and she just doesn't look happy enough." He tossed the picture aside and fit another photo into the design.

Ms. Simpson's office looked like Catherine's mother's old kitchen in Memphis. The rug was a cropped indoor/outdoor green, the wallpaper a plaid vinyl. Ms. Simpson was sitting at a round table in the center of the room. Catherine could barely swallow, and, turning to shut the door, she swung back around, looked Ms. Simpson in the eye, and said, "I don't want to be the Enterainment editor, Ms. Simpson."

She heard her own voice and thought, Why did I just do that? Why did I just throw everything out the window? "Please," Ms. Simpson said, getting up. "Sit down."

Catherine took a seat in a hard-backed chair opposite Ms. Simpson at the round table in the center of the room. The table didn't belong in an editor's office. It didn't even belong in New York. It belonged in one of those *I* states in the middle of the country—Iowa, Indiana, or Illinois. There was a spidery brass sculpture on the center of the table, a General Excellence Award Ms. Simpson had received a few years ago from the Association of Magazine Editors.

"We're going to stop running the Entertainment section," Ms. Simpson said, walking over to the little window in the wall. She slid the thick glass window shut. Catherine could see the murky dark figure of Ms. Simpson's assistant on the other side. "I'd rather incorporate celebrities into Fashion and Beauty, maybe even into the How-To guide." Ms. Simpson paused and looked at Catherine for a response. Catherine nodded. "Leave the gossip to *People*," Ms. Simpson went on. "Women will have to find out who's sleeping with whom someplace else now."

Ms. Simpson walked a few steps to her right, to the corner of the room, and there she plugged in her green rock.

She's firing me, Catherine thought, trying to smile, trying to remain calm. Ms. Simpson is firing me.

"How do you like it here?" Ms. Simpson asked, sitting down. There was an old Underwood typewriter on another smaller table beside her. It was said that she kept it around, not for luck, but because she liked the way it felt. She still used it. She typed all her editorial comments on it because, it was said, Simpson wrote like a doctor.

Catherine stared at Ms. Simpson's typewriter. She had never seen it up close before, but it suddenly occurred to her that she would miss it. What would she do? She could get a job at a soup kitchen for the homeless. Maybe then she would learn how to cook.

Entertainment journalism was the only thing Catherine had any training in. She could work at another magazine. She thought of what it might be like to work at *People*. She heard that on nights before deadlines, everybody in the office stayed over and slept on cots. She thought of more screenings and press parties. The word "star" used to bring goose bumps to her skin—why didn't that word do anything for her anymore?

She could take a crash course in dental hygiene, stand beside Dr. Panter, and dab while he drilled. For a moment, Catherine had a mental picture of herself giving air to a patient.

"I like it here," Catherine said. She wanted to weep and cry out, "You don't understand, Ms. Simpson. This job is my life. Working for *Women* has saved me. You see, I don't have a life outside these offices. This is my family. You are my mother. Please don't abandon me. Please don't kick me out of the house."

"I like it here a lot."

"I understand you're not from around here. That you're from the Midwest," Ms. Simpson said. "I'm from Monroe, Wisconsin, myself."

Catherine nodded and looked at her, wondering if this was supposed to mean something.

"I've been enjoying your How-To guide pieces."

"My guide pieces?"

" 'Twenty-seven Ways to Get through a Crisis.' 'Five Ways to Pry Yourself out of Bed.' 'How to Touch a Person with AIDS.' " Ms. Simpson was reading from a sheet of paper rolled in her typewriter. " 'What You Can Learn from a Best Friend.' " Catherine scanned the tabletop. She saw the casting-couch piece. In bold red ink, she saw Ms. Simpson's scrawl. "I hate these kind of stories," she had written. "Pay $1000 kill fee." At the upper left-hand corner of the first page, Catherine saw that her name had been whited out and Fran's name had been written in with gold ink.

"You got a letter, too," Ms. Simpson said, picking up a flowery Hallmarkish card. " 'Dear *Women*. Thank you for the story about AIDS. My son Ian is dying with the disease. He joined a support group and he was the 'wellest' one there. Now they have all gone (six of them) and only Ian is left. I can touch Ian—I am his mother—but I know other mothers who are scared of their own sons who have AIDS. I have Xeroxed your piece and put it up in the lobby of the hospital where I work. Sincerely, Mary Ann Whitehead, Rolla, Missouri.' " Ms. Simpson put the letter down. "I'm glad we rushed that piece for August."

She looked over Catherine's shoulder towards the wall behind her, lined with gold-framed *Women* covers.

"You remind me a little of what Ann Bartel was like when she first started here," she said. "Maybe a little brassier. But still, this work here"—she patted the How-To copy—"It's poignant."

Poignant. Ms. Simpson said she was *poignant.*

"Let me get to the point. I've been having a problem with How-To. All the ideas are old, and the editors, well, they've been too soft."

She was going to ask Catherine to be How-To.

Some would consider it a demotion of sorts: Catherine would be responsible for the pages nobody else at *Women* wanted or even read. The only people who read the How-To guide were women in places like Iowa or Nebraska. Would becoming the How-To editor be like taking on a suicide mission? Everybody at *Women* knew about the How-To editors. They were the losers, women who thought they knew enough to fill that section every month but never could. Could she? Did she know enough now?

Catherine watched Ms. Simpson's mouth as she gave Catherine her new job description. At that moment, Catherine couldn't think of anything else in the world she would rather be in charge of than the How-To guide for *Women*.

She wouldn't have to fetch brownies from Zaro's for Fran. And she wouldn't have to sleep on a cot at *People*. Maybe she could even have her own assistant after a while. The Greek girl with the one arm. For a moment Catherine imagined herself, the one-armed girl beside her, wearing a white dentist's coat, holding a respirator and an oxygen tank, giving air to millions of *Women* readers.

When Ms. Simpson had compared Catherine with Ann Bartel, Catherine's heart had skipped a beat. Fran would have been insulted, but Catherine had had a sudden, vivid image of catching up with Ann after all those times she had been unable to on Madison Avenue—of grabbing hold of Ann's hand, running across the street, and catching the first express bus uptown.

She looked at Ms. Simpson. Who was this woman? It was said that she was married, but that she had cheated on him. It was said that she drank. Catherine wondered where and how she lived now. Did she take the subway? She was the editor-in-chief of a major women's magazine—how come she didn't wear a fur?

Ms. Simpson got up and put her hand on the green rock, her fingers turning a Martian fluorescent green. She was standing next to all those framed *Women* covers, row upon row of women. Only recently had they showed their teeth when they smiled. In the old days models couldn't afford to get their teeth fixed, so they kept their mouths shut. Catherine had a theory that that's why everyone pouted through the 1960s.

Ms. Simpson straightened a cover from the eighties. These were her babies, Catherine thought. Fran had her celebrity photos. Daniel had had his art objects. Joey had had his clothes and his *Interview* covers which he never had the chance to help produce. Catherine considered what she had produced that year. The interview with the Disney actor that had gotten her on Page Six. All those Entertainment pieces on the Beatrix Potter PBS special, Barbie dolls, dance movements, and the extra work she had put in for Food on peas. Then there was the baby that was never born. Michael's baby. Her baby. She wondered what it would look like now. She wished she had it right now, in her arms, dabbing at its mouth the way Ms. Simpson was wiping away a bit of dust on the glass over one of her girls.

Lewis Lipman had once told her that some day she would have to ask herself: What is important? Who is important?

"I know what you're thinking," Ms. Simpson said. "This wouldn't be as glamourous a job as you're used to."

Catherine wanted to leap up from her chair and kiss Ms. Simpson right then and there. Please please please, she wanted to say. Please let me throw glamour out the window. Allow me that much.

"I can give you a twenty-five-percent raise," Ms. Simpson said, picking up the Health page from her table to read over. "Let me know your decision Monday."

Fran was putting away her gold-framed celebrity photos. She wrapped each one carefully in newspaper first and stacked them together in boxes.

"A man who said he represented Mick Jagger called," Fran said. "He asked if I was Catherine with a C, the Entertainment editor." Fran waited for Catherine to say something, then went on. "Mick's free tommorrow at noon."

Catherine laughed. It suddenly occurred to her: She had nothing whatsoever she wanted to ask Mick Jagger.

"Take him," Catherine said. She brought her Rolodex over to Fran. "Take this, too."

"Are you sure?

"I'm doing How-To from now on."

"Well, at least keep this," Fran said, giving her back her Rolodex. "You've earned it." Then she laughed and admitted that she had Xeroxed all of it the night before.

"We never talked about Joey's death," Fran said after a minute. "I'm sorry."

Catherine nodded thanks. She looked at her bulletin board, trying to decide if she should start taking things down. She started with the sheet of adjectives, where she had once crossed out "comeuppance."

"Jesus, and now you've got to do How-To." Fran shook her head and took down the last of the pictures, an old one Catherine had forgotten about. It was the head shot of Lewis Lipman. "Have you noticed we always get screwed when we're away? You went to Hawaii and boom, you're How-To. I keep reading a person's supposed to take vacations—you know, relieve stress and work will go so much better. They never tell you how you'll get screwed over while you're away."

Fran had put Lewis' picture up a few months after he had appeared posthumously in *People*. "Yeah. He was a great guy," she would tell people who stopped by the office and commented on his photo.

"Don't worry," Fran said. She wrapped Lewis in a sheet of old newspaper and dropped him into her box. "There'll be other jobs."

That weekend Catherine prepared to move. She started with her closet, and there, on the top shelf, she came across some of Daniel's old shirts. So this is what you're left with, she thought. His old shirts—the ones you wore home on the days you didn't want to put on the clothes from the night before. And he had loved that—that first time—seeing her in his things. And she had loved it, too—the comfortable bigness of all his cotton shirts.

So then what were you supposed to do with them—wear them on weekends? Wear them until someone else came along and gave you his shirts? Was that what it all came down to? You love someone and then you stop, get a new pair of earrings, maybe a perm, then go and love someone else? Like a career switch? Was it just a matter of deciding not to break up anymore because neither one of you has any more energy?

In her closet, at the bottom behind a basket full of shoes, she found the papier-mâché parrot Michael had bought her that day she had gotten lost in Tijuana, and next to that, wrapped in a torn piece of tissue paper, were pieces of driftwood she and Joey had found that day on the beach. Behind the wood was Joey's red sequined dress, folded neatly inside the Bendel's bag.

"You wanna go to dinner or something?" she said over the phone to Daniel. "Lunch? Brunch? Crudités?"

"Hold on a minute, will you?"

The phone dropped. Catherine heard voices. Was that a woman's voice she heard? Daniel, she wanted to shout out, never mind. Never mind about dinner. She knew she no longer had any claim on him. But still.

Ever since Lewis had died, Daniel had been the only person in New York Catherine had wanted to talk to. When Joey was sick, Catherine had met Daniel at an Indian restaurant somewhere in the Eighties and over dinner she told him everything about Joey and about Michael. She told Daniel that she wasn't sure if she had AIDS, but the chances were slim that he had it—they had been careful, after all, that one time. They left the restaurant together and she shook his hand outside. She had never been so honest with anybody in her life and she felt wonderfully relieved not only because she had told him virtually everything, but also because she assumed he would probably never want to see her again. She had walked a whole block away from him until he caught up with her, turned her around, and he had held her then, right there at the corner of Lexington and Eightieth.

"Sorry about that," Daniel said. "I was in the middle of something. We just got a new delivery—a piece from South Africa."

We? Catherine wanted to say, but she bit her lip. She had called Daniel a few times since she had gotten back from Maui, but each time she had gotten his answering machine. Daniel had an answering machine now. And in his message his voice said "we," as in "We are not in right now." Catherine had just assumed Daniel had caught on to the royal "we."

"I've got a new assistant," he quickly added.

Catherine nodded without saying anything. That he had said that, she thought, was his way of saying, I am still free.

He didn't want to go to dinner. Daniel wanted to buy a headboard for his new house in upstate New York, so the following Saturday morning, Catherine went with him to a salvage place near the garment district. It was a warehouse with five floors of stuff from buildings that had been torn down. First floor was frames and pews. Second was sinks with a few lamps here and there. Third was cabinets and bars.

Catherine followed Daniel, and the salesman followed Catherine. They went past the doors and the moldings, past a twenty-foot long green marble frieze called *The Green Man* for twelve hundred dollars, and another called *Green Man with Damaged Face* for two hundred. They skipped the cabinet doors/marine salvage/windows and mirrors floor, and went on up to the fourth floor. Next to a stack of brass doors, they passed six roaring lions' heads. Seven hundred dollars each. Next to those was a pulpit with a red SOLD tag taped to the rim.

In the back, past the telephone booths and Saint Christopher statues, there were stacks of wrought-iron gates, some of them twisted, some painted, some still caked with dirt.

"Right up ahead," the salesman said. "This is what I was talking about." He picked up one of the gates. It was obviously heavy. "Good stuff," he said. "Feel the weight."

Daniel lifted another gate and nodded. "It's heavy, all right."

"So these were all in cemeteries?" Catherine said. There was a white garden bench near a stone statue of an angel that had a face like Liza Minnelli's. Catherine sat down. She looked at Daniel, who was picking up another gate. He propped it up against Liza's head to get a better look.

"You really want to sleep under a cemetery gate?" Catherine asked. Daniel had read about making an old cemetery gate into a headboard in an issue of *Arts & Antiques*.

"This is great-looking," Daniel said.

"French," the salesman said.

"Nineteenth century?"

"Eighteenth."

"Looks nineteenth."

Catherine shifted on the bench. She knew what Daniel was doing. He would try to convince the salesman that the iron was nineteenth century so that he could get a better price. She imagined Daniel and her sleeping under a cemetery gate.

He had said that there really wasn't that much to do to a gate to change it into a headboard—just weld some legs on and attach it to the bed frame. She wondered if spirits would creep in through the wrought iron, seep into the mattress and haunt them. She wondered if they were going to be good, French, eighteenth-century spirits. She wondered if Daniel would argue with them too, convince them that they were nineteenth-century spirits.

"Look at this twist here," Daniel said. "It's coming apart."

"Yeah. But feel the weight."

Daniel went to another pile of iron, pretending not to be interested anymore. The salesman looked at Catherine.

"That's a good bench," he said. "I found it on some property in Ohio, of all places."

"Really?" Catherine said. "It looks English." Daniel looked at her and then at the bench.

"It's comfortable, isn't it?" The man sat down next to Catherine. "It's got this back, see. Most garden benches don't have a back. I like this curve at the top. You can put your arm right here, see?" The man put his arm so that his fingers were touching her shoulder. "It's a romantic bench."

Catherine nodded. "Perfect for two."

"The kind of bench where you might propose," he said.

Catherine and the salesman looked at Daniel. The salesman was not coming on to her, he was trying to make a sale, and that was fine with Catherine. Daniel was across the room, near a pile of stone angels, lifting up another gate. There was more grey in his hair now. He was wearing a sweatshirt he said he had picked up in Rome. *I* ♥ *Firenze* was written in fuchsia across his chest—a fuchsia which probably wouldn't come to New York until the spring collections. It was only a color, she knew, but for the first time since she had known him, Catherine realized Daniel was at least five months ahead of her.

She had on an old sweatshirt, too, a big, bland, comfortable grey one Michael had left behind at her place that weekend they had made up.

"This one's good." Daniel was holding up a gate that had just been painted. It didn't need any scraping. It even had the legs to post to a bed frame. Ready-made, Catherine thought.

"It doesn't have much character," Catherine said. "I like the one that looks like it's falling apart better."

"I'm not looking for character in a headboard," he said. The salesman went over and held the gate so Daniel could examine it more closely. "Look at this," Daniel said, running his hands over the smooth wrought-iron sides. "It doesn't even need any work."

They couldn't get a cab standing there on the curb with the gate, so they took the subway.

"What should I call it now, a gate or a headboard?" Catherine said. They sat side by side, the iron knocking against their knees. Her whole side was next to his—shoulder, arm, hip, thigh, foot. Their calves weren't touching because, she remembered, he was slightly bowlegged. Sometimes, after they had made love, Daniel used to put his hand over her belly and slide it down. "That's mine," he would whisper. She wondered now, bumping against his shoulder, his headboard bumping against her knee, if he ever thought of moments like that with her. She wondered if he was thinking of her now, there, next to her, in the subway.

A black man, rolling a pair of dice on top of his leg, stared across the aisle at them. His girlfriend, a black girl with purple nails, kept her eye on the dice. Behind them stood a figure of a man spray-painted black on the subway car, his hands on his hips, waiting.

"I'm moving, you know," Catherine said after a while. "I figured I needed a repotting."

"Cat, we need to talk."

"It's a one-bedroom, but there's still enough room for two. You'd love it. High ceilings, a little balcony. You can see the whole sky—all the stars in the world are right outside my window. The water pressure's weird, though. I figure that's when Dr. Panter has just asked someone downstairs to rinse. Maybe you could spend some time there with me."

"Catherine."

"I loved when that salesman kept saying, 'Feel the weight.' I mean if weight makes things more valuable, how come everybody's not fat?"

"Cat."

"It makes me hungry. Are you hungry? Let's go get some lunch. We can bring this with us. What do we call it? When's it going to make the transition? Should we get an exorcist or something?"

"Sweetie. I'm getting married. I'm engaged."

Catherine looked at Daniel. Her mouth opened and a "Ha" came out. It came out loud. Too loud. The black girl looked at them.

"That's great. Really. That's great. That's just so . . . great." Catherine was nodding her head. She couldn't stop nodding her head. She held on to the steel pole to her right, but it felt oily and she let go. Why did all the handrails on buses and subways in New York always feel oily? You can blame everything on Manhattan, Joey had said.

"You don't have to say anything," Daniel said.

"No, really. It's so . . . So you're going to invite me to the wedding?"

Daniel looked at her, then he looked at the gate. He brushed away a piece of dirt near the bottom. "I don't think that would do anybody any good."

"Oh," Catherine said. "Well." Her mouth was open again, but she thought if she closed it she might start crying and never stop. She kept on nodding her head. She shifted her leg from the weight of the gate. His gate. His headboard. His and somebody else's. Not hers. She would not have to worry about French eighteenth-century spirits. Good. But still she felt vaguely nauseous. How could he sleep under this cemetery gate with another woman after he and Catherine had bought it together?

"Guess lunch is out, huh?" she said, looking at him in the reflection in the window. He was looking down at the gate. It wasn't a headboard yet, she told herself. It was still just a gate.

They went to a crowded place on Third and Eighty-second and left the gate with the cashier. Catherine ordered a cheeseburger and a glass of wine even though she felt sick and ashamed. She could barely look at him. But she wanted to sit there, across the table from him, to let what he had said sink in.

An old couple sat at the table to their right.

"How about a plain omelette?" the man yelled out across their little table.

"Why not?" his wife yelled back. She laid down her menu and took the silverware out of her napkin, placing the fork to her left, the knife and spoon to her right. She made sure they were straight, even though her head and hands were shaking vigorously. Then, with a great deal of effort, she got up, went to the other side of the table where her husband sat, and arranged his forks and knives in the same manner. Catherine was so moved she wanted to cry.

Daniel was going on about how he had met his wife-to-be. They had met in front of a Caravaggio at the Uffizi in Firenze—he was still calling Florence "Firenze." The Caravaggio had been an annunciation scene. Oh, pulease, Catherine almost said out loud. They had spent whole days comparing Pietas. She was Italian, of course. She probably had hips, Catherine thought, watching Daniel sip his wine and suck the ends of his mustache. She probably had olive skin, hips, and dark eyes. She was probably all hair and clothes.

He was careful not to give away too much. He was like a little boy with a secret. He pulled his sweatshirt out, fingering the heart. She had given it to him, he said.

When he said her name, he pronounced it the way the Italians would have. Laura. The *au* came out *ou*, as in *ouch*.

"We work together," he said.

"She's your new assistant," Catherine said, thinking, Great, so now it all finally dawns on me. Daniel nodded.

"That's so great," she kept saying. "Really." She wished she would shut up. She wished he would, too. Sometimes, she thought, a person can know too much. She flagged down the waiter and ordered another glass of wine.

In *Sweet Charity,* when the guy says he can't marry her, Shirley MacLaine just walks off and goes back to the dance hall. Nothing changes. She gets dumped at the beginning of the movie and then again at the end. But it's not the same with me, Catherine told herself. The circumstances are different here. First off, she thought, I was the one who started the breaking-up process a long time ago.

The old woman next to Catherine was drinking her coffee through a straw. She put in a second and offered it to her husband. Sitting there in the restaurant, watching this old couple, Catherine wondered if she should have tried harder to make what she and Daniel had had work.

Daniel went on yakking about the *Last Judgment,* how it was such a disappointment, and the Sistine Chapel, how powerful it was now that it was getting cleaned—all those bright colors.

"Man is so great," he said, licking the ketchup from the tips of his fingers. He picked up his hamburger and bit into it. "We're always getting ourselves into trouble, but still, we are the most impressive thing we've got."

Funny, she thought, last time he went on about Italy, we landed up in bed.

"Do you mind?" Catherine said. "All your bullshit's making me queasy."

"Look," he said. He threw down his burger so that it came apart on his plate. "I loved you, and maybe you loved me, too. For a little while. Now why don't you just leave me alone?"

Catherine couldn't look at him. She knew he was right. He had found someone—someone else—and he didn't want to blow it this time. She understood that. And she also understood that if there was not another woman in the picture, she and Daniel would have gone on as they had always gone on—seeing each other for the occasional week or weekend. But nothing more. She knew that about them and about herself.

She had been someone else altogether when she had loved Daniel. She was not that person anymore. And Daniel was not the same man. Looking at the old man and the old woman sitting at the table next to theirs, Catherine wondered how some couples arranged it so that they grew together instead of apart.

Maybe it was the age difference, or maybe it had something to do with the fact that he lived for the past while she wondered about it, was haunted by it, and grieved over it.

Maybe she had begun to love too young. She was twenty years old when she had met Daniel. He was forty then. She knew a few lines from Keats. "Heard melodies are sweet, but those unheard / Are sweeter." He had memorized all the odes and a good portion of "Endymion," and had come to the conclusion that he preferred Yeats.

She had had a vague notion of what she wanted to do with her life. He was already doing what he had always wanted to do. Maybe you had to know everything there was to know about yourself before you went off and fell in love. Maybe you had to season and toughen yourself before you gave yourself to anybody.

Catherine looked at Daniel, who was looking across the table at her. His brown eyes were shiny with tears that had not yet fallen. Or maybe, maybe she just had to get used to saying good-bye.

How to Keep Living When Those You Love Have Gone Away. How to Keep Loving When the One You Once Loved No Longer Loves You. *Proceed as usual,* as Dr. Crotchcough once adviced breast-cancer patients who wanted to make love during chemotherapy, *but carefully. Tenderly.*

"OK," Catherine whispered. "I'm OK."

Later, after Daniel had paid the bill and reclaimed his gate from the cashier, they stood outside in front of a hot dog stand. Daniel put the gate down, letting it lean against his leg. Catherine said that it wouldn't have worked anyway.

A Rastafarian was standing next to a blanket he had spread out on the sidewalk. On the blanket were earrings.

"We don't grow up where we're born," she said. "We don't even live where we grow up. How can we be expected to stick with one person? We can't even stay in one place long enough to hang curtains."

She looked at Daniel. She could feel tears coming to her eyes. "I mean, I'm still sleeping in a pull-out sofa, for Chrissakes."

He nodded and blew his nose.

She put her hand in her pocket, brought out two dollar bills, and bought a pair of earrings from the Rastafarian. The ones she selected had tiny brass bells on the ends of the hoops. For one split second, she hoped Daniel would admire her spontaneity, compare her to his fiancee and call the whole thing off.

Her hair got tangled up in the earrings while she tried to get them on her ears. Daniel told her to hold still. His fingers were warm on her earlobes and she held her breath.

"I did love you," she whispered.

He held his breath and then let it out.

"When did it stop?" he said.

She shrugged. "I don't know. Maybe . . . maybe when we went out dancing that one time at Danceteria. You were doing all that tai chi shit. I stopped and you just kept on going."

She looked at him in the way that she knew he knew, and he took her in his arms. The cemetery gate came between them and he moved it, leaning it against the hot dog stand, and then he turned back around and he and Catherine held each other there on the sidewalk, wearing sweatshirts they had received from other lovers, sighing and swaying back and forth.

On her way home, Catherine passed a rent-a-car place. She stood outside, looking in, watching the line of men exchanging their credit cards for keys.

In the middle of Midtown Tunnel rush-hour traffic, Catherine worried; the rent-a-car people had given her a stick shift because that was all they had left. Catherine had driven a VW bug in high school and she figured it would all come back. But now, she was bumper to bumper with what seemed like all of Manhattan, in a dark tunnel, which she knew happened to be under the East River. She checked the walls for leakage. There were little puddles all around, just as there had been before her apartment had caved in. I'm almost there, Catherine thought. She took a deep breath. She thought of the calm look on Kimberly's face behind her mask underwater near the coral reef off Kapalua Bay. Slow. Calm. OK, now breathe. Breathe deep, Catherine said to herself. I'm almost to the other side.

It felt odd being behind the wheel again. She wished she had taken a driver's ed. class before she had come up with the idea of renting a car. She felt she needed to relearn the rules of the road. The least she could have done was read up on how to drive a stick shift.

Catherine turned on the radio. Jagger was singing "Undercover of the Night" and it sounded terrible. She played her old game: of all the people I want to know something from, who do I want to call up and talk to this very minute? She thought of Ann Bartel. She thought of Ms. Simpson and she thought of her mother. Catherine smiled to herself. She couldn't think of one celebrity with whom she wanted to talk.

Maybe it was because she didn't have any questions to ask them. For the first time in a long time, Catherine felt as though she knew a few things. She knew she didn't have to be "up" on anything ever again. She would go to movies at her leisure, good-looking, intelligent, obscure movies that had dialogue. She would go and buy her own albums and cassettes and none of them would have *For Promo Only* stamped in gold on the cover. She wouldn't have to keep up with who was alive or dead on "Dynasty," "Knot's Landing," or "Dallas." And she knew that she would never ever be too soft for the likes of Ms. Simpson.

If there had been a phone booth there in the Midtown Tunnel, Catherine would have pulled over, gotten out of her rented car, and called Ms. Simpson to say, "I'll take it. I'll be How-To." Monday seemed too far away.

And then Catherine thought of Mary Ann Whitehead, the woman from Missouri who had written about her son Ian. It was Catherine's first piece of reader mail, and for the first time Catherine knew why she was still there, in New York, working for *Women.* Lewis had said this would happen to her—that someday she would have to ask herself, What have I got here? Whom do I have here? And why am I still here?

I have my mother. I have myself. I have a cat named Damn It and I have Mary Ann Whitehead.

Catherine thought of all the things she would buy with her twenty-five-percent raise and her lowered monthly rent. First, she would get a big desk calendar and she would mark all of her How-To due dates on it in red and she would never ever get behind.

She would write and assign good, solid, instructive How-To pieces, and she would go to lunch every week with Ann Bartel and they would try out ideas on each other. Ann would nod or shake her head and remind Catherine, "No, no. That's not it. That's not the truth. That's not what's important." They would do that—they would keep each other on track. They would remind each other of what's important.

And Catherine would start a garden, perhaps, and buy guest towels, good, expensive ones from a store that only sold things for bathrooms. She would hang curtains. She would buy a real bed.

She would call her mother and she would say, "Mom. I think it's time you widened your horizons. I think it's time you paid me a visit." And her mother would say, "Oh yeah? It's not like I've been waiting all my life for this. But OK. What's the weather like? What would I wear if I were to come?" And Catherine would say, "Whatever you feel comfortable in,

Mom. I want you to feel at home." Because that is what Catherine would have. She would have a home.

Traffic was moving again and suddenly Catherine was out of the Midtown Tunnel and moving fast on the Long Island Expressway. She shifted into third. She wasn't sure where she was going. She only knew she was headed east towards the ocean. She pressed the clutch and shifted into fourth, then, after grinding the gears, she finally found fifth. She looked at the other drivers, but it wasn't as if they had heard. She was alone and she was heading for the ocean and she figured whatever she needed to know from here on, she would figure out.